Dear Reader,

Welcome to the to[...] [...]'ll join me there to me[...] [...] friends and wives-to[...] [...]es, originally published [...]6, that led me to write the six-book *Heart of Texas* series, and eventually its sequel, *Promise, Texas*.

I discovered with the Midnight Sons stories how much I enjoyed creating a town and the personalities that populate it. Once the characters were established in my mind, I loved taking them from one story to the next, never fully certain what role they would play. I soon learned that my readers enjoyed it, too.

I've never worked harder on a project. Nor have I enjoyed my research more. In the summer of 1994, my husband and I traveled to Alaska and I fell in love with the state— its sheer magnificence, the warmth of its people, the excitement of life on the "last frontier." We flew with bush pilots, trekked across the tundra and talked with anyone and everyone willing to share their experiences.

Now I invite you to sit back and allow me to introduce you to some proud, stubborn, wonderful men—Alaska men—and show you what happens when they meet their real matches. Women from the "lower forty-eight." Women with the courage to change their lives and take risks for love. Women a lot like you and me!

Love,

Debbie

P.S. But wait—there's more! For a follow-up story to Midnight Sons, look for Superromance #936 (available in September 2000), celebrating the twenty-year anniversary of this popular Harlequin line. I'm pleased to tell you that *Midnight Sons and Daughters* is part of this anthology, entitled BORN IN A SMALL TOWN. Enjoy!

New York Times bestselling author Debbie Macomber always enjoyed telling stories—first to her baby-sitting clients, and then to her own four children. As a full-time wife and mother and an avid romance reader, she dreamed of one day sharing her stories with a wider audience. In the autumn of 1982 she sold her first book, and then began making regular appearances on the *USA Today* bestseller list. Now her heartwarming stories have conquered the *New York Times* bestseller list, and there are over forty million copies of her books in print worldwide!

DEBBIE MACOMBER

FAMILY MEN

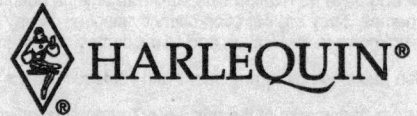
HARLEQUIN®

TORONTO • NEW YORK • LONDON
AMSTERDAM • PARIS • SYDNEY • HAMBURG
STOCKHOLM • ATHENS • TOKYO • MILAN • MADRID
PRAGUE • WARSAW • BUDAPEST • AUCKLAND

ISBN 0-373-83435-7

FAMILY MEN

Copyright © 2000 by Harlequin Books S.A.

The publisher acknowledges the copyright holder of the original works as follows:

DADDY'S LITTLE HELPER
Copyright © 1995 by Debbie Macomber

BECAUSE OF THE BABY
Copyright © 1996 by Debbie Macomber

CONTENTS

The History of Hard Luck, Alaska

Hard Luck, situated fifty miles north of the Arctic Circle, near the Brooks Range, was founded by Adam O'Halloran and his wife, Anna, in 1931. Adam came to Alaska to make his fortune, but never found the gold strike he sought. Nevertheless, the O'Hallorans and their two young sons, Charles and David, stayed on—in part because of a tragedy that befell the family a few years later.

Other prospectors and adventurers began to move to Hard Luck, some of them bringing wives and children. The town became a stopping-off place for mail, equipment and supplies. The Fletcher family arrived in 1938 to open a dry goods store.

When World War II began, Hard Luck's population was fifty or sixty people, all told. Some of the younger men, including the O'Halloran sons, joined the armed services; Charles left for Europe in 1942, David in 1944 at the age of eighteen. Charles died during the fighting. Only David came home—with a young war bride, Ellen Sawyer (despite the fact that he'd become engaged to Catherine Fletcher shortly before going overseas).

After the war, David qualified as a bush pilot. He then built some small cabins to attract the sport fishermen and hunters who were starting to come to Alaska; he also worked as a guide. Eventually, in the early seventies, he built a lodge to replace the cabins—a lodge that later burned.

David and Ellen had three sons, born fairly late in their marriage—Charles (named after David's brother) was born in 1960, Sawyer in 1963 and Christian in 1965.

Hard Luck had been growing slowly all this time, and by 1970 it was home to just over a hundred people. These were the years of the oil boom, when the school and community center were built by the state. After Vietnam, ex-serviceman Ben Hamilton joined the community and opened the Hard Luck Café, which became the social focus for the town.

In the late 1980s, the three O'Halloran brothers formed a partnership, creating Midnight Sons, a bush-pilot service. They were awarded the mail contract, and also deliver fuel and other necessities to the interior. In addition, they serve as a small commuter airline, flying passengers to and from Fairbanks and within the North Arctic.

At the time these stories start, there are approximately 150 people living in Hard Luck—a preponderance of them male....

DADDY'S LITTLE HELPER

CHAPTER ONE

THE NEW SCHOOLTEACHER wouldn't last.

It didn't take Mitch Harris more than five seconds to make that assessment. Bethany Ross didn't belong in Alaska. She reminded him of a tropical bird with its brilliant plumage. Everything about her was *vivid,* from her animated expression to her sun-bleached hair, which fell to her shoulders in a frothy mass of blond. Even blonder curls framed her strong, classic features. Her eyes were a deep, rich shade of chocolate.

She wore a bright turquoise jumpsuit with a wide yellow band that circled her trim waist. One of her skimpy multicolored sandals dangled from her foot as she sat on the arm of Abbey and Sawyer O'Halloran's sofa, her legs elegantly crossed.

This get-together was in her honor. Abbey and Sawyer had invited the members of the school board to their home to meet the new teacher.

To Mitch's surprise, she stood and approached him before he had a chance to introduce himself. "I don't believe we've met." Her smile was warm and natural. "I'm Bethany Ross."

"Mitch Harris." He didn't elaborate. Details wouldn't be necessary because Ms. Ross simply wouldn't last beyond the first snowfall. "Welcome to Hard Luck," he said almost as an afterthought.

"Thank you."

"When did you get here?" he asked, trying to make conversation. He twisted the stem of his wineglass and watched the chardonnay swirl against the sides.

"I flew in this afternoon."

He hadn't realized she'd only just arrived. "You must be exhausted."

"Not really," she was quick to tell him. "I suppose I should be, considering that I left San Francisco early this morning. The fact is, I've been keyed up for days."

Mitch strongly suspected Hard Luck was a sorry disappointment to her. The town, population 150, was about as far from the easy California life-style as a person could get. Situated fifty miles north of the Arctic Circle, Hard Luck was a fascinating place with a strong and abiding sense of community. People here lived hard and worked harder. Other than Midnight Sons, the flight service owned and operated by the three O'Halloran brothers, there were a few small businesses, like Ben Hamilton's café. Mitch himself was one of a handful of state employees. He worked for the Department of the Interior, monitoring visitors to Gate of the Arctic National Park. This was in addition to his job as the town's public-safety officer—PSO—which meant he was responsible for policing in Hard Luck. Trappers wandered into town now and again, and an occasional pipeline worker. To those living on the edge of the world, Hard Luck was a thriving metropolis.

Lately the town had piqued the interest of the rest of the country, as well. But Bethany Ross had nothing to do with that. Thank heaven, although Mitch suspected she'd stay about as long as some of the women the O'Halloran brothers had brought to town.

Until recently only a small number of women had lived here. Not many were willing to endure the hardship of living this far from civilization. So the O'Hallorans had spearheaded a campaign to bring women to Hard Luck. Abbey was one of their notable successes, but there had been a few equally notable failures. Like—who was it?—Allison somebody. The one who'd lasted less than twenty-four hours. And only last week, two women had arrived, only to return home on the next flight out. Bethany Ross had actually applied for the teaching job last spring, though, before all this nonsense.

Unexpectedly she smiled—a ravishing smile that seemed to say she'd read his thoughts. "I plan to fulfill my contract, Mr. Harris. I knew what I was letting myself in for when I agreed to teach in Alaska."

Mitch felt the heat rise to his ears. "I didn't realize my...feelings were so transparent."

"I don't blame you for doubting me. I don't quite blend in with the others, do I?"

He was tempted to smile himself. "Hard Luck isn't what you expected, is it?"

"I'll adjust."

She said this with such confidence he began to wonder if he'd misjudged her.

"Frankly, I didn't know *what* to expect. With Hard Luck in the news so often, the idea of moving here was beginning to worry me."

Mitch didn't bother to conceal his amusement. He'd read what some of the tabloids had written about the town and the men's scheme to lure women north.

"My dad was against my coming," Bethany continued. "It was all I could do to keep him from flying up here with me. He seems to think Hard Luck's populated with nothing but love-starved bush pilots."

"He isn't far wrong," Mitch said wryly. If Bethany

had only been in town a few hours, she probably hadn't met the pilots currently employed by Midnight Sons. He knew Sawyer had flown her in from Fairbanks.

It was after repeatedly losing their best pilots for lack of female companionship that the O'Hallorans had decided to take action.

"Midnight Sons is the flight service? Owned by the O'Hallorans?" she asked, looking flustered. "Sawyer and his brothers?"

"That's right." Mitch understood why she was confused. Immediately following her arrival, she'd been thrust into the middle of this party, with twenty names or more being thrown her way all at once. In an effort to help her, Mitch explained that Charles O'Halloran, the oldest of the three brothers, was a silent partner.

Charles, hadn't been so silent, however, when he learned about the scheme Sawyer and Christian had concocted to lure women to Hard Luck. He'd changed his tune, though, since meeting Lanni Caldwell. Earlier in the week, they'd announced their intention to marry.

"Is it true that Abbey—Sawyer's wife—was the first woman to come here?" Her eyes revealed her curiosity.

"Yes. They got married earlier this summer."

"But...they look like they've been married for years. What about Scott and Susan?"

"They're Abbey's children from a previous marriage. I understand Sawyer's already started the adoption process." Mitch envied his friend's happiness. Marriage hadn't been nearly as happy an experience for him.

"Chrissie's your daughter?" Bethany asked, glancing over at the children gathered around a Monopoly game.

Mitch's gaze fell fondly on his seven-year-old daughter. "That's right. She's been on pins and needles waiting for school to start."

Bethany's eyes softened. "I met her earlier with Scott and Susan. She's a delightful little girl."

"Thank you." Mitch tried hard to do his best for Chrissie. Sometimes he wondered, though, whether his best would ever be enough. "You've met Pete Livengood?" he asked, gesturing toward a rugged-looking middle-aged man on the other side of the room.

"Yes. He owns the grocery?"

"That's right. Dotty, the woman on his left, is another one who answered the advertisement."

Bethany blinked as if trying to remember where Dotty fit into the small community. "She's the nurse?"

He nodded. "Pete and Dotty plan to be married shortly. The first week of October, I believe."

"So soon?" She didn't give him an opportunity to answer before directing her attention elsewhere. "What about Mariah Douglas? Is she a recent addition to the town?"

"Yup. She's the secretary for Midnight Sons."

"Is she engaged?"

"Not yet," Mitch said, "but it's still pretty early. She only arrived last month."

"You mean to say she's lived here an entire month without getting married?" Bethany teased. "That must be some sort of record. It seems to me the virile young men of Hard Luck are slacking on their duties."

Mitch grinned. "From what I've heard, it isn't for lack of trying. But Mariah says she didn't come to Hard Luck looking for a husband. She's after the cabin and the twenty acres the O'Hallorans promised her."

"Good for her. They've fulfilled their part of the

bargain, haven't they? I read that news story about the cabins not being anywhere close to the twenty acres. Sure sounds misleading to me.'' Fire flashed briefly in her eyes, as if she'd be willing to take on all three O'Hallorans herself.

"That's none of my business. It's between Mariah and the O'Hallorans.''

Bethany flushed with embarrassment and bent her head to sip from her wine. "It isn't my business, either. It's just that Mariah seems so sweet and gentle. I hate the idea of anyone taking advantage of her.''

They were interrupted by Sawyer and Abbey. "I see you've met Mitch," Sawyer said, moving next to Bethany.

"He's been helping me keep everyone straight,'' she said with a quick smile.

"Then he's probably told you that in addition to his job with the Department of the Interior, he's our public-safety officer.''

"Hard Luck's version of the law," Mitch translated for her.

She leveled her gaze with his. "My father's a member of San Francisco's finest.''

"Well," said Sawyer, "Mitch was one of Chicago's finest before moving here.''

"That's right," Mitch supplied absently.

"I imagine your head's swimming right about now," Abbey said. "I know mine was when I first arrived. Oh—'' she waved at a woman just coming in the door ''—here's Margaret. Margaret Simpson, the high school teacher.''

Margaret, a pleasant-looking brunette in her thirties, joined them. She greeted Bethany with friendly enthusiasm, explained that she lived on the same street as

Sawyer and Abbey did and that her husband was a pipeline supervisor who worked three weeks on and three weeks off.

Mitch hardly heard the conversation between Margaret and Bethany; the words seemed to fade into the background as he found himself studying Bethany Ross.

He wanted to know her better, but he wouldn't allow himself that luxury. Although she claimed otherwise, he didn't expect her to last three months, not once the brutal winter settled in.

But still, she intrigued him. Tantalized him. The reasons could be as basic as the fact that he'd been too long without a woman—six years to be exact. He'd buried Lori when Chrissie was little more than an infant. Unable to face life on the Chicago police force any longer, he'd packed their bags and headed north. As far north as he could get. He'd known at the time that he was running away. But he'd felt he had no choice, not with guilt and his own self-doubts nipping at his heels. He was out of money and tired of life on the road by the time he reached Hard Luck.

And he'd been happy here. As happy as possible, under the circumstances. He and Chrissie had made a new life for themselves, made new friends. For Mitch, the world had become calm and orderly again, without pain or confusion. Without a woman in their lives.

He certainly hadn't anticipated meeting a woman like Bethany—a tropical bird—in Alaska.

She wasn't exactly beautiful, he decided. She was...striking. He struggled to put words to his assessment of her attributes. Feminine. Warm. Generous. Somewhat outrageous. Fun. The kids would love her. He'd spent ten, possibly fifteen, minutes chatting with her and immediately wanted more of her time, more of her attention.

But he refused to indulge himself. He'd learned all the lessons he ever wanted to learn from his dead wife. The new schoolteacher could tutor some other man.

Bethany yawned and tried to hide it behind the back of her hand.

"You must be exhausted," Abbey said sympathetically. "I can't believe we've kept you this long. I feel terrible."

"No, please, it was wonderful of you to make me feel so welcome." To her obvious chagrin, Bethany yawned again. "Maybe it would be best if I did leave now."

"She's dead on her feet," Sawyer said to no one in particular. "Mitch, would you be kind enough to escort her home?"

"Of course." He immediately set down his wineglass, but truth be known, he'd rather have declined. He was about to suggest someone else do the honor when he realized Bethany might find that insulting.

She studied him, and again he had the impression she could read his mind. He looked away and searched the room until he found his daughter. Chrissie was sitting near the door to the kitchen with her best friend, Susan. The two were deep in conversation, their heads close together. He didn't know what they were discussing, but whatever it was seemed terribly important. Yet another scheme to outsmart the adults, no doubt. Heaven save him from little girls.

He turned to Bethany Ross. "If you'll excuse me a moment?" he asked politely.

"Of course. I'll need a few minutes myself."

While Mitch collected Chrissie, Bethany bade the members of the school board good-night.

They met just outside the front door. He didn't have to ask where she lived—the teacher's living quarters were supplied by the state and were some of the best accommodations in town. The small two-bedroom house was located on the far side of the school gymnasium.

Mitch held open the passenger door so Chrissie could climb into the truck first. He noticed how quiet his daughter had become, as if she was in awe of this woman who would' be her teacher.

"I appreciate the ride," Bethany told him once he'd started the engine.

"It's no trouble." Well, it was, but not because of the extra few minutes' driving. But then he decided he might as well let himself enjoy her company. It was a small thing and not likely to be repeated. Once the eligible men in Hard Luck caught sight of her, he wouldn't stand a chance. Which was just as well.

"Would you mind driving me around a bit?" Bethany asked. "I didn't get much of a chance to see the town when I arrived."

"There's not much to see." It occurred to him that he might enjoy her company too much, and that could be a dangerous thing.

"We could show her the library," Chrissie said eagerly.

"Hard Luck has a library?"

"It's not very big, but we use it a lot," said the girl. "Abbey's the town librarian."

Sawyer's wife had worked for weeks setting up the lending library. The books were a gift from the O'Hallorans' mother and had sat in a disorganized heap for years—until Abbey's arrival. She'd even started ordering new books, everything from best-selling fiction to cook books; the first shipment had arrived a week ago, occasioning great excitement. It seemed everyone in town had become addicted to books. Mitch often heard lively discussions revolving around a novel. An avid reader himself, he was often a patron, and he encouraged Chrissie to take out books, too.

"Ms. Ross should see the store, too," Chrissie suggested next. "And the church and the school."

"What's that building there?" Bethany asked, pointing to the largest structure in town.

"That's the lodge," he said without elaborating.

"Matt Caldwell's fixing it up." Again it was Chrissie who supplied the details. "He's Lanni's brother."

"You didn't meet Lanni Caldwell," Mitch explained. "I told you about her—she's engaged to Charles O'Halloran."

"I met Charles?"

"Briefly. He was in and out."

"The tall man wearing the Midnight Sons sweatshirt?"

"That's right."

Chrissie leaned closer to Bethany. "No one lives at the lodge now because of the fire. Matt bought it, and he's fixing it up so people will come and stay there and pay him lots of money."

"The fire?"

"It happened years ago," Mitch told her. "Most of the damage was at the back, so you can't see it from here." He shook his head. "The place should either have been repaired or torn down long before now, but I guess no one had the heart to do either. The

O'Hallorans recently sold it to Matt Caldwell, which was for the best all around.''

"Matt's going to take the tourists mushing!'' Chrissie said, excitement raising her voice several decibels. "He's going to bring in dogs and trainers and everything!''

"That sounds like a lot of fun.''

"Eagle Catcher's a husky,'' Chrissie added.

Mitch caught Bethany's questioning look. "That's Sawyer's dog.''

"He belongs to Scott,'' his daughter corrected him.

"True,'' Mitch said with a smile at Chrissie. "I'd forgotten.''

"Scott and Susan are brother and sister, right?'' said Bethany. "Abbey's kids?''

"Right.''

Mitch could tell Bethany was making a real effort to keep everyone straight in her mind, and he thought she'd done an impressive job so far. Maybe a memory for names and faces came with being a teacher.

"Are there any restaurants in town?'' Bethany asked. "I'm not much of a cook.''

Mitch glanced her way. Their eyes met briefly before he looked back at the road. "The Hard Luck Café.''

Bethany smiled, amused by the name, he suspected.

"Serves the best cup of coffee in town, but then Ben hasn't got much competition.''

There was a pause. "Ben?''

"Hamilton. He's an ugly cuss, but don't let that fool you. He's got a heart of gold, and he's a lot more than chief cook and bottle washer. Along with everything else, he dishes up a little psychology. You'll like him.''

"I—I'm sure I will.''

Mitch drove to the end of the road. A single light

shone brightly in the distance. "That's where the cabins are," he explained. "Mariah's place is the one on the far left." Mitch had lost count of the number of times the youngest O'Halloran brother, Christian, had tried to convince his secretary to move into town. But Mariah always refused. Mitch was just glad *he* wasn't the one dealing with her stubbornness.

He turned the truck around and headed back toward the school. When he pulled up in front of Bethany's little house, she turned to him and smiled.

"Thanks for the tour and the ride home."

"My pleasure."

"Chrissie," Bethany said, her voice gentle, "since I'm new here, I was wondering if you'd be my helper."

His daughter's eyes lit up like sparklers on the Fourth of July, and she nodded so hard her pigtails bounced wildly. "Can Susan be your helper, too?"

"Of course."

Chrissie beamed a proud smile at her father.

"Well, good night, Chrissie, Mitch," Bethany said, then opened her door and climbed out.

"Night," father and daughter echoed. Mitch waited until she was inside the house and the lights were on before he drove off.

So, he thought *the new school teacher has arrived.*

BETHANY WAS even more tired than she'd expected. But instead of falling into a sound sleep, she lay awake, staring at the ceiling, fighting fatigue and mulling over the time she'd spent with Mitch Harris.

The man was both intense and intelligent. That much had been immediately apparent. He stood apart from the others in more ways than one. Bethany strongly suspected he wouldn't have bothered to introduce himself, which was why she'd taken the initiative. She'd noticed him right away, half-hidden in a corner, watching the events without joining in. When it looked as if the evening would pass without her meeting him, she'd made the first move.

There was something about him she found intriguing. Having lived with a policeman all her life, she must have intuitively sensed his occupation; she certainly hadn't been surprised when Sawyer told her what it was. In some remote way, he reminded her of her father. They seemed to have the same analytical mind. It drove her mother crazy, the way Dad carefully weighed each decision, considered every option, before taking action. She'd bet Mitch was the same way.

It was one personality trait Bethany *didn't* share.

She would've liked to know Mitch Harris better, but she had the distinct impression he wasn't interested. Then again...maybe he was. A breathless moment before she'd introduced herself, she'd recognized some glint of admiration in his eye. She'd been sure of it. But now she wondered if that moment had existed only in her imagination.

All the same, she couldn't help wondering what it would be like to see his eyes darken with passion just before he kissed her.

She was definitely too tired; she wasn't even thinking straight. Bethany closed her eyes and pounded the pillow, trying to force herself to relax.

But even with her eyes shut, all she saw was Mitch Harris's face.

She hadn't come to Hard Luck to fall in love, she told herself sternly.

Rolling onto her other side, she cradled the pillow in her arms. It didn't help. Drat. She could deny it till doomsday, but it wouldn't make any difference. There was just something about Chrissie's father....

"Ms. Ross?"

Bethany looked up from the back of her classroom. Chrissie and Susan stood just inside the doorway, their faces beaming with eagerness.

"Hello, girls."

"Um, we're here to be your helpers," Chrissie said. "Dad told us we'd better make sure we *are* helpers and not nuisances."

"I'm sure you'll be wonderful helpers," Bethany said.

The two girls instantly broke into huge grins and rushed into the room. Bethany soon put them to work sorting out textbooks. This was the first time she'd taught more than one grade, and the fact that she'd now be handling kindergarten through six intimidated her more than a little.

"Everyone's looking forward to school," Chrissie announced, "especially my dad."

Bethany chuckled. Mitch wasn't so different from other parents.

The girls had been working for perhaps twenty minutes when Chrissie suddenly asked, "You're not married or anything, are you, Ms. Ross?"

A smile trembled on her mouth. "No."

"Why not?"

Leave it to a seven-year-old to ask that kind of question. "I haven't met the right man," she explained as simply as she could.

"Have you ever been in love?" Susan probed.

Bethany noticed that both girls had stopped sorting

through the textbooks and were giving her their full attention. "Yes," she told them with some hesitation.

"How old are you?"

"Chrissie." Susan jabbed her elbow into her friend's ribs. "You're not supposed to ask that," she said in a loud whisper. "It's against the human-rights law. We could get charged with snooping."

"I'm twenty-five," Bethany answered, pretending she hadn't heard Susan.

The girls exchanged looks, then immediately started using their fingers to count.

"Seven," Chrissie breathed, as if it were a magic number.

"Seven?" Bethany asked curiously. What game were the girls playing?

"If a man's seven years older than you, is that too old?" Susan asked, her eyes round and inquisitive.

"Too old," Bethany repeated thoughtfully. She sat on the edge of a desk and crossed her arms. "That depends."

"On what?" Chrissie moved closer.

"On age, I suppose. If I was fourteen and wanted to date a man who was twenty-one, my parents would never have allowed it. But if I was twenty-one and he was twenty-eight, it would be okay."

Both girls looked pleased with her answer, and gave each other a high five.

Bethany decided to respond to their odd behavior with a joke. "You girls aren't thinking about dating fourteen-year-old boys, are you?" she asked, narrowing her eyes in pretend disapproval.

Chrissie covered her mouth and giggled.

Susan rolled her eyes. "Get real, Ms. Ross. I don't even know what the big attraction to boys is." Then, as if to explain her words, she added, "I have an older brother."

"Would you tell us about the man you were in love with?" This came from Chrissie. Her expression had grown so serious Bethany decided to answer, despite her initial impulse to change the subject.

"The man I was in love with," she began, "was a guy I dated while I was in college. We went out for about a year."

"What was his name?"

"Randy."

"Randy," Chrissie repeated with disgust, turning to look at her friend.

"Did he do you wrong?"

Bethany laughed, although she was uncomfortable with these questions. "No, he didn't do me wrong." If anyone was to blame for their breakup, it had been Bethany herself. She wasn't entirely sure she'd ever really loved him, which she supposed was an answer in itself. They'd been friends, and that had developed into something more—at least on Randy's part.

He'd started talking marriage and children, and at first she'd thought it sounded like a good idea. Then she'd realized she wasn't ready for that kind of commitment. Not when she had two full years of school left to complete. Not when she'd barely begun to experience life.

They'd argued and broken off their unofficial engagement. The breakup had troubled Bethany for months afterward. But now she couldn't help thinking that what she'd really regretted was the loss of the friendship.

"Do you still see him?" Chrissie asked.

Bethany nodded.

"You *do?*" Susan sounded as if this was a tragedy.

"Sometimes."

"Is he married?"

"No." Bethany grew a little sad, thinking about her longtime friend. She did miss Randy, even now, five years after their breakup.

Both Chrissie and Susan seemed deflated at the news of Bethany's lost love.

"Would it be all right if we left now?" Chrissie asked abruptly.

"That's fine," Bethany told them. "Thanks for your help."

The two disappeared so quickly all that was missing was the puff of smoke.

If nothing else, the girls certainly were entertaining, Bethany decided. She returned to the task of cutting large letters out of colored paper.

The sun blazed in through the classroom windows, and she tugged her shirt loose, unfastened the last few buttons and tied the ends at her midriff. Then she pulled her hair away from her face and used an elastic to secure it in a ponytail.

Half an hour later, most of the letters, all capitals, for the word "September" were pinned in an arch across the bulletin board at the back of the classroom. She stood on a chair and had just pinned the third *E* in place when she felt someone's presence behind her. Twisting around, she saw Mitch standing in the open door.

"Hi," she said cheerfully, undeniably pleased to see him. He was dressed in the khaki uniform worn by the Department of the Interior staff. His face revealed none of his emotions, yet Bethany had the distinct feeling he'd rather not be there.

"I'm looking for Chrissie."

Bethany pinned the *R* in place and then stepped down from the chair. "Sorry, but as you can see she isn't here."

Mitch frowned. "Louise Gold told me this was where she'd be."

Bethany remembered that Louise Gold was the woman who watched Chrissie while Mitch was at work. She'd briefly met her the day before. In addition to her other duties, Louise served on the school board.

"Chrissie was here earlier with Susan."

"I hope they behaved themselves."

Bethany recalled their probing questions and smiled to herself. Pushing the chair back into place, she said, "They were fine. I asked Chrissie for her help, remember?"

Mitch remained as far away from her as possible. Bethany suspected he'd rather track a cantankerous bear than stay in the same room with her. It was not a familiar feeling, or a pleasant one.

"She's probably over at Susan's, then," he said.

"She didn't say where she was headed."

He lingered a moment. "I don't want Chrissie to become a nuisance."

"She isn't, and neither is Susan. They're both great kids, so don't worry, okay?"

Still he hesitated. "They didn't, by chance, ask you a lot of personal questions, did they?"

"Uh...some."

He closed his eyes for a few seconds and an expression of great weariness crossed his face. He sighed. "I'll look for Chrissie over at Susan's. Thanks for your trouble."

His gaze held hers. By the time he turned away,

Bethany felt a little breathless. She was certain of one thing. If it were up to Mitch Harris, she would never have left San Francisco.

Well, that was unfortunate for Mitch. Because Bethany had come to Hard Luck for a reason, and she wasn't leaving until her mission was accomplished.

Come hell or high water.

CHAPTER TWO

"DADDY?"

Mitch looked up from the Fairbanks newspaper to smile at his freckle-faced daughter. Chrissie was fresh out of the bathtub, her face scrubbed clean, her cheeks rosy. She wore her favorite *Beauty and the Beast* pajamas.

His heart clenched with the depth of the love he felt for her. No matter how miserable his marriage had been, he'd always be grateful to Lori for one thing. She'd given him Chrissie.

"It's almost bedtime," he told the seven-year-old.

"I know." Following their nightly ritual, she crawled into his lap and nestled her head against his chest. Sometimes she pretended to read the newspaper with him, but not this evening. Her thoughts seemed to be unusually grave. "Daddy, do you like Ms. Ross?"

Mitch prayed for patience. He'd been afraid of this. Chrissie had been using every opportunity to bring Bethany into the conversation, and he realized she was hoping something romantic would develop between him and the new teacher. "Ms. Ross is very nice," he answered cautiously.

"But do you *like* her?"

"I suppose."

"Do you think you'll marry her?"

It was all Mitch could do to keep from bolting out

of the chair. "I have no intention of marrying anyone," he said emphatically. As far as he was concerned, the subject wasn't open to discussion. With anyone, even his daughter.

Chrissie batted her baby blues at him. "But I thought you liked her."

"Sweetheart, listen, I like Pearl, too, but that doesn't mean I'm going to marry her."

"But Pearl's old. Ms. Ross is only twenty-five. I know because I asked her. Twenty-five isn't too old, is it?"

Mitch gritted his teeth. After they'd driven Bethany home that first night, Chrissie had been filled with questions about the new teacher. No doubt she'd subjected Bethany to a similar inquisition that morning, despite his telling her not to be a nuisance.

Mitch supposed all this talk about marriage was inevitable. The summer had been full of romantic adventures. Certainly Sawyer had wasted no time in marrying Abbey; it didn't help that Abbey's daughter was Chrissie's best friend. Then Charles had become engaged to Lanni, followed by Pete and Dotty's recent announcement. To Chrissie, it must have seemed as if the whole town had caught marriage fever. Bethany, however, had been hired by the school board last spring and had nothing to do with recent influx of women to Hard Luck.

"I like Ms. Ross *so* much," Chrissie said with a delicate sigh.

"You barely know her. You might change your mind once you see her in the classroom." Mitch felt he was grasping at straws, but he was growing more and more concerned. He could hardly forbid his daughter to mention Bethany's name!

He wasn't sure what the woman had done to sprout wings and a halo in his daughter's mind. Nor did he understand why Chrissie had chosen to champion Bethany instead of, say, Mariah Douglas.

Perhaps she'd intuitively sensed his attraction to the young teacher. That idea sent chills racing down his spine. If Chrissie had figured it out, others wouldn't be far behind.

"I won't change my mind about Ms. Ross," Chrissie told him. "I think you should marry her."

"Chrissie. We've already been over this. I'm not going to marry Ms. Ross."

"Why not?"

There was something very wrong with a grown man who couldn't out-argue a seven-year-old child. "First, we don't really know each other. Remember, sweetheart, she's only been in town two days."

"But Sawyer fell in love with Abbey right away."

"Yes..." he muttered warily.

"Then I don't understand why you can't get your word in about Ms. Ross before any of the other men decide they like her, too."

"Chrissie—"

"Someone else might marry her if you don't hurry up."

Mitch calmed himself. It was clear that his daughter had an argument for every answer. "This is different," he explained reasonably. "I'm not Sawyer and Ms. Ross isn't Abbey. She came here to teach, remember? She isn't looking for a husband."

"Neither was Abbey. I really want you to marry Ms. Ross."

Mitch clenched his jaw. "I'm not marrying Ms. Ross, and I refuse to discuss it any further." He rarely used this tone with his daughter, but he wanted it understood that the conversation was over. He wasn't getting married. End of story. No amount of begging and pleading was going to change his mind.

Chrissie was quiet for several minutes. Then she said, "Tell me about my mommy."

Mitch felt like a drowning man. Everywhere he turned there was more water, more trouble, and not a life preserver in sight. "What do you want to know?"

"Was she pretty?"

"Very pretty," he answered soothingly. Normally he found the subject of Lori painful, but right now he was grateful to discuss something other than Bethany Ross.

"As pretty as Ms. Ross?"

He rolled his eyes; he'd been sucker-punched. "Yes."

"She died in an accident?"

Mitch didn't know why Chrissie repeatedly asked the same questions about her mother. Maybe the child sensed he wasn't telling her the entire truth. "Yes, your mother died in an accident."

"And you were real sad?"

"I loved her very much."

"And she loved me?"

"Oh, yes, sweetheart, she loved you."

His daughter seemed to soak in his words, as if she needed reassurance that she'd been wanted and loved by the mother she'd never known.

After that, Chrissie grew thoughtful again. Mitch returned to his newspaper. Then, when he least expected it, she resumed her campaign. "Can I have a brother or sister someday?" she asked him. The question came at him from nowhere and scored a direct hit.

"Probably not," he told her truthfully. "I don't plan to remarry."

"Why don't you?" She wore that hurt-little-girl look that was guaranteed to weaken his resolve.

Mitch made a show of checking his wrist-watch. He was through with answering questions and finding suitable arguments for a child. Through with having Bethany Ross offered up to him on a silver platter—by his daughter, the would-be matchmaker.

"It's time for bed," he said decisively.

"Already?" Chrissie whined.

"Past time." He slid her off his knee and led her into her bedroom. He removed the stuffed animals from the bed while Chrissie got down on her knees to say her prayers. She closed her eyes and folded her hands, her look intent.

Mitch could see his daughter's lips move in some fervent request. He didn't have to be a mind reader to know what she was asking. If God joined forces against him, Mitch figured he'd find himself engaged to the tantalizing Ms. Ross before the week was out.

CHRISTIAN O'HALLORAN, youngest of the three brothers, walked into the Hard Luck Café and collapsed in a chair. He propped his elbows on the tabletop and buried his face in his hands.

Without asking, Ben picked up the coffeepot and poured him a cup. "You look like you could use something stronger," he commented.

"I can't believe it," Christian muttered, running one hand down his face.

"Believe what?" Ben assumed it had something to do with Christian's secretary. He didn't understand what it was about Mariah that Christian found so objectionable. Personally he was rather fond of the young lady. Mariah Douglas had grit. She had the gumption to live in one of those rundown cabins. No power. No electric lights. And for damn sure, nothing that went flush in the night.

"You won't believe what just happened. I nearly got my head chewed off by some feminist attorney."

Now this was news. Ben slid into the chair opposite Christian's. "An attorney? Here in Hard Luck?"

Christian nodded. Even now his face remained a smoldering shade of red. "I was accused of everything from false advertising to misrepresentation and fraud. *Me*," he said incredulously.

"Who hired her?"

Christian's eyes narrowed. "My guess is Mariah."

"No." Ben found that hard to accept. Mariah might have been the cause of some minor troubles with Christian, but there wasn't a vindictive bone in her body. From everything he'd seen of her, Mariah was a sweet-natured, gentle soul.

"It isn't exactly clear who hired the woman," Christian admitted, "but odds are it's Mariah."

"I don't believe that."

"I do!" Christian snapped. "I swear to you Mariah's been looking for a way to do me in from the moment she arrived. First off, she tried to cripple me."

"She didn't mean to push that filing cabinet on your foot."

"Is that a fact? I don't suppose you noticed how perfect her aim was, did you? She's been a thorn in my side from day one. Now this."

"Seems to me you're getting sidetracked," Ben said. He didn't want to hear another litany of Mariah's supposed sins, not when there was other, juicier information to extract. "We were discussing the attorney, re-member?"

Christian plowed all ten fingers though his hair. "The lawyer's name's Tracy Santiago. She flew in from some high-falutin' firm in Seattle. Let me tell you, I've seen sharks with duller teeth. This woman's after blood, and from the sound of it, she wants mine."

"And you think Mariah sent for her?" Ben asked doubtfully.

"I don't know what to think any more. Santiago's here, and when she's through discussing the details of the lawsuit with Mariah, she wants to talk to the others. To Sally McDonald and Angie Hughes." He referred to the two most recent arrivals—Sally, who worked at the town's Power and Light company, and Angie, who'd been hired as an administrative and nursing as-sistant to Dottie. Both of them were living in the house owned by Catherine Fletcher—Matt and Lanni Cald-well's grandmother.

"Are you going to let her?"

Christian raised his eyes until they were level with Ben's. "I can't stop her, can I? But then, I don't think a freight train would slow this Santiago woman down."

"Where is she now? At your office?" Ben asked, craning his neck to look out the window. The mobile office of Midnight Sons was parked next to the airfield, within sight of the café. He couldn't see anything out of the ordinary.

"Yeah, I had to get out of there before I said or did something I'd regret," Christian confessed. "I feel bad about abandoning Duke, but he seemed to be holding his own."

"Duke?"

"Yeah. Apparently he flew her in without knowing

her purpose for coming. He made the fatal mistake of thinking she might have been another of the women I hired. Santiago let him know in no uncertain terms who and what she was. By the time they landed, the two of them were at each other's throats.''

That they'd been able to discuss anything during the flight was saying something, given how difficult it was to be heard above the roar of the engines.

"If I were this attorney," Christian said thoughtfully, "I'd think twice before messing with Duke."

Ben had to work hard to keep the smile off his face. When a feminist attorney tangled with the biggest chauvinist Ben had ever met, well...the fur was guaranteed to fly.

The door opened. Christian looked up and groaned, then covered his face with his hands.

Ben turned around and saw that it was Mariah. He lumbered to his feet, reached for the coffeepot and returned to the counter.

"Mr. O'Halloran," the secretary said as she timidly approached him.

"How many times," Christian demanded, "have I asked you to call me by my first name? In case you haven't figured it out, there are three Mr. O'Hallorans in this town, and two of us happen to spend a good deal of time together in the same office."

"Christian," she began a second time, her voice wavering slightly. "I want you to know I had nothing to do with Ms. Santiago's arrival."

"And pigs fly."

Mariah clenched her hands at her sides. "I didn't know anything about her," she insisted, "and I certainly had nothing to do with hiring her."

"Then who the hell did?"

Ben watched as Mariah closed her eyes and swallowed hard. When she spoke again, her voice was a low whisper. "I suspect it was my dad. He must have talked to her about my being here."

"And why, pray tell, would he do something like that?" Christian asked coldly.

Mariah went pale. "Would you mind very much if I sat down?"

The look Christian threw her said he would. After an awkward moment or two, he curtly gestured toward the seat across from him.

"You want any coffee?" Ben felt obliged to ask.

"No." Christian answered for her. "She doesn't want anything."

"Do you have orange juice?" Mariah asked.

"He has orange juice," Christian told her, "at five bucks a glass."

"Fine."

Another awkward moment of strained silence passed while Ben delivered the four-ounce glass of juice.

"You had something you wanted to tell me?" Christian asked impatiently.

"Yes," she said, her voice gaining strength. "I'm sure my family's responsible for Ms. Santiago's visit. You see...I didn't exactly tell them I'd accepted your job offer. They didn't know—"

"You mean to tell me you were in hiding from your parents?"

"I wasn't hiding," she argued. "Not exactly." She brushed the long strand of hair away from her face, and Ben noticed that her hands were shaking badly. "I wanted to prove something to them, and this seemed the only way I could do it."

"What were you trying to prove?" Christian demanded. "How easy it is to destroy a man and his business?"

"No," she replied, and squared her shoulders. "I wanted to demonstrate to my father that I'm perfectly capable of taking care of myself. That I can support myself, and furthermore, I'm old enough to make my own decisions without him continually interfering in my life."

"So you didn't tell him what you'd done."

"No," she admitted, chancing a quick look in Christian's direction. "Not at first. It's been a while since my family heard from me, so I wrote them a letter last week and told them about the job and how after a year's time I'll have the title to twenty acres and the cabin."

"And?"

"Well, with Hard Luck being in the news and everything, Dad had already heard about the deal Midnight Sons was offering women. He..." She paused and bit her lower lip. "He seems to think this isn't the place for me, and the best way to get me home is to prove you're running some kind of scam. That's why he contacted Ms. Santiago. I think he may want to sue you." She closed her eyes again, as if she expected Christian to explode.

Instead, he stared sightlessly into space. "We're dead meat," he said tonelessly. "Sawyer and I can forget everything we've ever worked for because it'll be gone."

"I explained the situation as best I could to Ms. Santiago."

"Oh, great. By now I'm sure she thinks I've kidnapped you and that I'm holding you for ransom."

"That's not true."

"Think about it, Mariah. Tracy Santiago would give her eyeteeth to cut me off at the knees—and all because you wanted to *prove something* to your father!"

"I'll take care of everything," Mariah promised. Her huge eyes implored him. "You don't have to worry. I promise I'll get everything straightened out. There won't be a lawsuit unless I'm willing to file one, and I'm not."

"*You'll* take care of it?" Christian repeated, and gave a short bark of laughter. "*That's* supposed to reassure me? Ha!"

LANNI CALDWELL glanced at her watch for the third time in a minute. Charles was late. He'd promised to pick her up in front of the *Anchorage News,* where she was working as an intern. She should wait outside for him he'd said. It had been ten days since they'd last seen each other, and she'd never missed anyone so much.

They'd agreed to postpone their wedding until the first week of April. At the time, that hadn't sounded so terrible, but she'd since revised her opinion. If these ten days were any indication of how miserable she was going to be without him, she'd never last the eight months. Her one consolation was that his travel schedule often brought him to Valdez, which was only a short airplane trip from Anchorage.

Just when she was beginning to really worry, Lanni saw him. He was smiling broadly, a smile that spoke of his own joy at seeing her.

Unable to stand still, Lanni hurried toward him, threading her way through the late-afternoon shoppers crowding the sidewalks.

When she was only a few feet away, she started to run. "Charles! Oh, Charles!"

He caught her around the waist and lifted her off the ground. They were both talking at once, saying the same things. How lonely the past days had been. How eight months seemed impossible. How much they'd missed each other. She stopped, simply because there wasn't enough air in her lungs to continue.

It felt so incredibly good to be in his arms again. She hadn't *intended* to kiss him right there on the sidewalk with half of Anchorage looking on, but she couldn't stop herself. Charles O'Halloran was solid and handsome and strong—and he was hers.

His mouth found Lanni's and her objections, her doubts, her misery all melted away. She hardly heard the traffic sounds, hardly noticed the smiling passersby.

Slowly Charles lowered her to the ground. He dragged in a giant breath; so did she. "When it comes to you, Lanni," he whispered, "I haven't got a bit of self-control."

They clasped hands and started walking. "Where are we going?" she asked.

"We have to go somewhere?" he teased.

Lanni leaned her head against his shoulder. "No, but dinner would be nice. I'm starved."

"Me, too, but I'm even more starved for you."

Lanni smiled softly. "I'm dying to hear what came of the lawyer's visit to Hard Luck. What's this about Mariah being the one who's filing the lawsuit? I don't know her well, but I can't see her doing that."

"I'll explain everything later," he promised, wrapping his arm around her, keeping her close to his side.

"All I can say is that Christian deserves whatever he gets. He's been so impatient with her."

Charles's eyes met Lanni's, then crinkled in silent amusement. "Just whose side are you on in this fiasco?"

"Yours," she said promptly. "It's just that I find it all rather…entertaining."

"Is that a fact?" He brought her hand to his lips and kissed her knuckles. "Christian's convinced we're in a damned-if-we-do and damned-if-we-don't situation."

"Really?" Her eyes held his. This could well be more serious than it sounded. "Is Midnight Sons in legal trouble?"

Charles held open the door of her favorite Chinese restaurant. "I don't know. Frankly it's not my problem. Sawyer and Christian are the ones who came up with this brilliant plan to bring women to Hard Luck. I'm sure that between them they'll find a solution."

They were promptly seated and the waiter took their order. "Don't look so worried," Charles said, gripping her hand across the table. "As far as I'm concerned, this is a tempest in a teacup. Mariah's parents are the ones who started this, so I suggested we let Mariah work this out with them. Her father doesn't want to ruin Midnight Sons; all he really cares about is making sure his daughter's safe and sound."

"I'd say Mariah can look after herself very well indeed. She's bright and responsible and—"

"Christian might not agree with you, but I do."

A smile stole across Lanni's features. "You're going to make me a very good husband, Charles O'Halloran."

For long moments they simply gazed at each other. To Lanni there was no better man than Charles, and her heart swelled with love and pride. Of all the women in the world, he'd chosen to marry *her*—but then, she was convinced their falling in love had been no accident.

"I talked to your mother," she said, suddenly remembering the lengthy conversation she'd had earlier with Ellen Greenleaf. Ellen had remarried a couple of years ago and was now living in British Columbia.

"And?"

"And she's absolutely delighted that you came to your senses and proposed."

"I proposed?" he chided. "It seems to me it was the other way around."

"Does it really matter who asked whom?" she said in mock disgust. "The important thing is I love you and you love me."

Charles grew serious. "I do love you."

Lanni would never doubt him. Slowly he raised her hand to his lips and kissed her palm. The action was both sensual and endearing.

"Does your grandmother know about us?" Charles asked.

Lanni shook her head. "Her health has deteriorated in the last couple of weeks. Mom said Grammy doesn't even know who she is half the time. Apparently she slips in and out of consciousness. The doctors...don't expect her to live much longer."

Charles frowned and his eyes grew sad. "I'm sorry, Lanni."

"I know you are."

"I spent a lot of years hating Catherine Fletcher for what she did to my family, but I can't any longer. It's because of her that I found the most precious gift of my life. You. Remember what you said a few weeks ago about the two of us being destined for each other? I believe it now as strongly as I believe anything."

BETHANY HAD PURPOSELY waited three days before making her way to the Hard Luck Café. She'd needed the time to fortify herself for this first confrontation. The night of her arrival, Mitch had confirmed what she already knew: Ben Hamilton owned the café.

Her heart scampered, then thudded so hard it was almost painful. Her palms felt sweaty as she pulled open the door and stepped inside. If she reacted this way before she even met Ben, what would she be like afterward?

"Hello."

Ben stood behind the counter, a white apron wrapped around his middle, a welcoming smile on his lips. Bethany felt as if the wind had been knocked out of her.

"You must be Bethany Ross."

"Yes," she said, struggling to make her voice audible. "You're Ben Hamilton?"

"The one and only." He sketched a little bow, then leaned back against the counter, studying her.

With her breath trapped in her lungs, Bethany made a show of glancing around the empty room. It was eleven-thirty, still early for lunch. The café sported a counter and a number of booths with red vinyl upholstery. The rest of the furnishings consisted of tables and mismatched chairs.

"Help yourself to a seat."

"Thank you." Bethany chose to sit at the counter. She reached for a plastic-coated menu and pretended to study it.

"The special of the day is a roast-beef sandwich," Ben told her.

She looked up and nodded. "What about the soup?"

"Split pea."

Ben was nothing like she'd expected. The years hadn't been as generous to him as she'd hoped. His hair had thinned and his belly hung over the waistband of his apron. Lines creased his face.

If he hadn't introduced himself, hadn't said his name aloud, Bethany never would have guessed.

"Do you want any recommendations?" he asked.

"Please."

"Go with the special."

She closed the menu. "All right, I will."

As he walked back into the kitchen, he asked, "How are things going for you at the school?"

"Fine," she said, surprised she was able to carry on a normal conversation with him. "The kids are great, and Margaret's been a lot of help."

She wondered what Ben saw when he looked at her. Did he notice any resemblance? Did he see how much she looked like her mother, especially around the eyes? Or had he wiped the memory of her mother from his mind?

"Everyone in Hard Luck's real pleased to have you."

"I'm pleased to be here," she answered politely. She was struck by how friendly and helpful he was, how genuinely interested he seemed. Was it because of that quality her mother had fallen in love with him all those years ago?

The door opened and Ben looked up. "Howdy, Mitch. Said hello to the new schoolteacher yet?"

"We met earlier." Bethany thought she detected a note of reluctance in his voice, as if he regretted coming into the café while she was there.

Mitch claimed the stool at the opposite end of the counter.

"I don't think she's contagious," Ben chided from the kitchen, and chuckled. "And she doesn't look like she bites."

Mitch cast Bethany an apologetic glance. Uncomfortable, she glanced away.

Ben brought her meal, and she managed to meet his eyes. "I...I meant to tell you I wanted to take the sandwich with me," she said, faltering over the words. "If that would be all right."

"No problem." He whipped the plate off the counter. "What can I get for you, Mitch?" he asked.

"How about a cheeseburger?"

"You got it." Ben returned to the kitchen, leaving Bethany and Mitch alone.

She looked at him. He looked at her. Neither seemed able to come up with anything to say. In other circumstances, Bethany would have found a hundred different subjects to discuss.

But not now. Not when she was so distracted by the battle being waged in her heart. She'd just walked up to her father and ordered lunch.

No, he *wasn't* her father, she amended. Her father was Peter Ross, the man who'd loved her and raised her as his own. The man who'd sat at her bedside and read her to sleep. The man who'd escorted her to the father-daughter dance when she was a high school sophomore.

The only link Bethany shared with Ben Hamilton was genetic. He was the man who'd given her life, and nothing else. Not one damn thing.

CHAPTER THREE

ON THE FIRST DAY of school, Mitch swore his daughter was up before dawn. By the time the alarm sounded and he struggled out of bed and into the kitchen, Chrissie was already dressed.

She sat in the living room with her lunch pail tightly clutched in her hand. She was dressed in her flashy new jeans and Precious Moments sweatshirt.

"Morning, Daddy."

"Howdy, pumpkin." He yawned loudly. "Aren't you up a little early?" He padded barefoot into the kitchen, with Chrissie following him.

"It's the first day of school." She announced this as if it was news to him.

"I know."

"Ms. Ross said I could be her helper again."

Mitch had stopped counting the number of times a day Chrissie mentioned Ms. Ross. He'd given up telling her he wasn't interested in marrying the teacher. Chrissie didn't want to believe him, and arguing with her only irritated him. In time, she'd see for herself that there would never be a relationship between him and Bethany.

He'd heard that Bethany had stirred up a lot of interest among the single men in town. Good. Great. Wonderful. Soon enough, she'd be involved with someone else, and his daughter would get the message.

Mitch hated to disappoint his tenderhearted seven-year-old. But, he reasoned, disappointment was a part of life, and he wouldn't always be able to protect her. The sooner she accepted there would be only the two of them, the better.

"I packed my own lunch," she told him proudly, holding up her Barbie lunch pail.

"I'm proud of you."

She delighted in showing him what she'd chosen for her lunch. Ham-and-cheese sandwich carefully wrapped in napkins, an apple, juice, an oatmeal cookie. Mitch was pleased to see that she'd done a good job of packing a well-balanced meal and told her so.

He looked at his watch, gauging the time before they could leave. "What about breakfast?"

Although Chrissie claimed she was too excited to eat anything, Mitch insisted she try. "How about a bowl of cereal?" he suggested, pulling out several boxes from the cupboard. He wasn't much of a break-fast eater himself. Generally he didn't have anything until ten or so. More often than not, he picked up a doughnut or something equally sweet when he stopped in for coffee at Ben's.

"I'll *try* to eat something," Chrissie agreed with a decided lack of enthusiasm. He let her pour her own cereal and milk. His daughter was an independent little creature, which was fine with Mitch. He took pride in the fact that Chrissie could take care of herself.

By the time he'd finished dressing, she'd eaten her breakfast and washed and put away her bowl and spoon. She sat on the couch waiting for Mitch to escort her to school.

"Are you sure you need me, now that you're a sec-ond-grader?" Not that Mitch objected to walking his daughter to class. However, he had a sneaking suspicion that if the teacher had been anyone other than the lovely Ms. Ross, Chrissie would have insisted on walking without him.

"I *want* you to take me," she said with a smile bright enough to blind him. The kid knew exactly what she was doing. And being the good father he was, he had to go along with her. The way he figured it, he'd walk her to the school door and, if he was lucky, escape without seeing Bethany.

His plan backfired. Chrissie insisted on showing him her desk.

"I'm over here," she said, taking him by the hand and leading him to the front row. "Ms. Ross let me pick my own seat." Wouldn't you know, his daughter had chosen to sit directly in front of the teacher's desk.

He tried to make a fast getaway, but Bethany herself waylaid him.

"Good morning, Mitch."

"Morning." The tropical bird was back in full plumage. She wore a hot pink skirt with a colorful floral top; it reminded him of the shirt Sawyer had brought back from Hawaii. Her hair was woven into a thick braid that fell halfway down her back.

She did have beautiful hair, he'd say that much. It didn't take a lot of effort to imagine undoing her braid and running his fingers through the glossy strands. He could see himself with his hands buried wrist-deep in her hair, drawing her mouth to his. Her lips would feel silky soft, and she'd taste like honey and passion and—

"Are you picking me up after school?" Chrissie asked, interrupting his thoughts.

Thank heavens she had. Apparently all Chrissie's chatter about Bethany was having more of an effect on him than he'd realized. His heart pounded like an over-worked piston, his pulse thumping so hard he could feel it throb in his neck.

Bethany and Chrissie were both looking at him, awaiting his response. "Pick you up?" As a rule, Chrissie walked over to Louise Gold's house after school.

"Just for today," Chrissie said, her big eyes gazing up at him hopefully.

"All right," he agreed grudgingly. "Just for today." Chrissie's face shone with her smile.

He would've bidden Bethany farewell, but she was talking to other parents. Just as well. The sooner he got away from her, the sooner he could get a grip on his emotions.

Mitch wished to hell he knew what was wrong with him. After vehemently opposing all talk about becoming romantically involved, he found it downright frightening to discover the overwhelming effect she had on him. There was only one way he could account for it.

He'd been too long without a woman.

SAWYER DEBATED what exactly he should say to his brother. It wasn't often he felt called upon to take Christian to task. But enough was enough. Christian had Mariah so unnerved the poor girl couldn't do anything right.

"She did it again," Christian muttered as he walked past Sawyer's desk to his own.

Sawyer looked up. "Who?" he asked in an innocent voice.

Seething, Christian jerked his head toward Mariah. "She can't seem to find accounts receivable on the computer."

"It's here," Mariah insisted, her fingers on the keyboard. Even from where Sawyer was sitting, it looked as though she was randomly pressing keys in a desperate effort to find the missing data. "I'm just not sure where it went."

"Don't you have it on a backup disk?" Sawyer asked.

"Yes..."

"Who knows?" Christian tossed his hands in the air. "The backup disk might well be the same place as the missing file. We could be in real trouble here." Panic edged his voice.

"She'll find it," Sawyer said confidently.

Mariah thanked him with a brief smile.

"Let me look," Christian demanded, flying out of his chair. "Before you do something more serious and crash the entire system."

"I lost it, I'll find it." Mariah didn't budge from her seat. The woman had long since won Sawyer's admiration, not least for the mettle she'd shown in dealing with his brother.

"Leave her be," Sawyer said.

"And risk everything?"

"We aren't risking anything. There's a backup disk."

Christian sat down at his desk, but his gaze remained glued on Mariah. Sawyer watched Christian. And Mariah did her level best to ignore them both.

"Fact is, I could use a break," Sawyer said. "Why don't we let Ben treat us to a cup of his coffee?"

"All right," Christian agreed reluctantly.

As Sawyer walked past Mariah's desk, she mouthed a thank-you. He nodded and steered his irritable brother out the door.

"I wish you wouldn't be so hard on her," he said the minute they were alone. It annoyed him to see Christian treat Mariah as if she didn't have a brain in her head.

"Hard on her?" Christian protested loudly. "The woman drives me insane. If it was up to me, she'd be out of here in a heartbeat. She's trouble with a capital *T.*"

"She's a damn good secretary," Sawyer argued. "The office has never been in better shape. The files are organized and neat, and the equipment's been updated. Frankly I can't believe we managed without a secretary as long as we did."

Christian opened his mouth, then closed it. He didn't have an argument.

"Okay, so there was the one fiasco with that attorney," Sawyer said, knowing that part of Christian's anger stemmed from the confrontation with Tracy Santiago.

Christian's mouth thinned and his eyes narrowed. "Mark my words, she'll be back."

"Who?"

His brother eyed him as if he was dense. "The attorney. If for nothing more than pure spite. That woman's vicious, Sawyer. Vicious. And as if that's not bad enough, she took an instant dislike to all of us—especially Duke. She's out for revenge."

Sawyer didn't believe that. True, Christian had been the one who'd actually talked to her, but his brother's assessment of Tracy's plans for revenge sounded a little farfetched.

"It's my understanding that everything was squared once Mariah talked to her. I don't think there's any real threat."

"For now, you mean," Christian said meaningfully. "But don't think we've heard the end of this. Yup, you mark my words, Santiago's gone for reinforcements."

"Don't be ridiculous. Why would she do that if no one is paying her fee? We've seen the last of her."

"I doubt it," Christian muttered.

Instead of heading straight to Ben's, they strolled toward the open hangar. John Henderson, who served as a sometime mechanic and a full-time pilot, was servicing the six-passenger Lockheed, the largest plane in their small fleet.

When he saw them approach, John grabbed an oil rag from his hip pocket and wiped his hands. "Morning," he called out cheerfully.

Sawyer noticed that John had gotten his hair and beard trimmed. He wasn't a bad-looking guy when he put some effort into his appearance. Of course, there hadn't been much reason to do that until recently.

It occurred to him that Duke Porter might learn a thing or two from John. Duke might have fared better with the Santiago woman had he been a bit more gentlemanly. Sawyer had never seen any two people take such an instant dislike to one another.

"You're looking dapper," he commented, nodding at John, and to his surprise, the other man blushed.

"I was thinking of asking the new schoolteacher if she'd have dinner with me Friday evening," he said. Sawyer noted that John was looking at Christian as if he expected him to object.

"It's Thursday, John," Sawyer pointed out. "Just when do you plan to ask her?"

"That depends." Again John studied Christian.

"What are you looking at me for?" Christian

snapped, his mood as surly with John as it had been earlier with Mariah.

"I just wanted to be sure you weren't planning on asking her yourself."

"Why would I do that?" The glance Christian gave Sawyer said he had more than enough problems with *one* woman.

John's face broke into a wide grin of unspoken relief. "That's great."

Christian grumbled something under his breath as he headed out the other side of the hangar. Sawyer followed him to the Hard Luck Café.

As they sat down at the counter, Ben stuck his head out from the kitchen. "It's self-service this morning, fellows."

"No problem." Sawyer walked around the counter and reached for the pot. He filled two mugs. Meanwhile, Christian helped himself to a couple of powdered-sugar doughnuts from under the plastic dome.

"Getting back to Mariah," Sawyer said when he'd finished stirring his coffee. He felt obliged to clear this up; in his opinion, Christian's attitude needed a bit of adjusting.

"Do we have to?"

"Yes, we do. She's proved herself a capable secretary."

"The woman's nothing but a nuisance. She can't type worth a damn, she misfiles correspondence, and she habitually loses things. The accounts-receivable disaster this morning is a prime example."

"I've never had any trouble with her," Sawyer countered. "I've found Mariah to be hardworking and sincere."

"She makes too many mistakes."

"Frankly I don't see it. If you ask me, *you're* the problem. You make her nervous. She's constantly worried that she's going to mess up—it's a self-fulfilling prophecy. Besides," Sawyer added, "she's gone to a lot of trouble to work things out with her family and settle this lawsuit business. I admire her for that."

Apparently Christian didn't share his admiration. "I wish they'd talked her into heading back to Seattle. It's where she belongs."

Sawyer merely shrugged. "Face the fact that Mariah's going to stay the entire year. It's a matter of pride with her, and that's something we can both appreciate."

Christian looked away.

"She isn't so bad, you know." Sawyer slapped his brother affectionately on the back. "There's one other thing you seem to have conveniently forgotten."

"What's that?"

Sawyer snagged one of Christian's doughnuts. He grinned broadly. "You must have liked *something* about her. After all, you're the one who hired her."

"In other words, I don't have anyone to blame but myself."

"You got it." With that Sawyer walked out of the café, leaving his brother to foot the bill.

IN TWO WEEKS Bethany hadn't seen even a glimpse of Mitch Harris. The man made himself as scarce as sunlight in an Alaskan winter. He must be working overtime, and she had to wonder if it was—at least partly—in an effort to avoid her.

Bethany could accept that he wasn't attracted to her if indeed that was the case. But the night they'd met and each time afterward, she'd sensed a growing awareness between them. She knew he felt it, too, even though he doggedly resisted it. Whenever they were in a room together, no matter how many other people were present, their eyes gravitated toward each other. The solid ground beneath Bethany would subtly shift, and she'd have to struggle to hide the fact that anything was wrong.

"Can I clean the blackboards for you, Ms. Ross?" Chrissie asked, interrupting her musings. The youngster stood next to Bethany's desk. It would be very easy to love this child, she thought.

Chrissie had been her student for two weeks, and it became increasingly difficult not to make her a teacher's pet. The seven-year-old was so willing to please and always looked for ways to brighten Bethany's day.

If Bethany had any complaints about Mitch's daughter, it was the number of times Chrissie introduced her father into the conversation. Clearly the girl adored him.

"Can I?" she asked again, holding up the erasers.

"Certainly, Chrissie. What a thoughtful thing to ask. I'd be delighted if you cleaned the blackboards."

Chrissie flushed with pleasure. "I like to help my dad, too. He needs me sometimes."

"I'll bet you're good at helping him. You've been a wonderful assistant to me."

Once more the child glowed at Bethany's approval. "My dad promised to pick me up after school today," she said; she seemed to be watching for Bethany's reaction to that news. From other bits of information Chrissie had dropped, Bethany knew that Mitch occasionally came for his daughter after school. She herself hadn't seen him.

"With your dad coming, maybe you should skip cleaning the boards this afternoon," Bethany said. She didn't want Mitch to be kept waiting because Chrissie was busy, nor did she want to force him to enter the classroom.

"It'll be all right," Chrissie said quickly. "Don't worry, Dad'll wait."

Still, Bethany wasn't really confident she was doing the right thing, especially since Mitch seemed to be avoiding her so diligently.

The little girl was busy with the blackboards, standing on tiptoes to reach as far as she could, when Mitch walked briskly into the classroom. His movements were filled with impatience. His body language said he didn't appreciate having to come look for his daughter.

As had happened before, his eyes flew to Bethany's, and hers to his. Slowly she rose from behind her desk. "Hello, Mitch."

"Bethany."

"Hi, Dad. I'm helping Ms. Ross. I'm almost done," Chrissie said lightheartedly. "All I have to do is go outside and stamp the chalk out of the erasers. I promise I'll only take a minute."

Mitch opened his mouth as though to protest, but before he could utter a word, Chrissie raced out the door.

Bethany and Mitch were alone.

They couldn't stop staring at each other. Bethany would have paid good money to know what he was thinking. Not that she was all that clear about her own feelings. Their attraction to each other *should* have been uncomplicated. It wasn't as though either of them was involved with anyone else.

True, John Henderson, one of the bush pilots employed by Midnight Sons, had asked her to dinner. She'd accepted; there was no point in sitting around waiting for Mitch to ask her out, and John seemed pleasant.

The silence between them grew louder. Mitch's face was stern, his features set. Bethany sighed, uncertain how to break the ice.

"I understand you're going out to dinner with John Henderson this evening," Mitch surprised her by mentioning.

"Yes." She wasn't going to deny it.

"I think that's a good idea."

"My having dinner with John?"

"Yes."

Their eyes remained locked. Finally she swallowed and asked, "Why?"

"John's a good man."

It was on the tip of her tongue to ask the reason Mitch hadn't asked her out himself. Mitch was attracted to her, and she to him. The force of that attraction was no small thing. Surely it would be better to discuss it openly, even if they didn't act on their feelings. She longed to toss out the subject and see where it would take them. But in the end she said nothing. Neither did Mitch.

Chrissie reentered the classroom, and Bethany slowly moved her gaze from Mitch to his daughter.

"The erasers are clean," Chrissie announced. Her eyes were filled with expectation.

"Thank you, sweetheart."

"You're welcome. Can I clean them again next Friday?"

"That would be very thoughtful."

"Have a nice evening," Mitch said as he walked out the door, his hand on his daughter's shoulder.

"I will, thank you," she called after them, but she didn't think Mitch heard.

The encounter with Mitch left Bethany feeling melancholy. She accompanied Margaret Simpson to her house for a cup of coffee, hoping that a visit with the other teacher would cheer her up; however, despite herself, she remained distracted during their conversation. Once she arrived home, she turned on her CD player and lay down on the carpet in the living room, listening to Billy Joel—which said a good deal about her state of mind.

Instead of being excited about her dinner date, she was bemoaning the fact that it wasn't Mitch taking her out. It was time to face reality: he wasn't interested in seeing her. She told herself it didn't matter. It wasn't the end of the world. There were plenty of other fish in the sea. But her little pep talk fell decidedly flat.

Because John was afraid he might get back late from a flight into Fairbanks, he'd asked if they could meet at the Hard Luck Café. Bethany didn't object. She showered and changed into a knee-length, chocolate brown skirt, an extra-long, loose-knit beige sweater and calf-length leather boots. To dress up the outfit, she wove a silk scarf into her French braid. She looked good and knew it. Her one regret was that Mitch wouldn't see her. She'd like him to know what he was missing!

To her surprise, there were only two other people in the café when she arrived. The men, deeply engrossed in conversation, sat drinking beer at one of the tables.

"My, my, don't you look pretty," Ben hailed her when she took a seat in a booth near the window. Apparently he knew she was meeting John, because he filled two water glasses and tucked a couple of menus under his arm.

"Thank you."

"I heard John's got his eye on you."

Bethany didn't comment. Although she'd been into the café a number of times since her arrival, she was never completely comfortable with Ben. She'd moved to Hard Luck with an open mind about him. She had no plan other than getting to know this man who'd fathered her.

It was something she'd learned only a year ago. Despite the initial shock, this new knowledge didn't change her feelings toward either her mother or Peter Ross. She just wanted to discover for herself what kind of man Ben Hamilton was. She certainly didn't intend to interfere in his life. Nor did she intend to embarrass him with the truth. The year might well come to a close without his ever knowing who she was.

In all honesty, Bethany couldn't think of a way to casually announce that she was his daughter. For a giddy moment, she was tempted to throw open her arms and call him Daddy. But, no—he'd never been that.

Ben lingered at the table. "If you want the truth, I was surprised you were coming here with John."

"Really." Bethany picked up the water glass.

"I kinda thought you were sweet on Mitch."

The glass hit the table with an unexpected thunk, garnering the attention of the restaurant's two other occupants.

Ben rubbed the side of his face. "What I've seen, Mitch is taken with you, as well."

Bethany gazed down at the table and swallowed nervously. "I'm sure that isn't true."

Low laughter rumbled in Ben's chest. "I've seen the way you two send looks at each other. I'm not blind, you know. Yes, sir, I see plenty—lots more than people think." He tapped his finger on his temple to emphasize the point. "I might be a crusty old bachelor, but I—"

"You never married?" she interrupted him.

"No."

"Why not?" She turned the conversation away from herself, at the same time attempting to learn what she could of his life.

"I guess you could say I never found the right woman."

His answer irritated Bethany. Her mother was one of the finest women she'd ever known. The desire to defend her mother, tell this character about the heartache he'd caused, burned in the pit of her stomach.

"How...how long have you been in Alaska?" she asked, instead.

Ben seemed to need time to calculate his answer. "It must be twenty years now. The O'Halloran boys were still wet behind the ears when I made my way here."

"Why Hard Luck?" she asked.

"Why not? It was as good a place as any. Besides," he said, flashing her a grin, "there's something to be said for having the only restaurant within a four-hundred-mile radius."

Bethany laughed.

The door opened and John Henderson rushed in, a little breathless and a whole lot flustered. He hurried over to the table, and his eyes lit up at the sight of her. He seemed speechless.

"Hello again," Bethany said.

John remained standing there, his mouth open.

Ben slapped him on the back. "Aren't you going to thank me for keeping her company?"

John jerked his head around as if noticing Ben for the first time. "Thanks, Ben."

"No trouble." He turned to walk back to the kitchen, but before he did, Bethany's eye caught his and they shared a secret smile. It was a small thing, this smile, but for the first time Bethany felt as if she'd truly communicated with the man she'd come three thousand miles to meet.

DINNER TURNED OUT to be more of an ordeal than Bethany had expected. By the time he'd paid for their meal, Bethany actually felt sorry for John. During the course of their dinner, he'd dripped gravy down the front of his shirt, overturned the sugar canister and spilled his cup of coffee, half of which landed on her skirt. The man was clearly a nervous wreck.

"I'll walk you home," John said.

She waited until they were outside before she thanked him. Although it was only two weeks into September, there was a decided coolness, and the hint of snow hung in the air. Bethany was glad she'd worn her coat.

"Thank you, John, for a lovely evening."

The pilot buried his hands in his jacket pockets. "I'm sorry about the coffee."

"You didn't do it on purpose."

"What about your skirt?"

"Don't worry—I'm sure it'll wash out."

"You didn't get burned?"

She'd assured him she hadn't at least a dozen times. "I'm fine, John, really."

"I want you to know I'm not normally this clumsy."

"I'm sure that's true."

"It's just that it isn't often a woman as beautiful as you agrees to have dinner with me."

There was something touching about this pilot, something endearing. "What a sweet thing to say. Thank you."

"Women like to hear that kind of stuff, don't they?" John asked. "About being pretty and all."

Bethany hesitated, wondering where the conversation was heading. "I'd say it was safe to say we do."

It was difficult to keep from smiling. With someone else, she might have been irritated or worse. But not with John. Besides, the evening was so beautiful. The sky danced with a brilliant display of stars, and the northern lights seemed to sizzle just over the horizon. Bethany couldn't stop gazing up at the heavens.

"Is it always this beautiful here?"

"Yup," John said without hesitation. "But then they say that beauty's in the eye of the beholder."

"That's true," Bethany admitted, a little puzzled.

"It won't be long now before the rivers freeze," he explained soberly.

"So soon?"

"Yup. We're likely to have snow anytime."

Bethany could hardly believe it. "Really?"

"This is the Arctic, Bethany."

"But it seems as if I just got here. It's still summer at home."

"Maybe in California it is, but not here." He looked worried. "You aren't going to leave, are you?"

"No. I signed a contract for this school year. Don't

worry, I'm not going to break my commitment because of a little snow and ice."

They strolled past the school, and she glanced at the building with a sense of pride. She loved her job and her students.

Soon her house was within sight. Bethany was deciding how to handle the awkwardness that might develop when they reached her front door. She didn't plan to invite John in.

"Thank you," Bethany said again when at last they stood on the stoop.

"The evening would've been better if I hadn't…you know."

"Stop worrying about a little coffee."

"Don't forget the sugar canister." He grinned as if he'd begun to find the entire episode amusing.

"Despite a few, uh, mishaps, I really did enjoy dinner," she told him.

John kicked at the dirt with the toe of his shoe. "I don't suppose you'd consider going out with me again."

Bethany wasn't sure how to respond. She liked John, but only as a friend, and she didn't want to mislead him into thinking something more could develop between them. She'd made that mistake once before.

"You don't need to feel guilty if you don't want to," he said, his eyes avoiding hers. He cleared his throat. "I can understand why someone hand-delivered by the angels wouldn't want to be seen with someone like me." He glanced shyly at her.

"How about if we have dinner again next Friday night?" she asked.

John's head shot up. "You mean it?"

Bethany smiled. "This time it'll be my treat."

His smile faded and he crossed his arms on his chest. "You want to buy *me* dinner?"

"Yes. Friends do that, you know." A car could be heard in the distance slowly making its way down the street.

"Friends, you say?" The car was coming closer.

She nodded and leaned forward and very gently pressed her lips to his cheek. As she backed away, she noticed the car had stopped.

Silhouetted against the moonlight sat Mitch Harris. He'd just witnessed her kissing John Henderson.

CHAPTER FOUR

THE FIRST SNOWFALL of the year arrived in the third week of September. Thick flurries drifted down throughout the day, covering the ground and obscuring familiar outlines. Mitch thought he should have been accustomed to winter's debut by now, but he wasn't. However beautiful, however serene, this soft-looking white blanket was only a foretaste of the bitter cold to follow.

He looked at his watch. In a few minutes he'd walk over to the school to meet Chrissie. He'd gotten into the habit of picking his daughter up on Friday afternoons.

Not because she needed him or had asked him to come. No, he wryly suspected that going to the school was rooted in some masochistic need to see Bethany.

He rationalized that he was giving Chrissie this extra attention because he worked longer hours on Friday evenings, when Diane Hestead, a high school student, stayed with her. That was the only night of the week Ben served alcohol. Before the women had arrived, a few of the pilots and maybe a trapper or two wandered into the Hard Luck Café. But with the news of women coming to town, Ben's place had begun to fill up, not only with pilots but pipeline workers and other men.

For the past three Friday nights, John Henderson and

Bethany had dined at the café. They came and left before eight, when Ben opened the bar.

From the gossip circulating around town, Mitch learned that they'd become something of an item, although both insisted they were "only friends."

Mitch knew otherwise. On Bethany's first date with John, he'd happened upon them kissing. Friends indeed! Even now, his gut tightened at the memory.

For the thousandth time he reminded himself that he'd been the one to encourage her to see John. He couldn't very well reveal his discontent with that situation when she'd done nothing more than follow his advice.

He'd tried to convince himself that his discovering John and Bethany together—kissing—had been sheer coincidence. But it hadn't been.

As the public-safety officer, Mitch routinely checked the streets on Friday nights. He'd seen the two leave Ben's place on foot that first evening and had discreetly followed them. On subsequent Fridays he'd continued his spy tactics, always making sure he was out of sight. He wasn't particularly proud of himself, but he found it impossible to resist the compulsion.

Except for their first date, when he'd seen them kissing outside her house, she'd invited John in. The pilot never stayed more than a few minutes, but of course Mitch knew what the two of them were doing.

He kept telling himself he should be pleased she was dating John; Henderson was a decent sort. But Mitch *wasn't* pleased. At nights he lay awake staring at the four shrinking walls of his bedroom. Still, he knew it wasn't the walls that locked him in, that kept him from building a relationship with Bethany.

It was his guilt, his own doubts and fears, that came

between him and Bethany. This was Lori's legacy to him. She'd died and in that moment made certain he'd never be free of her memory.

Mitch checked his watch a second time and decided to head over to the school. The phone rang as he closed and locked the door, but he resisted the temptation to answer it. The machine would pick up the message, and he'd deal with the call when he returned to the office.

Mitch could hear excited laughter in the distance as the children frolicked in the snow. Chrissie loved playing outside, although there would be precious little of that over the next few months.

By the time Christmas came, Hard Luck would be in total darkness. But with the holidays to occupy people's minds and lift their spirits, the dark days didn't seem nearly as depressing as they might have.

Mitch had just rounded the corner to the school when he saw Bethany. She half trotted with her head bowed against the wind, her steps filled with frantic purpose. She glanced up and saw him and stopped abruptly.

"Mitch." Her hand pushed a stray lock of hair away from her face, and he noticed for the first time how pale she was. "It's Chrissie. She's been hurt."

The words hit Mitch like a fist. He ran toward her and gripped her by the elbows. *"What happened?"*

"She fell on the ice and cut herself. The school tried to phone you, but you'd already left the office."

"Where is she?"

"At the Clinic..." Bethany's voice quavered precariously. "I knew you were probably on your way to the school. Oh, Mitch, I'm so afraid."

It was bad. It had to be, otherwise Bethany wouldn't be this pale, this frightened. Panic galvanized him and he began running toward the clinic. He'd gone half a block before he realized that Bethany was behind him, her untutored feet slipping and sliding on the snow. Fearing she might stumble and fall, he turned back and stretched out a hand to her. She grasped his fingers with surprising strength.

Together they hurried toward the clinic. It couldn't have taken them more than two or three minutes to reach the building, but it felt like a lifetime to Mitch. He couldn't bear the thought of something happening to Chrissie. His daughter, his joy. It was she who'd given his life purpose following Lori's death, she who'd given him a reason for living.

He jerked open the clinic door, and the first thing he saw was blood. Crimson droplets on the floor. Chrissie's blood. He stopped cold as icy fingers crept along his backbone.

Dotty Harlow, the nurse who'd replaced Pearl Inman, was nowhere in sight; neither was Angie Hughes.

"Dotty!" he called urgently.

"Daddy." Chrissie moaned his name, and the sound of her pain cut at his heart.

Dotty stepped out of a cubicle in the back. Her soothing voice calmed his panic as she explained that Chrissie required a couple of stitches, which she was qualified to do.

Angie, who'd been talking to Chrissie, stepped aside when he came into the room. Chrissie sniffled loudly and her small arms circled his neck; when she spoke, her words came in a staccato hiccupping voice. "I... fell...and cut my leg real...bad."

"You're going to be fine, pumpkin." Gently he pressed his hand to the side of her sweet face and laid his cheek on her hair.

"I want Ms. Ross."

"I'm here," Bethany whispered from behind Mitch.

Chrissie stretched out her arms and Bethany hugged her close. Watching the two of them together threatened his resolve, as nothing else could have, to guard his heart against this woman.

"You were very brave," Dotty told Chrissie, as she put away the medical supplies.

"I tried not to cry," Chrissie said, tears glistening in her eyes, "but it hurt too bad."

"She's going to need to take this medication," Dotty said, distracting Mitch. The nurse rattled off a list of what sounded like complicated instructions. Possibly because he looked confused and uncertain, Dotty wrote everything down and reviewed it with him a second time.

"I can take her home?" he asked.

"Sure," Dotty said. "If you have any questions, feel free to call me or Angie."

"Thanks, I will."

"Can I go home now?" Chrissie asked.

"We're on our way, pumpkin."

"I want Ms. Ross to come with us. Please, Daddy, I want Ms. Ross."

Any argument he might have offered died at the pleading note in Chrissie's voice. There was very little he could have denied his daughter in that moment.

When they arrived at the house and went inside, Chrissie climbed on Bethany's lap, and soon her eyelids drifted shut.

"How'd it happen?" Mitch asked tersely, sitting across from Bethany. Even now, the thought of losing his child made him go cold with the worst fear he'd ever experienced. When he'd found Lori dead, he hadn't felt the panic that overcame him when a terrified Bethany told him his daughter was hurt.

"I'm not sure myself how it happened," Bethany said. "As she always does on Fridays, Chrissie offered to clean the boards and erasers. My guess is that she took them outside and slipped. She must have cut her leg on the side of the Dumpster. One of the other children came running to get me."

"Thank God you were close at hand."

Bethany squeezed her eyes shut and nodded. When she opened them again, he noticed how warm and gentle they were as she looked down at Chrissie. "I don't mind telling you, it shook me, finding her like that," Bethany admitted. "You have a very special child, Mitch."

"I know." And he did. He felt a strange and unfamiliar blend of emotions as he gazed at the two of them together. One he loved beyond life itself. The other he *wanted* to love, and couldn't. He had nothing to offer her—not his heart, not marriage. And it was because he'd failed Lori, just as she'd failed herself. And failed him, failed her daughter. Day in and day out, his wife had grown more desperate, more unhappy. Following Chrissie's birth, she'd fallen into a deep depression. Nothing he said or did had helped, and he'd finally given up. Mitch blamed himself; his resignation had cost Lori her life.

"She's fast asleep," Bethany whispered, smoothing Chrissie's hair away from her temple. Her words freed him from his bitter memories and returned him to the present.

Mitch stood, gently lifting his daughter from Bethany's arms. He carried her into her bedroom while

Bethany went ahead to turn down the covers, then placed his daughter in her bed.

As soundlessly as possible they left the room, keeping the door half-open.

There wasn't any excuse for Bethany to linger. She had a date with another man—but Mitch didn't want her to leave.

"I suppose you have to get ready for your dinner with John?" he said, tucking his hands in his back pockets.

"No." Her eyes held his and she slowly shook her head.

It was on the tip of his tongue to ask why, but he quickly decided he shouldn't question the unexpected gift that had been dropped in his lap.

"Chrissie and I rented a video to watch tomorrow," he said, hoping to hide his eagerness for her company. "We generally do that on weekends. This week's feature presentation is a three-year-old romantic comedy. Not my choice," he felt obliged to tell her. "Pete Livengood's movie selection isn't the most up-to-date, but I think you'd enjoy it. Would you care to stay and watch it with me?"

She gave a small, tentative smile and nodded.

Heaven knew, Mitch wanted her to stay. About as much as he'd wanted anything in his life.

"How about some popcorn?" she asked.

He grinned almost boyishly. "You got it."

It wasn't until the kernels were sizzling in the hot oil that he realized they hadn't bothered with dinner. It didn't matter. He'd fix something later if they were hungry. He had several hours before his patrol, and he didn't intend to waste them.

When the corn had finished popping, he drenched it

with melted butter, then carried the two heaping bowls into the living room. Bethany followed with tall, ice-filled glasses of soda. He set the bowls on the coffee table and reached for the remote control.

Normally he would have sat in the easy chair and propped his feet on the ottoman. He chose to sit next to Bethany, instead. For this one night, he was going to indulge himself. He needed her.

The movie began, and he eased closer to her on the comfortable padded sofa. He found himself laughing out loud at the actors' farcical antics and clever banter, which was something he didn't do often. Very rarely did he see the humor in things anymore. When he ran out of popcorn, Bethany offered him some of hers. Soon his arm was around her, and she was leaning her head against his shoulder. This was about as close to heaven as he expected to get anytime within the next fifty years.

Curiously time seemed to slow, not that Mitch objected. At one comical moment in the movie, Bethany glanced at him, laughing. Her eyes were a remarkably rich shade of brown. He wondered briefly if their color intensified in moments of passion.

He swallowed hard and jerked his head away. Such thoughts were dangerous and he knew it. He reverted his attention to the television screen. Another mistake. The scene, between the hero and heroine, played by two well-known actors, was the final one of the movie, and it was a love scene.

Mitch watched as the hero's lips moved over the heroine's, first in a slow, easy kiss, then with building passion. The actors were damn good at their craft. It didn't take much to convince Mitch that the two characters they played were going to end up in the bedroom.

His breathing grew shallow as a painful longing sliced through him. The scene reminded Mitch of what he would never have with Bethany. In the same second, he realized with gut-wrenching clarity how much he wanted to kiss her.

As though neither one of them could help it, their eyes met. In Bethany's he read an aching need. And he knew that what he saw might well be a reflection of his own.

There was a long silence as the credits rolled across the screen.

It was either throw caution to the winds and kiss her—or get the hell out while he could still resist her. Almost without making a conscious decision, Mitch leapt from the sofa.

He buried his hands deep in his pockets, because he couldn't trust them not to reach for her. "Good movie, wasn't it?" he asked.

"Wonderful," she agreed, but she couldn't hide the disappointment in her voice.

"MOM, I'M SO SORRY." Lanni Caldwell stood in the doorway of the Anchorage hospital room. Her grandmother had died there only an hour before. "I came the minute I heard."

Kate looked up from her mother's bedside, her eyes filled with tears, and smiled faintly. "Thank you for getting here so quickly." Lanni's father stood behind his wife, his hand on her shoulder.

Lanni gazed at Catherine Fletcher, the woman on the bed. *Grammy.* A term of affection for a woman Lanni barely knew, but one she would always love. Her heart ached at the sight of her dead grandmother. Over the past three months, Catherine's health had taken a slow but steady turn for the worse. Yet even in her failing physical condition, Catherine had insisted she would return to Hard Luck. Dead or alive.

She would return.

Not because it was her home, but because Catherine wanted to go back to David O'Halloran, the man she'd loved for a lifetime. The man who'd left her standing at the altar more than fifty years earlier, when he'd brought home an English bride. The man she'd alternately loved and hated all these years.

"My mother's gone," Kate whispered brokenly. "She didn't even have the decency to wait for me. Like everything else in her life, she had to do this on her own. Alone. Without family."

After spending the summer in Hard Luck, Lanni better understood her mother's pain. For reasons Lanni would never fully grasp, Catherine Fletcher had given up custody of Kate when she was only a toddler. In a time when such decisions were rare, Catherine had chosen to be separated from her daughter. Chosen, instead, to stand impatiently on the sidelines waiting for David's marriage to Ellen to disintegrate. When that didn't happen, Catherine had decided to help matters along. But Ellen and David had clung steadfastly to each other, and in the end, Catherine, following David's untimely death, had let her bitterness and disillusionment take control.

All her life, Kate Caldwell had been deprived of her mother's love. She'd known that her mother had married her father on the rebound. The marriage had lasted less than two years, and Kate's birth had been unplanned, a mistake.

"Matt's on his way," Lanni told her parents. She'd spoken to her brother briefly when he phoned to give her his flight schedule. Sawyer O'Halloran was flying him into Fairbanks, and he'd catch the first available flight to Anchorage that evening. Lanni had arranged to pick him up at the airport.

After saying her own farewell to her grandmother, Lanni moved into the empty waiting room, reserved for family, to wait for her parents. Her heart felt heavy, burdened with her mother's loss more than her own.

Light footsteps alerted her to the fact that she was no longer alone. When she glanced up, she discovered Charles O'Halloran.

"Oh, Charles," she whispered, jumping to her feet. She needed his comfort now, and before another moment had passed, she was securely wrapped in his embrace.

The sobs that shook her came as a shock. Charles held her close, his strength absorbing her pain, his love quieting her grief.

"How'd you know?" Although tempted, she hadn't phoned him even though he was currently working out of Valdez.

"Sawyer."

She should have guessed his brother would tell him.

"Why didn't you call me?" he asked, tenderly smoothing the hair away from her face.

"I...didn't think I should."

Her answer appeared to surprise him. "Why not?"

"Because...I know how you still feel about Grammy. I don't blame you. She hurt you and your family."

They sat down together and Charles gripped both of Lanni's hands in his own. "I stopped hating her this summer. How could I despise the woman who was indirectly responsible for giving me you?''

Lanni swiped at the tears on her cheeks and offered a shaky smile to this man she loved to the very depths of her soul.

"And after my mother told me the circumstances that led to her marrying my dad,'' Charles went on, "I have a better understanding of the heartache Catherine suffered. My father made a noble sacrifice when he married Ellen. I know he grew to love her. But in his own way, I believe he always loved Catherine.''

"I'd like to think they're together now,'' Lanni said. Charles's father and her grandmother. "This time, forever.''

"I'd like to think they are too,'' Charles said softly, and he dropped a gentle kiss on the top of her head.

Lanni pressed her face against his shoulder and closed her eyes.

"The memorial service will be in Hard Luck?'' he asked.

"Yes. And Grammy asked that her ashes be scattered on the tundra next spring.''

He nodded. "Do you know when the service is?''

"No.'' The details had yet to be decided. Lanni lifted her head and looked up at him. "I'm glad you came.''

"I'm glad I did, too. I love you, Lanni. Don't ever hold anything back from me, understand?''

She nodded.

He stood, offering her his hand. "Now let's go see about meeting your brother's plane.''

MITCH HEARD via the grapevine that Bethany had a date with Bill Landgrin. His pipeline crew was working at the pump station south of Atigun Pass. The men responsible for the care and upkeep of the pipeline usually worked seven days on and seven days off. During his off-time, Bill occasionally made his way into the smaller towns that dotted the Alaskan interior.

What he came looking for was a little action. Gambling. Drinking. Every now and again, he went in search of a woman.

Mitch didn't know when or how Bill Landgrin had met Bethany. One thing was sure—Mitch didn't like the idea of his seeing Bethany. In fact, he didn't want the man anywhere near her.

Mitch understood all too well Landgrin's attraction to Bethany. It had been hard enough to idly sit by and watch her date John Henderson. The pilot was no real threat; Bill Landgrin, on the other hand, was smooth as silk and sharp as a tack. A real conniver, Mitch thought grimly.

There was no help for it. He was obligated to warn Bethany of Bill's reputation. *Someone* had to.

He bided his time, waiting until two days before she was said to be meeting Bill. As if it was a spur-of-the-moment decision, he'd stop by to see her after school. He'd make up some fiction about being concerned with Chrissie's grades—which were excellent.

He waited until he could be sure there was no chance of running into Chrissie. The last thing he needed was to have his daughter catch him seeking out Bethany's company. The kid might get the wrong idea.

Mitch had intentionally avoided Bethany since the night of Chrissie's accident. There was only so much temptation a man could take, and that evening had stretched his endurance to the breaking point.

He found Bethany sitting at her desk. Her eyes widened with surprise as he walked into the classroom. "Mitch, hello! It's good to see you."

He smiled briefly. "I hope you don't mind, my stopping in like this."

"Of course not."

"It's about Chrissie," he said hurriedly, for fear Bethany would get the wrong impression. "I've been a little, uh, concerned about her grades."

"But she's excelled in all her subjects. She's getting top marks."

He was well aware that his excuse was weak. From the moment school had started, he hadn't had to hound Chrissie to do her homework. Not even once. She would've gladly done assignments five hours a night if it meant pleasing Ms. Ross.

"I've been wondering about her grades since the accident," he said.

"They're fine." Bethany flipped through her grade book and reviewed the most recent entries. "I've kept a close eye on her, looking for any of the symptoms Dotty mentioned, but so far everything's been great. Is there a problem at home—I mean, has she been dizzy or anything like that?"

"No. No," he was quick to reassure her.

"Oh, good." She seemed relieved, and he felt even more of a fool.

Mitch stood abruptly and turned as if to leave. "By the way," he said, trying to make it sound like an afterthought, "I don't mean to pry, but did I hear correctly? Rumor has it you're having dinner with Bill Landgrin this Friday night."

"Yes." She stared at him. "How'd you know that?"

"Oh," he said with a nonchalant shrug, "word has

a way of getting around. I didn't know you two had met.''

"Only briefly. He was on a flight with Duke and stopped in at the café the same time I was there,'' she explained.

"I see,'' he said thoughtfully. He started to leave, then turned back with a dramatic flourish. "What about John? Do you often date men you've just met?''

"What about him?''

"Why aren't you seeing him anymore?''

Bethany hesitated. "I don't think I like the tone of your question, Mitch. I have every right to date whomever I wish.''

"Yes, of course. I didn't mean to imply anything else. It's just that, well, if you must know, Bill has something of a...reputation.''

She stiffened. "Thank you for your concern, but I can take care of myself.''

He was making a mess of this. "I didn't mean to offend you, Bethany. It's just that I'm all this town's got in the way of law enforcement, and I thought it was my duty to warn you.''

"I see.'' She snapped the grade book shut. "And I'm a policeman's daughter. As I told you earlier, I can take care of myself.'' She made a production of looking at her watch. "Now if you'll excuse me?''

"Yes, of course,'' he said miserably, turning to go. And this time he left.

BETHANY WASN'T SURE why she was so angry with Mitch. Possibly because he was right. She had no business having dinner with a man she barely knew. Oh, she'd be safe enough. Not much was going to happen to her in the Hard Luck Café with half the town looking on.

It went without saying that she'd agreed to this dinner date for all the wrong reasons. John Henderson had started seeing another woman recently. One of the newer recruits, a shy young woman named Sally McDonald.

After nearly six weeks here, Bethany had to conclude that Mitch didn't want to become romantically involved. The night of Chrissie's accident, she'd felt certain they'd broken through whatever barrier separating them. Even now, she remembered the way his eyes had held hers following the love scene in the movie. Bethany knew darn well what he was thinking, because she was thinking it, too. Then, when things looked the most promising, Mitch had leapt away from her as if he'd been scorched. Since then, he'd had nothing to say to her. Bethany was left feeling frustrated and confused.

When Bill Landgrin had asked her out, she'd found a dozen reasons to accept. She'd always been curious about the Alaska pipeline. It was said to stretch more than eight hundred miles across three mountain ranges and over thirteen bridges. Having dinner with a man who could answer her questions seemed innocent enough.

In addition, it sent a message to Mitch, one he'd apparently received loud and clear. He didn't like the idea of her dating Bill Landgrin, and frankly she was glad. Unfortunately Mitch had to use his daughter's injury as an excuse to talk to her about Bill. That was what irritated Bethany most.

MITCH HONESTLY TRIED to stay away from Bethany on Friday night. Chrissie was spending the night at Susan's, and the house had never seemed so empty. By seven o'clock, the walls were closing in so tightly he'd had to grab his coat and flee.

He tried to look casual and unconcerned when he walked into Ben's café. A quick look around, and his mouth filled with the bitter taste of disappointment. Bethany was nowhere in sight.

"Looking for the new teacher, are you?" Ben asked as he dried a glass with a crisp linen cloth.

"What gives you that idea?" Mitch growled. He was in no mood for conversation. "I came here for a piece of pie."

"I thought you decided to cut back on sweets."

"I changed my mind," Mitch argued. If he'd known Ben was going to be such a pain in the butt, he would've stayed at home.

Ben brought him a slice of apple pie. "In case you're interested, she left not more than twenty minutes ago."

"Who?" he asked, pretending he didn't know.

"She wasn't alone, either. Bill insisted on seeing her home."

Agitated, Mitch slapped his fork down on the plate. "Who Bethany Ross dates is her own damn business."

"Maybe," Ben said, bracing both hands against the counter, "but I don't trust the man, and you don't either, otherwise you wouldn't be here. My feeling is maybe one of us should check up on Bethany—see that everything's the way it should be."

Mitch was convinced there was more to this scenario than Ben was telling him. His blood started to heat.

"Since you're the law in this town, I think you ought to go make sure she got home all safe and sound."

Mitch wiped his mouth with the back of his hand.

Ben was right. If anything happened to Bethany, Mitch would never forgive himself. In the meantime, if he did meet up with Bill, he'd impress upon the man that he was to keep away from Bethany.

"So, are you going to see her?"

No use lying about it. "Yeah."

"Then the pie's on the house," Ben said, grinning.

Mitch drove to Bethany's, grateful to see that the lights were still on. He knocked loudly on the door and would have barged in if she hadn't opened it when she did.

"Mitch?"

"May I come in?"

"Of course." She stepped aside.

He walked in and looked around. If Bill was there, he saw no evidence of it.

She'd been combing her hair, and the brush was still in her hand. She didn't ask Mitch why he'd come.

He suspected she knew.

"Did Landgrin try anything?" Mitch demanded.

Her eyes narrowed as if she didn't understand the question.

"Landgrin. Did he try anything?" he repeated gruffly.

She blinked. "No. He was a perfect gentleman."

Mitch shoved his fingers though his hair as he paced the confines of her small living room. He didn't need anyone to tell him what a fool he was making of himself.

"Will you be seeing him again?"

"That's my business."

He closed his eyes and nodded. Certainly he had no argument. "Sorry," he said. "I shouldn't have come." He stalked toward the door, eager to escape.

"Mitch?"

His hand was on the doorknob. He stopped but didn't turn around.

"I won't be seeing Bill Landgrin again."

Relief coursed through him.

"Mitch?"

She was close, so very close. He could feel her breath against the back of his neck. All he had to do was turn and she'd be there. His arms ached to hold her. His hand tightened on the doorknob as though it were a lifeline.

"I won't see Bill again," she said in a voice so soft he had to strain to hear, "because I'd much rather be seeing you."

CHAPTER FIVE

A WEEK FOLLOWING Catherine Fletcher's death, the town held a memorial service. Although she'd never met Catherine, Bethany felt obliged to attend. She slipped into the crowded church and took a place in the last row, one of the only seats left. It seemed everyone in Hard Luck wanted to say a formal goodbye to the woman who'd had such a strong impact on their community.

The moment news of Catherine's death had hit town, it was all anyone could talk about. Apparently the woman's parents had been the second family to settle in Hard Luck. Bethany knew that Catherine had grown up with David O'Halloran, although a lot of the history between the two families remained unclear to her. But it was obvious that Catherine Fletcher had played a major role in shaping the town. Folks either loved her or hated her, but either way, they respected her feisty opinions and gutsy spirit.

The mood was somber, the sense of loss keen. Hard Luck was laying to rest a piece of its heart.

A number of people attending the service were strangers to Bethany. The members of Catherine's family had flown in for the memorial. An older couple she assumed was Catherine's daughter and son-in-law. Matt Caldwell, Catherine's grandson, lived in Hard Luck. Bethany had met him one Saturday afternoon at

Ben's café. She remembered that Matt had bought out the partially burned lodge from the O'Hallorans and was currently working on the repairs.

When they'd met, Matt had told her he planned to open the lodge in time for the tourist traffic next June. It was on Bethany's mind to ask *what* tourist traffic, but she hadn't.

Matt's younger sister, Lanni, sat in the front pew, as well, Charles O'Halloran close by. Bethany had heard that they were engaged, with their wedding planned for sometime in April. Even from this distance, she could see how much in love they were. It was evident from the tender looks they shared and the protective stance Charles took at his fiancée's side.

Abbey had told her about Sawyer's older brother and Lanni, and a little of the story about O'Halloran brothers' father and Catherine Fletcher. Bethany gathered that for many years there'd been no love lost between Catherine and the O'Hallorans. Then again, she thought, perhaps that *was* the problem between the two families. *Love lost.* Maybe, just maybe, it had been found again through Charles and Lanni.

Silently Bethany applauded them for having the courage to seek out their happiness, despite the past.

Reverend Wilson, the circuit minister, had flown in for the service. He stepped forward, clutching his Bible, and began the service with a short prayer. Bethany solemnly bowed her head. No sooner had the prayer ended than Mitch Harris slipped into the pew beside her.

He didn't acknowledge her in any way. She could have been a stranger for all the attention he gave her. His attitude stung. It hurt to realize that if there'd been anyplace else to sit, he would have taken it.

As the service progressed, Bethany noticed how restless Mitch became. He shifted his position a number of times, almost as though he was in some discomfort. When she dared to look his way, she discovered that his eyes were closed and his hands tightly clenched into fists.

Then it hit her.

She knew little of his life, but she did know that he was a widower.

Reverend Wilson opened his Bible and read from the Twenty-third Psalm. "'Yea, though I walk through the valley of the shadow of death, I will fear no evil: for thou art with me; thy rod and thy staff they comfort me.'"

Mitch had traversed that dark, lonely valley himself, and Bethany speculated that he hadn't found the comfort the pastor spoke of. And she realized, as Reverend Wilson continued, that it wasn't Catherine Fletcher Mitch mourned. It was his dead wife. The woman he'd loved. And married. The woman who'd carried his child. The woman he couldn't forget.

How foolish she'd been! Mitch didn't want to become involved with her. How could he when he remained emotionally tied to his dead wife? No wonder he'd been fighting her so hard. He was trapped somewhere in the past, shackled to a memory, a dead love.

Bethany closed her eyes, amazed that it had taken her so long to see what should have been obvious. True, he was attracted to her. That much neither could deny. But he wasn't free to love her. Maybe he didn't *want* to be free. He probably hated himself for even thinking about someone else. His behavior at this memorial service explained everything.

Mitch leaned forward, supporting his elbows on his

knees, and hid his face in his hands. He was in such unmistakable pain that Bethany couldn't sit idly by and do nothing. Not knowing whether her gesture would be welcome, she drew a deep breath and gently laid her hand on his forearm.

He jerked himself upright and swiveled in his seat to look at her. Surprise blossomed in his eyes. Apparently he'd forgotten he was sitting next to her. She gave him a slight smile, wanting him to know only that she was his friend. Nothing more.

Mitch blinked, and his face filled with a vulnerability that tore at her heart. She wanted to help, but she didn't know how.

As if reading her thoughts, Mitch reached out and grasped her hand. The touch had nothing to do with physical desire. He'd come to her in his pain.

Then, as if he couldn't bear it any longer, he rose abruptly and hurried out of the church. Bethany twisted around and watched him leave, the doors slamming behind him.

MITCH STALKED into his office, his chest heaving as if the short walk had demanded intense physical effort. His heart hammered wildly and his breathing was labored.

He'd decided at the last minute to attend the memorial service. He hadn't known Catherine Fletcher well, but appreciated the contribution she and her family had made to the community.

Mitch had talked with her only a few times in the past five years. Nevertheless he'd seen his attendance at the service as a social obligation, a way of paying his respects.

But the minute he'd walked into the church, he'd

been bombarded with memories of Lori. They'd come at him from all sides, closing in on him until he thought he'd suffocate.

He remembered the day he'd first met her and how attracted he'd been to the delightful sound of her laughter. They'd been college sophomores, still young and inexperienced. Then they'd gotten married; they'd had the large, traditional wedding she'd wanted and he'd never seen a more beautiful bride. They were deeply in love, blissfully happy. At least he'd been. In the beginning.

When they learned she was pregnant, a new joy, unlike anything he'd experienced before, had taken hold of him. But after Chrissie was born, their lives had quickly slid downhill. Mitch covered his head. He didn't want to remember any more.

He continued to pace in the silence of his office. Attending the memorial service had been a mistake. He'd suffered the backlash caused by years of refusing to deal with the pain. Years of denial. Now he felt as though he were collapsing inward.

He'd never felt so desperate, so out of control.

"Mitch."

He whirled around. Bethany stood just inside the office, her eyes full of compassion.

"Are you all right?"

He nodded, soundlessly telling her nothing was wrong. Even as he did, he realized he couldn't sustain the lie. "No," he said in a choked whisper.

Slowly she advanced into the room. "What is it?"

He closed his eyes and shook his head. His throat clogged. He stood defenseless as his control crumpled.

Gently Bethany's hand fell on his arm. He might have been able to resist her comfort if she hadn't touched him. His body reacted immediately to the physical contact, and he lurched as if her hand had stung him. Only it wasn't pain he experienced, but an incredible sense of release.

"Let me hold you...please," he said. "I need...I need you." He didn't wait for her permission before he brought her into his arms and buried his face in her shoulder. She was soft and warm. Alive. He drew in several great lungfuls of air, hoping that would help stabilize his erratic heart.

"Everything's all right," she whispered, her lips close to his ear. "Don't worry."

Her arms were his shelter, his protection. The first time he'd met Bethany, he'd promised himself he wouldn't become involved with her. Until now he'd steadfastly stuck to that vow.

But he hadn't counted on needing her—or anyone—this badly. She was his sanity.

He knew he was going to kiss her in the same moment he acknowledged how desperate he'd been for her. With a hoarse groan that came from deep in his throat he surrendered to a need so strong he couldn't possibly have refused it.

Their lips met, and it was like a burst of spontaneous combustion. He'd waited so long. He needed her so badly. One hand gathering the blond thickness of her unbound hair, he kissed her repeatedly, working his mouth over hers, unable to get enough.

He feared his astonishing need had shocked her, and he sighed with heartfelt relief when she opened her mouth to him, welcoming the invasion of his tongue.

He moaned, wanting to tell her how sorry he was. But he was unwilling to break the contact, to leave her for even those short seconds.

Bethany coiled her arms tightly about his neck. Again and again he ran his hands down the length of her spine, savoring the feel of this woman in his arms. Their mouths worked urgently, frantically, against each other. He felt insatiable, and she responded with an intensity that equaled his own.

Mitch broke off the kiss when it became more than he could physically handle. He felt that the passion between them might never have burned itself out. At the rate things had progressed, the kiss would quickly have taken them toward something more intimate. Something neither one of them was ready to deal with yet.

Bethany gasped in an effort to catch her breath, and she pressed her hand over her heart as though to still its frenzied beat. Her lips were swollen. Mitch raised his index finger and gently stroked the slick smoothness of her mouth.

Slowly he raised his head and studied her.

She blinked, as if she was confused. Or dazed.

He was instantly filled with regret. "That should never have happened," he whispered.

She said nothing.

"I promise you it won't happen again," he continued.

Her eyes flickered with...anger? She opened her mouth, then abruptly closed it again. Before another second had passed, she'd turned and rushed out of his office.

MATT HAD FOUND the day long and emotionally exhausting. He'd attended the services for his grandmother and the wake that followed.

His mother mourned deeply, and in his own way

Matt did, too. His grief surprised him. Matt had barely known Catherine—Grammy, as Lanni called her. There'd only been a few visits over the years.

She'd always sent a card with a check for his birthday. Money again at Christmas. A Bible when he graduated from high school, and a trust fund she'd established for him. This was the money he'd used to buy the lodge from the O'Halloran brothers.

His grandmother had never known how he'd used the money in the trust fund. By the time he was able to collect it this past summer, her health had disintegrated so much she no longer recognized him. Somehow Matt felt she would have condoned his choice. He liked to think she would have, anyway.

The memorial service and wake had gone well. Virtually all the townspeople had offered condolences, and many had inquired about his progress with the lodge.

The people of Hard Luck had been open and friendly since his arrival, but Matt tended to keep to himself. He was too busy getting the lodge ready to socialize much. He didn't dare stop and think about everything that needed to be done before he officially posted an Open sign on the front door. The multitude of tasks sometimes overwhelmed him.

Readying the lodge was a considerable chore, but his success depended on a whole lot more than making sure the rooms were habitable.

He'd have to convince people to make the trek this far north, and he'd have to provide them with activities. Wilderness treks, fishing, dogsledding. If his first order of business was getting the lodge prepared for paying customers, his second was attracting said customers.

He'd do it. Come hell or high water or both. By God, he'd do it. He had something to prove to—

His mind came to an abrupt halt.

Karen.

He worked fifteen-hour days for one reason, and that reason was Karen. Just saying her name produced an aching sensation in his heart, an ache that had started the day she'd filed for divorce.

What the hell kind of wife filed for divorce without discussing the subject with her husband first? Okay, so maybe she'd mentioned once or twice that she was unhappy.

Well, dammit, he was unhappy, too!

He'd be the first to admit she had a valid complaint—but only to a point. True, he'd changed careers four times in about that many years. He was a man with an eye to the future, and opportunities abounded. But Karen had accused him of being self-indulgent and irresponsible, unable to settle down. That wasn't true, though. He'd always headed on to something new when the challenge was gone, when a job no longer held his interest.

In some ways he supposed he could understand her discontent, but he'd never thought she'd actually leave him. To be fair, she'd threatened it, but he hadn't believed her.

If she truly loved him, she would have stuck it out.

Matt shook his head. There was no point in reviewing the same issues again. He'd gone over what had led to the divorce a thousand times without solving anything. It wouldn't now, either.

The final blow had been when she left Alaska. Oh, he'd fully expected her to do well in her career. She was an executive secretary for some highfalutin engineering company. Great job. Great pay. When they'd offered her a raise and a promotion, she'd leapt at the chance. Without a word, she'd packed her bags and headed for California.

For the love of God, California? Even now he had trouble believing it.

He reached for a magazine and idly flipped through the pages, then slapped it closed. Thinking about Karen was unproductive.

California! He hoped to hell she was happy.

No, he didn't. He wanted her to be miserable, as miserable as he was. Damn, but he missed her. Damn, but he loved her.

A year. You'd think he'd be over her by now. He should be seeing new women, going out, making friends. He might have, too, if he wasn't so busy working on the lodge. But if he had some free time and if there were single women available—like that new teacher, maybe—he'd start dating again.

No, he wouldn't.

Matt wasn't going to lie to himself. Not after today when he'd stood with his family and mourned the loss of his grandmother. His parents had been married nearly thirty years now, high school sweethearts. Lanni and Charles had stood on his other side. Together.

Losing Grammy had been difficult for Lanni. Having spent part of the summer in Hard Luck cleaning out their grandmother's home, Lanni felt much closer to Catherine. She grieved, and Charles was there to lend comfort.

The way his father comforted his mother.

But Matt stood alone.

It pained him to admit how much he'd yearned to have Karen beside him. His agony intensified when he was forced to recognize how deeply he still loved her.

He wondered if it would always be this way. Would

he ever learn to let her go? Not that he had any real choice. The truth was, any day now he expected to hear she'd remarried.

There wasn't a damn thing to stop her. The men in California would have to be blind not to notice her. It wouldn't take long for her to link up with some executive who'd give her the stability she craved. There wasn't a man alive who could resist her, he thought morosely. He should know.

His ex-wife was beautiful, talented, generous and spirited. Was she spirited!

A smile cracked his lips. Not many people would believe that the cool, calm Karen Caldwell loved to throw things—mainly at Matt. She'd hurled the most ridiculous objects, too.

His shirt. A newspaper. Potato chips. Decorator pillows.

When her anger reached this point, there was only one sure method to cool her ire. One method that had never failed him.

He'd make love to her. The lovemaking was wild and wicked, and soon they'd both be so caught up in the sheer magic of it she'd forget whatever it was that had angered her.

Matt remembered the last time Karen had expressed her fury like a major-league pitcher. His smile widened as he leaned back in his chair and clasped his hands behind his head.

He'd quit his job. All right, he should have discussed it with her first. He hadn't planned to go into work that day and hand in his notice. It had just…happened.

Karen had been furious with him. He tried to explain that he'd found something better. Accounting wasn't for him—he should have realized it long before now.

He'd been thinking about something else, something better suited to his talents.

She wouldn't give him a chance to explain. Ranting and raving, she'd started flinging whatever she could lay hands on. Matt had ducked when she'd sent her shoes flying in his direction. The saltshaker had scored a direct hit, clobbering him in the chest.

That had given her pause, he recalled, but not for long. Braving her anger, he'd advanced toward her. She'd refused to let him near her. When she ran out of easy-to-reach ammunition, she'd walked across the top of the sofa and leapt onto the chair, all the while shouting at the top of her lungs and threatening him with the pepper mill.

It hadn't taken much to capture her and he'd let her yell and struggle in his arms for a few minutes. Then he did the only thing he could to silence Karen—kiss her.

Before long, the pepper mill had tumbled from her hands and onto the carpet, and they were helping each other undress, their hands as urgent as their need.

Afterward, he remembered, Karen had been quiet and still. While he lay on his back, appreciating the most incredible sex of his life, his wife had been plotting their divorce. Less than a week later, she moved out and he was served with the papers.

The smile faded as the sadness crept back into his heart.

He modified his wish. He didn't want Karen to be miserable. If someone had to be blamed, then fine, he'd accept full responsibility for their failure. He deserved it.

He missed her so much! Never more than now. Whatever happened in the future with this lodge and the success of his business venture seemed of little consequence. Matt would go to his grave loving Karen.

Like his grandmother before him, he would only love once.

"YOU'RE LOOKING PENSIVE," Sawyer said as he sat on the edge of the bed and peeled off his socks.

With her back propped against the headboard, Abbey glanced over the top of her mystery novel. "Of course I look pensive," she muttered, smiling at her husband. "I'm reading."

"You're pretending to read," he corrected. "You've got that look again."

"What look?" she asked him with an expression of pure innocence.

"The one that says you're plotting."

Abbey made a face at him. How was it Sawyer knew her so well? They hadn't been married all that long. "And what exactly am I plotting?" She'd see if he could figure *that* one out.

"I don't know, but I'm sure you'll tell me sooner or later."

"For your information, Mr. Know-It-All, I was just thinking about Thanksgiving."

Sawyer cocked his head to one side, as if to say he wasn't sure he should believe her. "That's weeks away. Tell me what could possibly be so important about Thanksgiving that it would occupy your mind now?"

"Well, for one thing, I was thinking we should ask Mitch and Chrissie to join us." She glanced at her husband in order to gauge his reaction.

Sawyer didn't hesitate. "Good idea."

"And Bethany Ross."

A full smile erupted on Sawyer's handsome face as he pointed his finger at her. "What did I say? You're plotting."

"What?" Once more she feigned innocence.

"You want to invite Mitch *and* Bethany to Thanksgiving dinner?"

"Right," she concurred, opening her eyes wide in exaggerated wonder that he could find anything the *least* bit underhand in such a courtesy. "And what, pray tell, is so devious about that?"

His finger wagged again as he climbed into bed. "A little matchmaking, maybe? You've got something up your sleeve, Abbey O'Halloran."

"I most certainly do not," she said with a touch of righteous indignation.

"I notice you didn't suggest inviting John Henderson."

"No," she admitted.

"Isn't he the one Bethany's been having dinner with the last few weeks?"

"They're friends, that's all."

"I see." Sawyer leaned over and deftly reached for one end of the satin ribbon tying the collar of her pajama top. He slowly tugged until it fell open.

"Besides, I heard from Mariah that John's interested in someone else now."

Sawyer idly unfastened the first button of her top. "Is that right?"

Her husband's touch was warm, creating feathery sensations that scampered across her skin.

Sawyer's eyes dropped to her mouth, and his voice lowered to a soft purr. "Mitch has lived here for a number of years now."

"True." Her second button gave way as easily as the first.

"If he was interested in remarrying, he'd have done something about it before now, wouldn't you think?"

Abbey closed her book and set it blindly on the table next to the bed. "Not necessarily."

"Do you think Mitch is interested in Bethany?" Sawyer slipped his hand inside the opening he'd created.

Abbey closed her eyes at the feel of her husband's fingers. "Yes." The word sounded shockingly intimate.

"As it happens," Sawyer said in a husky whisper, "I agree with you."

"You do?" Her voice dwindled to a whisper. With her eyes still closed, she swayed toward him.

Sawyer's kiss was long and deep. The conversation about Mitch Harris and Bethany Ross stopped there. Instead, Sawyer and Abbey continued their dialogue with husky sighs and soft murmurs.

BETHANY WALKED into the Hard Luck Café shortly after ten on Saturday and sat at the counter. The place was empty of customers. Ben wasn't in sight, either, which was fine; she wasn't in any hurry. Tired of her own company, she'd decided to take a walk and sort through what had happened between her and Mitch. Ha! she thought sourly. As if such a thing was possible.

There wasn't anyone she could ask about Mitch's past. And apparently *he* wasn't going to volunteer the information. He hadn't said word one about his life before Hard Luck, and no one else seemed to know much, either.

As for what had happened at the memorial service,

Bethany had given up any attempt to make sense of it. For whatever reason, Mitch had turned to her. He'd kissed her with such intensity, such hunger, that her heart had burst open with an incredible sense of joy.

Then he'd apologized. And she'd realized he had simply needed someone. Anyone. Any woman would have sufficed. She just happened to be handy. The minute he saw what he'd done, he regretted ever having touched her.

"Bethany, hello! How are you this fine day?" As always, Ben greeted her with a wide smile as he bustled up to the counter. "We missed you at the wake after Catherine's memorial service. The women in town put on a mighty fine spread."

There was probably some psychological significance in the fact that she'd seek out Ben now, Bethany decided. If she wasn't so sick of analyzing the situation between her and Mitch, she might have delved into *that* question. As it was, she felt too miserable to care.

"I'm fine."

"Is that so?" Without her asking, Ben filled a mug with coffee. "Then why are those little lines I see between your eyes?"

"What lines?"

He pointed to his own forehead. "When I'm stewing about something, these lines magically appear on my brow. Three of them. Seems to me you're cursed with the same thing. Can't fool a living soul, no matter how hard I try." He smiled, encouraging her to talk.

Bethany resisted the urge to tell him she'd come by those lines honestly. Inhaling a deep breath, she eyed him, wondering how much she dared confide in him about her feelings for Mitch. Darn little, she suspected.

That she'd even wonder was a sign of how desperate she'd become.

"What can you tell me about Mitch?" she asked.

"Mitch? Mitch Harris?" All at once, Ben found it necessary to wipe down the counter. He ran a rag over the top of the already spotless surface. "Well, for one thing, he's a damn good man. Decent, caring. Loves his daughter."

"He's lived in Hard Luck for how long?" She already knew the answer, but she wanted to ease Ben into the conversation.

"Must be five years now. Maybe a little longer."

She nodded. "I heard he worked for the police department in Chicago before that."

"That's what I heard, too."

"Do you know how his wife died?" Since Ben wasn't going to volunteer any real information, she'd have to pry it out of him.

"Can't say I do." His mouth twisted to one side, as if he was judging what he should and shouldn't tell her. "I don't think Mitch has ever talked about her to anyone. Hasn't mentioned her to me."

Bethany heard the door open behind her. Their conversation was over, not that she'd gleaned any new information.

"If you're curious about his wife," Ben whispered, "I suggest you ask him yourself. He just walked in."

For the briefest of seconds, she felt like a five-year-old with her hand caught in the cookie jar.

To her surprise, Mitch opted to sit on the stool next to hers. He studied her for what seemed an eternity. "Hello, Bethany," he finally said in a low voice.

"Mitch." She refused to meet his eyes.

"I'm glad I ran into you."

Well, that was certainly a change.

Ben strolled over and Mitch asked for coffee.

"I'd like to talk to you, Bethany." He gestured toward one of the booths, the steaming mug in his hand.

She followed him to the farthest booth, and they sat across from each other. For long moments, he didn't say anything, and when he lifted his head to look at her, his eyes were bleak.

"Bethany, I can't tell you how sorry I am. I don't know what else to say. I've lain awake nights worrying what you must think of me."

Confused and hurt, Bethany said nothing.

He gestured helplessly. "I'm sorry. What more can I say? Talk to me, would you? Say something. Anything."

"What are you sorry for?" she asked, her voice almost a whisper. "Kissing me?"

"Yes."

Even now he didn't seem to realize she'd been a willing participant. "You needed me. Was that why?"

"Yes," he said, as if this was his greatest sin.

She hesitated, searching for the words. "Any other woman would have done just as well. Isn't that what you're really saying? It wasn't *me* you were kissing. It wasn't *me* you needed. I just happened to...be available."

CHAPTER SIX

"YOU'RE GOING to do it, aren't you?" Duke Porter asked John for the second time. An incredulous look contorted the pilot's features. "You're *actually* going to do it?"

"Yes," John said, irritated. He jerked the grease rag from his back pocket and brusquely wiped his hands.

Duke followed him to the far end of the hangar while John put away the tools he'd used. "You're sure this is what you want?"

John didn't hesitate. "I'm absolutely, positively sure."

"But you barely know the woman."

"I know everything I need to know," he muttered. Duke was good at raising his hackles, but nothing was going to ruin this day. The engagement ring burned a hole in his pocket. The searing eagerness to propose was nothing compared to the way he felt about Sally.

This time it was *his* turn. Earlier, he'd fallen all over himself in an attempt to court Abbey Sutherland. What he hadn't known was that Sawyer O'Halloran had stolen her heart without giving any of the others a chance.

Then there was Lanni Caldwell. John had never seriously considered her wife material, believing she'd only be in town for the summer. Duke might have been more interested in striking up a relationship with her, but once again they'd been beaten out by one of the O'Halloran brothers.

John liked Mariah Douglas well enough, but it was plain as the nose on your face that she only had eyes for Christian. Besides, the last thing he wanted to do was tangle with *her*. Daddy Douglas just might sic that attorney on him.

He'd had a shot with Bethany, the schoolteacher. In the beginning he was quite drawn to her. He knew she didn't share his enthusiasm, but he'd figured that, given time, their friendship might grow into something more.

Then Sally McDonald had arrived.

Sally, with her pretty blue eyes and her gentle smile. He'd taken one look at her and his heart had stopped beating. In that moment, he'd recognized beyond a hint of a doubt that she was the one for him. After John had met Sally, he didn't resent Sawyer for stealing Abbey away from him and the others. It seemed like a little thing that Lanni was marrying Charles, or that Bethany Ross wasn't as keen on him as he'd been on her. Sally was the one for him.

"If you want my opinion…"

John glared at Duke. "I didn't ask for it, did I?"

"No," Duke argued, "but I'm going to give it to you anyway."

John sighed loudly. "All right. If you find it so important, tell me what you think."

"I can understand why you'd want to marry Sally—" Duke began.

"But you're thinking about her for yourself!" This explained why Duke was poking into something that was none of his concern.

"No way," Duke said, raising both hands. "I'm off

women. Too many of 'em are like that lawyer, looking for any excuse to chew on a man's butt.''

"Tracy Santiago wasn't like that.'' John grinned broadly at the memory of the way those two had clashed. To be fair, he wasn't interested in her for himself, but he kinda liked the way she'd cut Duke down to size. "She was doing her job, that's all.''

"Listen, if you don't mind, I'd rather not discuss that she-devil. She's gone, at least for now, and all I can say is good riddance. The woman was nothing but a damned nuisance.''

John swallowed back a laugh. He'd never seen Duke get this riled up over a woman. It seemed to his inexperienced eye that his friend protested too much. He figured that, this time, Duke had met his match. Too bad Tracy lived in Washington State and Duke in Alaska.

"About Sally…'' The other pilot broached the topic once more.

John could see there was no escaping his friend's unwanted counsel. "All right,'' he said, giving in. Duke was going to state his opinion whether John wanted to hear it or not. He might as well listen—or pretend to.

"Don't get me wrong here,'' Duke said, and stuffed his hands in his pockets as though he found this matter difficult. "I like Sally. Who wouldn't? She's a real sweetheart.''

"Exactly.''

"The thing that concerns me is…she's young.''

"Not that much younger than Bethany. Or Lanni.''

"True, only Sally's led a more sheltered life than either of them.''

John found he couldn't disagree. Sally had been

raised in a British Columbia town with a population of less than a thousand. From what he understood, her family was a closeknit one. She'd attended a small, private high school and a church-affiliated college. When finances became too tight for her to continue her education, she'd gotten a job working in an accounting office in Vancouver. That was where she'd read Christian's newspaper ad and applied for the job with Hard Luck Power and Light.

"You know why she came to Hard Luck, don't you?"

"Yeah." John knew, and frankly he was surprised Duke did, too. After moving to Vancouver, Sally had become involved with a fast-talking man who'd ultimately broken her heart. He'd been married; she'd found out because his wife had shown up at her door.

According to what she'd told him, Sally had walked away from the relationship feeling both heartsick and foolish. When she read about Midnight Sons offering land, housing and jobs, she'd jumped at the opportunity to start over. This time she'd do it in a small-town environment, the sort she was familiar and comfortable with.

"Are you sure she's over this other guy?" Duke asked.

"I'm sure." Although he made it sound like there could be no question, John wasn't entirely convinced. He was grateful Duke didn't challenge his response.

"What about her family?" the other pilot asked, instead.

"What about them?" John said defensively. He didn't much like where Duke's questions were leading.

"From what you've said, they're the old-fashioned sort. If you're serious about marrying their daughter, the thing to do is talk to her father first. Meet him face-to-face and tell him how you love Sally and—''

''How the hell am I supposed to do that?'' John wanted to know. ''Sal's dad lives in some dinky town on the coast. It isn't like I can leave here. Especially now.''

Winter had set in with full force. Temperatures had dipped into the minus range every day for a solid week. When it fell to minus thirty, Midnight Sons was forced to cancel all flights. The stress to the aircraft was too great a risk.

Snow accumulations measured forty inches or more in the past month alone. Thanksgiving was less than a week away, and there didn't seem to be any break in the weather ahead. In a word, they were snowed in. No matter how much he wanted to meet Sally's family, for the time being it was impossible.

''First,'' Duke said, and held up his hand. He pressed down one finger. ''You got a woman who's only recently turned twenty-one, so she's young. Younger than any of the others who've come to Hard Luck. Secondly—'' he bent down another finger ''—she moved here on the rebound, hoping to cure a broken heart.''

''Third,'' John said, fighting back his frustration, ''she comes from a family who wouldn't appreciate their daughter marrying a man they haven't personally met and approved.''

''If you start out on the wrong foot with her parents, it could take you years to make up for it,'' Duke said. ''If you truly love her—''

''I do,'' John insisted heatedly, then added in a lower voice, ''I've never felt this strongly about anyone.''

His friend nodded in understanding. ''Then do this

right. I can't think of a single reason to rush into marriage, can you?''

John could list any number of reasons to marry Sally that very day, but said nothing.

"If she's the one for you, then everything will work out the way it's supposed to, and you've got nothing to worry about.''

John shrugged. He didn't like it, but Duke had a valid point. The engagement ring could continue to burn a hole in his pocket until he'd had a chance to square matters with Sally's father. Until he could be sure she loved him for himself—and not as an instant cure for a broken heart.

"DADDY, I DON'T FEEL GOOD.'' Chrissie came slowly into the kitchen, clutching her Pooh bear to her chest. The stuffed animal was a favorite from her preschool days. Now she sought it out only on rare occasions.

Concerned, Mitch stuck the casserole in the oven, then pressed the back of his hand against his daughter's brow. She did feel warm. Her face was flushed and her eyes were unusually solemn.

"What's wrong, pumpkin?''

She shrugged. "I just don't feel good.''

"Does your tummy hurt?'' There'd been lots of flu going around.

Chrissie nodded.

"Do you have a sore throat?''

She bobbed her head and swallowed. "It hurts there, too.''

"You'd better let me take your temperature.''

Her eyes flared wide. "No! I don't want that thing in my mouth.''

"Chrissie, it isn't going to hurt.''

"I don't care. I don't want you to take my temperature. I'll...I'll just go to bed."

Mitch had forgotten how unreasonable his daughter could be when she was ill. "Don't you feel like eating dinner?"

"No," she answered weakly. "I just want to go to bed. Don't worry about me. I won't die."

Mitch sighed. He didn't know if she was being dramatic or was expressing some kind of anxiety about death. She'd known about Catherine's funeral, and maybe that had made her think about Lori....

"Will you tuck me in?"

"Of course." He followed her down the narrow hallway to her bedroom. While he pulled back her covers, Chrissie knelt on the floor and said her prayers. It seemed to take her twice as long as usual, but Mitch pretended not to notice.

Once she was securely tucked beneath the blankets, Mitch sat on the edge of her bed and brushed the hair from her brow. Her face seemed a little warm.

"Stay with me, okay?" she asked in a voice that suggested she was fading quickly.

Mitch reached for the Jack London story he'd been reading to her. Chrissie placed her hand on his forearm to stop him. "I want you to read the story about the Princess Bride. That's my favorite."

Mitch swore he'd read the book a thousand times. Chrissie could recite parts of it from memory, and Mitch knew he could repeat whole sections of it without bothering to turn the pages. Although his daughter was quite capable of reading on her own, there were certain stories she insisted he read to her.

He picked up the book and flipped it open. He made

it through the first page by merely glancing at it a few times.

"Daddy."

"Yes, pumpkin?"

"Are we going to Susan's for Thanksgiving?"

Mitch closed the book. "Sawyer asked this afternoon if we'd join them for dinner." Naturally Susan would have said something to Chrissie. Sawyer had also let it drop that Bethany would be there, then waited for his reaction. So Mitch had smiled politely and said he looked forward to seeing her again. Actually it was true.

"Did you tell Sawyer we'd come?"

Mitch nodded.

Chrissie's eyes lit up, as if this confirmation had given her a reason to live. "I hope I'm not still sick." She made a show of swallowing.

"You won't be."

Mitch didn't know what was wrong with his daughter, but he had a sneaking suspicion it wasn't nearly as serious as she'd like him to believe. He sat with her a few minutes more, then moved into the kitchen to check on dinner.

"Daddy!"

It was a deathbed call if ever he'd heard one. He made his way down the hallway and stuck his head inside her bedroom door. "Now what?"

"I want Ms. Ross."

Mitch's heart rate accelerated. "Why?"

Chrissie nodded. "I just want to talk to her, all right?"

Mitch hesitated. Of all the things he expected Chrissie to ask of him, Bethany wasn't it. A game of checkers. A glass of juice. Anything but her teacher.

"Please, oh, please, Daddy. Ms. Ross will make me feel *so* much better."

If Mitch was looking for an excuse to call Bethany, then his daughter had just offered it to him on a golden serving dish. They hadn't seen much of each other in the past few weeks, but Bethany seemed to be the one avoiding him. Embarrassed by what had happened in his office during Catherine Fletcher's service, Mitch had decided to let her be. He'd done enough damage.

But it didn't change the way he felt about her. They couldn't be in the same vicinity without his heart erupting. It had been years since he'd felt this vulnerable with a woman, and frankly it made him nervous.

Since their meeting at Ben's place, they'd greeted each other cordially—nothing personal. Just noncommittal chitchat, of the kind he might have exchanged with a near-stranger.

None of that, however, was enough for Mitch to forget the feel of Bethany in his arms, Bethany's lips on his, warm and welcoming. And so blessedly giving that he wanted to kick himself every time he thought about the way he'd treated her.

"Daddy." Chrissie gave him a long look. "Will you call Ms. Ross?"

He nodded helplessly. Walking into the kitchen, he reached for the phone. Chrissie couldn't possibly realize what she'd asked of him. Even while that thought formed in his mind, he realized he was grateful for the excuse to call Bethany.

He punched out the phone number and waited. Bethany answered on the second ring.

"Hello."

Now that he heard her voice, he felt a moment's panic. What could he possibly say? He didn't want to exaggerate and make it sound as if Chrissie was seriously ill, nor did he wish to make light of the request for fear that Bethany would see through it.

"It's Mitch."

No response.

"I'm sorry to trouble you."

"It's no trouble." She sounded friendly, but not overly so.

"Chrissie seems to have come down with the flu." Then, on a stroke of genius, he invented the reason for his call. "Did she mention not feeling well at school today?"

"No, she didn't say a word." Concern was more evident in her voice than irritation.

"It's probably nothing more than a twenty-four hour virus," he said.

"Is there anything I can do?" she asked.

He'd been born under a lucky star, Mitch decided. Without his having to say a word, she'd volunteered.

"As a matter of fact, Chrissie's feeling pretty bad at the moment and she's asking for you. I don't want you to go out of your way—"

"I'll be there in ten minutes."

"No." He wouldn't hear of her walking that far in weather this cold. "I'll come for you in the snowmobile."

She hesitated. "Fine. I'll watch for you."

Mitch went back into Chrissie's bedroom. "I talked to Ms. Ross."

"And?" Chrissie nearly fell out of the bed she was so eager to hear the outcome of the conversation.

"She'll come, but I didn't want her walking over here in the cold. I'm going to pick her up in the snowmobile. You'll be all right alone for five minutes, won't you?''

Chrissie's eyes filled with outrage. "I'm not a little kid anymore!"

"I'm glad to know that." If he'd actually been upset about asking Bethany to visit, he might have pointed out that someone who wasn't a little kid anymore wouldn't ask for her teacher.

Mitch called out to Chrissie that he was leaving. He pulled on his insulated, waterproof jacket and wound the thick scarf around his neck, covering his mouth, before he stepped outside. The snowmobile was the most frequently used means of transportation in the winter months, and he kept his well maintained. The minute he pulled up outside Bethany's small house, her door opened and she appeared.

She climbed onto the back of the snowmobile and positioned herself a discreet distance behind him. Nevertheless, having her this close produced a fiery warmth he couldn't escape—didn't *want* to escape.

She didn't say anything until they'd reached his house. He parked the snowmobile inside the garage and plugged in the heater to protect the engine.

Once in the house they removed their winter gear. Bethany was wearing leggings and an oversize San Francisco Police Department sweatshirt; her feet were covered in heavy red woollen socks. He stared at her, taking in every detail.

Mitch found he couldn't speak. It was the first time they'd been alone together since the scene in his office. This sudden intimacy caught him off guard, and he wasn't sure how to react.

Part of him yearned to reach for her and kiss her

again. Only this time he'd be tender, drawing out the kiss with a gentle touch that would—

"Where's Chrissie?" Bethany asked, mercifully breaking into his thoughts.

"Chrissie… She's in her bedroom."

The oven timer went off, and grateful for the excuse to leave her and clear his head, Mitch walked into kitchen. He opened the oven and pulled out the ground-turkey casserole to cool on top of the stove.

He entered his daughter's room and discovered Bethany sitting on the bed, with Chrissie cuddled close. The child's head rested against Bethany's shoulder as she read from the story he'd begun himself. When Chrissie glanced up to find Mitch watching, her eyes shone with happiness.

"Hi, Dad," she said, craning her neck to look up at Bethany. "Dad usually reads me this story, but you do it better because you love it, too. I don't think Dad likes romance stories."

"Dinner's ready," Mitch announced. "Are you sure you won't try to eat something, pumpkin?"

Chrissie's frown said that was a terribly difficult decision for her to make. "Maybe I could eat just a little, but only if Ms. Ross will stay and have dinner with us."

Before Bethany could offer a perfunctory excuse, Mitch said, "There's plenty, and we'd both enjoy having you." He wanted to be certain she understood that he wouldn't object to her company; if anything he'd be glad of it.

He saw her gaze travel from Chrissie and then back to him. He leaned against the doorway, his hands deep in his pockets, trying to give the impression that it made no difference to him if she joined them for dinner or not. But it did. He wanted her to stay.

"I... It's thoughtful of you to ask. I, uh, haven't eaten yet."

"Oh, goodie." Chrissie jumped up and clapped her hands, bouncing with glee. Then, as if she'd just remembered how ill she was supposed to be, she sagged her shoulders and all but crumpled onto the bed.

In an effort to hide his smile, Mitch returned to the kitchen and quickly set the table. By the time Chrissie and Bethany joined him, he'd brought the casserole to the table, as well as a loaf of bread, butter and some straight-from-the-can bean salad.

Dinner was...an odd affair. Exciting. Fun. And a little sad. It was as if he and Bethany were attempting to find new ground with each other. Only, they both seemed to fear that this ground would be strewn with land mines. He'd take one step forward, then freeze, afraid he'd said something that might offend her.

He noticed that Bethany didn't find this new situation any easier than he did. She'd start to laugh, then her eyes, her beautiful brown eyes, would meet his and the laugh would falter.

Following their meal, Chrissie wanted her to finish the story. Since Mitch was well aware of how the story ended, he lingered in the kitchen over a cup of coffee.

He had just started the dishes when Bethany reappeared.

"Chrissie's decided she needs her beauty sleep," she told him, standing at the far side of the room.

Mitch didn't blame her for maintaining the distance between them. Every time she'd attempted to get close, he'd shoved her away. Every time she'd opened her heart to him, he'd shunned her. Yet when he'd desperately needed her, she'd been there. And although she'd accused him of settling for any woman who happened to fall into his arms, *she* was the only one who could fill the need in him.

"I imagine you want to get back home," he said, experiencing a curious sadness. He dumped what remained of his coffee into the sink. Something about the way her eyes flickered told him she might have enjoyed a cup had he offered one.

"Stay," he said suddenly. "Just for a few minutes."

The invitation seemed to hang in the air. It took her a long time to decide; when he was about to despair, she offered him a small smile, then nodded.

"Coffee?"

"Please."

His heart reacted with a wild burst of staccato beats. He quickly poured her a mug, grabbing a fresh one for himself. His movements were jerky, and he realized it was because he felt afraid that if he didn't finish the task quickly enough, she might change her mind.

He carried the mugs into the living room and sat across from her. At first their conversation was awkward, but gradually the tension eased. It amazed him how much they had to talk about. Books, movies, politics. Children. Police work. Life in Alaska. They shared myriad opinions and stories and observations.

It was as though all the difficulties between them had been wiped out and they were starting over.

Mitch laughed. Damn, this felt good. He'd begun to feel warm and relaxed, trusting. Alive. She seemed curious about his past, but her occasional questions were friendly, not intrusive. And she didn't probe for more information than he was willing—or able—to give her.

He brought out a large photo album and sat next to

her on the sofa, with the album resting partially on his lap and partially on hers. Mitch turned the pages, explaining each picture.

He wondered what Bethany thought about the gap in his past. It was as if his and Chrissie's life had started when they moved to Hard Luck. There wasn't a single photograph of their lives before the move. Not one picture of Lori.

He turned a page and his hand inadvertently brushed hers. He hadn't meant to touch her, but when he did, it was as if something exploded inside him. For long seconds, neither moved.

Slowly Mitch's gaze sought hers. Instead of accusation, he found approval, instead of anger, acceptance. He released his breath, tired of fighting a battle he couldn't win. With deliberate movements, he closed the photo album and set it aside.

"Mitch?"

"We'll talk later," he whispered. He wrapped his hand around the back of her neck and gently pulled her forward. He needed this. Ached for this.

He kissed her slowly, sweetly, teasing her lips until her head rolled back against the cushion in abject surrender.

"Mitch..." She tried once more.

He stopped her from speaking by placing his fingertip against her moist lips. "We both know Chrissie manipulated this meeting."

She frowned as if she was about to question him.

"She's no sicker than you or I."

Bethany blinked.

"Let's humor her."

Her eyes darkened to a deep shade of melted chocolate. "Let's," she agreed, and wound her arms around his neck.

"THANK YOU SO MUCH for coming," Bethany said to Ben. It had taken a lot to convince him to speak to her students.

Ben had resisted, claiming he wasn't comfortable with children, never having had youngsters himself. But in the end Bethany's persistence had won out.

"You did a great job," she told him.

Ben blushed slightly. "I did, didn't I?" He walked about the room and patted the top of each desk as if remembering who had sat where.

"The children loved hearing about your job," she told him. "And about your life in the navy."

"They certainly had lots of questions."

Bethany didn't mention that she'd primed them beforehand. She hadn't had to encourage them much; they were familiar with Ben and fascinated by him.

Bethany wasn't especially proud of the somewhat underhand method she'd used to learn what she could of Ben's past. Still, inviting him to speak to her students was certainly legitimate; he wasn't the only community member she'd asked to do so. Dotty had been in the week before, and Sawyer O'Halloran had agreed to come the week following Thanksgiving. She found herself studying Ben now, looking for hints of her own appearance, her own personality.

"I haven't seen much of you lately," he said, folding his arms. He half sat on one of the desks in the front row. "Used to be you'd stop in once a day, and we'd have a chance for a nice little chat."

"I've been busy lately." In the past week, she'd been seeing a lot of Mitch and Chrissie.

"I kinda miss our talks," Ben muttered.

"Me, too," Bethany admitted. It was becoming increasingly difficult, she discovered, to talk to Ben about personal things. Her fear was that she'd inadvertently reveal their relationship. The temptation to tell him grew stronger with each meeting, something she hadn't considered when she'd decided to find him.

Ben stared at her a moment as if he wasn't sure he should go on. "I thought I saw you with Mitch Harris the other day." It was more question than statement.

She nodded. "He drove me to the library." He'd said he didn't want her walking. The piercing cold continued, but temperatures weren't as low as they'd been earlier in the week. Bethany could easily have trekked the short distance; Mitch's driving her was an excuse—one she'd readily grasped.

"Are you two seeing each other now?"

Bethany hesitated.

"I don't mean to pry," Ben said, studying her. "You can tell me it's none of my damn business if you want, and I won't take offense. It's just that I get customers now and again who're curious about you."

"Like who?"

"Like Bill Landgrin."

"Oh." It embarrassed her no end that she'd had dinner with the pipeline worker. He'd phoned her several times since, and the conversations had always been uncomfortable. Not because of anything Bill said or did, but because she'd dated him for all the wrong reasons.

Bethany walked from behind her desk and over to the blackboard. "I don't know what to tell you about Mitch and me," she said, picking up the eraser.

Ben's face softened with sympathy. "You sound confused."

"I am." Bethany found it easy to understand why people so often shared confidences with Ben; he was a good listener, never meddlesome and always encouraging.

With anyone else, Bethany would have skirted around the subject of her and Mitch, but she felt a strong connection with Ben—one that reached beyond the reasons she'd come to Hard Luck. It wasn't just a connection created by her secret knowledge. Since her arrival, Ben had become her friend. That surprised her; she hadn't expected to like him this much.

"I'm afraid I'm falling in love with Mitch," she said in a soft, breathless voice.

"Afraid?"

She lowered her gaze and nodded. "I don't think he feels the same way about me."

"Why's that?" Ben leaned forward.

"He doesn't *want* to be attracted to me. Every time I feel we're getting close, he backs away. There's a huge part of himself he keeps hidden. He's never discussed Chrissie's mother. I've never really questioned him about her or about his life before he moved to Hard Luck, and he never volunteers."

Ben rubbed one side of his face. "But we all have our secrets, don't you think?"

Bethany nodded and swallowed uncomfortably. She certainly had hers.

"Whatever happened to Mitch cut deep. He lost his wife, the mother of his child. I can tell you because I was living here when Mitch and Chrissie first arrived. Mitch was a wounded soul. Whatever happened, he's kept to himself. He'd been here five years now, and for the first time I've seen him smile. You're good for him and Chrissie. Real good."

"He and Chrissie would be easy to love."

"But you're afraid."

She nodded.

"Seems to me you two've come a long way in a short time. I could be wrong, but not so long ago all you did was send longing looks at each other. Now you're actually talking, spending time together." He paused. "I heard he told Bill Landgrin a thing or two recently."

"Mitch did?"

Ben grinned broadly. "Not in any words I'd care to repeat in front of a lady, mind you. Seems to me he wouldn't have done that if he wasn't serious about you himself. Give him time, Bethany. Yourself, too. You've only been here three months. Rome wasn't built in a day, you know."

Bethany exhaled. "Thank you for listening—and for your advice."

"No problem," Ben said. "It was my pleasure."

Smiling, she closed the distance between them and kissed his rough cheek.

Ben flushed and pressed his hand to his face.

She felt worlds better, and not only because Ben had given her good advice. He'd said the things her own father would have said.

The irony of that thought didn't escape her.

CHAPTER SEVEN

"Hi." BETHANY FELT almost shy as she opened her front door to Mitch that Saturday night. Chrissie was so often with them that any time Bethany and Mitch were alone together, an immediate air of intimacy developed between them.

"Hi yourself." Mitch unwound his scarf and took off his protective winter gear. He, too, seemed a little ill at ease.

They looked at each other then quickly glanced away. Anyone watching them would have guessed they were meeting for the first time. Tonight, neither seemed to know what to say, which was absurd, since they often sat and talked for hours about anything and everything.

This newfound need to know each other, as well as the more relaxed tenor of their relationship, came as a result of Thanksgiving dinner with Sawyer and Abbey. The four adults had played cards following dinner. Two couples. It had seemed natural for Bethany to be with Mitch. Natural and right. Conversation had been lively and wide-ranging, and Bethany felt at home with these people. So did Mitch, judging by the way he laughed and smiled. And somehow, whatever he'd been holding inside seemed less important afterward.

They'd all enjoyed the card-playing so much that it had become a weekly event. In the last couple of weeks

Bethany had spent a lot of time in Mitch's company, and she believed they'd grown close and comfortable with each other. But then, they were almost always with other people. With Chrissie, of course. With Sawyer and Abbey. The other O'Halloran brothers. Ben. Margaret Simpson. Rarely were they alone. It was this situation that had prompted her to invite him for dinner.

"Dinner's almost ready," she said self-consciously, rubbing her hands on her jeans. "I hope you like Irish stew."

"I love it, but then I'm partial to anything I don't have to cook myself." He smiled and his eyes met hers. He pulled his gaze away, putting an abrupt end to the moment of intimacy.

Bethany had to fight back her disappointment.

"I see you got your Christmas tree," he said, motioning to the scrawny five-foot vinyl fir that stood in the corner of her living room. She would have preferred a live tree, but the cost was astronomical, and so she did what everyone in Hard Luck had done. She ordered a fake tree through the catalog.

"I was hoping you'd help me decorate it," she said. It was only fair, since she'd helped him and Chrissie decorate theirs the night before. Chrissie had chattered excitedly about Susan's slumber party, which was tonight. Bethany wondered if Abbey had arranged the party so Bethany and Mitch would have some time alone together. Whether it was intentional or not, Bethany was grateful.

"Chrissie said the two of you baked cookies today."

"Susan helped, too," she said. Bethany had offered to take both girls for a few hours during the afternoon; Mitch was working, and Abbey wanted a chance to wrap Christmas gifts and address cards undisturbed.

Mitch followed her into the kitchen. They were greeted by the aroma of sage and other herbs. The oven timer went off, and she reached for a mitt to pull out a loaf of crusty French bread.

Mitch looked around. "Is there anything you need me to do?"

"No. Everything's under control." That was true of dinner, perhaps, but little else felt manageable. Mitch suddenly seemed like a stranger, when she thought they'd come so far. It was like the old days—which really weren't so old.

"I'll dish up dinner now," she said.

He didn't offer to help again; perhaps he thought he'd only be in the way. With his hands resting on a chair back, he stood by the kitchen table and waited until she could join him.

The stew was excellent, or so Mitch claimed, but for all the enjoyment she received from it, Bethany could have been eating boot leather. Disappointment settled over her.

"I imagine Abbey's got her hands full," she said, trying to make conversation.

"How many kids are spending the night?" Mitch asked. "Six was the last I heard."

"Seven, if you count Scott."

"My guess is Scott would rather be tarred and feathered than join a bunch of girls to decorate sugar cookies and string popcorn."

"You're probably right." She passed Mitch the bread. He thanked her and took another slice.

Silence.

Bethany didn't know what had happened to the easy camaraderie they'd had over the past few weeks. Each attempt to start a discussion failed; conversation simply refused to flow. The silence grew more awkward by the minute, and finally Bethany could stand it no longer. With her mouth so dry she could barely talk, she threw down her napkin and turned to Mitch.

"What's wrong with us?" she asked.

"Wrong?"

She gulped some water. "We're so blasted *polite* with each other."

"Yeah," Mitch agreed.

"We're barely able to talk."

"I noticed that, too." But he didn't offer any suggestions or solutions.

Bethany met his eyes, hoping he'd do *something* to resolve this dilemma. He didn't. Instead, he set his napkin carefully aside and got to his feet. "I guess I'm not very hungry." He carried his half-full bowl to the sink.

"Oh."

"Do you want me to leave?" he asked.

No! her heart cried, but she didn't say the word. "Do...do you want to go?"

He didn't answer.

Bethany stood up, pressing the tips of her fingers to her forehead. "Stop. Please, just stop. I want to know what's wrong. Did I do something?"

"No. Good heavens, no." He seemed astonished that she'd even asked. "It isn't anything you've done."

Mitch stood on one side of the kitchen and she on the other. "It's my fault," he said in a voice so quiet she could hardly hear him. "You haven't done anything, but—" He stopped abruptly.

"What?" she pleaded. "Tell me."

"Listen, Bethany, I think it would be best if I did leave." With that, he walked purposefully into the living room and retrieved his coat from the small entryway closet.

Although the room was warm and cozy, Bethany felt a sudden chill. She crossed her arms as much to ward off the sense of cold as to protect herself from Mitch's words. "It's back to that, is it?" she managed sadly. From the first day in September, Mitch had been running away from her. Every time she felt they'd made progress, something would happen to show her how far they had yet to go.

His hand on the doorknob, he abruptly turned back to face her. When he spoke his voice was hoarse with anger. "I can't be alone with you without wanting to kiss you."

She stared at him in disbelief. "We've kissed before." There had been those memorable passionate kisses. And more recently, affectionate kisses of greeting and farewell. "What's so different now?"

"We're alone."

"Yes, I know." She still didn't understand.

He shook his head, as if it was difficult to continue. "Don't you see, Bethany?"

Obviously she didn't.

"With Chrissie or anyone else around, the temptation is minimized. But when it's just the two of us, I can't think about anything else!" This last part was ground out between clenched teeth. "Don't you realize how much I want to make love to you?"

"Is that so terrible?" she asked quietly.

"Yes." The only sound she could hear was the too-fast beating of her heart. She could see Mitch's pulse hammering in the vein in his neck.

"I can't let it happen," he told her, his back straight, shoulders stiff.

"For your information, making love requires two people," Bethany told him simply. "I wish you'd said something earlier. We could have talked about this...arrived at some understanding. It's true," she added, "the thought of us becoming...intimate has crossed my mind—but I wouldn't have allowed it to happen. At least not yet. It's too soon for either of us."

Without a word, Mitch closed the distance between them. With infinite tenderness he wove his fingers through her hair, and buried his lips against the fragrant skin of her throat. "You tempt me so much."

She sighed and wrapped her arms around him.

"Feeling this way frightens me, Bethany. Overwhelms me."

"We can't run from it, Mitch, or pretend it doesn't exist."

His hands trembled as they slid down the length of her spine, molding her against him. His kiss was slow and melting, and so thorough she was left breathless. She buried her head in his shoulder.

"I guess this means I can put away the celery," she whispered.

"The celery?"

"When the catalog order came, I didn't receive the mistletoe. The slip said it's on back order. I talked to my mom earlier today and told her how disappointed I was—and she suggested celery as a substitute. So I nailed a piece over the doorway. Apparently you didn't notice."

Mitch chuckled hoarsely. "You know what I like best about you?"

"You mean other than my kisses?"

"Yes."

The look in his eyes was as potent as expensive whiskey. "You make me laugh."

The amusement drained from her eyes. "Don't close me out," she said, and her gaze drifted to his lips. "I can't bear it when you shut me out of your life. There isn't anything you can't tell me."

"Don't be so sure." Mitch eased her out of his arms and stared down at her, as if testing the truth of her words. It occurred to her that the expression on his face was like that of a man walking a tightrope over Niagara Falls—not daring to look down and not daring to look back.

"Mitch," she said gently, touching his face, "what is it?"

"Nothing." He turned away. "It's nothing."

Bethany didn't believe that. But she had no choice other than end this discussion, which apparently distressed him so much. When he was ready he'd tell her.

"Didn't you say something about decorating your Christmas tree?" he asked with feigned enthusiasm.

"I did indeed," she said, following his lead.

"Good. We'll get to that in a moment," he said, and took her by the hand.

"Where are we going?"

"You mean you don't know?" He grinned boyishly. "I'm taking you to the celery, er, mistletoe."

Soon she was in his arms, and all the doubts she'd entertained were obliterated the moment he lowered his mouth to hers. She felt only the gentle touch of his lips. Slow and confident. Intimate and familiar.

CHRISTIAN HAD EXPECTED Mariah to move away from Hard Luck before December. He wasn't a betting man, but he would've wagered a year's income that his secretary would high-tail it out of town right after the first snowfall. Not that he'd have blamed her, living as she was in a one-room cabin. He cringed every time he thought about her in those primitive conditions.

It wasn't the first time Mariah had proved him wrong. Christian was convinced she stayed on out of pure spite. She wanted to prove herself, all right, but at the expense of his pride.

He walked into the office to find Mariah already at her desk, typing away at the computer. Her fingers moved so fast they were a blur.

At the sound of the door closing, she looked up—and froze.

"Morning," he said without emotion.

"Good morning," she offered shyly. She glanced away, almost as if she expected him to reprimand her in some way. "The coffee's ready."

"So I see." He wasn't looking forward to this, but someone had to reason with her, and Sawyer had refused to take on the task.

Christian poured himself a cup of coffee, then walked slowly to his desk. "Mariah."

She stared at him with large, frightened eyes. "Did I do something wrong again?"

"No, no," he said quickly, wanting to reassure her. "What makes you think that?" He gave her what he hoped resembled an encouraging smile.

She eyed him as if she wasn't sure she could trust him. "It seems the only time you talk to me is when I've done something wrong."

"Not this time." He sat down at his desk, which wasn't all that far from her own. "It's about you living in the cabin," he said.

He watched her bristle. "I believe we've already discussed this subject," she answered stiffly. "Several times."

"I don't want you there."

"Then you should never have offered the cabins as living accommodations."

"I'd prefer it if you moved in with the other women—in Catherine Fletcher's house," he said, ignoring her comment. Actually having Catherine's house available to them had been a godsend. Two women—Sally and Angie—had moved into the house, and the arrangement was working out well.

The pilots Midnight Sons employed lived in a dormsize room. It was stark, without much more than a big stove for heating and several bunk beds and lockers, but the men never complained. The house was far more to the women's liking. As soon as it could be arranged they were bringing in two mobile homes for the women.

Until then Christian wasn't comfortable thinking about Mariah—or anyone else—living in a one-room cabin. Not with winter already here.

"I'm just fine where I am," Mariah insisted.

Sawyer thought she was all right there, too, but Christian knew otherwise. At night he lay awake, thinking of Mariah out there on the edge of town in a cabin smaller than a rich man's closet. It had no electric power and no plumbing, and was a far cry from what she'd been accustomed to.

"I'm asking," he said being careful to phrase the words in a way she wouldn't find objectionable, "if you'd move in with Sally and Angie. Just until the spring thaw."

"Why?"

Arguing with her was an exercise in frustration. And

the amount of time he wasted fretting over her! That in itself made no sense to him. The fact was, he didn't even *like* Mariah. The woman drove him crazy.

"I'm asking you to move in with them for a reason other than the cabin's primitive conditions." This, of course, wasn't true, but he had to find *some* way of getting her to move. He said the first thing that came to mind.

"I...I think one or two of the women are considering leaving Hard Luck. We don't want to lose them."

"Who?"

Christian shrugged. "It's just rumors at this point. But I need someone who can encourage them to stick out the winter. Someone the others like and trust."

She looked at him as if she wasn't sure she should believe him.

"The others need someone they feel comfortable with. They like you, and I think you could help."

Mariah paused. "But I don't believe it's necessary for me to move in with them."

"I do," he answered automatically. "How often do you get a chance to talk with your friends? I can't imagine it's more than once a week." He was stabbing in the dark now.

Mariah nibbled on her lower lip and seemed to be considering his words. "That's true."

"A few aren't having an easy time adjusting to life in the Arctic. Will you do it, Mariah?" he pleaded gently. Heaven knew, he'd tried every other means he could think of to get her to move out of that godforsaken cabin. "Will you move in with the other women?"

She hesitated. "I'll still get the deed to the land and the cabin at the end of the year, won't I?"

"You can have both now." It wasn't the first time he'd made that offer. The sooner she accomplished her goals, he figured, the sooner she'd leave Hard Luck.

"Giving me the title now wouldn't be right. The terms of my contract state that at the end of one year's time I'll be entitled to the cabin and the land. I wouldn't dream of taking the deed a moment sooner."

"Then I'll assure you in writing that the time you spend living with the other women will in no way jeopardize our agreement. You can type up the papers yourself."

He watched her and waited. Waited while the interminable minutes passed. He couldn't believe that one small decision would demand such concentration.

"Will you or won't you?" he demanded when he couldn't stand the silence any longer.

"I will," she said, "but on one condition. I want to talk to the others first and make sure I won't be intruding."

"For the love of heaven," Christian muttered, resisting the urge to bury his face in his hands. "Midnight Sons is paying the rent!"

"I'm well aware of that," Mariah said coolly.

"If I want to move the entire French Foreign Legion into that house, then I'll do it."

"No, you wouldn't," Mariah said with a know-it-all grin. "First, Sawyer wouldn't let you and—"

"It was a figure of speech." Christian now fought the urge to pull out his hair. No one on earth could anger him as quickly as Mariah Douglas. The year she was contracted to work for him couldn't end fast enough. Not until she left Hard Luck would he be able to sleep through the night again.

A WREATH HUNG inside the door of the Hard Luck Café. Flashing miniature lights were strung around the windows. Christmas cards were hung against one wall in a straggling triangle. Bethany guessed the shape was supposed to represent a Christmas tree.

The thank-you notes the children had written following his visit to the classroom were taped against another wall for everyone who came into the café to see. The worn look of those notes told her Ben had read them countless times himself.

"It's beginning to look downright festive around here," Bethany said as she stepped up to the counter.

"Christmas is one of my favorite times of the year," Ben declared. "How about a piece of mincemeat pie to go with your coffee? It's on the house."

"Actually I don't have time for either," Bethany said regretfully. She was on her way to church for choir practice and only had a few minutes. "I came to invite you to my house for Christmas dinner."

Ben's mouth opened and a look of utter astonishment crossed his face. "I'd thought... Me? What about Mitch and Chrissie? Aren't they spending the day with you?"

"I invited them, too. I'm sure I'm not half as good in the kitchen as you, but I should be able to manage turkey and all the goodies that go with it. Besides, it'll do you good to taste someone else's cooking for a change."

He frowned as though this were a weighty decision. "I like my turkey with sage dressing and giblet gravy."

"You got it. My mom always stuffs the bird with sage dressing, and my dad always makes giblet gravy. I wouldn't know how to do it any other way." When he seemed about to refuse, she added, "If you want to contribute something, you can bring one of those mincemeat pies you're trying to fatten me up with."

Ben turned away from her and reached for the rag. He began to wipe the already clean countertop. "I...I don't know what to say." His eyes continued to avoid hers.

"Just say yes. Dinner's at three."

He gestured weakly. "I always keep the place open."

"Close it this year." She almost suggested he should spend the holiday with family, then realized she couldn't. She admitted to herself that she felt close to Ben; she *did* feel that he was family. Perhaps this was emotionally dangerous, but being with him on Christmas Day might help ease the ache of missing her parents.

"Folks generally spend Christmas Day with family," he said. It was as if he'd been able to read her thoughts. "I don't have any left," he told her in a low voice. "At least, none that would want me dropping in unannounced at Christmas."

"I'll be your family, Ben," she offered, waiting for her heart to stop its crazy beating. He had no way of knowing how much truth there was in her words. "And you can be mine. For this one day, anyhow."

"Won't I be in the way? I mean, with you and—"

Bethany reached for his hand and patted it gently. "I wouldn't have invited you if that was the case."

"What about you and Mitch? You two seem to be spending a lot of time together lately—which is good," he hastened to add. "Don't think I've ever seen Mitch look happier, and what I hear folks saying, there's a night-and-day difference with Chrissie. She used to be a shy little thing."

Bethany had the feeling he would have rambled on for an hour if she hadn't stopped him.

"Ben!" She laughed outright. "I'm asking you to Christmas dinner. Will you or won't you come? I need to know how much food to prepare."

She watched his throat work convulsively. "No one ever asked me to Christmas dinner," he said in a strangled voice.

"Well, they are now."

He met her look and his eyes grew suspiciously bright. "What time do you want me there again?"

"Dinner's at three. You come as early as you like, though."

"All right," he said with some difficulty. "I'll be there, and I'll bring one of my pies."

"Good. I'll see you Christmas Day." Having settled that, Bethany left the café.

"Bethany," Ben stopped her. "If you need any help making that gravy, you let me know."

"I will. Thanks for offering."

Not until she was outside, with the cold clawing at her face, did she realize there were tears in her eyes. She quickly brushed them away and hurried on to the church.

CHRISTMAS WAS SUPPOSED to be a joyous time of year. It would be, Matt Caldwell thought, if Karen was with him. He glanced around the Anchorage church. The harder he tried not to think about his ex-wife, the more difficult it became to concentrate on the hymnbook in his hands.

Perhaps it was because the last time he'd been in church was when his grandmother died. The sadness that had taken hold of his heart then hadn't faded in the weeks since.

Matt hadn't made church a habit of late, either. The fact was, he and God weren't on the best of terms. He was quite comfortable ignoring the presence of an almighty being, since evidence of God had been sorely lacking in his life these past few years.

It didn't help that he was once again the only family member who was alone. His parents stood on one side of him, and Lanni and Charles on the other. Those two were so much in love it was painful just being around them.

Although Lanni enjoyed her work with the *Anchorage News,* she hated the long separations from Charles. April couldn't come soon enough as far as she was concerned.

The Christmas Eve church services continued, and the members of the congregation lifted their voices in song. But Matt wasn't in any frame of mind to join in. He'd worked hard during the past three months. Damned hard. Other than his obvious purpose of getting the lodge ready, he'd driven himself in a single-minded effort, but whether it was to impress Karen or to get her out of his system, he no longer knew.

He couldn't help wondering how his ex-wife was spending Christmas. He was pretty confident she wouldn't have a white Christmas in California, though.

Was she alone, the way he was? Did she feel empty inside? Was she thinking of him?

Somehow he doubted it, considering the impetuous way she'd left Alaska. It still bothered him that she hadn't so much as told him she was moving. Instead, she'd contacted his sister, knowing full well that Lanni would tell him.

Once the interminable singing ended, there was the predictable Christmas pageant. Despite his misery, Matt found himself smiling as the Sunday school children gave the performance they'd no doubt been rehearsing for months.

This year, instead of using a doll, they had a newborn infant playing the role of the baby Jesus. This child was anything but meek and mild. In fact, he let out a scream that echoed through the church and started all the children giggling.

Well, that was what they got for using a real baby. A baby.

His mind froze on the thought. Babies. Children. He glanced around the congregation and noticed a number of families with small children.

Karen had wanted children. They'd had more than one heated discussion on that subject. Matt had been the one against it; he didn't feel ready for fatherhood. Not when his future and career remained unsettled. In retrospect, he could see he'd been right. Dragging a child through a divorce would have been criminal.

Now the likelihood of his having a family was remote at best. He discovered, somewhat to his surprise, that the realization brought with it a new pain. Great. Just what he needed. Another resentment to harbor. Another casualty of his dead marriage. Something else to flail himself with.

He was relieved when the church service ended. At least he hadn't been subjected to a lengthy sermon on top of the singing and the pageant.

Once they were home, his family gathered around the Christmas tree. Traditionally they opened their gifts on Christmas Eve. It had taken some doing for him to dredge up enough spirit to spring for gifts, but he'd managed it.

"How about hot apple cider?" Lanni asked, sitting down next to him.

"Sure," he said, faking a smile. It didn't seem fair to burden everyone else with his misery.

His sister brought him a cup, then sat down next to him. Matt noticed that their mother was busy in the kitchen and his father was talking to Charles.

"I hoped we'd have a minute alone before we get started opening the gifts," Lanni whispered. She searched through the mound of gaily wrapped presents; beneath one of them she found what she was looking for. An envelope. She handed it to him.

Matt looked at his name on the envelope and instantly recognized the handwriting as Karen's. His heart skipped a beat, and he raised his eyes to his sister's, not sure what to think.

"How'd you get this?"

"Karen mailed a gift to me and to Mom and Dad. It was in the same package."

"I see." His hand closed tightly over the envelope.

"There's something else," Lanni said, her gaze avoiding his.

"Yes?" He was eager to escape to his room and read what Karen had written.

"Our wedding…"

"What about it?"

"Would you mind very much if Karen served as my maid of honor?"

Matt stared at his sister, not understanding. "You want her in your wedding party?"

"Yes," she said, then quickly added, "But only if you don't object. I wouldn't want it to be uncomfortable for you, Matt. You're my brother, after all, and she was your wife—but she's still my friend."

"Why should I care?" he mumbled. "It's your wedding." With that, he left the room.

Once he was inside his old bedroom, Matt threw himself onto the bed and tore open the envelope. A single sheet of paper fell from the card. Heart pounding, he unfolded it and read:

Merry Christmas, Matt.
It didn't seem right to mail gifts to Lanni and your parents and send you nothing. But at the same time, it's a bit awkward to buy my ex-husband a Christmas gift.
     I hope this card finds you well.
                                        Sincerely,
                                        Karen

Sincerely. She'd actually signed the note *sincerely*. Matt couldn't believe it. He picked up the Christmas card he'd discarded earlier and found she'd written nothing but her name.

Well, sending a Christmas card was more than he'd done for her. He supposed he'd have to add that to his long list of failures and regrets.

CHAPTER EIGHT

Mitch woke early Christmas morning.

Not wanting to wake Chrissie, he moved silently into the living room, where the miniature lights on the tree glittered like frosted stars. He smiled at their decorations—paper chains, strung popcorn and handmade ornaments.

He rearranged the gifts under the tree. He'd placed them there the night before, after Chrissie had gone to bed. He suspected she didn't believe in Santa Claus any longer, but it was more fun for them both to keep up the pretense.

The largest present wasn't from him, but Bethany. A Barbie thingamajig. Town house or some such nonsense. Only it wasn't nonsense to Chrissie; the kid took her Barbie seriously. She'd be thrilled with this. He knew Chrissie would be happily absorbed with her gifts all morning, and then later, in the afternoon, they were going to Bethany's place for a turkey dinner with all the fixings.

Bethany.

He needed these quiet early-morning moments to clear his thoughts and make sense of his feelings.

It had happened.

Despite his resistance, his best efforts to prevent it, despite his vows to the contrary, despite the full force of his determination, he'd gone and fallen in love with Bethany Ross.

He didn't *want* to love Bethany, and in the same breath, he found himself humbled that this remarkable woman had entered his life. Especially after Lori. Especially now.

Mitch paced the living room, too restless to sit. Admitting that he cared deeply for Bethany required some sort of decision. A man didn't come to this kind of realization without defining a course of action.

He knew he had nothing to offer her. While it was true that he made enough money to support a family, his financial status wasn't impressive enough to mention. Somehow he doubted this would matter much to Bethany, but still...

He was dismally aware, too, that he came to her with deep emotional scars and a needy child in tow. The mere thought of loving again, of trusting again, terrified him. It was enough to cause him to break out in a cold sweat. On top of everything else was the paralyzing fear that he'd fail Bethany the way he had Lori.

Then again, he reminded himself, he had options. He could do what he'd done for these past three months—deny his feelings. Ignore what his heart was telling him.

He might have continued that way for months, possibly years, if it wasn't for one thing.

Chrissie.

From the moment his daughter had met Bethany, she'd set her sights on making the teacher her mother and his wife. Watching the two of them together had touched him from the very first. In ways he'd never fully understand, Bethany ministered to his daughter's need for a mother in the same way she satisfied his own long-repressed desire for a companion. *A wife*...

As the weeks progressed, Chrissie had started looking to Bethany for guidance more and more often. There wasn't *anything* Chrissie wouldn't do to be with her—including feigning flu symptoms.

What confounded him was the fact that Bethany seemed to share his feelings. He felt her love as powerfully as those brief moments of sunlight everyday, brightening the world in the darkness of an Arctic winter.

Admitting his love for Bethany—to her and to himself—wasn't a simple thing. Love rarely was, he suspected. If he told her how he felt about her, he'd also have to tell her about his past.

Love implied trust. And he'd need to trust her with the painful details of his marriage. With that came the tremendous risk of her rejection. He wouldn't blame her if she *did* turn away. If the situation were reversed, he didn't know how he'd react. He was laying an enormous burden on her.

Telling her all this wasn't something he could do on the spur of the moment. Timing was critical. He'd have to wait for the right day, the right mood.

Not this morning, he decided. Not on Christmas. He refused to spoil the day's celebration with the ugliness of his past. No need to darken the holiday with a litany of his failures as a husband.

"Daddy?" Chrissie stood just inside the living-room doorway yawning. She wore her pretty new flannel pajamas—the one gift he'd allowed her to open Christmas Eve.

"Merry Christmas, pumpkin," he said, opening his

arms to her. "It looks like Santa made it to Hard Luck safely, after all."

Chrissie leapt into his embrace and he folded his arms around her, slowly closing his eyes. His daughter was the most precious gift he'd ever been given. And now, finding Bethany... His heart was full.

"I CAN'T BELIEVE I ate the whole thing," Ben teased, placing his hands on the bulge of his stomach and sighing heavily. He eased his chair away from the kitchen table. "If anyone else gets wind of what a good cook you are, Bethany, I'll be out of business before I know it."

Bethany smiled, delighted with his praise. "I don't think you have a thing to worry about. Those pies of yours were fabulous, especially the mincemeat. I'd like to get your recipe."

Ben gave her a wide grin. "Sure. No problem. It's one I came up with myself—I like to try new things when I cook. How about you? Have you always been this good in the kitchen?"

It was another trait she shared with her birth father, but once again this wasn't something she could mention.

"Almost always. While other little girls were playing with dolls and makeup, I was using my Betty Crocker Baking Center to concoct pastries and other sugary delights."

"Well, all that practice sure paid off," Mitch said.

Bethany blushed a little at the compliments. She'd done her best to put on a spread worthy of their praise. The meal had taken weeks of careful planning; she'd had to special-order some of the ingredients, and her mother had mailed her the spices. A lot of the dishes she'd made were traditional family recipes. Mashed sweet potatoes with dried apricots and lots of pure, creamery butter. Sage dressing, of course, and another rice-and-raisin dressing that had been a favorite of hers, one her grandmother made every year.

"You miss your family, don't you?" Mitch asked as he helped her clear the table.

"Everyone does at Christmas, don't you think?" This first year so far away from her parents and two younger brothers had been more difficult than she'd anticipated; this morning had been particularly wrenching. She knew they missed her, too. Bethany had spoken to her family in California at least once a day for the past week. She didn't care how high her phone bill ran.

"I must have chatted to Mom three times this morning alone," she told Mitch. "It's funny. For years I've helped her with Thanksgiving and Christmas dinners, but when it came to doing it on my own, I had a dozen questions."

"You need me to do anything?" Ben asked, getting up from the table. He carried his plate to the sink. "I've done plenty of dishes in my time. I wouldn't mind lending a hand, especially after a meal like that. Seems to me that those who cook shouldn't have to wash the dishes."

"Normally I'd agree with you, but not today. You're my guest."

"But…"

"I should think you'd know better than to argue with a woman," Mitch chided.

Laughing, Bethany shooed Ben out of the kitchen.

"We were going to continue our game of Monopoly,

remember?'' Chrissie reminded him eagerly. "You said you wanted a chance to win some of your money back.''

"Go play," Bethany said with a laugh. "I'll rope Mitch here into helping."

"You're sure?" Ben asked.

"Very sure," she told him, glancing over at Mitch with a gentle smile.

Mitch mumbled something she couldn't hear. She looked at him curiously as she reached for a bowl. "What did you say?"

His eyes held hers. "I said a man could get lost in one of your smiles and never find his way home."

Bethany paused, the bowl of leftover mashed potatoes in her hands. "Why, Mitch, what a romantic thing to say."

His face tightened ever so slightly, as though her comment had embarrassed him. "It must have something to do with the season," he said gruffly. He turned away from her and started to fill the sink with hot, sudsy water.

Bethany smiled to herself. It was a rare thing to see Mitch Harris flustered. Her hand fingered the polished five-dollar gold piece he'd had made into a pendant and placed on a fine gold chain. The coin had been minted the year of her birth, and Mitch had had it mounted in a gold bezel. The necklace was beautiful in its simplicity. The minute she fastened it around her neck, Bethany knew this was a piece of jewelry she'd wear every day for the rest of her life.

She felt that her gift for Mitch paled in comparison. Mitch was an avid Tom Clancy fan, and through a friend who managed a bookstore in San Francisco, she'd been able to get him an autographed copy of Clancy's latest hard cover.

When Mitch had opened the package and read the inscription, he looked up at her as though she'd handed him the stone tablets direct from Mount Sinai.

Chrissie had been excited about her Barbie town house, too.

The one who'd surprised her most, however, was Ben. He'd arrived for dinner with not one pie but four—all of them baked fresh that morning. In addition to the pies, he'd brusquely handed her an oblong box, as though he couldn't be rid of the thing fast enough. Bethany got a kick out of the way he'd wrapped it. He'd used three times the amount of paper necessary and enough tape to supply the U.S. Army for a year.

Inside the box was a piece of scrimshaw made from a walrus tusk. The scene on the polished piece of ivory was of wild geese in flight over a willow-filled marsh. Mountains rose in the distance against a sun-lit sky.

Ben had done his best to dismiss his gift as nothing more than a trinket, but Bethany knew from her brief stay in Fairbanks how expensive such pieces of artwork had become. She tried to thank him, but it was clear her words only served to embarrass him.

"I would have thought you'd want to fly home for Christmas," Mitch said, rolling up the sleeves of his long-sleeved shirt before dipping his hands in the dishwater.

"I thought seriously about it." Bethany wasn't going to minimize the difficulty of her decision to remain in Hard Luck. "But it's a long way to travel for so short a time. I'll probably stay in Alaska during spring break, as well. After all, my commitment here is only for the school year."

"You're going home to California in June, then?"

"Are you asking if I plan to return to Hard Luck for another school year?"

"Yes," he said, his back to her.

Something in the carefully nonchalant way he'd asked told her that her answer was important to him.

"I don't know," she said as straightforwardly as she knew how. "It depends on whether I'm offered a contract."

"And if you are?"

"I...don't know yet." She loved Alaska and her students. Most important of all, she loved Mitch and Chrissie. Ben, too. But there were other factors to consider. Several of them had to do with Ben—should she tell him he was her biological father and what would his reaction be if she did? More and more, she felt inclined to confront him with the truth.

"Well, I hope you come back" was all the response Mitch gave her. The deliberate lack of emotion in his voice was clearly intended to suggest that they'd been talking about something of little importance.

Why, for heaven's sake, couldn't the man just say what he wanted to say?

Hands on her hips, Bethany glared at him. Mitch happened to turn around for another stack of dirty dishes; he saw her and did a double take. "What?" he demanded.

"All you can say is 'Well, I hope you come back,'" she mimicked. "I'm spilling my heart out here and *that's* all the reaction I get from you?"

He gave her a blank look.

"The answer is I'm willing to consider another year's contract, and you can bet it isn't because of the tropical climate in Hard Luck."

Mitch grinned exuberantly. "The benefits are good."

"But not great."

"The money's fabulous."

"Oh, please," she muttered, rolling her eyes. She took an exaggerated breath. "My, my, I wonder what the appeal could be."

Mitch looked at her in sudden and complete seriousness. "I was hoping you'd say it was me."

She regarded him with an equally somber look. "I do enjoy the way you kiss, Mitch Harris."

The first sign of amusement touched his lips. He lifted his soapy arms from the water and stretched them toward her. "Maybe what you need to convince you is a small demonstration of my enjoyable kisses."

A second later Bethany was in his arms. The water seeped through her blouse, but she couldn't have cared less. What *did* matter to her was sharing this important day with the people she loved. And those who loved her.

JOHN HENDERSON wanted to do the right thing by Sally. He loved her—more than he'd thought possible. Proof of that was his willingness to delay asking her to marry him; he was determined to wait until he'd talked to her father.

The engagement ring continued to burn a hole in his pocket. He'd been carrying it with him for weeks now.

Every once in a while he'd draw it out and rub the gold band between his index finger and his thumb. He figured that his patience—difficult though he found it to be patient—was a measure of his love for Sally. Still, he cursed himself a dozen times a day for ever having listened to Duke.

John told himself that the other pilot didn't know any more about love than he did. But it wasn't true; Duke had given him good, sensible advice. John desperately wanted everything to be right between Sally and him, especially after her recent heartbreak.

It would've been selfish to rush her into an engagement and then a wedding without first knowing that she shared his feelings—and was sure of her own. He had to be certain she wasn't marrying him on the rebound. Duke was right about the other thing, too. Sally's family was traditional, old-fashioned, even, and it was important to meet them, to give them a chance to know him. Important—but the waiting had become harder with every week that passed.

Now he was ready to make his move. And ask his questions.

Naturally, John would rather have delayed this initial awkwardness. No man likes to be scrutinized by strangers, especially when he's about to ask these very people for permission to marry the most precious, beautiful woman God ever made. Their daughter.

If he were Sally's father, John thought, he wouldn't blame the man for booting him out of the house. He hoped, however, that it wouldn't come to that.

He'd bought a new suit for the occasion. It wasn't a waste of money, he'd decided, seeing that he'd probably need it for the wedding and all. If Sally agreed to marry him, and he hoped and prayed she would.

Sally's true feelings for him seemed to be the only real question. They'd been seeing each other on a regular basis, but John had noticed certain things about her that left him wondering. Her eyes didn't light up when she saw him, the way they had in the beginning.

If he didn't know better, he'd think she was avoiding him lately.

Mariah Douglas had recently moved into the house with her, and Sally seemed almost relieved to have an excuse not to invite him over so often. Of course, he'd been busy at Midnight Sons, with the holiday rush and all.

Other signs baffled him, as well. These puzzling changes in Sally's behavior had started after he'd spent the night with her. It wasn't like he'd *planned* they make love; it had just happened.

A hundred times since, John had regretted not waiting to initiate their lovemaking until after the wedding. He'd known for a long time how he felt about Sally. Immediately following their one night together, he'd gone out and bought the engagement ring, but then Duke had talked him out of proposing until he could meet her family.

It might not be such a good idea to show up unannounced on Christmas Day, but John didn't have a lot of spare time. Midnight Sons was short-handed in the wintertime as it was. The holidays had offered him the opportunity to make the trip. That was why he was in British Columbia, in a small town with an Indian name he couldn't pronounce, dropping in on Sally's family uninvited and clutching a somewhat travel-worn bouquet of roses.

Squaring his shoulders, John checked the address on the back of the Christmas card envelope and walked up to the split-entry white house with the dark green shutters and the large fir wreath on the door. He pressed the doorbell, swallowed nervously and waited.

His relief was great when Sally answered the door

herself. Her eyes grew huge with surprise and, he hoped, with happiness when she saw who it was.

"John? What are you doing here?"

He thrust the flowers into her hand, grateful to be rid of them. "I've come to talk to your father," he told her.

"My dad?" she asked, clearly puzzled. "Why?"

"That's between him and me." He found it difficult not to stare at her, seeing she was as pretty as a model for one of those fashion magazines. They'd only made love that once and although he cursed himself for his lack of self-control, he couldn't make himself regret loving Sally. He looked forward to making love to her again. Only this time it would be when his ring was around her finger and they'd said their "I do's."

"John?" She closed the door and stepped onto the small porch steps, hugging her arms around him. Her pretty eyes questioned his. "What's this all about?"

"I need to talk to your father," he repeated.

"You already said that. Is it because I've decided not to return to Hard Luck? Who told you? Not Mariah, she wouldn't do that, I know she wouldn't."

John felt as if someone had punched him. For one shocking moment, he thought he might be sick. "You didn't plan on coming back after Christmas?"

"No." She lowered her gaze, avoiding his.

"But I thought...I hoped—" He snapped his mouth shut before he made an even bigger fool of himself. He was about to humble himself before her father and request Sally's hand in marriage. Yet she'd walked out of his life without so much as a word of farewell.

"You mean you didn't know?"

He shook his head. "You weren't planning on telling me?"

"No." She tucked her chin against her chest. "I...I couldn't see the point. You'd gotten what you wanted, hadn't you?"

"What the hell is that supposed to mean?" he shouted. Standing outside her family home yelling probably wasn't the best way to introduce himself to her father, but John couldn't help it. He was angry, and with damn good reason.

"You know exactly what I mean," she replied in a furious whisper.

"Are you referring to the night we made love?"

Mortified, Sally closed her eyes. "Do you have to shout it to the entire neighborhood?"

"Yes!"

Sally glared at him. "I think we've said everything there is to say to each other."

"Not by a long shot, we haven't," John countered. "Okay, so we made love. Big deal. I'm not perfect, and neither are you. It happened, but we haven't gone to bed since then, have we?"

"John, please, not so loud." Sally glanced uneasily over her shoulder.

His next words surprised him, springing out despite himself. "I wasn't the first, so I don't understand why you're making a federal case over it. Too late now, anyway." He would never have said this if he hadn't been so angry, so much in pain.

Tears instantly leapt into her eyes and John would have given his right arm to take back the hurtful words. He'd rather suffer untold tortures than say anything to distress Sally, yet he'd done exactly that.

The door behind her opened and a burly lumberjack of a man walked out onto the porch. "What's going on here?"

Sally gestured weakly toward John. "Daddy, this is John Henderson. He—he's a friend from Hard Luck."

Finding his daughter sniffling back tears wasn't much of an endorsement, John thought gloomily. He squared his shoulders and offered the other man his hand. "I'm pleased to meet you, Mr. McDonald."

"The name's Jack. I don't understand why my daughter hasn't seen fit to invite you into the house, young man." He cast an accusatory glance in Sally's direction. "Seems you've come a long way to visit my daughter."

"It doesn't look like I was as welcome as I thought I'd be," John muttered.

"Nonsense. It's Christmas Day. Since you've traveled all this way, the least we can do is ask you to join us and offer you a warm drink."

John didn't need anything to warm him. Spending time with the McDonald family would only add to his frustration and misery, but Jack McDonald gave him no option. Sally's father quickly ushered him inside.

Swallowing his pride, John followed the brawny man up a short flight of stairs and into the living room. The festivities ceased when he appeared. Sally's father introduced him around, and her mother poured him a cup of wassail that tasted like hot apple cider.

"I don't believe Sally's mentioned you in her letters home," Mrs. McDonald said conversationally as a chair was brought out for John.

He felt his heart grow cold and heavy with pain. Forcing himself to observe basic good manners, he thanked Sally's brother for the chair. All those months while he was pining over Sally, he hadn't managed to rate a single line in one of her letters home. Although he'd told her their making love had been no big deal, it *had* been. For him. He loved her. But apparently their relationship wasn't important enough to Sally to ever tell her his name.

"I told you about John," Sally said weakly.

John wondered if that was true, or if she was attempting to cover her tracks.

"John's the bush pilot I wrote you about." Sally sat across the room from him and tucked her hands awkwardly between her knees as if she wasn't sure what to do with them.

"Oh yes, now I remember. Don't think you mentioned his name, though." Her father nodded slowly. And her mother gave him a sudden, bright smile.

John drank down the cider as fast as his throat would accept it. It burned going down, but he didn't care. He drained the cup, stood and abruptly handed it to Sally's mother.

"Thank you for the drink and the hospitality, but I need to be on my way."

Jack bent down to the carpet and retrieved something. "I believe you dropped this, son," he said.

To John's mortification, Sally's father held out the engagement ring.

He checked his pocket, praying all the while that there were two such rings in this world, and that the second just happened to be in Sally's home. On the floor. Naturally, the diamond Jack held was the one he'd brought for Sally. Without a word, he slipped it back inside his suit pocket.

"It was a pleasure meeting everyone," he said, anxiously eyeing the front door. He'd never been so eager to leave a place. Leave and find somewhere to be by himself.

Well, he told himself bitterly, he'd learned his lesson

when it came to women. He was better off living his life alone. To think he'd been one of the men eager to have the O'Hallorans bring women north!

One thing was certain, he didn't need this kind of rejection, this kind of pain.

"John?" Sally gazed at him with those big, beautiful blue eyes of hers. Only this time he wasn't about to be taken in by her sweetness.

He ignored her and hurried down the stairs to the front door. He'd already grasped the door handle when he realized that Sally had followed him. "You can leave without explaining that ring, but I swear if you do I'll never speak to you again."

"I don't see that it'd matter," he told her, boldly meeting her eyes. "You weren't planning on speaking to me anyway."

He gave her ample time to answer, and when she didn't, he made a show of turning the knob.

"Don't go," Sally cried in a choked whisper. "I thought...that you'd gotten what you wanted and so you—"

"I know what you thought," he snapped.

"Maybe we could talk this out?" It sounded like she was struggling not to break into tears. Damn, but she knew he couldn't bear to see her cry. He dug inside his back pocket, pulling out a fresh handkerchief and handing it to her.

"Could we talk, John?" she asked and walked down the second flight of stairs to the lower portion of the house. "Please?"

John guessed he was supposed to follow her. He looked up to find her mother, father, brother and a few cousins whose names he'd forgotten leaning over the railing staring at him.

"You'd better go," Sally's younger brother advised, "it's best to do what she wants when she's in one of these moods."

"Do you love her, son?" Jack McDonald demanded.

John looked at Sally, thinking a response now would be premature, but he couldn't very well deny it, carrying an engagement ring in his pocket. "Yes, sir. I meant to ask Sally to marry me, but I wanted everything to be right with us. I thought I'd introduce myself and ask your permission first."

"It's a good man who speaks to the father first," Sally's mother said, nodding tearfully.

"Marry her with my blessing, son."

John relaxed and grinned. "Thank you, sir." Then he figured he'd better give himself some room in case things didn't go the way he hoped. "In light of what's happened, I'm not sure Sally will say yes. She wasn't planning on returning to Hard Luck—I'm not sure why, but she hadn't said a word about it to me."

"I believe my daughter's about to clear away any doubts you have, young man. She'll give you plenty of reasons not to change your mind."

"Daddy!" This drifted up from the bottom of the stairwell.

John winked at his future in-laws. "That's what I was hoping she'd do," he said and hurried down the stairs, his steps jubilant. "Oh, and Merry Christmas, everyone!"

Whether it had to happen or not, was beyond God knows how. Randy knew how things had gone for all the years when she knew I didn't know the future, his loss.

So now was know, and if that had such...

how, and which that, and anything, essentially at least, it was the world, every, everything, he was he...

CHAPTER NINE

IT SHOULDN'T UPSET HER. If anything, Bethany thought, she should be pleased that Randy Kincade was getting married. The invitation for the March wedding arrived the second week of January, when winter howled outside her window and the promise of spring was buried beneath the frozen ground.

Bethany wasn't generally prone to bouts of the blues. But the darkness and the constant cold nibbled away at her optimism. Cabin fever—she'd never experienced it before, but she recognized the symptoms.

Her hair needed a trim, and she longed to see a movie in a real theater that sold hot, buttered popcorn. It was the middle of January, and she'd have killed for a thick-crust pizza smothered in melted cheese and chunks of spicy Italian sausage.

The craving for a pizza brought on a deluge of other sudden, unanticipated wants. She yearned for the opportunity to shop in a mall, in stores with fitting rooms, and to stroll past kiosks that sold delights like long, dangling earrings and glittery T-shirts. Not that she'd buy a lot of items. She just wanted to *see* them.

To make everything even worse, her relationship with Mitch had apparently ground to a standstill. As each week passed, it became more and more obvious that her feelings for him were far stronger than his were for her.

Whimsically she wondered if this was because God wanted her to know how Randy must have felt all those years ago when she didn't return the fervor of his love.

So now she knew, and it hurt like hell.

Not that Mitch had said anything. Not directly at least. It was his manner, his new reserve, the way he kissed her—as if even then he felt the need to protect his heart.

It frustrated Bethany. It angered her, but mostly it hurt. In many ways, she felt their relationship had become more honest and open, yet in others—the important ones—he still seemed to be holding back. He seemed to fear that loving her would mean surrendering a piece of his soul, and she'd begun to wonder if he'd always keep the past hidden from her.

On another front, she increasingly felt an urge to let Ben know she was his daughter. Perhaps this was because she missed her family so much. Or maybe it was because she'd come to terms with Ben's place in her life. Then again, maybe it was because she felt frustrated in her relationship with Mitch. She didn't know.

This wasn't to say the soulful kisses they shared weren't wonderful. They were. Yet they often left her hungering, not for a deeper physical relationship, but for a more profound emotional one. She longed for Mitch to trust her with his past, and clearly he wasn't willing to do that.

Their times alone, she noted, seemed to dwindle instead of increase. It almost seemed as though Mitch encouraged Chrissie's presence to avoid being alone with Bethany. It almost seemed as though dating Bethany satisfied his daughter's needs, but not his own.

On this January Saturday evening, when Bethany joined Mitch and Chrissie for their weekly video night, she couldn't disguise her melancholy. She tried, she honestly tried, to be upbeat, but it had been a long-drawn-out week. And now Randy was engaged, while her own love life had stalled.

Mitch must have noticed she hadn't touched the popcorn he'd supplied. "Is something wrong?" he asked, shifting in his seat beside her on the couch.

"No," she whispered, fighting to hold back the emotion that bubbled up inside her, seeking escape. Tears burned for release, and she feared she was about to weep and could think of no explanation that would appease him. No explanation, in fact, that would even make sense.

Mitch and Chrissie glanced at each other, then at her. Mitch stopped the movie. "You look like you're about to cry. I understand this movie's a tearjerker, but I didn't expect you to start crying while the previews were still playing."

She smiled weakly at his joke. "I'm sorry," she said. Her throat closed up, and when she tried to speak again, her voice came out in a high-pitched squeak.

"Bethany, what's wrong?"

She got to her feet, then didn't know why she had. She certainly didn't have anything to say, nor did she know what to do.

"I—I need a haircut," she croaked.

Mitch looked to Chrissie, as if his daughter should be able to translate that. Chrissie regarded Bethany seriously, then shrugged.

"And a pizza—not the frozen kind, but one that's delivered, and the delivery boy should stand around until he gets a tip and act slightly insulted by how little it is." She attempted a laugh, but that failed miserably.

"Pizza? Insulted?" Her explanation, such as it was, seemed to confuse Mitch even more.

"I'm sorry," she said again, gesturing forlornly with her hands. "I really am." She tucked her fingers against her palms and studied her hands. "Look at my nails. Just look. They used to be long and pretty—now they're broken and chipped."

"Bethany—"

"I'm not finished," she said, brushing the tears from her face. Now that they'd started, she couldn't seem to stop them. "I feel like the walls are closing in on me. I need more than a couple of hours of light a day. I'm sick and tired of watching the sun set two hours after dawn. I need more *light* than this." Even though she knew she wasn't being logical, Bethany couldn't stop the words any more than she could the tears. "I want to buy a new bra without ordering it out of a catalog."

"What you're feeling is cabin fever," Mitch explained calmly.

"I *know* that, but…"

"We all experience it in one way or another. It's not uncommon in winter. Even those of us who've lived here for years go through this.

"What you need is a weekend jaunt into Fairbanks. Two days away will make you feel like a new woman."

Men always seemed to have a simple solution to everything. For no reason she could explain—after all, she *wanted* to visit a big city—Mitch's answer only irritated her.

"Is a weekend trip going to change the fact that Randy's getting married?" she argued. Her hands clenched into fists, and her arms hung stiffly at her sides.

It took Mitch a moment or so to ask, "Who's Randy?"

"Bethany was engaged to him once a long time ago," Chrissie supplied.

"Do you love him?" Mitch asked in a gentle tone.

His tenderness, his complete lack of jealousy, infuriated her beyond reason. "No," she cried, "I love you, you idiot! Not that you care or notice or anything else." Convinced she'd made an even bigger fool of herself, Bethany reached for her coat and hat.

"Bethany—"

"You don't understand *any* of what I'm feeling, do you? Please, just leave me alone."

To add insult to injury, Mitch stepped back and did precisely as she asked.

By the time Bethany had walked home—having refused Mitch's offer of a ride—she was sobbing openly. Tears had frozen to her face. The worst part was that she *knew* how ridiculous she was being. Unfortunately it didn't seem to matter.

She was weeping uncontrollably—and all because she couldn't have a pizza delivered. Mitch seemed to think all she needed was a weekend in Fairbanks. It didn't escape her notice that he didn't suggest the two of them fly in together.

"Fairbanks, my foot," she muttered under her breath.

Restless and discontented, Bethany found she couldn't bear to sit around the house and do nothing. She was lonely and heartbroken. This type of misery preyed on itself, she realized. What she needed was some kind of distraction. And some sympathy...

Then, on impulse, she phoned Mariah Douglas, who was living in Catherine Fletcher's house now. She hoped she could talk Mariah into inviting her over. Mariah sounded pleased to hear from her and even said she had a bottle of wine in the fridge.

Before long, the two sat in the living room, clutching large glasses of zinfandel and bemoaning their sorry fate. It seemed the secretary of Midnight Sons shared Bethany's melancholy mood. Not long afterward, Sally McDonald and Angie Hughes, Mariah's housemates, showed up and willingly raided their own stashes of wine and potato chips.

Bethany acknowledged that it felt good to talk with female friends, to compare her list of woes with others who appreciated their seriousness. Soon it wasn't the lack of a decent pizza they were complaining about, but a more serious problem: the men in their lives.

"He wants me gone, you know," Mariah said, staring into her wineglass with a woebegone look. "He takes every opportunity to urge me to leave Hard Luck. I don't think August will come soon enough for him. I've…tried to be a good secretary, but he flusters me so."

Bethany knew Mariah was referring to Christian O'Halloran and wondered what prompted the secretary to stay when her employer had made his views so plain.

Then Bethany realized that Mariah stayed for the same reasons she did.

Bethany swirled the wine in her goblet. Her head swam, and she realized she was already half-drunk. A single glass of wine and she was tipsy. That said a lot about her social life.

"Let's go to Fairbanks!" she suggested excitedly. Although she'd rejected Mitch's suggestion out of hand, it held some appeal now. Escape by any means available was tempting, especially after a sufficient amount of wine.

"You want to leave for Fairbanks now?" Mariah asked incredulously.

"Why not?" Sally McDonald asked. Of them all, Sally was the one with least to complain about—at least on the male front. Sally and John Henderson had become engaged over the Christmas holidays.

"I don't fly. Do you?" Mariah asked. They looked at each other, then broke into giggles.

"I don't fly," Bethany admitted. "But we aren't going to let a little thing like a lack of a pilot stop us, are we? Not when we live in a town chock-full of them."

"You're absolutely right." Mariah's eyes lit up and she wagged her index finger back and forth. "Duke'll do it. He's scheduled for the mail run first thing in the morning and we'll tag along. Now, which of you girls is coming? No, *are* coming. No…"

There were no other volunteers. "Then it's just Beth and me. No, Beth and *I*…"

It was at this point that Bethany realized her friend was as tipsy as she was herself. "How will we get back?"

"I don't know," Mariah said, enunciating very carefully. "But where there's a way there's a will."

Bethany shut her eyes. That didn't sound exactly right, but it was close enough to satisfy her. Especially when she was half-drunk and her heart dangled precariously from her sleeve.

"He doesn't love me, you know," she said, making her own confession.

"Mitch?"

It was time to own up to the truth, however painful.

"He cares for you, though." This came from Sally.

Bethany fingered the gold coin that hung from the delicate chain around her neck. The gift Mitch had given her for Christmas. Touching it now, she experienced a deep sense of loss.

"Mitch does care," she agreed in a broken voice, "but not enough."

Mariah looked at her with sympathy and asked with forced cheer, "Who wants to go to Ben's? A few laughs, a dance or two..."

MITCH LOST COUNT of the number of times he'd tried to reach Bethany by phone. He'd left Chrissie with a high school girl who lived next door and walked over to Bethany's house. He stood on the tiny porch and pounded on the door until his fist hurt, despite the padding provided by his thick gloves.

Clearly she wasn't home. He frowned, wondering where she could possibly have gone.

Even as he asked the question, he knew. She'd gone to Ben's. Folks tended to let their hair down a bit on Fridays and Saturdays.

It wasn't uncommon to find Duke and John lingering over a cribbage board, while the other pilots shot the breeze over nothing in particular. Every now and again, one or more of the pipeline workers would wander in on their way to Fairbanks for a few days of R and R. Things occasionally got a bit rowdy; Mitch had broken up more than one fight in his time. He didn't like the idea of Bethany getting caught in the middle of anything like that.

When he stepped into the Hard Luck Café, he found the noise level almost painful. He couldn't recall the last time he'd seen the place so busy. It was literally hopping.

He caught sight of Bethany dancing with Duke Porter. Mariah Douglas was dancing with Keith Campbell, a pipeline employee and a friend of Bill Landgrin's. Mitch didn't trust either man.

Christian O'Halloran sat brooding in the corner, nursing a drink. Mitch noted that he was keeping a close eye on Mariah. Mitch suspected she wouldn't tolerate or appreciate Christian's interference and that Keith knew it and used it to his advantage.

Frowning, Mitch made his way into the room. He wanted to talk to Bethany, reason with her if he could. He understood her complaints far better than she realized. Her accusations had hit him like a…like a fist flying straight through time. Those were the words Lori had said to him day after day, week after week, month after month.…

Before he'd realized that it was Bethany talking to him and not his dead wife, Bethany had left. He needed to explain to her that he *did* know what she was experiencing. He'd been through it himself.

In January when daylight was counted in minutes, instead of hours, it did feel as though the walls were closing in.

He wanted to sit down and talk to her and say what had been burdening his heart for weeks now. Since Christmas. *He loved her.* So much it terrified him. He wanted to tell her about Lori; he hadn't, simply because he was afraid of her response. Most of all, he wanted to tell her he loved her.

Bill Landgrin saw him, and the two eyed each other malevolently. From the looks of it, Bill was more than a little put out over their last meeting. From the gleam in his eyes, he'd welcome a confrontation with Mitch.

Mitch wasn't eager for a fight, but he wouldn't back away from one, either.

Bill's gaze traveled from Mitch to Bethany and then back again. He set his mug on the counter and made his way to the other side of the café, where Bethany was sitting, now that her dance with Duke was over. Mitch started in her direction himself, scooting around tables.

Bill beat him to the punch.

"Beth, sweetheart." Mitch heard the other man greet her. "How's about a dance?"

It seemed to Mitch that she was about to refuse, but he made the mistake—a mistake he recognized almost immediately—of answering for her.

"Bethany's with me," he said, his words as cold as the Arctic ice.

"I am?" she asked.

"She is?" Bill echoed. He rubbed his forehead as though to suggest he found it hard to believe Bethany would align herself with the likes of Mitch. "Seems to me the lady's intelligent enough to make her own decisions."

It took Bethany an eternity to make up her mind. "I don't imagine one dance would hurt," she finally said to Bill.

Mitch's jaw hardened. He didn't blame her for defying him; he'd brought it on himself. Somehow the fact that she'd dance with another man, for whatever reason, didn't sit right with him. Not when she'd said she loved him!

He sat down in the chair she'd vacated, and as he watched Bill draw Bethany into his arms, his temperature rose. He wasn't a drinking man, but he sure could have used a shot of something strong right about then.

The song seemed to drone on for a lifetime. When he couldn't bear to sit any longer, Mitch got to his feet and restlessly prowled the edges of the dance area. Not once did he let his eyes waver from Bethany and Bill.

Something that gave him reason to rejoice was the fact that she didn't seem to be enjoying herself. Her gaze found his over Landgrin's shoulder, and she bit her lower lip in a way that told him she was sorry she'd ever agreed to this.

He resisted the urge to cut in.

Although Bethany was in another man's arms, Mitch found himself close to laughter. She'd said she loved him and in the same breath had called him an idiot. He was beginning to suspect she was right. He *was* an idiot. Love seemed to reduce him to that.

The music finally ended, and as Landgrin escorted Bethany to her table and reluctantly left her there, the tension eased from Mitch's body.

He made a beeline for her, regretting now that he hadn't been waiting for her when she returned. But he didn't want to give her reason to think he didn't trust her.

Unfortunately Keith Campbell reached her before he did. "A dance, fair lady?" Keith asked, bowing from the waist.

Again Mitch was left cooling his heels while Bethany frolicked across the dance floor in the arms of yet another man. While he waited, he ordered a soda and checked his watch.

He'd told Diane Hestead, the high school girl staying with Chrissie, that he wouldn't be more than an hour or so. He'd already been gone that long, and it didn't look like he'd be back home any time soon.

With the music blaring, he found the phone and

made a quick call to tell Diane he'd be longer than expected.

"Bethany certainly seems to be have captured a few hearts, hasn't she?" Ben commented, slapping Mitch good-naturedly on the back.

"I don't know why she needs to do that," he grumbled. "She's had mine for weeks."

"Does she know that?" Ben asked.

"No," Mitch blurted.

"What do you expect her to do, then?"

Ben was right, of course. Mitch returned to the table to wait for her. When the dance finished, he made damn certain he was there. "My turn," he announced flatly the minute the two of them were alone.

Bethany's gaze narrowed; she promptly ignored him and sat down. She finished the last of her soda and set the glass aside.

"Let's dance," he said, and held out his hand to her.

"Is that a request or a command?" she asked, staring up at him.

Mitch swallowed. This was going from bad to worse. "Do you want me to put on a little performance for you the way Keith did?"

"No," she answered simply.

It was now or never. "Bethany," he said, dragging air into his oxygen-starved lungs, "I love you. I have for weeks. I should have told you before now."

She stared at him, her eyes huge and round. Then, as though she found reason to doubt his words, she hastily looked away. "Why now, Mitch?"

He could hardly hear her over the music. "Why now what?"

"Why are you telling me now?" she asked, clarifying her question. "Is it because you're overwhelmed by the depth of your feelings?'' She sounded just a little sarcastic, he thought. ''Or could the truth be that you can't bear to see me with another man?''

He frowned, not because he didn't understand her question, but because he wasn't sure how to answer. Certainly she had a point. He might well have been content to leave matters as they were if he hadn't found her dancing with Landgrin.

''Your hesitation tells me everything I need to know,'' she whispered brokenly. She stood then, in such a rush that she nearly toppled the chair. ''Duke,'' she called, hurrying toward the pilot. ''Didn't I promise you another dance?''

Mitch ground his teeth in frustration.

He'd started toward the door when Bill Landgrin stopped him. ''Looks like you're batting zero, old friend. Seems to me the lady knows what she wants, and it isn't you.''

''I BLEW IT,'' Bethany muttered miserably. She'd lingered behind and was helping Ben clear the last remaining tables. Mariah had disappeared hours earlier after a confrontation with Christian, and she hadn't seen her friend since.

''What do you mean?''

''Mitch and me.''

''What's with you two, anyway?'' Ben asked as he set a tray of dirty glasses on the counter.

''I don't know anymore. I thought… I'd hoped…'' She felt tongue-tied, unable to explain. Slipping onto the stool opposite Ben, she let her shoulders sag in abject misery. She was still feeling a little drunk and a lot discouraged—not to mention suffering from a near-fatal bout of cabin fever.

"Here," Ben said, reaching behind the counter and bringing out a bottle of brandy. "I save this for special occasions."

"What's so special about this evening?" she asked.

"A number of things," he said, but didn't elaborate. He brought out a couple of snifters and poured a liberal amount into each one. "This will cure what ails you. Guaranteed."

"Maybe you're right." At this point she figured a glass of brandy couldn't hurt.

"Cheers," Ben said, and touched the rim of his glass to hers.

"To a special...friend," she said and took her first tentative sip. The liquid fire glided over her tongue and down her throat. When it came to drinking alcohol, Bethany generally stuck to wine and an occasional beer, rarely anything stronger.

Her eyes watered, and this time it had nothing to do with her emotions.

"You all right?" Ben asked, slapping her on the back.

She pressed her hand over her heart and nodded breathlessly. She found her second and third sips went down far more easily than the first. Gradually a warmth spread out from the pit of her stomach, and a lethargic feeling settled over her.

"Have you ever been in love?" she asked, surprising herself by asking such a personal question. Perhaps the liquor had loosened her tongue; more likely it was simply the need to hear this man's version of his affair with her mother. This man who'd fathered her....

"In love? Me?"

"What's so strange about that?" she asked lightly, careful not to let on how serious the question really was. "Surely you've been in love at least once in your life. A woman in your deep, dark past maybe—one you've never been able to forget?"

Ben hesitated, then chuckled. "I was in the navy, you know?"

Bethany nodded. "Don't tell me you were the kind of sailor who had a woman in every port?"

He grinned almost boyishly and cocked his head to one side. "That was me, all right."

Although she'd solicited it, this information disturbed Bethany. It somehow cheapened her mother and the love she'd once felt for Ben. "But surely there was one woman you remember more than any of the others," she pressed.

Ben scratched the side of his head as though to give her question heavy-duty consideration. "Nope, can't say there was. I was the kind who liked to play the field."

Bethany took another sip of the brandy. "What about Marilyn?" she asked brazenly, tossing caution to the winds. "You do remember her, don't you?"

"Marilyn?" Ben repeated, surprise in his eyes. "No...I don't recall any Marilyn." He sounded as though he'd never heard the name before.

Ben might as well have reached across the counter and slapped her face. Hard. She hurt for her mother, and for herself. Before she met him, she'd let herself imagine that her mother's affair with Ben had been a romantic relationship gone tragically awry.

In the past few weeks, she'd began to think she shared a special friendship with Ben. A real bond. Because of that, she'd lowered her guard and come close to revealing her secret.

Bethany clamped her mouth shut. She wanted to

blame the wine. The brandy. Both had loosened her tongue, she realized, but she'd been on the verge of telling him, anyway. She brushed the hair out of her face and looked past him.

"Three years ago," she began resolutely, struggling to find the right words, knowing she couldn't stop now, "the doctors found a lump in my mother's breast."

"Cancer?"

Bethany nodded.

Ben glanced at his watch. "It's getting kind of late, don't you think?"

"This story will only take a couple more minutes," she promised, and to fortify her courage, she drank the rest of the brandy in a single gulp. It raged a slick, fiery path down her throat.

"You were talking about your mother," Ben prodded, and it seemed he wanted her to hurry. Bethany didn't know if she could. Those weeks when her mother had been so sick from the chemotherapy had been the most traumatic of her life.

"It turned out that the cancer had spread," Bethany continued. "For a while we didn't know if my mother was going to survive. I was convinced that if the cancer didn't kill her, the chemotherapy would. I was still in college at the time. My classes let out around two, and I got into the habit of stopping off at the hospital on my way home from school."

Ben nursed his drink, his eyes avoiding hers.

"One day, after a particularly violent reaction to the treatment, Mom was convinced she was going to die. I tried to tell her she had to fight the cancer."

"Did she die?" Ben asked. For the first time since starting her story she had his full attention. Either she was a better storyteller than she realized, or Ben did remember her mother.

"No. She's a survivor. But that day Mom asked me to sit down because she had something important to tell me." At this point, Bethany paused long enough to steady herself. After all this time, the unexpectedness of her mother's announcement still shocked her.

"And?"

"My mother told me about a young sailor she'd once loved many years ago. They'd met the summer before he shipped out to Vietnam. By the end of their time together, they'd became lovers. Their political differences separated them as much as the war had. He left because it was his duty to fight, and she stayed behind and joined the peace movement, protesting the war every chance she had. She wrote him a letter and told him about it. He didn't answer. She knew he didn't approve of what she was doing."

"Whoever this person was, he probably didn't want to read about what she was doing to undermine his efforts in Southeast Asia, don't you think?" Ben asked stiffly.

"I'm sure that's true," Bethany said, and her voice vacillated slightly. "The problem was that when he refused to open her next letter, he failed to learn something vitally important. My mother was pregnant with his child."

The snifter in Ben's hand dropped to the floor and shattered. His eyes remained frozen on Bethany's face.

"I was that child."

The silence stretched taut to the breaking point. "Who took care of her?" he asked in a choked whisper.

"Her family. When she was about four months pregnant, she met Peter Ross, another student, and she confided in him. They fell in love and were married shortly before I was born. Peter raised me as his own and has loved and nurtured me ever since. I never would have guessed... It was the biggest shock of my life to learn he wasn't my biological father.''

"Your mother's name is Marilyn?''

"Yes, and she named you as my birth father.''

"Me,'' Ben said with a weak-sounding laugh. "Sorry, kid, but you've got the wrong guy.'' He continued to shake his head incredulously. "What'd your mother do—send you out to find me?''

"No. Neither of my parents know the reason I accepted the teaching contract in Hard Luck. I gave your name to the Red Cross, and they traced you here. I came to meet you, to find out what I could about you.''

"Then it's unfortunate you came all this way for nothing,'' he said gruffly.

"It's funny, really, because we *are* alike. You know the way you get three lines between your eyes when you're troubled or confused? I get those, too. In fact you're the one who mentioned it, remember? And we both like to cook. And we—''

"That's enough,'' he snapped. "Listen, Bethany, this is all well and good, but like I already said, you've got the wrong guy.''

"But—''

"I told you before and I'll tell again. I never knew any woman by the name of Marilyn. You'd think if I'd slept with her, I'd remember her, wouldn't you?''

His words were like stones hurled at her heart. "I don't want anything from you, Ben.''

"Well, don't count on a mention in my will, either, understand?''

She nearly fell off the stool in her effort to escape. She retreated a step backward. "I...I should never have told you."

"I don't know why you did. And listen, I'd appreciate it if you didn't go spreading this lie around town, either. I've got a reputation to uphold, and I don't want your lies—and your mother's—besmirching my character."

Bethany thought she was going to be sick.

"It's a damn lie, you hear? It's a lie!" This last part was shouted at her.

"I'm sorry. I shouldn't have said anything."

He didn't answer her right away. "I don't know anything about any Marilyn."

"I made a mistake," Bethany whispered. "A terrible mistake." She turned and ran from the café.

CHAPTER TEN

IN ALL THE YEARS Mitch had lived in Hard Luck, he'd seen very few mornings when Ben wasn't open for business.

Mitch wasn't the only disgruntled one. Christian met him outside the café. "Do you think Ben might have overslept?"

Mitch doubted it. "Ben?" he asked. "Ben Hamilton, who says he never sleeps past six no matter what time he goes to bed?"

"Maybe he decided to take the day off. He's entitled, don't you think?" Christian asked.

Mitch had thought of that, too. "But wouldn't he put up a sign or something?"

Christian considered this, then said, "Probably." He checked his watch. "Listen, I'm supposed to meet Sawyer at his place."

"Go ahead." It was clear Christian was thinking the same thing as Mitch. Something was wrong. "I'll check things out and connect with you later," he promised.

Ben's apartment was situated above the café. Mitch had never been inside, and he didn't know anyone who had. Ben's real home was the café itself. He kept it open seven days a week and most holidays. Occasionally he'd post a closed sign when he felt like taking off for a few days' fishing, but that was about it.

The Hard Luck Café was the social center of town, the one place where people routinely gathered. Ben was part psychologist, part judge, part confidant and all friend. Mitch didn't know a man, woman or child in town who didn't like him.

Frowning, and growing increasingly worried, Mitch went around to the back door that led to the kitchen. After a couple of tentative knocks, he walked into the dark, silent café. Flicking on the light switch, the first thing Mitch noticed was shattered glass on the floor.

"Ben!" Mitch called out, walking all the way into the café.

Nothing.

The door to the stairs leading to Ben's apartment was open, and Mitch started up, his heart pounding in his ears. In an effort to compose himself, he paused halfway, fearing what he might find. If Ben was dead, it wouldn't be the first time he'd come upon a body. The last time had been when he'd found Lori.

He broke out in a cold sweat, and his breathing grew shallow. "Ben," he said again, not as loudly this time. It was another moment before he could continue upward.

The apartment itself was ordinary. A couch and television constituted the living room furniture. Small bath. Bedroom. Both doors had been left ajar.

"Ben?" he tried once more.

A moan came from the bedroom.

More relieved than words could express, Mitch hurried into the room. Ben was sprawled across the top of the bedspread. It took him a full minute to sit up. He blinked as if the act of opening his eyes had pained him.

"Are you all right?" Mitch asked.

Ben rubbed a hand down his face and seemed to give the question some consideration. "No," he finally said.

"Do you need me to call Dotty? Or take you to the clinic?"

"Hell, no. She can't do anything about a hangover."

"You're hung over?" To the best of his knowledge, Ben rarely drank.

Ben pressed both hands to his head. "Do you have to talk so blasted loud?" He grimaced at the sound of his own voice.

"Sorry," Mitch said in an amused whisper.

"Make yourself useful, would you?" Ben growled. "I need coffee. Make it strong, too. I'll be downstairs in a few minutes."

Mitch had the coffee brewing and had swept up the broken glass by the time Ben appeared, his eyes red-rimmed and clouded. His gaze shifted toward Mitch before he claimed a stool at the counter.

Mitch brought him a cup of coffee the minute it finished brewing.

"Thanks," Ben mumbled.

"I've never known you to get drunk," Mitch said conversationally, curious as to what had prompted Ben's apparent binge.

"First time in ten years or more," he muttered. "It was either that or...hell, I don't know what. There didn't seem to be a whole lot of options. Fight, I guess, but there wasn't anyone around to punch. Not that it would've done any good, since there wasn't anyone to blame but myself. Damn, but I messed up."

"Can I help?" Mitch asked. There were any number of times he'd come to Ben for advice about something or other, including his feelings for Bethany. Most of his visits had been on the pretext of wanting a cup of coffee. It appeared that the tables were turned now, and if he could assist Ben in some way, then all the better.

"Help me? No." Ben shook his head and instantly seemed to regret the movement. He closed his eyes and waited a couple of moments before opening them again.

"You want me to make you breakfast?" Mitch asked. "I'm not a bad cook."

He couldn't tell whether Ben was taking his offer into consideration. Lowering his head, Ben mumbled something Mitch couldn't hear.

Mitch leaned closer. "Did you say something?"

"Have, ah…have you seen Bethany this morning?"

"No." He'd actually come to tell his friend what had happened between them last night and seek his advice.

"Have you tried phoning her?"

"No."

Ben gave a slight nod in the direction of the phone. "Go ahead, okay?"

Mitch checked his watch. "It's a little early, isn't it?"

"Maybe, but try, anyway."

Mitch wasn't keen on the idea. "Is there anything in particular you'd like me to ask her?"

Ben propped his elbows on the counter and covered his face with both hands. He rubbed his eyes, and when he glanced in Mitch's direction they seemed to glisten. "I didn't know," he said in a frayed whisper. "I… never knew."

"What didn't you know?" Mitch asked gently.

"Marilyn was pregnant."

Ben might as well have been speaking in a foreign

language for all the sense he made. "And who's Marilyn?" Mitch asked in calm tones.

Ben dropped his hands. "Bethany's mother." He paused. "Bethany's my daughter. I'm the reason she came to Hard Luck, and when she told me...I pretended I never knew any Marilyn."

"You mean—"

"Yes," Ben shouted, and pounded his fist on the counter, hard enough for his hand to bounce away from the surface. "I'm Bethany's father."

Mitch swore under his breath.

"It was the shock. I...I never guessed. Maybe I should have...I don't know."

Mitch's mind buzzed with the information. He sat on the stool next to Ben, feeling the weight of his friend's burden as if it were his own.

"When she told me, I denied ever knowing her mother and then—" his face contorted with guilt "—I said some things I regret and sent Bethany away." Ben wiped impatiently at his eyes. "She ran out of here, and now I'm afraid she won't be back."

"I'll talk to her if you like." Although Mitch was happy to make the offer, he didn't know if he'd be a help or a hindrance. His own track record with Bethany wasn't exactly impressive.

"Would you?" Ben clung to Mitch's offer like a lifeline in a storm-tossed sea.

"Sure." Mitch needed to see her for his own reasons, anyway. "I'll do it right away," he said, eager now to find her. They'd parted on such cool terms Bethany might not be as eager for his company. But Mitch was willing to risk her displeasure. She needed him. When he'd been in pain and grief, she'd been there to comfort him. Ben's rejection must have left her reeling. Mitch suddenly understood how important it was to be the one to console her.

"Tell her..." Ben hesitated, apparently not knowing how to convey his message. "Tell her..." he began a second time, his voice weak. His eyes brightened again and he drew in a deep, shuddering breath. "That I'm proud to have her as my daughter."

To Mitch's way of thinking, Bethany would be better off hearing those words from Ben herself.

MITCH LEFT the café, and Ben was alone once again to deal with the pain and the guilt that had accompanied him most of the night. Even the brandy hadn't dulled the shock.

He had a daughter.

Even now, the words felt awkward on his tongue. Getting used to the idea was going to require some doing. What bothered him most was the thought of Marilyn's struggling alone, without him. It stung a little to know she'd married someone else so soon after his departure. But he couldn't blame her. What was she to do, pregnant with his child and unable to let him know?

Even if he'd learned the truth, he didn't think he could have helped her the way she needed. He might have been able to marry her. Maybe that could've been arranged. But he was involved in a war, and it wasn't like he could call time-out while he dealt with his personal problems. The navy wouldn't have released him from his obligations because he got a college girl pregnant.

If there was any single thing Ben regretted most about the past, it was returning Marilyn's letter unopened. It pained him almost to the point of being physically ill to think about her alone and pregnant, believing he didn't care. The truth of the matter was that he'd loved her deeply. It had taken him years to put his love for her behind him.

She'd done the right thing in marrying this other man, he decided suddenly. Ben wouldn't have been a good husband for her, or for any woman. He was too stubborn, too set in his own ways. "It was easier to comfort himself with those reassurances, he supposed, than deal with all the might-have-beens.

The fact was, he'd fathered this child. Except that Bethany wasn't exactly a child. She was an adult, and a mighty fine one at that. Any man would be proud to call her daughter.

Bethany. Ben would give anything to take back the things he'd said to her. It was the shock. The fear, too, of her wanting something from him when he had nothing to give—emotionally or financially. He couldn't change the past or make up to Marilyn and Bethany for what he'd done—and hadn't done.

Ben poured himself a second cup of coffee in an attempt to clear his head. His temples still throbbed—enough to convince him not to seek his solution in a bottle again anytime soon.

There was a knock at the front door. He'd forgotten that he'd left it locked. With a decided lack of enthusiasm, he shuffled across the café and unlatched the bolt. To his surprise, he found it was Mitch.

"She's gone," Mitch announced, sounding like a man in a trance.

"Bethany gone? What do you mean, gone?"

"I just saw Christian. Duke flew her out this morning."

Pain shot through Ben's chest and he felt the sudden

need to sit down. He'd only just found her and now—now he'd lost her.

THE PIZZA HAD HELPED, Bethany decided, but not nearly enough. Sorry that Mariah had decided not to join her, after all, she sat on top of the big hotel bed in front of the television. She was halfheartedly watching a movie she'd seen before she'd left for Alaska and paying the same price now as she had in a California theater.

Earlier in the day, she'd had her hair trimmed, and while she was at it, she'd sprung for a manicure.

Following that, she'd found a shopping mall and lingered for hours, just poking about the shops and watching the people. It didn't take long, however, for the doubts and regrets to crowd their way back into her mind.

She'd ruined everything. With Ben feeling the way he did, she wasn't comfortable returning to Hard Luck, and at the same time she couldn't leave. Not with everything between her and Mitch still unresolved. If the situation had been different, she could have phoned her parents, but of course neither of them knew the real reason she'd accepted the teaching assignment in Alaska. She hadn't wanted them to know.

What about Chrissie? And Susan and Scott and Ronnie… She couldn't leave her students or break the terms of her contract. She had a moral and a legal obligation to the people who'd hired her. The state and the town had entrusted her with these young lives. She couldn't just walk out and leave.

On the other hand, how could she return? It was all she could do not to bury her face in her hands and weep. Even now, she didn't know what had possessed her to confront Ben with the truth last night. Her timing couldn't have been worse. The information had come at him with the stealth and suddenness of a bomb, exploding in his life. She hadn't prepared him in any way to learn she was his daughter.

No wonder he— Her thoughts came to a crashing halt at the loud knock on her door.

"Bethany."

"Mitch?"

"Please open up."

She hadn't a clue how he'd learned where she was staying. She scrambled off the bed and ran to unlatch the door.

He stood on the other side as though he was surprised he hadn't been forced to kick the door open. He blinked, then blurted, "Don't leave."

"Leave?" She followed his gaze to her small suitcase.

"You've packed your things."

True, but only for a short stay in Fairbanks. She wondered where Mitch thought she was going. Then she realized he must think she wasn't planning to return. That was it. He assumed she was leaving for good.

"Give me one good reason to stay," she invited.

He walked past her and into the room. As he moved, he shoved his fingers through his hair and inhaled sharply. Unable to stand still, he paced the area like a man possessed.

"I love you, and I'm not saying it because there's another man wanting to dance with you. I'm saying it because I can't imagine living without you." He stopped, his eyes imploring. "I need you, Bethany. I didn't realize how much until I found you gone."

"You love me?"

"I haven't given you much reason to believe that, have I? There are reasons... I know you don't want to listen to excuses, and I don't blame you. Bethany, I'm not saying any of this for Chrissie. I need you for *me*. I love you for *me*." He paused and dragged in an uneven breath.

All at once it didn't seem fair to mislead him any further. "I'm not going anywhere," she confessed. "I was coming back, and when I did, I planned to try to work all this out with you."

He closed his eyes as if a great weight had been lifted from him.

"I need to settle matters with someone else, too," she said.

"Ben." His eyes held hers. "He wants to talk to you."

Bethany struggled for a moment to control her emotions before she asked, "He told you?"

Mitch nodded. "You're his daughter."

"He admitted that?" Her eyes welled with tears.

Again he nodded.

"Is he all right? I shouldn't have said anything— you don't know how much I regret it." She found it difficult to maintain her composure. "It was unfair to confront him the way I did. I can only imagine what he must think. Please," she begged, "tell him I don't expect anything of him. I realized he lied, but I understand. I don't blame him. Who knows what any of us would have done in similar circumstances."

"He very badly wants to talk to you himself."

"He doesn't need to say a word. I understand. Please assure him for me that I don't want anything from him," she said again.

"You can tell him yourself. He's here."

"Here?"

"Actually he's downstairs in the bar waiting. We tossed a coin to see which of us got to speak to you first. I won."

He gestured at the bed. "Please sit," he instructed. "This seems to be a time for confessions." Bethany obediently perched on the edge of the mattress and looked up at him expectantly.

"There's something important you need to know about me," he said. "I should have told you sooner— I'm sorry I didn't. After I've told you, you can decide what you want to do. If you'd rather not see me again…well, you can decide that later."

"Mitch, what is it?"

He couldn't seem to stay in one place. "I love you, Bethany," he said urgently. "I'm not a man who loves easily. There's only been one other woman I've ever felt this strongly about."

"Your wife," she guessed.

"I—I don't know where to start." Mitch threw her a look of anguish.

"Start at the beginning," she coaxed gently, patiently. She'd waited a long time for Mitch to trust her enough with his past.

He resumed his pacing. "I met Lori while we were in college. I suppose our history was fairly typical. We fell in love and got married. I joined the Chicago Police Department, and our lives settled down to that of any typical young couple. Or so I thought."

He paused, and it seemed to Bethany that the light went out of his eyes.

"I see," she said quietly. "Go on."

Moving to stand in front of her, he said, "Chrissie

was born, and I was crazy about her from the first. Lori wanted to be a good mother. I believe that, and she tried. She honestly tried. But she was accustomed to being in the workforce and mingling with other people, and staying home with the baby didn't suit her. About this time, I was assigned to Narcotics. From that point, my schedule became erratic. I rarely knew from one week to the next what my hours would be."

He stared somewhere above her head, as if the telling of these details was too painful to do directly.

"Lori became depressed. She saw a physician about it, and he explained that new-mother blues were fairly common. He prescribed something to help her feel better. He also gave her tranquilizers. A light dose to take when she had trouble sleeping."

"Did they help?"

"For a while, but then Lori found she couldn't sleep nights at all. It didn't help that Chrissie suffered from repeated ear infections, and Lori had to stay awake with her so often."

He frowned. "I don't know when she started doubling up on the tranquilizers, or even how she was able to get so many of them. I suspect she went to a number of different doctors."

Bethany held out her hand to him and Mitch gripped it hard between both of his own. Then he sat on the bed beside her, turning his body to face her. "What's so tragic about all this is that time and time again Lori told me how unhappy she was, how miserable. She didn't like being home. She didn't like staying with the baby so much. She wanted me home more often. She clung to me until I felt she was strangling me, and all along she was so terribly sick, so terribly depressed."

"Did you know she was hooked on the tranquilizers?"

"I suppose I guessed. But I didn't want to deal with it. I couldn't. I was working day and night on an important case," he said, his eyes bleak with his sorrow. "If she wanted to dope herself up at night with tranquilizers, then fine. I'd deal with it when I could, but not then." He closed his eyes and shook his head. "You see, I might have saved her life had I dealt with the problem immediately, instead of ignoring it and praying she'd snap out of it herself."

"What happened?" Bethany asked. She intuitively realized there was more to the story, and that it would only grow worse.

"If the signs had been any plainer, they would've hit me over the head."

"It happens every day."

"I worked with addicts. I should have known."

It was clear this was one thing Mitch would never forgive himself for.

"She killed herself," he said in a stark whisper. "Her family thought it was an accident, but I know better. She needed me, but I was too involved in chasing down a drug dealer to help my own wife. She was depressed, unhappy, miserable, and addicted to tranquilizers. I'm convinced she felt she had nothing left to live for. Certainly not a caring, tender husband. I turned my back on my own wife. I might as well have poured the pills down her throat."

"Oh, Mitch, you were under so much stress yourself. You can't blame yourself for Lori's weakness."

"Yes, I can," he said, "and I have. I should've realized what was happening to her. She paid the penalty for my neglect—with her life. I can understand if you don't want to marry me…''

"Is that what you're asking me, Mitch? To be your wife?''

"Yes.'' His gaze held hers. "I realize how much Chrissie loves you, but like I told you last night, it isn't for my daughter I'm asking. It's for me.''

The lump in Bethany's throat refused to dissolve. She nodded and swallowed back her tears.

"Is that a yes?'' he asked in a harsh whisper, as if he was afraid of the answer.

She nodded vigorously.

Mitch briefly closed his eyes. "I live a simple life, Bethany. I don't want to leave Hard Luck.''

"I don't want to leave, either. My home is wherever you are.''

"You're sure? Because I don't think I could let you go. Not now.'' He reached for her and kissed her with a hunger and a longing that left her breathless. A long time passed before he released her.

"We'd better stop while I've got the strength to let you go,'' he told her. "Besides, Ben's waiting.''

"Ben.'' She'd almost forgotten.

"He's downstairs bragging to the bartender about his daughter,'' Mitch said with the hint of a smile. "Would you like to join him there? I know he wants to talk to you.''

"In a little while,'' she whispered and pressed her head against his shoulder. They'd both come to Hard Luck for a purpose. His had been to hide; hers had been to locate the man whose genes she shared. Together they'd discovered something far more precious than the gold that had drawn generations of prospectors to Alaska.

Together they'd found each other. And love.

EPILOGUE

HALF AN HOUR LATER, Bethany made her way into the dimly lit cocktail lounge and found Ben sitting alone at a table, nursing a bottle of beer. His shoulders slumped forward and his head was bowed. It looked, she thought sadly, as if the weight of nearly thirty years of regret rested solidly on his back.

He raised his eyes to meet hers when she walked over to his table. "Do you mind if I sit down?" she asked, feeling tentative herself. She understood now that the way she'd confronted Ben had been a mistake; she wished more than anything that they could start over again.

He nodded, his expression concerned as she slid out the chair and sat across from him.

"Do you want something to drink?" he asked.

"No, thanks." The wine and brandy last night had loosened her tongue. She didn't want to repeat *that* mistake. "I'm so very sorry…"

"I'm the one who's sorry," Ben cut in. "I'm not proud of the way I reacted yesterday—my only excuse is shock."

"I couldn't have done a worse job of it," she said.

His face tightened, and his eyes grew suspiciously bright. "It's so hard to believe I could have a daughter as beautiful as you, Bethany. My heart feels like it's going to burst wide open just looking at you."

Bethany smiled tremulously, close to tears herself.

"Your mother...the resemblance between you is striking. I didn't see it at first, but I do now." He took a swallow of his beer and Bethany suspected he did it to hide his emotion. He set the bottle back on the table. "How is Marilyn? The cancer?"

"She's better than ever, and there's no sign of the cancer recurring."

"She's...she's had a good life? She's happy?"

Bethany nodded. "Very happy. Mom and Dad have a good marriage. Like any relationship, it's had its ups and downs over the years, but they're deeply in love, and they're truly committed to each other." She paused and drew in a deep breath. "They don't know that I've—that I found you."

He lowered his head. "Do you plan on telling them?"

"Yes, and you can be assured I'll handle it a lot more delicately than I did with you. I accepted the teaching contract in Hard Luck because I knew you were here, but originally I'd never intended to tell you."

"Not tell me?"

"All I wanted was to get to know you, but once I'd done that, it didn't seem to be enough. We're very alike, Ben, in many important ways. But before I knew that, I was afraid of the kind of man you'd be."

He sipped from the beer bottle. "I'm probably a disappointment..."

"No," she rushed to tell him. "No! I'm *proud* to be your daughter. You're a warm, generous, caring human being. Hard Luck Café is the heart of the community, and that's because of you."

"I can't be your father," Ben murmured with regret,

"Your mother's husband—Peter—he'll always be that."

"That's true. But you could be my friend."

His face brightened. "Yes. A special friend."

Bethany stretched her hand across the table and Ben squeezed her fingers. "Where's Mitch?"

"He's in the lobby waiting for us." Bethany smiled, and the happiness bloomed within her. "This seems to be a day for clearing the air."

Ben placed some money on the table and together they walked out of the lounge. "Are you going to marry that young buck and put him out of his misery?"

"Oh, yes. I came to Hard Luck wanting to meet you, and instead I found *two* men I'll love all my life."

Mitch hurried toward them, and they met him halfway. Grinning widely, Ben slung an arm around their shoulders, drawing them close. "Well, my friends. This seems to be an evening to celebrate. Dinner's on me!"

BECAUSE OF THE BABY

PROLOGUE

SHE WOULD ALWAYS BE his valentine, according to the card.

The man was a low-down, dirty rat! Furiously Karen Caldwell tossed the card into the garbage. She stood there in the middle of her kitchen, with the Californian sun pouring through her windows, and battled down tears.

Leave it to her ex-husband to do something like this. In the four years of their marriage Matt hadn't once bought her a valentine card. *Or* an anniversary card. Oh, no, he waited until they were divorced to do that. Waited until she was convinced he was finally out of her life—and her heart. Only then had he bothered to send her a card. A sweet, funny card celebrating a day meant for lovers. He'd purposely postponed contacting her until she'd managed to persuade herself she was almost happy.

Karen drew a deep, shaky breath, determined to put the man and the valentine out of her mind.

Her ex-husband infuriated her. This was just another example. Put a hundred, a thousand, of these examples together, and it explained why she'd divorced him. Matthew Caldwell was irresponsible. Thoughtless. Unreliable. In the four years of their marriage he'd changed careers five times. Five times!

Without fail, whenever she'd begun to think he'd

finally found his niche, Matt would casually announce he'd quit his job. Not once had he discussed his plans with her. He seemed to believe his decision was none of her concern.

Over and over he'd tell her he didn't know how unhappy he was until the moment he quit, as if that should be all the explanation she'd need.

Giving his notice at Curtis Accounting had been the final straw. When that happened Karen had done the only sensible thing a woman could do in the circumstances. She left him.

No one blamed her, least of all Matt's family. His parents and sister were as exasperated with his penchant for shifting careers as she was herself.

Right after the divorce Karen had been offered the transfer to California. Leaving Alaska just then had sounded like a perfect solution, and it didn't hurt that a promotion went along with the relocation. The move was sure to help her put the unpleasantness of her failed marriage behind her. Sunny California was just the distraction she needed.

Or so Karen had thought.

Now she wasn't so sure. She missed Alaska. Missed her friends. And damn it all, she missed Matt.

Karen avoided looking at the garbage can. Every time she thought of the valentine card, it made her mad. What irritated her most was that she knew he'd had to go out of his way to buy it.

Karen had been to Hard Luck, where Matt was living now. In a town that small, there wouldn't be anyplace that sold greeting cards. Matt would've had to order it by mail, or fly into Fairbanks.

He'd moved to Hard Luck because of the lodge— his latest folly.

Karen rolled her eyes at the thought. Her ex-husband had used the trust fund his grandmother had left him to purchase the burned-out lodge from the O'Halloran brothers. What Karen understood from a conversation with his sister was that Matt had begun to renovate it and hoped to attract tourists. Tourists north of the Arctic Circle!

But then, it made as much sense as anything else Matt had done in the past few years. If he wanted to waste his inheritance on another one of his grand schemes, *she* wouldn't try to stop him. Besides, it was none of her business.

When she couldn't stand it any longer Karen pulled the valentine out of the garbage. Below the printed message, he'd written "love" and his name.

Tears blurred her eyes. If this was how she reacted to a simple card, what would happen at the wedding? Matt's sister, Lanni, had asked Karen to serve as her maid of honor, and she'd agreed.

True, it might be a bit uncomfortable, since Matt was attending the wedding, but Lanni had assured her that she'd discussed the situation with him. Matt hadn't objected. They might be divorced, but they were both adults.

It had been eighteen months since she'd last seen her ex-husband. The wedding wouldn't be so bad, Karen decided. She'd smile a lot and let him know how happy she was. How much she liked California. How well she was doing at her job.

She'd make sure she looked her best, too. Lose five pounds, get her hair trimmed, buy some new clothes. After one glance, he'd be ready to hand her his heart on a silver platter.

And Karen? She'd hand it right back.

CHAPTER ONE

"SHE'S JUST BEAUTIFUL," Pearl Inman whispered to Matt as his sister walked down the center aisle, escorted by their proud father. "A perfect spring bride."

"Yes, she is," Matt agreed, but his eyes weren't on Lanni. He hadn't been able to stop watching Karen from the moment she'd entered the church.

Matt had been too busy getting the lodge ready for his first guests to give much thought to his sister's wedding. He knew Lanni had asked his ex-wife to serve as her maid of honor. He'd gone so far as to assure her it didn't matter to him. He'd managed to sound downright nonchalant about it, too.

It wasn't any big deal, he'd told Lanni. Their marriage was over. Finished. Kaput. Nope, it wouldn't bother him if Karen came to Hard Luck. He didn't plan to give it another thought.

All right, if he was being honest—and he should be, since he was in a church—he *had* thought about Karen coming to Hard Luck. Okay, so he'd counted the days. The hours. The minutes. But he wasn't going to beat himself up because of it. They'd been married for four years and divorced nearly two. It was only natural he'd be anxious about seeing her.

To his dismay, Matt soon discovered he was completely unprepared for the emotional impact of being with Karen again.

Especially at a wedding.

Damn, she was beautiful. His heart ached just looking at her. She wore an elegant rose-colored dress that was perfect for her tall, lithe frame. A halo of flowers circled her glossy brown hair and Matt was convinced he'd never seen a more beautiful maid of honor.

A more beautiful woman.

The church was packed. It surprised and pleased Matt that Lanni and Charles had decided to be married in Hard Luck. He'd assumed his sister would choose Anchorage, where the majority of their friends and family lived. When he'd asked her, Lanni said she'd chosen Hard Luck since this was where she and Charles would make their home. She'd met and fallen in love with Charles O'Halloran here, so it seemed fitting to have the wedding here, as well. In time, Lanni hoped to start a community newspaper, but until Hard Luck was large enough to support a weekly, she'd be content to write free-lance articles.

Matt was happy for his sister. He didn't doubt that Charles and Lanni were deeply in love. But watching them together had been almost painful. Their closeness, their delight in each other—he remembered what those feelings were like. Before his marriage fell apart...

With effort Matt pulled his gaze away from Karen.

This winter had been a long bleak one, with only his hopes for the lodge to sustain him.

The wedding was the one bright spot in an otherwise bleak winter. It would be another six weeks before the snow melted. Another month before he got any response to the advertising he'd mailed to travel agencies around the country.

Matt had risked a whole lot more than his inheritance in buying the lodge. He closed his eyes, refusing to allow any worries to crowd his mind. On the positive side, every room had been booked for the night. Never mind that his guests were family and friends and that he wasn't getting a dime for his hospitality. Never mind that his ex-wife was one of those guests.

The wedding was a sort of dry run for the lodge. Unfortunately the kitchen wasn't in working order yet, but he'd have everything up and running by mid-June. Just in time to welcome his first real customers.

Love. Honor. As Charles O'Halloran repeated his vows, Matt felt a wrenching ache in his chest. He'd purposely let his mind wander in an effort to avoid just this.

The marriage vows were a painful reminder of how he'd failed Karen. Difficult as it was to admit, he'd never been the right husband for her. She wanted a man who was content to hold down a nine-to-five job. A husband who'd work forty years for the same company and retire with a decent pension.

Matt had tried to give her the stability she'd craved. It just hadn't worked. Within months of taking on a job, he'd grow restless and bored. He'd always brought real effort and creativity to every new position; if he put that kind of effort into something, Matt wanted to be the one who profited from the outcome. Karen had never understood or appreciated that.

Lanni's sweet voice echoed Reverend Wilson's words. His sister's eyes lovingly held her husband's. It was a poignant moment, and more than one person was fighting back tears. Charles and Lanni had bridged the pain and anger of two families to find happiness. The O'Hallorans and Catherine Fletcher—Matt and Lanni's grandmother—had become bitter and enduring enemies when Charles's father married another woman. But the enmity was over now. And it was largely due to Lanni, Matt reflected, looking at her with pride.

Despite his best effort, his eyes wandered back to Karen. Her head was bowed as if she, too, had a hard time listening to the exchange of vows.

They hadn't spoken since her arrival in Hard Luck. He didn't think she was actually avoiding him, but he couldn't be sure. Her flight had landed in Fairbanks early that morning; Sawyer O'Halloran had picked her up, along with the other two bridesmaids, who'd flown in from Anchorage. The three women had been closeted with Lanni ever since, getting ready for the wedding.

He knew Karen was scheduled to fly out first thing the next morning. But for this one night she'd be sleeping in the lodge. *His* lodge.

Matt had made sure when he assigned the rooms that Karen got the most elaborate one. The one with the big brass bed and feather mattress. He'd polished the hardwood floor himself until it shone like new. Matt wondered if she'd guess all the trouble he'd gone to—then decided he didn't want her to know.

The ceremony was soon over, and Matt heaved a sigh of relief. Nothing like a wedding to remind him of his own shortcomings in the husband department. In failing Karen, he'd failed himself.

He and Karen had once been as much in love as Lanni and Charles. In fact, he'd still loved her when she left him and filed for divorce. And despite everything, he loved her now.

His jaw tightened as he remembered the night he'd come home to find she'd packed her bags and moved out—and then had him served with the divorce papers.

It rankled to this day that she hadn't so much as talked to him first.

He'd asked her about that once, and she'd shrugged as if it was of little concern. She'd warned him, she'd said. Besides, he'd never talked to *her* about quitting his jobs. Now it was his turn to see how it felt.

In all these months his bitterness hadn't faded. It would be best if they didn't talk to each other, Matt decided. Nothing would be served by dredging up the past, especially when that was all they had to discuss.

Music crescendoed, filling the church as Lanni and Charles turned to greet their guests. His sister's face radiated happiness. Arm in arm, the couple strolled down the aisle.

Karen followed with Sawyer O'Halloran, one of Charles's younger brothers. It didn't escape Matt's notice that his ex-wife did everything humanly possible to avoid looking in his direction.

So she didn't want any eye contact? Well, he wasn't too keen on it himself. This whole affair was difficult enough without their having to confront each other. He'd managed to get through the wedding; now all he needed to do was survive the reception. That shouldn't be so difficult.

It took Matt all of ten minutes to retract those words.

He delayed going to the school gymnasium, where the reception was being held, as long as he could. By the time he arrived, the music had started and a half-dozen couples were already on the area cleared for dancing.

The first person Matt saw was Karen—dancing with Duke Porter, one of the pilots for Midnight Sons, the Arctic flight service owned and run by the O'Hallorans. The sight of another man with his arms around Karen made Matt so damn mad he walked directly over to the bar and downed a glass of champagne. He wasn't sure that getting drunk would serve a useful purpose, but it might help cut the pain. This probably wasn't the first time a man had held her since their divorce, but it was the only time he'd been around to witness it. He didn't like the experience one bit.

"Where were you?" The question came from his mother, Kate. "I was beginning to get worried."

"I'm fine." It was another moment or two before he could pull his gaze away from Karen and Duke. "I, uh, was making sure everything was ready at the lodge."

"Your aunt Louise is looking for you."

Matt didn't bother to disguise a groan. "Mother, please, anyone but Aunt Louise." The first thing his meddling aunt would do was quiz him about his divorce. Matt figured he'd need more than one glass of champagne if he was going to be trapped in a conversation with his father's oldest sister. He doubted an entire bottle would fortify him for Aunt Louise and her shamelessly prying questions.

His rescue came from the most unlikely source. Chrissie Harris, eight-year-old daughter of Mitch, the town's public-safety officer.

"Will you dance with me?" the child pleaded, widening her dark, seal-pup eyes.

"Sure thing, kiddo." He grinned. The kid's timing couldn't have been better.

"Dad's dancing with Bethany," Chrissie explained, sounding a little disappointed. "Dad and Bethany are getting married this summer."

Great, another wedding. "I know."

"I think Scott would like to ask me, but he's afraid."

Scott was Sawyer O'Halloran's adopted ten-year-old son—one of his wife's two children by a previous marriage.

Matt held out his arms to the girl. "Well, we can't let the prettiest girl here be a wallflower," he said. Mitch's daughter slipped off her patent-leather Mary Janes and stepped onto the tops of his shoes. He waltzed her from one end of the dance floor to the other. For a whole minute, perhaps longer, he was able to enjoy the dance without thinking of Karen.

His pleasure was short-lived, however. The next time he happened to catch sight of her, Karen was with Christian O'Halloran, Charles and Sawyer's younger brother. At the end of the dance, Matt thanked Chrissie and refilled his glass.

The second glass of champagne gave him enough courage to approach his ex-wife. It was ridiculous to pretend they weren't aware of each other.

Karen was sitting, probably for the first time since the music had started. He picked up two full champagne glasses and walked over to her. Although she wasn't looking in his direction, she knew he was coming. Matt could tell by the way her body stiffened.

"Hello, Karen," he said evenly.

"Matt."

He handed her one of the glasses and claimed the empty seat beside her. "You look like you could use something to drink."

"Thanks."

Neither seemed to have anything more to say. Matt struggled to find some safe, neutral topic.

"How's California?" he managed finally.

She stared into the champagne as if she expected to

find her response written in the bottom of the glass. "Wonderful."

"You look good." It was best to start off with a compliment, he decided; besides, it was the truth. She looked fantastic.

"You, too."

It was nice of her to lie. He'd lost fifteen pounds because he'd been working his butt off for months. He rarely got enough sleep and wasn't eating properly.

She took a sip of champagne, then asked, "Why'd you mail me a valentine card?" He thought her voice shook ever so slightly.

He regretted sending that stupid thing the moment he'd slipped it into the mailbox. If there'd been a way to retrieve it, he would have.

"We were married for four years," she said, "and not once in all that time did you buy me a card."

He didn't have an argument, so he said nothing.

"You claimed cards were silly commercial sentiments, remember?"

He wasn't likely to forget.

"Why this year?" she demanded, and the tremble in her voice was more apparent than ever.

"Maybe I was trying to make up for the years I didn't give you one." It wasn't much of an explanation, but the only one he had to offer. When he hadn't heard back from her—not that he'd expected to—Matt knew she hadn't appreciated the gesture.

"Don't mail me any more...sentiments, Matt. It's too little and it's much too late."

He frowned. "Fine, I won't."

They both stood up, eager to escape one another. Unfortunately they came face-to-face with his aunt

Louise. Karen looked to Matt to rescue her, but he was fresh out of ideas.

"Dance, you two."

Aunt Louise issued the order like a drill sergeant. The woman always did enjoy meddling in other people's affairs. It was either follow her dictates or be trapped in a thirty-minute question-and-answer ordeal.

Karen glanced at Matt and he stared at her. "Shall we?" he asked, motioning toward the dance floor. Judging by the look she gave him, Karen had weighed her choices and decided that dancing with him was the lesser of two evils.

Matt had often observed that when one thing went wrong, others were sure to follow. The music, which to this point had been fast and lively, abruptly changed to something slow and soft. Matt couldn't avoid touching Karen, nor could he avoid holding her close.

He slipped his arm around her waist and she held herself stiffly in his embrace. Matt did his utmost to concentrate on moving to the slow beat of the music and not on the woman in his arms.

He could feel her reluctance with every step.

"Don't worry," he whispered, "I promise not to bite."

"Your bites don't worry me."

"What does?" he asked.

"Everything else."

He smiled to himself and unconsciously moved his head closer to hers until his jaw pressed against her temple. Matt never had been light on his feet, but when he danced with Karen he somehow managed to look as though he knew what he was doing. It was as though the two of them were born partners.

Neither spoke for the rest of the dance. The second

the music stopped he released her and stepped back. The ache in his chest intensified, and he wondered how much longer he'd have to stay at the reception. He didn't want to slight his sister and brother-in-law, but being with Karen was pure agony. Pretending he didn't still love her was becoming impossible.

"Lanni and Charles are getting ready to leave," Karen said quickly. He sensed that she felt as awkward as he did. "I'd better see if she needs my help."

"Thanks for the dance."

Her eyes briefly met his and filled with an unmistakable sadness. "It was good to see you again, Matt," she mumbled, then hurried away.

Much as he longed to escape, Matt observed the proprieties—he kissed his sister and shook hands with Charles. They were honeymooning in the Virgin Islands for two weeks. He wished them a great trip, made the rounds to say his farewells and returned to the lodge.

Because he felt about as low as he ever had since his divorce, he brought out a dusty bottle of whiskey and poured himself a stiff drink. He wasn't a drinking man, but there were times when little else would do.

This was one of those times.

He sat on the leather sofa in front of the massive stone fireplace, his feet propped up on the raised hearth. He held the glass in one hand and the bottle in the other.

Soon his guests began to arrive. His parents came in first. It had been a long, exhausting day, and after a few words of greeting, they wandered up the stairs. The two bridesmaids followed and then another couple, married friends of Lanni's.

Karen was the last to arrive. Matt didn't ask who'd

escorted her to the lodge. Probably Duke, but he didn't want to hear that.

She paused in the large hall and looked around. Plenty of work remained to be done, but it was a pleasant, inviting room. Besides the sofa, Matt had placed a couple of big overstuffed chairs close to the fireplace. The other half of the room was set up with hardwood tables and chairs.

"This is very nice," Karen said, sounding surprised.

"Thanks." He'd worked damn hard, getting this place in presentable shape. For just a moment he wondered what she thought when she heard he'd purchased the lodge. Years before, a fire had destroyed much of the kitchen, plus a number of rooms upstairs.

Following the fire, the O'Hallorans had boarded up the place, unable to decide what to do with it. So the lodge had sat vacant and deteriorating for years. None of the brothers was interested in running a tourist business, and repairs would've been costly and time-consuming.

"Your room's at the top of the stairs. The farthest one down on the left-hand side." He gestured with the shot glass, afraid that if he stood, he might fall over.

"You've been drinking." Karen moved closer to the fireplace.

"Nothing gets past you, does it?" he muttered, too drunk to bother keeping the sarcasm out of his voice.

"You hardly ever drink." The problem was, the woman knew him too well.

"That's true, but sometimes the occasion calls for it." He raised his glass to her with a sardonic smile and downed the last of the whiskey. It burned a trail down the back of his throat. He squeezed his eyes shut, clenched his teeth and shook his head like a wet dog.

When he opened his eyes Karen sat on the other end of the sofa. "What's wrong?" she asked gently—as if she didn't know.

"Nothing," he answered cheerfully. "What could possibly be wrong?"

She didn't make the obvious reply. "I think I must have had a little more to drink than usual myself." Her eyes seemed unnaturally bright.

She got up and headed toward the stairs, and Matt realized he didn't want her to leave. "Do you want to see what I've spent the last few months doing?" he asked.

"Sure." Her eager response surprised him.

He gave her a quick tour of the downstairs area, pointing out the renovations. He was pleased with them, and didn't conceal his pride. "The kitchen should be ready soon," he explained when he'd finished showing her around. "The stove's what's holding me up, but I expect it in the next month or so."

"Who's going to do the cooking?" she asked.

"Right now, me." Matt shrugged. "I don't have a budget to hire anyone else. At least not yet. It's important to bring in paying guests first."

"Well, you're certainly qualified to cook."

She was referring to his stint as a chef. He'd enjoyed cooking school well enough, but had lost interest during his first restaurant job. He'd gone on to commercial fishing shortly after that, abandoning his sketchy plans to open a restaurant of his own.

"I wish you the very best with this venture, Matt."

"Thanks." He knew he sounded flippant.

"I mean that," she insisted.

He'd probably offended her, and he hadn't meant to. "But you don't believe it'll last, do you?"

"No." She didn't so much as hesitate. "You'll grow bored with the lodge just like you did with everything else."

"Maybe." He wasn't going to argue with her. Time would prove her wrong. He'd worked harder on this lodge than anything he'd done in his life. For the first time, he had something that was entirely his. The business would sink or succeed by his own efforts, no one else's.

"I'll show you to your room," he said without emotion, and led the way to the staircase.

He hadn't gone more than a few steps when she stopped him. "Matt." His arm tingled where her fingers touched him. "I apologize—I didn't mean to discourage you. I can tell you've put a lot of thought and effort into this lodge. I hope it succeeds. I really do."

He turned to face her. "Do you, Karen?"

Her eyes had never been more intent. In them he found a reflection of the loneliness he'd felt these past eighteen months. He hadn't wanted to admit, even to himself, how much he'd missed her. For months he'd worked himself into a state of exhaustion, rather than face a night without her.

This evening, for the first time since their divorce, he was forced to admit how good it felt to hold her. He couldn't deny how empty his arms felt without her. How empty his *life* felt.

Her face was slightly flushed. She still wore the rose-colored dress. The neckline was scooped, and it was impossible to ignore the gentle thrust of her breasts.

"I've missed you, Karen." She must know what it had cost him to admit that.

Her eyes drifted shut, and when she spoke her voice

was so low the words were hardly discernible. "I've missed you, too."

His breath caught in his throat, and Matt figured if he didn't touch her soon he'd die. He raised his hand and cradled her cheek with his callused palm. She was so smooth, so soft.

Karen moistened her lips.

It was the invitation Matt had been waiting for. He drew her toward him, and to his surprise, to his delight, she came without resistance.

He was almost afraid to kiss her, fearing she'd pull away from him, fearing she'd throw the past in his face. Karen did neither. When she brought her arms up to circle his neck, Matt nearly shouted for joy.

He didn't give her time to object. His kiss was raw with need. He'd intended to be gentle, to coax her, but it wasn't what either of them wanted. He possessed her mouth. No other words described their kiss. His lips slanted over hers, twisting, seeking, urgently needing the taste of her.

When her lips parted in unspoken welcome, he groaned and thrust his tongue deep into the waiting warmth.

Controlling the kiss was beyond him. Matt didn't know how long it continued. Too long. *Much* too long, he decided. When he did find the strength to ease his mouth from hers, they were both breathless.

He held her and waited for her to say something. Like telling him he shouldn't have done that. Perhaps she expected an apology. If so, she wouldn't be getting one.

He felt her shift, and afraid that she was about to move out of his arms, he tightened his grip. She snuggled close to him, creating a new kind of torture.

They'd been intimate too many years for him not to be affected by the sensation of her body stirring against his.

When she ran her tongue along the underside of his jaw Matt was forced to pull away. They stared at each other. Neither spoke, and he suspected it was because they both feared what the other would say. Her lips were moist and slightly swollen; her breath came in soft, disjointed gasps, as if she was struggling not to weep. His own was ragged and made a light hissing sound through his clenched teeth.

He kissed her again and this time forced himself to keep it slow and gentle. But when he ended the kiss the sensual impact had stripped him of all his painfully gathered control. He pulled her close against him, knowing she'd feel his arousal.

"I never was much good at these kinds of games," he said, his eyes holding hers.

"Games?"

"You know what I mean."

She lowered her lashes and her face filled with color.

"Don't expect me to silently steer you into my bedroom," he said. "If we're going to make love, I need to know you want me as much as I want you."

Still she said nothing.

"What's it to be, Karen? You can share my bed or go upstairs alone." The temptation to kiss her again was strong, but he resisted.

Tears brightened her eyes, and she bit her lower lip. "I don't want to be alone," she whispered.

He shook his head. "That's not good enough. Tell me you want me."

"Yes," she said stiffly, "I want you, Matt. I've missed you."

CHAPTER TWO

KAREN AWOKE with Matt's arm securely tucked around her waist. In the carefree state between sleep and complete wakefulness, she reveled in the comfort of being held in her husband's arms.

Husband.

It took her far longer than it should have to remember that he *wasn't* her husband. Not anymore. Her eyes flew open as her brain started putting together the events of the night before.

The wedding.

She was in Hard Luck for Lanni and Charles's wedding. She should never have agreed to serve as Lanni's maid of honor. That had been her first mistake. The divorce had been final for more than eighteen months. Karen had thought, no, hoped that any lingering emotion she carried for Matt was long dead. Her reaction to the valentine card should have told her otherwise. If she'd had a whit of common sense, she'd have phoned Lanni and begged off. Instead, she'd set out to prove she was over Matt.

She'd proved that all right, by spending the night with him. Mortified, Karen closed her eyes and forced back a sob. She'd had more to drink than usual, but she hadn't been even close to drunk, and she knew it.

She wanted to blame Matt for this. In fact, she'd feel a whole lot better if she could accuse him of seducing her, of luring her into his bedroom. But bless his black heart, he'd made sure she knew exactly what she was doing before they'd gone to bed.

The lovemaking had been incredible. It had always been good between them, but she'd forgotten just how good. They'd been so hungry for each other, so needy.

Afterward, Matt had held her in his arms and she'd silently wept. Not because she felt any regrets—she hadn't, not then. But because she had to admit how miserable she'd been without him. It wasn't fair; she loved him so much, yet she realized how wrong they were for each other. Just as her own mother must have realized at some point how wrong her own marriage had gone, how mismatched she and Karen's father were. Yet she'd steadfastly hung on for reasons Karen had never understood.

She and Matt had such contradictory expectations and needs. She had to have some predictability in her life, some certainty. He preferred just to drift along, following his whims. Of course, she hadn't known, when she first met him, that he'd have trouble staying in a job. It wasn't until after they were married that he started his pattern of changing from one occupation to the next. Karen felt blindsided.

Every time Matt quit a job, Karen faced an unhappy memory from her childhood. Her father had shared the same lack of ambition. Her mother's meager paycheck had supported the family. It wasn't that Eric Rocklin was lazy; far from it. His garden had been the neighborhood showpiece, and his model airplanes won contests. He was a good father, an attentive husband, a decent person.

His one failing was his inability to keep at a job.

Her family had declared bankruptcy when Karen and

her brother were in high school. One of her most humiliating memories was of the time her friends were visiting and two men came to repossess the family car. Later they were turned out of their rental house.

From the moment she introduced them, Matt and her father had gotten along famously. Now Karen knew why. As the saying goes, they were two peas in a pod.

Wearily she closed her eyes. She refused to make the same mistakes her mother had, refused to allow her husband's weakness to destroy her future. Painful though it was, she'd taken the necessary steps to correct the problem and get on with her life.

One small lapse wasn't the end of the world. It was only natural, she decided, to still have feelings for Matt. He was a gracious, compassionate person. And she was undeniably attracted to him. But he wasn't right for her. She'd put their night together behind her and go back to California, her lesson well learned. The farther away she was from Matt the better.

As carefully as she could, Karen folded back the covers and slipped one leg over the edge of the mattress. She eased herself from under Matt's arm and glanced around for something to cover herself. She caught sight of her dress, carelessly discarded in last night's haste; it lay crumpled on the floor across the room. She blushed, remembering how eager they'd been for each other. They hadn't been able to remove their clothes fast enough.

"Mornin'," Matt rolled onto his back, stretched his arms high above his head and yawned.

Karen rolled back into bed, covered herself with the sheet and ground her teeth in frustration. She'd hoped to be gone by the time Matt awoke.

Her ex-husband slid over to her side and propped up

his head with one hand. "Did I ever tell you how beautiful you look in the morning?"

"No." She wanted to groan aloud. It would have saved them both a good deal of embarrassment if she could've silently slunk away.

"Then let me correct that error." Brushing the hair from her face, he bent forward to kiss her gently. "You're beautiful in the morning. You brighten my life, Karen. Without you—"

"Don't say it. Please don't say it."

"Don't say it?"

"Last night was a mistake," she said coldly.

Matt looked stunned. "That's not what you said when—"

"I was drunk," she interrupted him, offering the first excuse that came to mind, although she'd already rejected it earlier.

He laughed harshly. "And pigs fly. Neither one of us had *that* much to drink."

"But enough—"

"Yes," he said, "enough to loosen our inhibitions. It was a good thing, too, because we belong together, Karen. We always have. I never did understand why you left me."

His words reminded her of the decision she'd already made—the decision to leave again. And why. "That says it all, don't you think?"

He ignored her question, something he'd often done. "Sure you were upset about me quitting my job, but I hated it. Would you really want me to continue working someplace that made me miserable?"

"Yes!" she cried. It was too late for this, but he'd drawn her in the way he always had. "If it was the first time I wouldn't have cared, although you might have talked it over with me, but it *wasn't* the first time. It was the fourth time in as many years, and now you're running a lodge. You'll never find the perfect job. Twenty years from now you'll still be searching for a career that suits you. Nothing's going to change.''

"Come off it, Karen. I'm only thirty-one."

"I don't have the time or energy to argue with you." There was no other option, so she tossed back the sheets and hurried across the room to retrieve her dress. With the zipper in the back, she had two choices—to either ask him to close it for her, or scurry to her room with the dress gaping open. She chose the latter.

"All right, all right," he muttered, lying on his back and staring at the ceiling. "I don't want to argue with you, either."

As fast as she could Karen gathered together the rest of her things, stuffing them in her arms.

"You aren't leaving, are you?" He sounded shocked.

"Yes." The sooner she retreated to her room, the better. Then she'd change clothes and get out of here.

"What about last night?"

Karen didn't know what to tell him. "Let's say it was for old times' sake."

His jaw tightened. "Do you do this sort of thing often?"

It would have hurt less if he'd punched her in the stomach. "That was a cheap shot, Matt, and unworthy of you. You've been my only lover and you damn well know it." Then, with as much dignity as she could marshal, she marched barefoot out of his bedroom. Halfway up the stairs she met Matt's parents. They stared at her, mouths open.

"Good morning," she greeted as if she were dressed

for a church meeting, ignoring the panty hose and underthings bunched in her arms.

"Karen." Matt's father nodded; his mother managed a belated good-morning.

As she continued up the stairs, Karen heard Kate call out to her son. "Matt, is everything all right with you and Karen?"

Matt didn't respond right away. "Nothing's changed."

His father's warm chuckle followed Karen into her room. "You could've fooled me."

TWO HOURS LATER, Karen was sitting in the Midnight Sons mobile office, waiting for the pilot to fly her out of Hard Luck. She stared at the worn floor, impatient to be gone and fully aware of why.

Matt made her weak when she believed she was strong.

Pressing her hands to her face, Karen closed her eyes and drew several deep, calming breaths. It was better for them both that she lived in California now. The temptation to be with him would be too great if she'd stayed in Alaska. Even Anchorage, which was hundreds of miles from Hard Luck, was too close.

Sick at heart, Karen willed herself to forget the night with Matt. Before she knew it, she'd be back in Oakland where she belonged.

Paragon, Inc., the engineering company she worked for, had been more than generous in giving her these vacation days for Lanni's wedding, but now the time had come to prove to her boss, Mr. Sullivan, that he'd invested the company's money wisely when he promoted her. She'd throw herself into the job, and she'd forget Matt once and for all.

Her heart ached at the thought of him. She did wish him well. Contrary to what he might believe, she wanted him to succeed. She just didn't think he would. If Matt was anything like her father, and he was, he'd find some way to sabotage himself. Only she refused to be like her mother, refused to stick around and pick up the pieces. She'd gotten out while she could and was determined to make a better life for herself.

To be on the safe side, Karen decided to curtail any contact with his family. It would be difficult, though. Karen loved Matt's parents as much as she did her own. They were generous, caring, loving people, and Lanni was like the sister she'd never had.

If this wedding had taught Karen anything, it was that she'd never get Matt out of her head, or out of her life, if she clung to his family.

The decision made, she swallowed her disappointment and decided to make more of an effort to meet new people once she got back to California. It was time. Past time. Matthew Caldwell wasn't the only attractive man in the world.

"YOU'RE LOOKING a little down in the dumps," Ben Hamilton, owner of the Hard Luck Café, said as he automatically filled Matt's coffee mug.

"What do you expect the day after a wedding?" Matt returned, fending off Ben's inquisitiveness. Matt hadn't come to socialize, but to escape.

His parents had been full of questions after seeing Karen parade barefoot up the stairs in the dress she'd worn to the wedding. It was all too clear where she'd spent the night.

"I must say your sister made a mighty pretty bride," Ben said casually.

Matt cupped the thick ceramic mug with both hands. "Thanks."

"Two weddings in Hard Luck within the space of a year. Now that's something."

Matt merely grunted in reply.

"Mitch and Bethany set their wedding date for this summer," Ben added conversationally.

Mitch Harris, the public-safety Officer—usually described as "the law around here"—and teacher Bethany Ross had announced their engagement earlier in the winter. Leave it to Matt to settle in a community where Cupid had run amuck. While he was divorced and miserable, everyone around him was stumbling all over themselves, falling in love. Not Matt. Once was enough for him, and damn it all, he loved Karen. Truly loved her.

"Bethany and Mitch's wedding's going to take place in San Francisco, but we're throwing a big reception for them when they come back from their honeymoon."

San Francisco was across the bay from Oakland. Karen lived in Oakland.

Karen. Karen. Karen.

No matter what he said or did, everything seemed to point back to Karen. At this rate he'd never be free of her.

Was that what he wanted, though?

Ben wiped the perfectly clean counter with slow, methodical strokes, patiently waiting for Matt to confide in him. Matt was well aware that a lot of the men in Hard Luck used Ben Hamilton as a sounding board. He was the kind of guy who made it easy to talk about one's troubles, but Matt wasn't interested. But then, he wasn't in the mood to talk to anyone. About anything.

He was half tempted to take his coffee and move to one of the tables. He might have, if Duke Porter hadn't chosen that moment to walk into the café. The bush pilot sidled up to the stool next to his and sat down.

Matt glared at the other man.

Duke glared back. "What's your problem?"

It was unreasonable and irrational to take his frustration out on Duke just because he'd had the gall to dance with Karen. "I've got woman troubles."

Duke snorted. "Me, too."

"You?" Ben poured a cup of coffee for the pilot and set it on the counter. "What're you talking about?"

"Well, not me personally. It's that attorney again. Tracy Santiago." His eyes narrowed as he mentioned the lawyer Mariah Douglas's family had hired to investigate Hard Luck after the town started advertising for women. Their daughter, Mariah, was the Midnight Sons secretary. "She's looking to stir up trouble. Mariah got a phone call from her on Friday. Christian told me the Santiago woman's threatening to fly up here again—probably in a couple of months—to check everything out."

"That's Christian and Sawyer's problem, isn't it?"

"Yes," Duke agreed, "but it makes me mad, you know? The way that woman keeps butting her nose into everyone's business. Here the O'Halloran brothers've done everything on the up and up—giving women jobs and housing—and what do those poor guys get in return? Hassles from some troublemaker who's accusing them of exploiting women and... and..."

"She's not your worry," Ben reminded him.

Duke didn't respond. "What's eating you?" he asked Matt, instead.

Matt wasn't keen on discussing his ex-wife, especially with Duke.

Duke didn't wait for Matt to answer him. "I imagine it's got something to do with Karen. What's with you two, anyway? The entire time she was dancing with me, Karen was asking about you."

"Me?" From the way she'd behaved, Matt had assumed he was the farthest thing from her mind.

"Oh, she tried to be subtle about it, you know, but I could see through her questions. She wanted to know about the lodge and what I thought of your plan. I told her it was a damn good one."

Matt was grateful. "I appreciate that."

"So, what's going on with you and your ex?" Duke asked again.

Matt frowned. He wasn't accustomed to discussing his personal business with anyone, not even his family. He certainly had no intention of confiding in a casual acquaintance. "We're divorced. What else do you need to know?"

"It's pretty damn obvious that you're still in love. I don't know what it is with couples these days," Duke complained to Ben. "Can anyone tell me why people who care about each other decide to call it quits? It just doesn't make sense."

Matt would've liked to argue the point, but he couldn't come up with a single, solitary thing to say. There was only one thought in his mind—what happened last night had proved beyond a doubt that he still loved Karen.

He leapt off the stool. Duke was right; instead of sitting here bemoaning his fate, he should confront

Karen. She loved him. She must. Otherwise she'd never have gone to bed with him.

All she needed was a little reassurance. Okay, he'd made a few errors in judgment, but that was behind them now. The lodge was their future, and if she'd give him another chance he'd prove he could make a go of it. If she needed stability, he'd give it to her.

Matt was going after her. When he found her, he'd convince her they'd both be fools to throw away the love they shared.

He was tired of pretending he didn't care, tired of pretending he didn't miss her. His life was on course now, and once she was back everything would be perfect.

All he had to do now was explain that to Karen.

"Has she left yet?" he demanded of Duke.

"Karen?" Duke asked.

"Who the hell else do you think I'm asking about?"

Duke checked his watch. "My guess is John's about to take off. You'd better hurry if you want to catch her."

Matt didn't need any further incentive. He slapped some money down on the counter, grabbed his coat and flew out the door. The mobile unit that housed the Midnight Sons office was close by, and he sprinted the distance.

He saw John Henderson heading in the same direction, and noticed the Baron 55 sitting on the gravel runway, ready to depart for the flight to Fairbanks.

Both men reached the door to the office at the same time. "I need a few minutes alone with Karen," Matt said. He blocked John's way.

The pilot began to complain bitterly about messing up his plans, but Matt didn't care. "Listen." Matt pulled a five-dollar bill out of his pocket. "Go have a cup of Ben's coffee and give me ten minutes alone with Karen. That's all I'm asking."

John stared at the money, then scratched the side of his head. "All right, all right, just be quick, will you? I'm on a schedule." He turned away mumbling, waving away Matt's profuse thanks. "Ten minutes," he called over his shoulder. "Not a second more."

Matt waited until he'd composed his thoughts before walking inside to confront his ex-wife. Karen sat on a worn vinyl couch, staring at the floor. She glanced up when he stepped into the waiting area, and her eyes widened dramatically when she saw who it was.

"What are you doing here?" she demanded, jerking herself upright. She shrank back from him, almost as if she was afraid.

"We need to talk," he said gently.

"No, we don't. Everything's already been said. It's over. It was over a long time ago."

"Last night says otherwise."

She shook her head. "Last night was a big mistake. Please, Matt, just let me go. I don't want to talk about what happened. It didn't change anything."

"I think it did." He eased his way toward her. Pulling out a chair, he twisted it around and straddled it. "I'd been thinking about buying the lodge for a while. I saw it shortly after the fire; and I'd forgotten about it till Lanni came up here. I finally made a deal with the O'Halloran brothers. I've spent nine months now, working fifteen-hour days, doing my damnedest to have it ready for the summer tourist trade."

"Matt, listen—"

"Let me finish," he pleaded. "The reason I'm telling you about the lodge is because I consider it our future."

Karen squeezed her eyes shut.

"I realize you've heard those words before, but this time it's true. This isn't just another one of my ideas. I sank the entire trust fund my grandmother left me into this venture. I'm so far out on a limb I could pick fruit. I'm giving this my best shot, Karen. I'm risking everything for us."

"There is no us," she reminded him in a whisper.

"But there *should* be! If last night proved anything, it's that we belong together. We always have. Come back to me, Karen. You want promises? I'll give you promises. You want reassurances? Fine, you've got them. Everything will be different. We'll start over again—"

Tears rolled down her face as Karen leaned forward and brought her fingers to his mouth, silencing him. "Don't. Please, don't." She pressed her lips tightly together and swiped at the tears, then continued. "You want me to give up my job and come back here, right?"

He nodded. Of course he wanted her back here—as his wife. He wanted them to work together to build their marriage and their business. He needed her, wanted her, loved her. That had never changed.

"I've heard all this before. My mother heard it from my father, too. She loved him. She believed him every time, and he led her down one garden path after another."

"Karen, I'm not your father."

She looked away. "I'm not my mother, either. I can't—I *won't* do what you're asking. My future is with Paragon. My home isn't in Alaska anymore, it's in Oakland. Don't you realize how many times you've said almost those identical words to me? Six months from now, you'll be bored again and you'll have some other wonderful dream to follow. I can't live that way. I tried. I honestly tried."

"But—"

"Matt, stop, please. The bottom line is that I'm not willing to throw my career down the drain for another one of your madcap schemes, no matter how promising it sounds."

Matt stood, his mind racing frantically as he tried to find a way of convincing her to stay.

"I have my own life now," she said. "I won't give up everything I've worked to achieve. Not for your dreams. Because for the first time in years, Matt, I have dreams of my own."

He was fighting a losing battle and he knew it.

"I'm going to find a man with a steady job and a savings account. I'm going to settle down in a house with a white picket fence and raise a passel of children." A sob shook her shoulders. "And I'm going to do everything I can to put our marriage behind me." Having said that, she reached for her suitcase and rushed out the door.

"MOM!" TEN-YEAR-OLD Scott O'Halloran burst in the front door with Eagle Catcher, his husky and faithful friend, trotting behind him.

Abbey looked up from the magazine she was reading.

"Sawyer—I mean Dad—let me fly his plane this afternoon," her son announced proudly.

Abbey's gaze instantly connected with that of her husband as he followed her son into the house.

"I didn't actually fly the plane," Scott quickly amended, "but Sawyer let me hold the control stick, and he told me all about the different instruments on the panel."

"It's time, honey," Sawyer said, kissing her on the cheek.

Abbey wasn't convinced of that. "But, Sawyer, he's only ten."

"Aw, Mom, you gotta stop treating me like a little kid."

Abbey swallowed a laugh. She recalled the day she'd arrived in Hard Luck with her two children in tow. She'd been one of the first women lured to town with the promise of a job, a house and land. She'd come hoping to make a new life for herself and her children.

The last thing either she or Sawyer had been looking for was love. But they'd found it, with each other. They must have had the fastest courtship in Hard Luck's history, Abbey mused. In retrospect, she wouldn't change a thing. Not only was she deeply in love with her husband, but Sawyer had legally adopted Scott and Susan, and he worked hard at being a good father.

"My dad was teaching me the basic elements of flying when I was ten," he assured her. "Trust me, I'm not going to do anything to put either of us in danger."

Abbey knew that went without saying; nevertheless, she couldn't help worrying.

"I'm going to find Ronny Gold," Scott told them. "I'll be back before dinner." He was out the door with another burst of speed. The silver-eyed husky raced along at his side.

"I wonder what Charles and Lanni are up to about now," Sawyer said with a cocky grin.

"They're probably lying on a sandy beach soaking up the sunshine."

Sawyer sat next to her on the sofa. "Remember our honeymoon?"

Abbey smiled. They hadn't actually seen too much of Hawaii.

"If you recall, we didn't spend a lot of time on any of those beaches. As far as I was concerned, all we needed was a bed and a little privacy."

"Sawyer!"

"I'm crazy about you, woman."

"Good thing, because I'm crazy about you, too." She turned, sliding her arms around his waist. The happiness she'd found with him continued to astound her. When she'd least expected it, Sawyer had given her back her heart, given her a second chance at love.

"Don't worry about cooking tonight," he said. "I thought I'd treat us all to dinner."

"On a Monday night?"

"Sure." He grinned. "Ben's started a frequent-eater program, and—"

"A *what?*"

"You know, like the airlines' frequent-flyer clubs."

"Oh. Of course."

"He's trying to drum up a little business, and I thought we should support his creativity."

Abbey gave Sawyer a quick kiss. "And have some of Ben's apple pie in the bargain."

"Then, later," Sawyer said, cozying up to her, "I thought you and I could relive some of those wonderful moments from our own honeymoon."

Abbey had a feeling he wasn't talking about lazing around the beach, either.

KAREN HAD NEVER felt worse, emotionally or physically. Bad enough to make a doctor's appointment.

Spring was generally one of her favorite times of year. The changes in the California weather weren't as dramatic as those in Alaska, but the heavy Oakland air seemed to hold less smog.

She'd been living in California for several months now, and she wondered if she'd ever grow accustomed to looking at the horizon and seeing nothing but a brown haze.

She'd hoped to adjust more quickly to life in California, but so far she hadn't. True, there were compensations—a staggering variety of stores and restaurants, lots of TV channels, consistently moderate weather. But daylight in the winter months had taken some getting used to. Freeways continued to unnerve her. Traffic intimidated her. And so many people! It boggled her mind. The contrast between California and Alaska was never more striking than on the freeways.

Karen had made friends. All female. It might have helped if she'd been able to get involved in another relationship. But she wasn't ready, and she didn't know how long it would be before she was.

Still, no matter how many months or years it took, she was determined to forget Matt.

First, though, she had to get over this strange malady of hers. A woman friend in her office had recommended Dr. Perry, and if the patients filling his waiting room were any indication, he must be good.

She flipped through a glossy women's magazine as she waited for the nurse to call her name. Checking her watch, she saw that it was already twenty minutes past her appointment time. Actually Karen didn't mind the wait because she didn't know what she'd say once she saw him. She didn't have any real symptoms. She just felt...bad. She slept more than she should. Her appetite was nonexistent. And she cried at the drop of a hat. Just the other night she found herself weeping over a television advertisement for a camera. A camera, for heaven's sake!

Her real fear was that Dr. Perry would announce she suffered all the symptoms of someone chronically depressed and tell her she should make an appointment with a mental-health professional. She was prepared to do that if he suggested it.

When her name was finally called, she followed the nurse to the cubicle and sat on a molded plastic chair. Considering what this appointment was costing her, she'd think Dr. Perry could at least afford a decent chair.

The nurse, Mrs. Webster, according to her nameplate, read over the questionnaire Karen had completed earlier. "It says here you haven't been feeling well."

"Yes," Karen responded crisply. "I think it might be the smog."

"The smog." Mrs. Webster made a notation on the chart.

"You see, I'm from Alaska. I've never been exposed to smog before. My lungs don't like it."

"I don't imagine they do."

"Personally I believe it's affecting my general health. I just feel crummy." Although she felt fine at the moment, Karen found herself battling back tears. "And I—I seem to have developed the ability to weep at nothing."

Mrs. Webster's eyes searched out hers. "Oh?"

Karen fumbled in her purse for a tissue and blew her

nose. "I tear up at the most ridiculous things. I can't tell you how embarrassing it is."

"You miss Alaska?"

"Yes…no. I don't want to go back…I mean I do, I really do, but I can't. You see, I accepted this promotion, and Paragon, Inc., the company I work for, moved me here." She stopped and blew her nose a second time. "Sorry."

"Let's go back to the part about feeling crummy. Do you have any other symptoms the doctor should know about?"

She shrugged. "Not really."

Mrs. Webster walked over to the drawer and took out some medical instruments. "I'm sure Dr. Perry's going to want to get a blood sample from you."

"Fine." She held out her arm for the nurse. "I feel sluggish. That's one of my symptoms," she clarified. "I wake up in the morning and I don't want to get out of bed."

"I'll mention that to the doctor."

"Do you think it might be the smog?" she asked hopefully, watching the older woman.

"I don't know. I'll let the doctor decide. But we've recently seen several people with low-grade flu symptoms."

That was reassuring. Maybe all she had was a simple case of the flu.

Ten minutes later, after the nurse had taken some blood and Karen had changed out of her clothes and into a flimsy paper gown, she met Dr. Perry. He was much younger than she'd expected. Maybe thirty, if that.

"Hello, Karen," he said. His voice was kindly.

"Hi." She felt more than a little ridiculous in her blue paper outfit.

While she tucked the gown more securely over her thighs, Dr. Perry read her chart. "I understand you haven't been feeling much like your usual self lately."

"No, not at all. I think it must be the smog."

"Tired. Sluggish. Weepy."

"That about sums it up."

He glanced up from the chart and held her gaze.

"Mrs. Webster said there's been a low-grade flu going around," she suggested.

"Yes," Dr. Perry agreed, "but this sounds like something else. Tell me, Karen, is there any possibility you could be pregnant?"

CHAPTER THREE

MATT STOOD in the main room of the lodge and handed Lanni the glossy brochure he'd produced. He studied her closely, eager for his sister's response. Since Lanni was a writer, he'd gone to her for advice about the text and even the design. Now the brochure was ready to mail out.

"Matt, this is really great!"

"Yeah, it looks good, but does it make you want to spend several thousand dollars to fly to northern Alaska?"

"Sure," she said.

Matt remained unconvinced. "What about the section on dogsledding?"

"I think it's a good idea." But her enthusiasm sounded forced, and when she hesitated, Matt wondered if she'd be honest or just tell him what she thought he wanted to hear.

"Do you really believe people want to learn how to run a dog team?" she asked after an awkward moment.

"Positive. It's the in thing. Men, and plenty of women, too, are looking for more than relaxation when they take their vacations." He strived to keep his voice calm and matter-of-fact. "They want adventure. Sure, lazing on a beach might sound good, but after two or three days most folks with A-type personalities are bored to tears. The people who can afford this kind of pricy vacation are generally professional people who're driven to succeed. Always looking for new challenges. I'm offering them something unique.''

Lanni grinned. ''I'll say. But city folks aren't going to know how to harness dogs or hitch them to a sled.''

''That's where the mushers come in, and I've got the real McCoy.'' Matt was thrilled with the response he'd gotten from the professional mushers. ''Anyone who signs on is going to learn it all. That's part of the thrill.''

''I hope this works.'' But it was plain Lanni remained skeptical.

''My gut instinct tells me this is going to catch on big.''

Matt sincerely hoped he was right. The survival of the business depended on his ability to convince travel agents across the United States to book their clients into Hard Luck Lodge. His vacation packages included guided fishing tours during the summer months and dogsledding in the winter.

''Imagine taking a hundred-mile trek above the Arctic Circle, driving your own team of dogs,'' Matt said, struggling to control his excitement. He figured if he could convince his sister, then he could sell this package to just about anyone. ''I've got everything spelled out right here,'' he said, pointing to the listing of six- and eight-day trips between February and April.

''Several of my guides have run the Iditarod themselves. They know all there is to know about dogs and sledding. This venture helps them, too. The mushers can use the money, and I've been more than fair in giving them a cut of the action.''

Lanni's attention returned to the brochure. ''I like the way you mention the history of the Iditarod. 'In

January 1925, Leonhard Seppala, a Norwegian musher,'" she read aloud, "'rushed diphtheria serum 675 miles from the end of the Alaska Railroad to Nome. The trip took just over five days.'"

"Even now the Iditarod is called the most rugged race on earth." Matt wasn't telling Lanni anything she didn't already know. "People dream about this kind of adventure."

"Then it's that thrill-seeking vacationer you're hoping to attract?"

"Exactly." Matt wanted this venture to succeed for more reasons than he cared to contemplate. He had something to prove to himself—and to Karen. "But it'll appeal to lots of other people, too.

"I'm listed with the Airline Report Corporation now," he said, although he suspected his sister didn't fully understand the significance of this. It meant that Hard Luck Lodge was formally listed with professional travel agents around the country. If a client came in looking for a place to fish, he or she would learn about the lodge.

"Good."

"I'm mailing out literally thousands of the brochures and offering plenty of incentives to agents to book their clients."

"Incentives? Like what?"

"Well, for one thing," he said, "the first ten agents who call me with reservations will receive a two-night fishing package."

"That's a great idea."

"I thought so." He leaned against the registration counter, crossing his arms, and surveyed the room. A gentle fire flickered in the massive stone fireplace. What the room really needed was those little touches a woman gave a home. He'd wanted to ask Lanni, but she'd already helped with the brochure; besides, she and Charles were newlyweds and he didn't want to intrude in their lives.

Karen had always been great with that sort of thing. It amazed him the way she could turn a dinky apartment into a real home, with the colors she used and plants and the placement of a few carefully chosen things. She had a gift for making a room look inviting.

"Now tell me about this trip you're taking," Lanni said, breaking into his thoughts. Actually he was grateful. He didn't want to think about Karen. She'd made her position clear—she didn't want him in her life—and he was determined to accept that.

"It's a ten-city West Coast tour to meet personally with travel agents," he explained. "I'll be giving a presentation in each city, along with other lodge owners. That way, the agents can ask me any questions they have."

Lanni nudged him playfully. "One thing's for sure, no one else is going to offer dog-sledding."

"Probably not," Matt agreed.

Lanni glanced over his travel itinerary and slowly raised her eyes to connect with his. "You'll be in Oakland."

"Yeah." He didn't pretend not to know what that meant. Karen lived in Oakland. Well, he'd made up his mind a long time ago that he wasn't going to see her.

A man had his pride, and she'd trampled his for the last time. Despite their night together, she wasn't interested in a reconciliation; fine, then that was the way things would be.

"I mailed Karen one of your brochures."

Matt stifled a groan. This was the problem with

Lanni and Karen's being such good friends. A part of him wanted Karen to see the brochure because he was damn proud of it. Proud of everything he'd accomplished in less than a year. But at the same time he didn't want to hear her tell him that his venture was another—what had she called it?—madcap scheme. Contrary to what his ex-wife felt, buying the lodge wasn't a passing fancy.

"Don't you want to know what Karen said?" Lanni asked.

"No," he lied. "She's out of my life now."

"But you still care about her."

Matt wasn't about to let his sister meddle in his life. "Stay out of it, Lanni. What's happened between Karen and me is none of your business."

"Don't be so quick to shut me out, big brother," his sister said, making her eyes wide and innocent, "As I remember, *you* tried to interfere in my relationship with Charles. You manipulated us into meeting so we'd settle our differences."

"As I remember," he echoed, "you didn't appreciate my interference. Karen and I won't, either. I love you, Lanni, but I want you to stay out of this."

Lanni suddenly looked uncomfortable.

"What did you do?" Matt demanded.

"I...I wrote and told her you were going to be in Oakland."

That wouldn't make the least bit of difference, Matt figured. "She won't look me up, and I'm certainly not going out of my way to see her, if that's what you're thinking." And he wouldn't. Karen wanted nothing more to do with him.

Fine. Great. He'd adjust. It wasn't like this was earth-shattering news. He'd been a little slow to get the message; he should have taken the hint when she filed for divorce.

"Whether or not you see her is up to you," Lanni assured him softly, almost as if she was aware that she'd risked offending him, "but I gave Karen the name of your hotel."

The anger caused him to clench his fists. He didn't want *anyone* interfering in his life, least of all his kid sister. Irritated though he was, he understood that her intentions were good. Lanni and Charles were so much in love themselves, it influenced the way they looked at everyone else's life.

"Don't be angry with me," she pleaded.

Matt said nothing.

"Remember, I'm the one who volunteered to take reservations when you're down in the lower forty-eight rounding up business."

It could be wishful thinking on his part, but Matt hoped this tour would generate enough interest in Hard Luck Lodge that bookings would immediately start pouring in. Lanni had offered to run the office while he was away. Actually the arrangement suited them both, since she needed a quiet place to write.

His sister left soon afterward, and Matt wandered into the kitchen with its gleaming new appliances. He was eager for paying guests. Eager to host tourists from all over the world.

So far, he'd managed to acquire only a handful of reservations. His listing in the ARC had been entered late—too late to attract much of the lucrative fishing business. He had a lot to learn about attracting tourists, but he was willing and able. And determined. He would make a go of this lodge or die trying.

"MATT HAS A RIGHT to know about the baby." Lanni's voice sounded tinny on Karen's telephone line. "You don't know how close I came to telling him myself this afternoon."

"But you didn't, did you?" Karen cried in alarm. If anyone told her ex-husband she was two months pregnant, it should be her. Except that it was turning out to be even harder than she'd thought.

"No, I didn't," Lanni assured her. "Listen, Karen, if you don't want to tell him face-to-face, why don't you write him a letter?"

"I can't." After the things she'd said to him, she wouldn't blame him if he returned her letter unopened. Besides, this was the kind of news that was better given in person.

"You should have called him right away." The censure in Lanni's voice was strong. It might have been a mistake to confide in her ex-sister-in-law, but Karen had had to tell *someone*.

"You've already waited a month longer than you should have," Lanni reminded her.

Karen had no defense. "I know."

"But you have the chance to rectify it all now. He's going to be in Oakland on Friday."

Karen bit her lower lip. "So you said."

The pause lasted long enough for Karen to wonder if Lanni was still on the line. When she spoke again, her voice was gentle. "How are you feeling?"

Karen rested her hand on her abdomen. "Better." No one had warned her how dreadful morning sickness could be. The first few weeks of the pregnancy she'd suffered few such symptoms, but now...

At the time of her original doctor's appointment she'd felt tired and restless and rather depressed. But that had changed dramatically after the first month. She wasn't depressed anymore—but not a day passed when she didn't view parts of a toilet that were never meant to be seen at such close range.

Despite the past month's discomforts, Karen was thrilled to be pregnant. She'd always wanted children but hadn't started a family with Matt because she'd wanted him to settle into a permanent job first; but he'd always dragged his feet. Furthermore, he'd seemed reluctant to have a child, and that was one reason she'd delayed telling her ex-husband he was about to become a father.

To some women this pregnancy would have been a disaster, but Karen couldn't help being excited. She wanted this child. Despite everything, she loved Matt. And as far as their relationship was concerned, the baby would be an additional complication to an already complicated situation.

"I hope you'll reconsider," Lanni said, and Karen realized she hadn't been listening.

"Reconsider?"

"Going to see Matt. You should, if for no other reason than to view his presentation. He had Charles and me sit through it before he left, and I have to tell you, Karen, I was impressed."

"He's talking to travel agents?"

"That's right. He's put together this wonderful slide show. I was so busy this winter finishing up my commitments to the newspaper in Anchorage that I didn't pay a lot of attention to what Matt was doing. Did you know he spent ten days on the tundra with nothing more than a tent and a team of sled dogs?"

"Matt?"

"He told me he couldn't very well sell the adventure

if he hadn't experienced it himself. I couldn't believe his pictures. They're fabulous."

Karen could easily imagine Matt standing in front of an audience. He was good with people, outgoing, friendly. And a persuasive kind of guy.

"When he talked about the dogs," Lanni went on, "his eyes just sparkled with excitement. If the number of phone calls I'm getting here is any indication, he's doing a good job of selling the winter packages."

"You mean to say he's actually convinced people to visit the Arctic in winter?" Karen had trouble believing it, but then, what did she know about vacations? In the entire four years of their married life, they hadn't been able to afford even one.

"I've taken at least ten reservations, and Matt's only been gone a week," Lanni announced proudly. "More are coming in every day."

"Lanni, please don't tell me he's actually planning to guide a group of innocent tourists himself. With a pack of highly excitable dogs, no less."

"Of course not," Lanni answered with a short laugh. "He's hired professional mushers."

"Oh." Karen felt ridiculous for having asked.

"Are you going to see him or not?"

"I...don't know yet."

"Well, you'd better decide soon because he'll only be in Oakland one night. He's scheduled to go to—" Karen heard a rustle of papers "—Portland, Seattle and then home."

"I'm not making any promises," Karen said, but she knew Lanni was right. Matt deserved to know that he would be a father in seven months. She just didn't know how he'd react to the news.

MATT SAW KAREN the moment she slipped into the back row of the meeting room. Even from this distance, the first thing he noticed was how pale she looked. He sat on the stage with a number of other lodge operators, all working hard to sell their tour packages. Luckily he'd already given his presentation, so the pressure was off and he could study his ex-wife.

She'd lost weight, and he wondered if that was intentional. If so, she was too thin, but she wouldn't appreciate hearing that from him.

The temptation to walk off the stage and confront her then and there was almost overwhelming. He might have done it if not for their last conversation.

Well, this time, damn it, she could come to him. He was tired of having his teeth shoved down his throat every time he attempted to reason with her.

Then again, maybe she didn't intend to seek him out. Maybe she was only here to satisfy her curiosity. Or because she'd promised Lanni. Fine, so be it, he decided. With effort he managed to keep his eyes resolutely trained on the current speaker. But again and again, his gaze drifted back to her, and he experienced a twinge of regret.

The moderator walked to the microphone. "Are there any questions?"

A hand went up in the middle of the room. "I have one for Mr. Caldwell."

Matt stood.

"Do you have any response to the animal-rights people who question using dogs to pull sleds?"

Matt had gotten the same question in almost every city. "First, I want to assure you that the dogs are loved and cared for the way most people look after their own children. As for the rigors of life on the trail, the huskies are thoroughly happy. Running was what they were born to, and they love it. Their comfort range is amazing. Until the weather drops to around thirty below, many sled dogs don't even care to sleep in a kennel.''

''Are the dogs dangerous?'' someone called out.

''No way,'' Matt said, smiling. ''Mostly they're playful and fun. At rest stops along the winter trails they cool down by rolling in the snow. For the first mile of a run, they're excited and excitable, but even then an inexperienced musher can learn to manage them. After the first day or so, everyone will come to know the dogs by name and personality.''

Since he offered something new and interesting, Matt fielded the majority of the questions. As with his audiences in other cities, he felt he'd accomplished his purpose. The travel agents certainly seemed enthusiastic. But even as he was speaking, his gaze was drawn back to Karen. Pride be damned. He wasn't letting her off the hook so easily. If she wanted to walk out, fine, but he made sure she knew he'd seen her.

Following the question-and-answer session, the applause was vigorous. Matt gathered his notes, glancing up only once to see if he could find Karen. His heart fell when he realized she was nowhere in sight.

Then, when he was convinced she'd run away like a frightened rabbit, he turned around and found her standing no more than a foot away.

At close range, she looked paler than she had from the other end of the room. His concern was immediate.

''Karen, have you been ill?''

''No. Well, you wouldn't call it ill.''

The woman spoke in riddles.

''Matt, do you have time for a drink?''

She was actually inviting him. That was progress.

He glanced at his watch, wanting her to sweat it out. "I suppose." He tried to make it sound as if he was squeezing her in between appointments.

Carrying his briefcase, he led the way to the hotel's cocktail lounge and ordered two glasses of white wine.

"No, just one glass," Karen said to the waitress. "I'll have an herbal tea. Any kind."

Matt looked at her in astonishment. "Tea? I thought you liked wine."

"I'm avoiding alcohol," she explained, keeping her gaze averted.

He couldn't imagine why, and he wasn't going to ask. She was the one with the agenda here, and frankly he was more than a little curious about what she wanted to say.

"I was impressed with your answers to the questions," she began. "I'd hoped to be here for your presentation, but...I wasn't feeling well earlier," she began, sounding shaky and uncertain. She rallied and continued, "Karen mailed me one of your brochures. They look terrific."

"Thanks." He was coldly determined not to make this easy for her. Not after the grief she'd given him, the pain she'd caused.

"She told me you've been getting a number of reservations since you went on tour."

"So I understand."

Their drinks arrived and Matt signed the bill with his room number. He noticed that when Karen sipped her tea, her hand trembled. Now he was beginning to get worried.

"Karen, what did you mean earlier about being sick?"

"I'm not sick."

"Oh, yeah, I can tell. How much weight have you lost?" He hadn't intended to be sarcastic, but he hated cat-and-mouse games. If she had something to say, he'd prefer she just spit it out.

He waited for her answer, determined not to speak again until she'd said something relevant; she remained silent. His resolve lasted all of one minute.

"How's the career coming?" he asked, hoping she noticed his choice of words. She'd worked for the engineering firm for three years. She was an employer's dream—conscientious, organized, efficient. It hadn't surprised him that when her boss was promoted he'd made her his executive assistant and moved her to California with him.

"Great."

Somehow Matt didn't believe her.

"Mr. Sullivan giving you problems?" he asked. In some ways, the older man was more like a father to Karen than her own. Matt couldn't imagine Sullivan creating difficulties for her.

"Actually he's been very understanding about the amount of time I've missed from work."

"Missed work?" That didn't sound like Karen, either. In the four years of their marriage, he couldn't recall her taking a single day of sick leave.

"I've been having some trouble…mostly in the mornings." She leveled her gaze at him, as though she expected him to make some logical deduction from that bit of information.

"Ah, you've got PMS," he said, attempting a small joke.

From the disapproving glare she sent him, he gathered she didn't find it humorous. "Matt, you can really be obtuse."

"Me? Listen, Karen, you're the one who wouldn't allow me to finish our last conversation. As far as I'm concerned, if you've got something to say, just say it, because I've got a flight to catch in the morning."

Lifting her chin to a dignified angle, she reached for her purse and stood. "You're absolutely right," she said in a clear voice. "I've been beating around the bush." Her purse strap slipped off her shoulder and she quickly secured it. "I don't have a perpetual case of PMS, Matt, as amusing as you appear to find that. The reason I've lost weight can be attributed to something else. I have what's known as morning sickness. Now, if you'll excuse me, I'll leave you to mull that one over." She turned abruptly and walked out of the lounge.

"Morning sickness," Matt repeated, and downed the last of his wine in one swallow. The words echoed in his brain and his gaze flew to her retreating figure. He bolted upright. "You're pregnant?"

Karen turned the corner and was gone.

"She's pregnant," Matt shouted to the cocktail waitress. Then, before he completely lost Karen, he raced to the lobby in enough time to see her walking out the front doors.

"Karen, wait!"

Either she didn't hear him or she was determined to ignore him. It was just like her to drop that kind of bombshell and then leave him to deal with the shrapnel all on his own.

He didn't catch up with her until she'd reached her car.

"What the hell do you mean you're pregnant?" he demanded. "How did something like this happen?"

She turned around and glared at him.

"Weren't you on the pill?"

"Why should I be?" she asked. "We were divorced, remember?"

As if he'd forgotten that!

"Don't you dare suggest birth control is entirely up to the woman," she said between gritted teeth.

Matt was having trouble taking all this in. "But how?"

"Well," she muttered sarcastically, "here's what I remember from biology class. The woman provides the egg and the man supplies the sperm."

"I know all that!" he snapped. "What I'm talking about is us. We're both responsible adults. I can't believe we didn't consider the possibility of your getting pregnant." He pushed the hair away from his face and leaned against the side of her car. His legs felt like gelatin.

"It might have helped if you'd broken the news a bit more gently," he accused.

"It would help if you weren't looking for someone to blame."

"That's not true," he flared. He rubbed his hand along the back of his neck. "You're going to need financial help." Since his budget was tight, money was the first thing that came to mind.

Karen made a growling sound, and he looked up to find her glaring at him again, her eyes bright with unshed tears. "You're impossible!" she shouted.

"What did I say now?"

"Nothing." She shook her head. "I've fulfilled my obligation. I told you about the baby. I do apologize for any inconvenience this might cause you." Sarcasm dripped from every word. "Perhaps the best alternative is to have my attorney talk to your attorney. Goodbye, Matt.''

With that, she unlocked her car door and climbed in.

"You can't leave," he shouted as she started the car's engine. "We have to talk." But she ignored him as if he hadn't even spoken. "Karen, damn it, would you listen to me?"

She twisted around to look over her shoulder before shoving the car into reverse. Then she backed out of the space and drove off, leaving him standing in the middle of the parking lot, seething with frustration.

KAREN BARELY SLEPT that night. She wasn't sure what she'd expected from Matt, but not the sarcastic arrogance he'd dished up and served her while they were in the cocktail lounge. He'd seemed to take delight in her discomfort.

When she'd finally garnered enough courage to tell him about the pregnancy, he'd reacted as if she'd plotted against him. As if it was important to somehow assign blame for the unexpected pregnancy.

What really bothered her, Karen decided, sometime in the wee hours of the morning, was the fact that his reaction was completely contrary to the romantic picture she'd painted in her mind. For weeks she'd envisioned telling Matt about their baby and watching his eyes go all soft as he regarded her with tenderness and love.

After being married to Matt for four years, she should've known better. The man didn't possess a romantic bone in his body. Furthermore, why should he be excited and pleased because she was pregnant? *He'd* never wanted a baby.

He didn't want a child now any more than he had

when they were married. A baby was an inconvenience. A baby got in the way of his plans.

She'd listened to his arguments about financial security often enough to know exactly what he'd been thinking. If Matthew Caldwell lived to be a hundred, he'd never be financially secure—simply because he'd never hold a job long enough to make it possible.

She was better off without him. On a conscious level she knew that, but on an emotional one, it hurt. Damn it, it really hurt. If ever there was a time in her life she needed coddling and comfort, it was now.

Although the doctors assured her the morning sickness would lessen with time, she hadn't seen any evidence of it. The following morning, like every other morning for weeks, she rose, managed to down a simple breakfast of tea and soda crackers and promptly lost it. Spending most of the night stewing about Matt hadn't helped her physical condition.

By nine she was stretched out on the sofa with a blanket. She'd placed a bucket on the floor beside her because of the queasiness in her stomach.

The doorbell chimed, but she was in no mood for company, and ignored it.

"Damn it, Karen! Open the door."

Matt.

"Leave me alone," she shouted, draining what little energy she had left.

Disregarding her demand, Matt opened the door himself and stepped into her small apartment. She never had learned to keep her door locked. Unfortunately the habit had followed her to California.

Matt looked as pale as she had the night before. He wore the same clothes he'd had on then. If she was guessing, she'd say he hadn't been to bed.

He lowered himself into the chair across from her, and his gaze fell on the bucket.

"No one told me getting pregnant was like suffering the worst case of flu known to womankind," she muttered. She sipped flat soda pop through a straw.

"Is it always like this?"

"Every morning for the past four weeks. And the occasional evening."

He frowned, and although he didn't say anything his look was apologetic. "That's the reason you've missed so much work?"

She nodded. "Listen," she said, rallying somewhat, "I'm sorry for hitting you with the news. Lanni's been telling me for weeks that you had a right to know. I—"

"Lanni knows?"

Karen nodded again.

He expelled his breath loudly. "Anyone else?"

"No. I wouldn't have told her, but—"

"Never mind," he said, cutting her off. "It's not important." He leaned forward and rubbed his palms together. "I've been giving this a lot of thought. For the past twelve hours, as a matter of fact."

She stared at him, waiting.

"I want you to move up to Hard Luck with me. The sooner we can remarry the better and—"

"No," she returned adamantly. "The baby is the last reason on earth for us to remarry."

CHAPTER FOUR

"YOU WON'T REMARRY ME?" Matt had the audacity to look shocked. "What about the baby?"

Karen closed her eyes. She wasn't feeling well enough to argue with her ex-husband. The nausea seemed to be worse this morning than usual and it was difficult enough to think clearly without Matt's questions.

"Karen—"

"I'm fine." She wasn't, but explaining how awful she felt required more strength than she could muster.

His brow creased with concern. "Will you be this sick the entire pregnancy?"

"I don't know." Good heavens, she prayed that wouldn't be the case. Her doctor seemed to think the bouts of vomiting would pass after the first three months. Eight weeks into the pregnancy, and Karen had experienced no lessening of symptoms. Why they should hit her so forcefully in the second month baffled her.

"Are you able to work?"

"Yes...no. I've used up all my sick leave." It hurt to admit that. Her boss had been wonderfully understanding, but she knew being away from her desk days on end was a terrible inconvenience to Mr. Sullivan.

In the past four weeks, Karen had spent an average of only two to three hours a day at the office. Even when she did manage to show up, she was unable to give one hundred percent.

As if he couldn't bear to remain seated, Matt got to his feet and started pacing. "Who's your doctor? Maybe I should talk to him myself. You shouldn't be this ill. Is there something you're not telling me?"

"Like what?"

"There's no possibility this will be a multiple birth, is there?"

Twins? Triplets? Karen hadn't given the matter a thought. "Of course not," she assured him, but it made her wonder. Good grief, how could she ever manage alone with twins? Then, because he'd raised the question, she asked, "What makes you think I could be having twins?"

"I read about something like this once where the wife—the woman suffered acute bouts of morning sickness and it ended up she had quints."

"Quintuplets!" The thought horrified Karen, but when she glanced up at Matt, he was grinning from ear to ear as though the idea brought him considerable enjoyment. "Just think of all the publicity that would bring the lodge."

Naturally he'd think of his precious lodge and not her. "Wipe that smile off your face, Matthew Caldwell."

Matt sat back down and leaned forward. "This is pretty incredible, you know."

That wasn't the impression he'd given her the night before. Okay, the news had come as a shock, but he had a long way to go to play his part in her fantasy. She'd pictured him bringing her a huge bouquet of flowers and a large teddy bear. So far, all he'd brought her was a bunch of silly questions and an outrageous demand. He assumed that because she was pregnant they should remarry as soon as possible. Sweep their difficulties under the rug and pretend they didn't exist—that was Matt's way of dealing with her pregnancy.

"Think about it, Karen," he continued, cocky grin firmly back in place. "In all the years we've known each other, the night of Lanni's wedding was probably the first time we ever made love without protection."

That was the last thing she wanted to be reminded of, especially when she felt so wretched. She remained on the sofa with her head dangling over the edge to be sure her aim for the bucket was on target.

"The odds of your getting pregnant from our one and only...lapse must be astronomical."

Leave it to Matt to get egotistical over something like this. The man was marinating in his own testosterone. Men and their pride! Karen would never understand it.

"Trust me, Matt, this is not the time to gloat." The nausea worsened and she closed her eyes, fearing she was about to lose whatever was left in her stomach.

He chuckled, then seemed to realize she wasn't joking. She must have gone even paler, because he reached over and brushed the hair from her brow.

"What can I do to help?" he asked gently.

It was his tenderness that nearly did her in. Karen had to fight back tears. "Nothing," she whispered, and breathed in deeply. "It'll pass in a moment." Sometimes it did, and other times it didn't. "It might be best if you left—I don't feel up to company."

"Oh, no, you don't," Matt warned. "I'm not walking out of this apartment until you and I have made some decisions."

"We have nothing to decide."

"What about the doctor and hospital bills?"

Karen hated to admit she was hurting in the pocketbook. The medical bills were beginning to mount. The health insurance provided through Paragon, Inc., paid eighty percent, but the twenty percent she had to pay grew with each doctor's visit. She didn't need a calculator to realize that with the difficulties she'd already experienced, she would soon run into the thousands. And the fact that her attendance at work was sporadic at best didn't help her financial situation.

"Are you offering to help?" she asked stiffly. Matt had never been good with money. It used to drive her crazy the way he'd write checks without keeping a balance in their checkbook. He'd often stack up two or three months' worth of bank statements before he'd reconcile their account. He wasn't irresponsible or reckless; he just wanted to make the effort worth his while. At least, that was what he always claimed.

Karen should have realized the moment he mentioned his plans to be an accountant that the effort was doomed. He'd never been interested enough in numbers.

"The baby is my responsibility, too," he reminded her.

But it went without saying that Matt was in no position to be giving her money. Not with launching Hard Luck Lodge. He'd sunk every penny he could scrounge plus his entire inheritance in this venture. Knowing Matt the way she did, Karen doubted there was anything left.

"I know, but—"

"Karen." He clasped her hand between his and got down on his knees beside her. "It makes sense to put aside this nonsense once and for all. We belong together. We always have—now more than ever.''

''Nonsense?'' Did he honestly believe that the agony of their divorce had been a trivial decision on her part? Leaving Matt and filing for divorce had been the most difficult painful thing she'd ever done. For him to make light of what it had cost her emotionally proved he'd never understand her.

''Okay, so you don't want to move to Hard Luck,'' he said as if living in the Arctic was all that held her back.

She closed her eyes, stunned that he knew so little about her.

''Do you?'' he asked hopefully.

She opened her eyes, confused by his question.

''Would you agree to marry me and move to Hard Luck?''

''Oh, Matt, please don't ask that of me. Not now when I feel this wretched.''

''I want to take care of you.''

He was going to have his hands full running the lodge. As for taking care of her, well, she'd been doing a fair job of that for years.

''No,'' she said fighting herself, as well as him. She needed him, really needed him, perhaps for the first time. Yet as hard as she tried, Karen couldn't put the past behind her. Matt had fallen short of her expectations so often. He'd made promises in the past and let her down. There was so much more at stake now.

''No,'' Matt echoed, his face tense. He stood and moved to the living room window, staring quietly out for several minutes. When he turned around, anger and frustration seemed to radiate from him in waves. The tightness around his mouth and eyes made his expression piercing and grim.

"I've never understood what I did that was so terrible," he said, his voice low. "Okay, I agree I fumbled around for a while looking for the right career. I knew that bothered you but, Karen, I'm not your father. You complain about my tendency to bounce from job to job, but was that really so bad? We never went hungry, the rent was paid and we had a decent life."

Karen wanted to argue that it was pure luck he found work so easily and you couldn't always count on luck. It was the uncertainty of the situation that drove her crazy. She'd fret and worry about the rent, although somehow, they'd always managed.

"I'm faithful and loyal. I never drank or abused you in any way."

"Matt, please—"

"I've always loved you. The day we stood before the judge and he pounded his gavel and solemnly proclaimed we were no longer married, I still loved you. You're carrying my child, and I love you more now than I thought possible—but I can't force you to care for me."

Karen covered her face in an effort to hold back the words that would tell him how much she cared.

"You want to shut me out of your life," he said starkly. "You want to ignore the fact that the child you're carrying is mine, too. I never thought I'd say it, but maybe you were right—having my attorney talk to yours might be the best way to handle this." Without another word, he walked to the door and left.

The sharp and sudden pain in Karen's abdomen took her by surprise. The unexpectedness of it was one thing, but the intensity of the attack took her breath away. She gasped and doubled up.

Something was very wrong.

Edges of darkness crowded her vision, and she feared she was about to faint. With what little strength she possessed, Karen heaved herself from the sofa and stumbled to the front door.

"Matt." She screamed his name, frantic now with fear.

He was halfway to the parking lot when he heard her.

"Help me..." she pleaded, sobbing uncontrollably. She stretched one arm toward him and clutched her stomach with the other. "I think I'm losing the baby."

MATT SAT in the waiting area outside the emergency room at Oakland Hospital. He'd tried a dozen times in the past two hours to see Karen but had been told the doctor was still with her. Two hours!

The waiting room was packed. There were several crying, sick children, a man with a bloody towel wrapped around his hand and a young mother gently singing a lullaby to her fussing two-year-old. A couple of girls were staring at the fish in an aquarium, while two or three men seemed glued to the lone TV, which was tuned to CNN.

Matt hadn't glanced at the television or the aquarium once. He was too worried about Karen and the baby. He was afraid the length of time she'd been with the doctor didn't bode well for the pregnancy.

He closed his eyes and forced himself to concentrate on breathing. A crushing sadness lodged in his chest. He'd known about the baby less than twenty-four hours, yet he deeply grieved the loss of his son or daughter. He would never hold this baby in his arms, never change a diaper or hear his child's first word.

Glancing toward the swinging doors, Matt willed someone—anyone—to come and tell him what was happening with Karen.

What he'd said earlier about loving her had never seemed truer than at this moment. He hurt more now than he had when she'd served him with the divorce papers. She'd made it clear that she wanted nothing to do with him, and heaven help him, he'd abide by her wishes. But no matter what the outcome of this day, it would be damn hard.

He leaned forward and clasped his hands, bracing himself against a fresh wave of pain. The hurt was so sharp, so constricting, that for a moment he found it difficult to breathe.

Distracted by his thoughts, Matt wasn't immediately aware of the doctor who entered the room and called his name.

"Matthew Caldwell."

Matt leapt to his feet and nearly tripped over a toddler sitting on the floor, stacking wooden blocks.

"I'm Matt Caldwell," he told the lanky older man in the white coat. "What's happened with Karen? What about the baby?" He prepared himself to receive the news that they hadn't been able to save the pregnancy.

"Your wife is resting comfortably."

Matt didn't bother to explain that Karen was his ex-wife.

"We've run a number of tests, and as far as we can tell the pregnancy is progressing just fine."

Matthew was too stunned to respond. "The baby's fine? What happened? Karen thought she was having a miscarriage."

The other man patted him on the back. "Your wife has a severe bladder infection."

"But...she was in such dreadful pain."

"I suspect the infection was complicated by stress and fatigue. To be on the safe side, we've decided to admit her for the night. Her obstetrician will call on her later."

"She's been dreadfully ill with morning sickness. Is this normal?"

"Sometimes. You might talk with Dr. Baker when he's in. Would you like to see your wife now?"

"Please."

Matt followed the ER physician down a corridor crowded with gurneys and IV stands to a semidarkened room. He pulled aside the thin curtain around the bed. Karen lay there, her hands resting protectively over her abdomen.

Matt barely noticed the doctor's leaving. He gazed down at Karen; their eyes met and held. She looked deathly pale against the white sheets and terribly drawn. Matt figured he probably didn't look much better. He'd never spent a more harrowing two hours in his life.

"How're you feeling?" he asked gently. Needing to touch her, Matt reached for her hand and brought it to his lips. It wasn't until her fingers closed around his that he remembered their disagreement.

"Oh, Matt," she whispered, "I'm so sorry for causing you all this trouble."

"I'd never consider helping you trouble." He kissed the back of her hand.

Tears filled her eyes and she turned her face away from him.

"The doctor said you should sleep," he urged her softly. "Don't worry about a thing."

"What about your plane? You were supposed to have left Oakland long before now." She shifted her position to look at him again.

"I called and canceled my reservation. Now stop worrying about it."

Ever so lightly, he touched her tear-stained face.

"But the tour—what about your presentations in Portland and Seattle?"

That she knew so much about his schedule surprised him. "There'll be other tours."

"I feel terrible about messing up your plans..." Her voice faded. Whatever drug the hospital had given her seemed to kick in just then, because she closed her eyes and was asleep within seconds.

Matt sat next to her bed until the orderly arrived. Then he followed Karen to the room she'd been assigned. He stayed until she started to stir, at which point he quietly slipped out. The way Matt figured it, he was the last person she'd want to see.

KAREN STARED into the emptiness, sluggish from drugs and a sleepless night spent fretting over her future and the baby's. She felt more rested now than she had in weeks. She pressed her hand against her stomach, forever grateful that the pregnancy remained intact. She'd been so afraid.

A brief smile touched her lips. Generally she was the calm, cool one in a crisis, not Matt. The reverse had happened that morning. Consumed as she was with the pain, weeping and nearly hysterical, Karen had been convinced she was suffering a miscarriage.

Although he hadn't known where to even find a hospital, Matt had been clearheaded and efficient, calling 911 for instructions and accompanying her in the ambulance. Not until they arrived at the emergency room had he displayed any emotion. And then only because the medical staff insisted he wait in the outer room.

She caught a movement out of the corner of her eye, and she turned her head to see her boss, Doug Sullivan, entering the room.

"Karen, how are you feeling?" He'd brought a large bouquet of arranged flowers and set the vase down on the nightstand.

Karen was so surprised to see him she didn't answer. "How did you know I was here?"

"Matt called me."

"Matt?" At the sound of her husband's name she swallowed hard. Apparently he'd left Oakland, because she hadn't seen him again. She'd asked the nurses about him, but no one seemed to know where he'd gone or when.

"Matt thought he should tell me you'd been hospitalized, and he was right." Doug moved to the foot of her bed. "What happened?" he asked gently.

"I don't know for sure, but all at once I had these excruciating pains. The doctors seem to think they're related to stress and fatigue."

"So Matt said."

"Was there anything else he told you?" she asked, resenting the way her ex-husband had taken it upon himself to interfere in her life. It wouldn't bother her nearly as much if he hadn't up and disappeared without a word—which just went to prove what she'd been saying all along. The man wasn't reliable.

"Matt did happen to mention that he wanted you to return to— What's the name of that town again?"

"Hard Luck," Karen supplied.

"Right, Hard Luck." Doug Sullivan paused, then said in a kind voice, "It might not be such a bad idea, Karen."

"But—"

He raised his hand, stopping her. "Just until the baby's born. Matt has every right to be concerned about you...and his baby."

The last person Karen had thought would side with her ex-husband was her boss. Typical of Matt to have someone else do his arguing for him! "Do you realize how far Hard Luck is from Fairbanks or a town of any real size?" she asked. "There isn't a doctor within a five-hundred-mile radius."

"True, but Matt says the public-health nurse is a fully qualified midwife. I believe he said her name was Dotty something. She's one of the women who went up there last year—she married the shopkeeper, I think."

Karen looked away, annoyed that Matt had brought Doug in to make a case on his behalf. He was obviously very serious about getting her to move to Hard Luck.

Doug's blue eyes twinkled as he spoke. "We got quite a chuckle out of that story, remember?"

Karen wasn't likely to forget. The news article about a group of lonely bush pilots advertising for women had attracted national attention. Her own connection with Alaska had made the topic especially fascinating for everyone at the Paragon office. Karen had laughed and joked with her friends—until she'd learned that Matt had moved to Hard Luck. Then the whole story had ceased to amuse her. With women said to be arriving each and every week—a gross exaggeration, according to Lanni—Matt could easily fall in love with one of the newcomers. Why that should concern her, Karen didn't care to question.

"So this Dotty was recruited by the O'Hallorans?" Karen asked, reining in her memories.

"Yes, and then she married a guy named, let me see, Pete. Unusual last name. Lively or Liver or something."

"Livengood," Karen remembered. A man with a thick gray beard came into her mind. She'd briefly danced with him at Lanni and Charles's wedding reception.

"In addition, a doctor flies in once a month."

"You sound like you want to be rid of me," Karen complained.

"Not at all," the older man assured her, patting her hand. "You know as well as I do that I'm a mess without you. Why else do you think I personally requested you for my executive assistant when I was promoted? You deserved it as much as I did—heaven knows I wouldn't have gotten my promotion without your help."

"Nonsense." But hearing him say so helped smooth her ruffled ego.

"Come back to work next spring after the baby's born," Doug suggested. "You've been frightfully ill these last few weeks."

Karen bit down on her lip, upset at the way everyone was making decisions for her. She felt trapped and helpless. And angry.

"Nancy's doing a reasonable job of filling in for you. She's not you, but she'll do until you're back on your feet."

Karen said nothing, unwilling to agree.

"Your job will be waiting for you," Doug promised. "But right now, you need to take care of yourself and the little one."

"Did Matt put you up to this?" she asked.

"No." Once again her boss was quick to set her straight. "He came to me with a number of questions, told me what had happened and left it at that. He's worried about you, the way any husband would be."

"Matt is no longer my husband."

"I realize that, my dear, but did anyone bother to tell him? He's fiercely protective of you, Karen. I know it's bothersome, but in this instance I agree with the young man. Your health and that of the baby is what's most important."

"Yes, but—"

"Now, because I want you back, I've talked with the good people in the employment office, and if you agree, I'll arrange to have your furniture and other personal belongings placed in storage. Then later, when you're ready to return to California, everything will be here waiting for you."

The resentment she'd experienced earlier flared back to life. She didn't want anyone making that kind of decision for her. But her anger died a quick death as Karen realized Doug was acting out of genuine concern and affection. Besides, she would have come to the same conclusion herself. Her health and that of her baby's had to take priority over her distrust of her ex-husband.

Moving to Hard Luck with Matt wasn't the ideal situation, but it made more sense than any of her other options.

"What do you say, Karen?" Doug prompted.

"All right, but just until the baby's born."

"Take as long as you like," he told her, patting her hand again. "When you're ready to move back to Oakland, your job will be waiting for you."

Doug Sullivan left following their discussion, and Karen must have fallen asleep, because the next thing she knew a small noise jarred her awake. It took her a moment to realize she wasn't alone in the room.

"Sorry." Matt stood at the foot of her bed, looking sheepish. "I guess this wasn't meant to be used as a flower vase, huh?" He'd thrust a bouquet of roses into the water pitcher.

Karen couldn't keep from smiling. "You brought me flowers?"

He seemed almost embarrassed to have been caught. He shrugged and mopped up the spilled water with his handkerchief.

"Doug Sullivan was in to see me," she announced.

Matt's hand stilled as he raised his eyes to meet hers. "I suppose you're angry because I talked to him. You might as well know I phoned Dr. Baker while I was at it. You've made it plain that you don't want me meddling in your life, but there's more to consider here than—"

"I'm not angry."

His head came up as if he wasn't sure he'd heard her correctly. "You're not?"

"No. I've decided the best thing for me and the baby is to do as you suggested and move to Hard Luck with you. But I want it understood right here and now that I'm returning to California as soon as the baby's born."

Matt's expression was astonished, then ecstatic. "Whatever you say."

"Don't think you're going to change my mind, Matthew Caldwell, because it isn't going to happen."

"Whatever you say, sweetheart."

Karen groaned. "I'm not your sweetheart or anything else."

"Maybe not, but you're the mother of my baby, and for now that's all that matters."

MATT FELT LIGHTHEARTED. If he'd ever needed to prove that sometimes the quickest route to what you want is an indirect one, he'd done it with Karen. He was convinced he could have argued with her until the twelfth of never and gotten nowhere. Only when he'd received Doug Sullivan's support did he get the results he wanted.

He stared out the window of the small aircraft as it passed over the rugged Arctic terrain, heading due north toward Hard Luck. The Midnight Sons plane, piloted by Ted Richards, had picked them up in Fairbanks.

Karen slept peacefully at his side. He restrained himself from placing an arm around her, although he'd been dying to do that from the moment they'd left Oakland a day earlier.

She wasn't happy about all this, but she'd finally been willing to listen to reason. The way he figured it, once she was in his home, he'd have her back in his bed in no time, and the rest would fall naturally into place.

To begin with, he'd make sure she understood that he wasn't going to ask anything from her physically. Sexually. They'd need to sleep in the same room, though, so he'd be able to look after her properly when she was ill. That made perfect sense. Still, it might take some talking to persuade her to share a room—and a bed—with him, but he'd talk as long as he had to. Wear her down, if nothing else, he thought wryly.

Getting Karen back in his bed had haunted Matt from the night of his sister's wedding. Nothing had ever felt so right to him. That Karen should get pregnant from their one time together struck him as a kind of poetic justice.

Their lovemaking had always been incredible. That night was no exception. But it *was* an exception in another sense—they'd made love without arguing first. During the last two years of their marriage, that had become a negative pattern. They'd had a lot of fights—and always ended up in bed afterward.

No one would guess that his sweet-natured wife had such a temper. Their fights used to escalate quickly to physical comedy, with Karen throwing anything she could lay her hands on. Over the years he'd dodged books, cups, pillows. A turkey drumstick, once. And the madder she got, the more passionate she became. The hotter her temper, the hotter her desire. The fact that, with them, passion was always tied to anger disturbed him.

And it was something Karen hated about herself, this tendency to flail at her husband in anger, then reconcile in bed.

They'd broken the pattern the night of Lanni's wedding. The reality that they'd created a baby still hadn't fully sunk in. Every time he thought about it he grinned.

In the airport that very day he'd found himself watching mothers with youngsters. It was all he could do to keep from approaching total strangers and declaring that he and Karen were having a baby.

"We're almost there," he whispered. He slid his arm

carefully around her; if she was going to be angry with him, then so be it.

Her beautiful long lashes fluttered open and she glanced out the small window on the opposite side of the plane. "How long have I been asleep?"

He was tempted to tell her that the amount of time she'd been awake would have been easier to calculate. "Not long," he assured her with a straight face.

She raised her eyebrows. "I'll bet. Well," she said, stretching, "I hope I can rest tonight."

She would—he'd make sure of that. Once upon a time they'd slept spoon fashion, cuddled up against each other, perfectly content. Now they would again. Every night, if he had anything to say about it.

The plane slowly descended, aligning itself with Hard Luck's narrow gravel runway. A number of planes lined the field, and several more were parked alongside nearby homes, like cars in a carport.

Matt resisted the urge to point out that the wildflowers were in bloom, to exclaim how beautiful the countryside looked with the snow all gone. June was probably his favorite month here in the high Arctic. The days were long now; night lasted only enough time for the stars to blink a couple of times and then disappear over the horizon, blinded by the light of approaching day.

"Lanni should be there to greet us," Matt assured her. When Matt had called his sister to tell her that Karen was returning with him, Lanni had shrieked with delight. She'd advised him to go slow with Karen, but he didn't need anyone to tell him that.

The Baron came down gently on the runway and coasted to a stop.

Sawyer O'Halloran was there to open the side door

and lower the steps. He offered Karen his hand as she climbed out of the aircraft, then greeted her with a warm hug.

"It's *great* to see you again."

"Thanks, Sawyer," she said a bit shyly.

It gave Matt a small degree of pleasure that she didn't just blurt out that she wasn't staying once the baby was born.

Sawyer loaded the luggage into his trunk, and ten minutes later they were at the lodge. Matt was eager to see the place after his two-week absence—and eager to learn how many new reservations Lanni had taken. Thanking Sawyer, he lugged in their suitcases and set them in the lobby, then called, "Lanni!"

"She's not here," Karen informed him with perfect logic after he'd called for his sister another two times. Then he saw a note propped up on the registration desk.

"So I see," Matt said, not entirely concealing his frustration. "Well, make yourself comfortable while I put our suitcases in the bedroom." He lifted the heavy bags and headed toward the master bedroom in his private quarters—a small apartment on the main floor.

"Matt."

He set the cases back down. "Yes?"

"Where are you taking my things?"

He'd just explained that, but he was a patient man. "To the bedroom."

"You appear to be carrying them into *your* bedroom."

"Mine? It's ours now, darlin'."

Her mouth thinned in that way of hers that told him she wasn't pleased. "I believe *my* room is up the stairs—*darlin'*."

Matt's gaze followed the staircase that led to the second level and the rooms beyond. "But I thought—"

"I know exactly what you thought, Matthew Caldwell, and it's not going to happen."

CHAPTER FIVE

ABBEY HUMMED SOFTLY to herself as she arranged the new books on the front display table. The town council had allotted her a small budget, and she'd quickly purchased the latest hardcover releases. She didn't expect them to remain on display for very long. Now that the Hard Luck Library was in full operation, most everyone in town took advantage of it. Abbey had been hired to organize the library, but it was thanks to the generosity of Sawyer's mother, Ellen O'Halloran—now Ellen Greenleaf—who had donated a vast majority of the books, that the place even existed. It had been Ellen's dream. And now the people of Hard Luck had access to fiction of all kinds and for all ages, as well as a variety of resource materials.

Abbey squatted down to replace one of the children's books and experienced a dizzy sensation. The room started to spin. She lost her balance and flopped onto the floor.

"Honey, I've been thinking..." Sawyer walked into the library, halting abruptly when he found his wife sitting, dazed, on the floor. "Abbey? Are you okay?"

She offered him a wan smile. "My goodness, that came as a shock."

"What happened?" Sawyer asked, helping her to her feet. He framed her face between his large hands and studied her intently. His frown deepened. "You're pale."

"I'm a little light-headed, that's all," she said, dismissing his anxiety.

"Light-headed?" His voice turned gravelly with concern. "I think you'd better talk to Doc Gleason the next time he flies in."

"Sawyer," she said, smiling softly, "I already know why this happened."

"You do?"

"I'm about ninety-nine percent sure I'm pregnant."

"Pregnant?" Her husband's mouth fell open. "You think we're going to have a baby?" He pulled out a chair, one she thought was meant for her, then promptly sat in it himself.

Abbey laughed out loud when Sawyer placed his hand over his heart and croaked, "You might have prepared me for this."

"Sawyer, we've talked about having a baby."

"I know, but this is different... You're pregnant!"

Abbey poured him a glass of water, which he swallowed in giant gulps. "We're going to have a baby." His eyes were loving as he gazed up at her. "Oh, Abbey, I can't begin to tell you how—"

"Stunned," she said.

"No, pleased. Happy. *Thrilled..*" His lips curved in a slow smile.

She smiled back. "I know." She'd never seen her husband react quite this way to anything.

"Have you told anyone else?"

"No. Sawyer, I would tell you first. Anyway, it's still early—I'm not entirely sure myself." But she was. The joy and excitement that swelled up inside her were as unmistakable as the physical symptoms of pregnancy.

"Can I tell someone? This news is too good to keep to myself. We should let Charles and Lanni know, don't you think? My mother!" he cried. "Mom will go bananas. She's dying for a granddaughter. Just look at the way she's taken to Scott and Susan, and after three sons who can blame her for wanting a girl? We should tell Christian." He was talking so fast the words nearly blended together. "I remember the morning he started talking about bringing women to Hard Luck. I kept thinking this was the craziest idea I'd ever heard. Then I met you, and now I'm so grateful for my brother's loony ideas. Charles is grateful too—he'd never have met Lanni if we hadn't needed more housing for the—"

"Sawyer," she said, interrupting gently. She touched his arm. "Don't you think we should let Scott and Susan know before we tell anyone else?"

"Scott and Susan...of course. You mean they don't already know?"

"No, sweetheart. Of course not." He made such a comical sight it was all Abbey could do to keep from laughing.

Sawyer stood up, then immediately sat back down. "Scott can help me build the cradle. But I don't want to ignore Susan, so maybe we should—"

She placed her arms around his neck and did the only thing she could think of to silence him. She kissed him.

Slowly Sawyer eased his mouth from hers. "Abbey, we've got to—"

Determinedly she brought his mouth back to hers and kissed him again, revealing without words how much she loved him and how joyful she was to be carrying his child. This time she met with far less resistance.

Sawyer groaned and his arms circled her waist as he pulled her onto his lap. "Abbey…"

"Hmm?"

"I love you, sweetheart."

"I've never doubted that. We can tell the kids about the baby this evening, and then we'll phone your mother and let the rest of the family know."

Her kisses had mellowed him considerably. "All right, but I think you should come home and rest first."

Abbey sighed and pressed her forehead against his. "Someone needs to be at the library. Besides, we both know that if I went home neither one of us would rest."

"This is the trouble with having a wife," Sawyer muttered, grinning broadly. "You know me far too well. You're right—resting *wasn't* what I had in mind."

AS SOON AS SHE HEARD that Abbey O'Halloran was pregnant, Karen stopped by the library. She knew the building had originally been the home of Adam O'Halloran, Hard Luck's founder, and she looked around with interest.

"Karen, it's good to see you." Abbey was sitting at the large desk in the main room, working on the card catalog. "You're looking great."

"Thanks. You, too." To Karen's mixed relief and chagrin, her bouts of morning sickness had all but disappeared in the two weeks since her arrival in Hard Luck. Matt gloated, certain that her return to health could be attributed to him. Karen preferred to believe it was the fresh Alaska air.

"I understand congratulations are in order," she said to Abbey, pleased that another woman in town was pregnant, too.

"So you heard about the baby," Abbey said, smiling happily. "But then, I can't see how you *wouldn't* know. I swear, Sawyer's personally announced our news to everyone in Alaska. You'd think I was the only woman in the world who ever got pregnant."

"And I thought Matt was the one who believed that."

The two women chuckled. "I'm happy for you," Karen said, "and on a purely selfish note, I'm glad there's someone I can talk to about all this."

"The morning sickness is better?"

"Oh, yes," Karen said with a deep, grateful sigh. "I can't understand it. When I was in California I considered it an accomplishment if I managed to get out of bed and dress. I arrive here, and it's like a miracle cure. Oh, I still have an occasional bout of nausea, but it's nothing like what I suffered before." She didn't mention how much Matt wanted to take credit for that.

"It happens that way sometimes," Abbey told her with the wisdom of two pregnancies behind her. "Can I help you find something?" she asked. "I can recommend a couple of good books on pregnancy and infant care."

"Matt bought about a dozen books in California," Karen said with a quick grin. "Actually I came to volunteer my services."

"At the library?"

"If I could." She was eager to find something to occupy her time. Matt was busy with the lodge, and she rarely saw him more than twenty minutes a day. Although she was living with her ex-husband, Karen was lonelier than before. The first set of guests had arrived, and Matt had left for a two-day fishing expedition; he wouldn't return until sometime that afternoon. But before leaving he'd hired Diane Hestead, a high school girl, as a part-time maid.

"I'd like to volunteer my services for the wedding reception for Mitch and Bethany Harris, too." Lanni had told Karen that the couple had been married ten days earlier in San Francisco. A huge welcoming party was planned for them when they returned from their honeymoon.

"We'd love to have you if you're sure you feel up to it," Abbey said excitedly.

Karen was tired of sitting around the lodge with nothing to do—no defined tasks. No responsibilities. Twiddling her thumbs. She'd even taken to organizing Matt's office, although she wasn't sure how he'd feel about it. He might have studied accounting, but the man didn't know the meaning of the words "filing system." Earlier that morning, Karen had gone into his office to set the mail on his desk and couldn't find a bare space.

How he could manage anything in such clutter was beyond her. She'd left the mail, determined to remind her ex-husband that this was no way to run a business. Ten minutes later she'd returned to the office and tackled the mess herself. Before she realized it, the morning was gone and she'd set up a filing system for him.

Although she told herself she'd done it out of her own need for organization, she knew that wasn't entirely true. She wanted to help Matt. Contribute.

He hadn't asked one thing of her. He treated her like a guest, and that wasn't what she wanted. If she was going to make the lodge her home for the next five or six months, then it was important to do something in return. She wanted to be part of the community, too, and helping with this reception was a good start.

Abbey beamed. "Ben insisted on doing all the cooking. Mariah Douglas—she's the Midnight Sons secretary, in case you haven't met her—is working on the decorations. Dotty Livengood's helping, too."

Karen was eager to make friends with the other women in Hard Luck. She hadn't ventured far from the lodge and was still finding her way around the small community. Everyone seemed to know her, though, thanks to Matt.

"The reception's on Saturday," Abbey continued, "and from what I understand, Mariah and Dotty are hoping to get everyone together Friday evening around seven to decorate. We'd love it if you'd come."

"I'll be there," Karen promised.

The July sun shone brightly as she wandered slowly back to the lodge, enjoying the day's warmth and the friendly greetings. Matt hadn't given her a specific time to expect him home, but she hoped it would be soon.

The first thing Karen noticed when she stepped into the lodge was the inviting smells coming from the kitchen. Savory spices mingled with the scent of simmering beef and vegetables.

"Matt?" She found her husband in the kitchen, wearing a starched white apron. He stood in front of the stove and grinned wryly when he saw her.

"Hi, honey, I'm home."

Karen begrudged the way her heart leapt with excitement just to see him again. She was lonely, she told herself, that was all. What did she expect when family and friends were in Anchorage, hundreds of miles away?

"How'd everything go?" she asked in an effort to take her mind off her pleasure at having him home.

"Great. The guys are showering up now. We had a fabulous time."

"Did you catch any fish?" Matt wasn't likely to get much repeat business unless he supplied the fishing experience of a lifetime. Karen had read in one of those glossy travel publications that it was cheaper to go on a safari in Africa than an expedition in Alaska.

"Both men said this was the best fishing of their lives. They've already given me a deposit for next year."

Karen couldn't help sharing in his pride. "That's wonderful!"

Matt added chopped potato to the stew. "Did you miss me?"

She had, but she wasn't about to admit it. "You were only gone two days."

"That doesn't answer my question."

She knew what he was hoping to hear; she just didn't think it was a good idea to let him know how lonely she'd been. "It was quiet around here," she said unwillingly.

He couldn't seem to take his eyes off her. "I swear you're looking more beautiful every day. Pregnancy obviously becomes you."

Compliments generally made Karen uncomfortable. "I can't button my jeans. And I'm only three months along," she complained. "At this rate, I'll end up resembling a battleship."

He stepped away from the stove and made a show of studying her. He twisted his head one way and then the other. When he'd finished, he said in a thoughtful tone, "Maybe, but you'll be the prettiest battleship around."

Matt always knew how to cheer her up. But she didn't *want* to laugh and joke with him; that kind of camaraderie was dangerous. She had to remind herself repeatedly that after the baby was born, she was returning to California. It was becoming more and more difficult to think about her life away from Matt.

"Let me help you with dinner," she insisted.

"No way." He was prepared to chase her out of the kitchen, but she stood her ground.

"Matt, I want to help. If you don't let me I'll go crazy with nothing to do."

He gave in. "All right, all right. You can set the table."

Then, because she was pleased to see him, and because she forgot for a moment that they were divorced and living together as brother and sister, she stood on her tiptoes and briefly brushed his mouth with hers.

Matt stared at her as though she'd suddenly sprouted wings. Or antennae. His expression said he didn't understand why she'd done this. She wasn't sure herself. But it felt right. It felt more than right—it felt *good.*

THE FOLKS IN HARD LUCK were getting to be experts at celebrating weddings, Ben Hamilton mused contentedly. He worked in the compact kitchen beside the school gymnasium, assembling hors d'oeuvres for Bethany and Mitch. First there'd been a wedding and reception for Sawyer and Abbey, and almost directly afterward another for Pete and Dotty. Come spring there was Charles and Lanni's, and now a reception for Bethany and Mitch.

His gaze followed the couple as they circulated

among their guests. A swell of pride filled him as he regarded Bethany—his daughter. The realization still took some getting used to. He actually had a daughter. One he'd never known about until she'd arrived in Hard Luck last year.

It saddened Ben to acknowledge that he hadn't been there for either Bethany or her mother, Marilyn. Instead, he'd spent twenty-odd years in the United States Navy, first in Vietnam and later on various ports around the world. When he retired ten years ago, only in his forties, he'd come here to Alaska and opened his café. He'd never married; his affair with Marilyn was a brief episode he'd never forgotten. One that, it turned out, had left him with a daughter.

And my, oh my, Bethany was a pretty thing. Looking at her now with her husband and stepdaughter, Chrissie, Ben wondered how he could have produced such a charming, caring woman.

With more than a touch of regret, he realized he hadn't. Her mother and Peter Ross, the man who'd loved Marilyn, had raised Bethany; they were the ones responsible for the woman she'd become. His contribution to the effort had been strictly genetic. Still, he took a good deal of pleasure in the woman she'd become. It thrilled him no end that Bethany and Mitch had decided to continue living in Hard Luck. He hadn't defined what role he would play in her life yet, but he was grateful for the opportunity to know her.

"What are you doing in the kitchen?" Christian O'Halloran demanded. "You should be out there with everyone else, enjoying the party."

Ben wasn't comfortable outside of a kitchen. He found he related to folks far more easily when he had something to occupy his hands, when he had coffee to pour and food to serve. He never had been one to mix and mingle at parties.

"I've got plenty to do right here," he insisted. He had the hors d'oeuvre platters ready, plus the fruit and vegetable trays. Fine-looking trays, too, even if he said so himself.

He'd spent a lot of time making sure everything was as appealing to the eye as it was to the palate. That he'd borrowed a cookbook by Martha Stewart from the library was his and Abbey's secret.

"But this is Bethany and Mitch's reception," Christian told him, as if he didn't already know.

"Ben, what can I do to help?" Mariah Douglas stepped into the kitchen and stopped abruptly when she saw Christian O'Halloran. The two regarded each other like wary dogs.

Ben had never considered himself much of an expert when it came to dealing with women. He was a crusty old bachelor, set in his ways. Nevertheless, he liked to think he was a good judge of what was happening between people. It seemed to him that Mariah Douglas was sweet on Christian—which was unfortunate, because the youngest O'Halloran brother avoided Mariah like a communicable disease.

"Hello, Christian," she greeted him stiffly.

Considering they worked together every day, it amazed Ben that Mariah was actually blushing.

"Mariah." Christian nodded once, formally, and Ben noticed that he backed up several steps.

Mariah returned her attention to Ben. "Can I help?"

"I've already offered," Christian said.

If Christian hoped those curt words would dismiss her, his plan failed. Ben decided it was time to intervene. "These trays could do with replacing, and that punch bowl needs to be refilled and set out on the table," he said briskly. Someone had brought the almost empty bowl into the kitchen. "Must be plenty of thirsty folks."

Ignoring Christian, Mariah headed for the punch bowl.

Christian started to lift a tray, then hesitated when he saw Mariah. "Don't do it like that."

"Like what?" she snapped.

Ben didn't blame her for using that tone. He wasn't privy to what was going on between them, but he'd listened to Christian's complaints about his inept secretary often enough to feel some sympathy for her.

"Don't fill the punch bowl here," Christian muttered as if that should have been obvious. "Did you stop to think how much easier it would be to carry the bowl to the table first and *then* mix the punch?" He gestured to the wine, soda water and fruit juice lined up on the counter.

"Yes, but—"

"Here, I'll do that and you carry the trays out."

"No," Mariah insisted. "I said I'd take care of this. Stop worrying about me."

Christian and Mariah reached for the punch bowl at the same time. Ben could see it coming even before it happened. As they tugged at opposite sides of the bowl, the bright red remains of the punch swirled around the bottom and upward in a wave—which slapped Christian's white dress shirt and ran down the front of his pants. He gasped and leapt back.

"Christian!" Mariah cried with alarm. "Oh, no."

"Now look what you've done!" Christian shouted.

"Me? As far as I'm concerned, you brought this on yourself."

Ben was proud to see that Mariah had learned to hold her own against her employer. She didn't even blink as he glared at her.

Christian's eyes narrowed and he whirled around to leave the kitchen. "Tell Mitch and Bethany I'll be back as soon as I've changed clothes," he said to Ben.

The instant Christian was out the door, Mariah sagged against the counter.

"You all right?" Ben asked.

"I'm fine," she muttered. "It's just that Christian and I... Oh, never mind. I'm sorry, Ben."

"No need to apologize to me." He picked up the food tray himself and carried it out to the table, then stepped back to admire his work. He grinned, inordinately pleased with his effort. It was a small thing, but he felt pride in being able to contribute to his daughter's reception.

"Ben." Bethany joined him. "I don't know how Mitch and I can possibly thank you. Everything looks so beautiful."

Ben decided he could live on those words and the happiness gleaming in her eyes for at least a week. "It's nothing," he said with a nonchalant shrug, as if he'd whipped up the entire display that morning. In actuality, he'd been planning and working on it for weeks.

"The food's fabulous," Bethany told him, "And I know what those grapes and watermelons cost. You've done such a beautiful job." She stood on tiptoe to kiss his cheek.

"I wanted your party to be special," he said, uneasy with emotion, even positive emotion. Damn, but he was proud of Bethany.

She'd chosen a good man in Mitch, too. Ben

grinned. He was pretty gauche about this romance business, but he was well aware that Mitch's daughter was responsible for bringing her father and Bethany—her teacher—together. It amazed him that an eight-year-old girl could be so smart. Ben was convinced he couldn't have picked a better man for Bethany had he sought out a husband for her himself.

"Dad told me what you did," Bethany said, slipping her arm around Ben's waist. "Writing Mom and Dad that letter was really thoughtful."

He shrugged again, making light of the single most difficult letter he'd ever written. "It was nothing."

"Dad told me you thanked him for raising me so well. It wasn't easy telling my folks I'd found you, and I think Dad might have harbored some fear that you'd replace him in my life."

Ben had given that some consideration, too. Peter Ross deserved a lot of credit for marrying a young woman pregnant with another man's child, and raising that baby to be the beautiful, generous woman Bethany had become. Ben wanted to thank this man he'd never met, and at the same time reassure him that he had no intention of stealing his daughter away. Peter was her real father; he respected that. Ben felt it was time to clear the slate with Marilyn, too. He'd written his regrets to Bethany's mother and asked her to forgive him for having left her to deal with the pregnancy alone.

"Dad said he'd be pleased to count you as a friend," Bethany told him, eyes glistening with tears.

Ben already knew that. Peter's letter had arrived two days before Bethany's wedding, and Marilyn had written him, also. He'd loved her, Ben realized; perhaps he still did. But he was content; she was happy and he'd discovered a woman who was not only his daughter but his comfort, his friend. Everything had worked out for the best.

"Are you going to dance with me?" Bethany asked, hugging him.

"Dance? Me?" Ben experienced a fleeting moment of panic. "Not on your life. That's what you've got a husband for. Now let me get back to the kitchen before your guests get hungry." He hurried back to where he felt most at home, but he turned around to study his daughter one last time. His heart seemed to expand a bit as Bethany stepped onto the dance floor with Mitch.

MATT KNEW Karen was having a good time. He'd been counting on this wedding reception for Bethany and Mitch. The last time the people of Hard Luck had gathered to celebrate a wedding was the night Karen had spent with him. Matt sincerely hoped that history was about to repeat itself.

He'd certainly been restraining himself with his ex-wife—he'd been as good as a choirboy! In three weeks he'd hadn't even *tried* to kiss her, which was a real feat, considering how he felt about her.

Matt feared she was looking for an excuse to leave, something that would prove she'd be better off living elsewhere. True, her options were limited right now; nevertheless she did have some. For example, he knew that her parents had invited her to move home if things became too uncomfortable. But Matt had decided he wasn't going to give Karen any reason to leave Hard Luck. He had five and a half months to prove himself. Five and a half very short months.

His hands-off policy was working, too; Matt could tell. She was much more relaxed with him. And almost against her will, she was beginning to appreciate the simple life in Hard Luck. She'd become part of the community, made new friends. And having his sister in town had proved more of an advantage than he'd anticipated. The two women got together at least twice a week.

Because she wanted to keep busy, Karen had started volunteering two afternoons a week at the library. In a matter of days she was more familiar with the townsfolk than he was after living in Hard Luck for nearly a year.

Another thing that boded well was the interest she'd taken in the lodge itself. Without his saying a word, Karen had started adding those small feminine touches he'd hoped for.

Before he knew it, she'd draped a patchwork quilt over the back of the sofa. A vase of wildflowers magically appeared at the registration desk. She'd even brought in a number of pieces of scrimshaw and some jade figurines. One day, out of the blue, a hand-carved totem pole appeared over the fireplace; it looked perfect, as though it had always stood there. She never said where she got it or how much she'd paid. Now and again, he found her looking at it and smiling happily to herself.

Over dinner a couple of nights before, she'd offered him a suggestion—a damn good one too. She'd pointed out that the lodge was attracting tourists from all over North America, and in order to reach Hard Luck they had to fly over the Arctic Circle. Karen came up with the idea of having certificates printed for everyone who stayed at the lodge, making them official members of the Arctic Circle Club. The next thing he knew, she was flipping through catalogs and making more suggestions. Like selling coffee mugs with the lodge's name and logo. That was a good idea, he agreed, especially if people took them home and used them at the office. Nothing like free advertising.

He was encouraged by all these indications of her growing attachment to Hard Luck and the lodge. But the most promising sign so far was the difference in her attitude toward him. Even if their relationship was more comradely than romantic. Or possibly because of that.

Okay, so he'd been out of line thinking they should sleep together right away. It was an innocent mistake. They weren't exactly strangers; besides, she was pregnant with his child. He'd assumed…and he shouldn't have. It was taking far longer than he'd expected for her sensibilities to right themselves.

Damn it all, Matt wanted her with him. His bed had never seemed so big…and empty. Every night he lay on his back and stared at the ceiling, knowing the woman he loved, the woman pregnant with his child, slept in the room directly above him. If ever there was a guarantee of insomnia, Karen had provided it.

On a more positive note everything else in his life seemed to be falling satisfactorily into place. With reservations coming in for the dogsledding tours and the business he'd managed to pick up this summer, there was a good possibility he'd break even. Well, perhaps not this year, but the next for sure. At the moment he was content to meet his expenses. The lodge was an investment, and for the first time since he'd told Karen about it, she was beginning to see the promise.

He watched her now, laughing with her friends, hugging Bethany, wishing the young couple well, and Matt grew impatient. Dancing had started an hour ago, and he wanted her in his arms.

Joining Karen, he slipped an arm around her waist. If he hadn't known she was pregnant, it would have been hard to tell. But he did know, and he found himself conscious of the thickening about her middle. Matt was convinced that this baby was giving him a second chance with Karen.

"How about a dance?" he asked. He'd had a couple of beers with the guys and was feeling mellow. Mellow enough to put aside his inhibitions.

"A dance?" She gazed up at him, frowning slightly as if she wasn't sure they should.

"One dance," he pleaded softly. They were halfway onto the dance floor already; she could hardly refuse.

"One dance," she echoed.

God was on his side, Matt decided, because the song was a lovely old ballad from the sixties, the music slow and sultry. Matt drew Karen into the circle of his arms, maintaining a respectable distance between them. Just enough to reassure her.

To his delight she leaned closer and pressed her head against his shoulder. "I love weddings," she murmured.

Matt was beginning to share her feelings. She hummed along with the music, and he closed his eyes, remembering the days when she came to him without restraint, without reserve. Remembering the times she'd freely shared her love.

One dance quickly became two, and then three. It felt so familiar—as if she'd never left him, never stopped loving him, never gone through with the divorce.

When Matt looked up, he noticed that a good number of the townsfolk had already left. By tacit agreement, he led Karen outside; together they strolled back to the lodge.

Once home it seemed only natural to kiss her. It was what he'd longed to do for weeks, what had been on his mind for days, ever since he'd learned they'd be attending the reception.

Karen sighed when his lips met hers. She tasted of summer and sunshine, tasted of heaven. Knowing this was what they both wanted, Matt deepened the kiss. His heart nearly flew out of his chest at the way her arms tightened around him. He caressed her back, savoring her softness. He investigated the slender curve of her spine and sought the curved fullness of her hips. He pulled her closer, needing her, wanting her to know exactly how much.

"Karen, I love you. I'm so damned crazy about you," he whispered between kisses.

"Oh, Matt..."

He kissed her again with a sweet desperation. "You know what I want," he murmured huskily when the kiss ended.

Karen braced her forehead against his shoulder and drew in several deep breaths. "I...I think it's time I went upstairs."

"Upstairs? You mean you aren't—you won't—" He stopped abruptly. He opened his mouth to argue with her, then closed it, knowing it would do no good.

"Good night, Matt," she said, and kissed his cheek. "Thank you for a lovely, romantic evening." With that, she turned and walked up the stairs. Alone.

CHAPTER SIX

KAREN HAD BEEN more tempted to sleep with Matt than she ever wanted him to know. It shocked her how easily he could take her in. How susceptible she was. She'd been in Hard Luck less than a month, and already he'd half persuaded her to accept his dream, the same way he had so many times before.

Already he had her believing in the lodge, in the feasibility of its success. Only, Karen should have known better—*did* know better. She'd walked that path too often not to recognize what awaited her at the end.

This latest scheme would be like all the others. Matt would completely win her over and then, when she least expected it, he'd abandon the entire venture for some ridiculous reason. Their past was riddled with such incidents. Her father had repeatedly done the same thing to her mother. It still astonished Karen that out of all the men in the universe, she had to marry one just like him. Yet, Karen reminded herself, she dearly loved her father. He had his faults, true, and they were glaring, but like Matt, he was a good man.

She could feel herself weakening. She loved living in Hard Luck and had quickly formed friendships. The sense of community and family was strong, and that appealed to her, especially now. People cared about each other. And like all of Alaska, the scenery was spectacular.

From her bedroom window she had a stunning view of the Brooks Mountains. She could see blooming tundra, awash with colorful wildflowers. The beauty of the landscape was almost more than any one person could absorb.

It went without saying that in January, when the baby was due, the world outside her window would be a different one. In the dead of winter, daylight would be minimal. Temperatures would dip to thirty and forty below. She'd lived in Alaska a long time, though, and that didn't really alarm her.

Karen stood gazing out her window at the morning and mulled over the situation with Matt. What was it about weddings and slow dancing that made her weaken her resolve every time?

A bright red warning light had started flashing in her mind the moment Matt led her onto the dance floor. She'd known even before he kissed her what was likely to happen. Yet, wanting him the way she did, she'd been powerless to stop.

If she didn't develop some control over her strong sexual attraction to him, it could quickly become a problem.

The obvious solution was to accept her parents' offer to move to Anchorage with them until the baby was born. The thought depressed her so much she immediately dismissed it. She closed her eyes, remembering all the places she'd lived as a child. They'd moved so often, never planted roots in any one town. Karen refused to live that migratory existence ever again. And she didn't want to be reminded of all those distressing emotions, all those sad childhood times—especially when she was about to have a child of her own.

It took some doing to own up to the truth: she didn't

want to leave Hard Luck. Nor did she want to be separated from Matt, not now, not while she was pregnant.

Later, she told herself, after the baby was born she'd visit her parents before she headed back to California.

She dressed and wandered downstairs. Yawning, she stretched her arms high above her head, surprised by how good she felt.

Matt, who stood behind the reservation desk, glanced up at her. "You look well rested," he murmured dryly.

"I am." Briefly she wondered what had happened to his usual cheerful greeting. She'd heard a joke long ago that said there were two kinds of people in the world—those who woke up in the morning and said, "Good morning, God," and those who said, "Good God, morning!" Karen had her own observation to add; she'd noticed that these two very different types of people often found one another—and married.

Matt fell into the chipper, lighthearted category and she into the other. Mornings had never been her favorite time of day, although it was easier when she had a regular schedule. This basic difference between them went further than simply the way they reacted to mornings. Matt was an optimist; she, however, was a realist. Or so she'd always insisted.

This particular morning she felt good—for no particular reason. Humming softly to herself, she poured a glass of orange juice and carried it to the front desk. "I'm meeting Lanni today," she said, sipping the juice.

Matt gave her a perfunctory nod of acknowledgment, then returned his attention to the ledger.

"Is something bothering you?" she asked.

"Not a damn thing," he snapped.

"My, my, we're in a grumpy mood this morning."
He glared at her.

Then it hit Karen like a ton of glacial ice. Her ex-husband was actually sulking because she'd refused to go to bed with him. This wasn't like Matt, either. As long as she'd known him, he'd never been subject to mood swings. Rarely, if ever, was Matt in a bad mood.

Some of the difficulties in their marriage had come from his almost childish insistence that everything would work out. Everything would be fine. He refused to look at any problem seriously, or even acknowledge there *was* a problem. This moody self-absorption was a side of him she hadn't seen, and frankly it amused her. She smiled.

"What's so funny?" he demanded.

"You. Matthew Caldwell, you're pouting."

"I most certainly am not." He slammed the ledger closed. "If there's anything wrong with me—and rest assured there isn't—it's that I didn't sleep well last night."

Karen didn't ask why; she knew. Their pattern had been broken. The fighting, followed by the intense lovemaking. They'd made progress, whether Matt recognized it or not.

He released a long sigh and shook his head. With a quick wave Karen started out the door, eager to see Lanni.

"Karen." Matt stopped her. "You said something last night that intrigued me."

"I did?"

"Before you went upstairs, you thanked me for the romantic evening."

"Yes?" she asked, not understanding his question.

"What made last night romantic?"

She shrugged. "I don't know. The way we danced, I guess. The way you held me, the way we kissed..."

"But you didn't spend the night with me."

This was another area of dissension that had often annoyed Karen. "Don't confuse sex with romance. A woman likes to be...wooed." She shrugged. "It's an old-fashioned word, I know, but it's what I mean."

"Wooed." Matt repeated the word as if it contained magic. His eyes brightened.

"I suspect it's not a good idea to tell you this, but you tempted me last night," Karen said. "It was all I could do to refuse you."

A cocky grin spread across his face. "Really." Almost immediately he started to frown. "If that's the case, why didn't you? You've got to know how much I love you, how much I want us to get back together again."

She stared down at the floor, not ready to admit that she wanted it, too. "I need more time," she said, knowing that sounded lame. But it was the truth.

"What if I wooed you just like you said?" he suggested. "Would that help?"

She looked at Matt and trembled with dread. Because, without a doubt, it was already too late. She loved him, loved the lodge, loved living in Hard Luck.

"Karen?" he asked again.

"I think it might be a good thing for us both," she answered. And then, afraid of what the future held, she hurried out the door.

MATT GLEEFULLY TOSSED his ballpoint pen into the air and caught it. He didn't know why he hadn't thought of this sooner. The solution was so simple! All this time, and he'd overlooked the obvious.

Every woman wanted to be shown that she was loved and appreciated. He needed to prove this to

Karen, and he needed to do it clearly and conclusively. He had to give her a reason to marry him again—other than the obvious one that she was pregnant with his child. He'd assumed that should be enough, but if he'd learned anything in his four-year marriage it was that women were rarely practical when it came to matters of the heart.

With the same determination he'd brought to re-building the lodge, he decided to take on the project of wooing back his ex-wife.

Soon, however, his grin faded. He set the pen down on the registration desk and wiped a hand across his suddenly damp brow.

Karen wanted to be wooed. How the hell was he supposed to do that?

"WHAT DO YOU THINK?" Lanni asked, studying Karen as her friend turned to the last page. This was agony, and Lanni chewed her lower lip, anticipating Karen's reaction to her latest article.

Charles had read the piece and raved about it, but Charles was her husband and, crazy as she was about him, she doubted he was a good judge of her work. According to him, she was simply brilliant. Although she loved him for believing that, she needed a less biased opinion.

Karen, on the other hand, could have been an editor.

Her former sister-in-law sighed and straightened the stack of pages.

"Well?" Lanni asked, barely giving Karen time to breathe. She yanked out the chair and sat across the table from her. "Tell me what you think. You don't need to worry about upsetting me. I just want the truth."

"The truth," Karen repeated. "Lanni, this is a beautifully written piece."

Lanni loved hearing it. "You think so? You really think so?"

"Have you decided where you want to submit it?"

Lanni named a nationwide, glossy travel periodical and waited for Karen to suggest she aim for a regional magazine, instead.

"Sounds like a good idea."

"You think so?" Her vocabulary seemed to be limited to those three words.

"Lanni, you should have more confidence in your talent. This article about Mt. McKinley is one of the best-written and best-researched I've ever read. This past year…" She hesitated. "I'm not sure how to put it, but there's a maturity to your writing that was lacking earlier. I'm sure the apprenticeship program with the Anchorage newspaper helped, but you've acquired more than style or technical skill."

Lanni hung on every word.

"Your work shows a new…depth."

Loving Charles had done that for her; Lanni was convinced of it. Their love, their marriage, had changed her view of life, deepened her understanding of people, given her a greater sympathy and tolerance. Charles had also helped her develop a more profound appreciation for the land.

They'd waited eight months, until she was finished the apprenticeship program, before they'd married. If it had been her decision she would have married Charles last Christmas, but he'd been the one to insist they hold off until she'd fulfilled her obligation to the paper. He'd worried about the fact that he was ten years older, and it was almost as if he expected her to change her mind. But not once had she doubted that she was meant to be with Charles O'Halloran. Nor did she doubt his love.

For years their two families had hated each other. Catherine Fletcher, Lanni's grandmother, had brought nothing but pain into the O'Hallorans' lives. David O'Halloran, Charles's father, was the only man her grandmother had ever loved. Yet Catherine had done all she could to hurt him, because he'd hurt her. Wrongs had been committed on both sides.

David and Catherine were both dead now. Lanni was sure they'd approve of her marriage and the reconciliation it had brought. Despite the animosity between their families, she and Charles had fallen in love. In some ways, she believed they were soul mates, meant for each other. It sounded fanciful, but she'd come to think they'd been given this one opportunity to make up for the wrongs of the past.

"There're a couple of typos," Karen murmured, flipping through the pages. She pointed them out, then swallowed the last of her cold drink. "I wish I could put my finger on what's changed in your writing."

Lanni smiled to herself. She didn't need Karen to tell her. She already knew.

MATT SLID onto a stool in the Hard Luck Café. Anyone who needed advice sought out Ben Hamilton. Although he'd never been married most people thought of him as something of an expert when it came to relationships.

"Coffee?" Ben asked, gesturing with the pot.

"No, thanks. I came in for a little advice." Matt wanted to get straight to the point.

"You're not going to order anything?"

"No, I wanted to ask—"

"Listen, advice is no longer free," Ben said. "You sit back and chow down on a piece of my homemade applepie, and then I'll tell you whatever it is you want to know."

"I'm not hungry," Matt objected. He'd never known Ben to push food on anyone. "Business slow or something?"

"All these women in town aren't exactly helping, you know? Every one of them's got a kitchen, and if they haven't already got a family to cook for, they're inviting the men in town to dinner. Business is down twenty percent from a year ago."

It looked like Matt was going to be the one with the sympathetic ear.

"So that's what the frequent-eater program's all about?"

"Exactly."

Matt understood Ben's concern, and he did want to support the Hard Luck Café. "All right, give me a cup of coffee." He was desperate enough to pay for coffee he didn't want if Ben could help him win over Karen.

Ben nodded, obviously pleased. He filled Matt's cup, then pressed his hands against the counter. "What can I do for you?"

"It's about Karen."

Ben's mouth quivered with the telltale signs of a smile. "Goes without saying."

Once more Matt was as direct as possible. "She wants to be, uh, *wooed*."

"Wooed," Ben repeated as though he'd never heard the word before. "What exactly does that mean?"

Matt hadn't considered that Ben wouldn't know. It would be a damn shame to waste a couple of bucks on a cup of brew if Ben wasn't going to help him. "Why the hell do you think I'm asking you?"

The door opened and Sawyer O'Halloran walked in.

"Sawyer," Ben called out, looking relieved. "You got a minute?"

"Sure." Sawyer perched on the stool next to Matt's.

"Matt, here, has a problem. Maybe you could help."

"Be glad to do anything I can," he said, righting his mug.

"Karen wants to be wooed," Matt told him.

"Any ideas?" Ben asked the pilot.

Sawyer frowned as he took his first sip of coffee. "You're asking the wrong fellow. I know what the word means, in a general way, but how to go about it is another question."

"You convinced Abbey to marry you," Ben reminded him.

"Sure, but it wasn't easy."

"How'd you do it?" Matt asked. True, he'd been married himself, married to Karen, but they were both young then. He didn't remember that he'd done anything special. She'd apparently thought marriage was a good idea, and he'd gone along with it. God knew he loved her. There hadn't been any talk of this wooing business; it sure hadn't been the problem it was now.

"First I didn't realize I was in love with Abbey," Sawyer confessed. "All I knew was I didn't like any of the other men bugging her. When I heard Pete Livengood had proposed I went ballistic."

"Pete's married to Dotty," Matt said, confused.

"That was before Dotty arrived," Ben explained.

"Okay, so Pete proposed to Abbey."

"It made me damn mad," Sawyer muttered. "I told myself that Christian and I had brought these women up to Hard Luck and it had cost us a lot of money. I sure as hell hadn't gone through all that trouble and expense so the local grocer, twenty years Abbey's senior, could steal her away.''

"So what'd you do?" Matt asked.

"I did the only logical thing I could think of. I told her if she was that desperate to find a husband, I'd marry her myself.''

Wow, maybe this'll be easier than I assumed, Matt thought. "Great idea. And that worked?"

Ben chuckled. "It worked so good the next thing I heard, Abbey had packed her bags and was scheduled to leave on the first flight out of here.''

"You're joking." Matt could see they weren't. "So what'd you do next?''

Sawyer held his mug with both hands and frowned. "What could I do? I begged.''

"Begged?" Matt figured he'd already tried that and it hadn't worked.

"I'd never been lower in my life. If there'd been any bridges around here, I might have jumped," Sawyer said, chuckling. "One thing I knew for sure—if Abbey left I wouldn't be worth a damn. I loved her and Scott and Susan.''

"What did you say that convinced her?"

Sawyer mulled that over, then shook his head. "Hell if I know. I was just so grateful she agreed to marry me I never asked.''

The door opened again and ten-year-old Scott O'Halloran flew into the café.

"Don't be bringing that dog in here," Ben warned.

Scott said something to Eagle Catcher, who stopped abruptly, tail drooping between his legs, and turned around. With a backward glance he ambled out the door.

"I swear that husky understands English," Matt said.

"I'll only be a minute," Scott told the dog. He hurried to the counter and slapped down a dollar bill. "Have you got any of those ice-cream bars left, Ben?"

"Sure do." Ben turned and headed for the freezer in the kitchen.

"So Karen wants to be wooed," Sawyer said to Matt. "She wants to be courted."

Wooed. Courted. Whatever you called it, Matt still didn't have any clearer idea of what she was seeking than before he'd asked his friends. He knew the results he was after; he understood the general strategy, but he just didn't have any specific plans.

"That's a good idea," Scott murmured absently.

"What is?" Matt asked the boy.

"Courting Karen. I wish she would marry you again, because then Angie or Davey would have someone to play with after they're born."

"Those are the names Abbey, the kids and I've got picked out for the baby," Sawyer explained. "You might listen to Scott—he offered me some valuable advice when I needed it with Abbey.

"Really?" Matt said eagerly. He didn't believe a ten-year-old kid could supply him with the answer three adult men couldn't. "So you think it's a good idea for me to court my ex-wife?"

Ben returned with the ice-cream bar. Scott regarded the others suspiciously. "Yeah," he said as if he thought this might be a trick question.

"Got any ideas how a man's supposed to go about

that?'' Ben asked Scott, leaning halfway over the counter.

"Well," Scott said, clearing his throat, "he could flatter her."

The three men exchanged glances. "That sounds like a good idea," Ben said.

"Yeah. Tell her…tell her that her eyes are as brown as a bear's winter coat," Sawyer suggested.

"She's got blue eyes," Matt said.

"Blue…blue…" Sawyer repeated in an apparent effort to find something to compare to her blue eyes. He must have said the word ten times before he stopped, defeated. "Anyone else got any ideas? I'm not exactly a poet, you know."

Matt had already figured that out for himself.

"Be affectionate," Scott suggested next.

The three leapt on that like hungry wolves over fresh kill. Matt was the first one to realize it wouldn't work.

"But…Karen's already pregnant," he babbled. Good grief, he can't get any more affectionate than that.

"True," Sawyer agreed.

"What about flowers?" Ben threw out. "Women are supposed to be crazy about getting flowers."

Matt had already thought of that himself. First he didn't have the money for such extravagance. And second, "Why would she want flowers when the tundra's in full bloom?"

"Maybe you should pick her some," Ben said.

Matt dismissed the idea with a sharp shake of his head. "I've got better things to do than traipse around there looking for tulips."

"There aren't any tulips on the tundra," Sawyer told him.

"I know that!" Matt snapped, losing patience. He glanced at Scott again. "Got any other ideas?"

The kid was busy eating his ice-cream bar, and Matt could tell from the way Scott kept looking over his shoulder that he was eager to be back outside with his dog. "Romance her," he said tersely.

"Romance," Matt echoed. That was what he'd thought this entire conversation had been about in the first place.

"Can I go now?" Scott asked him.

"You can go." Matt removed the dollar bill from the counter and handed it back to the boy. "Put that on my tab, Ben," he instructed. "Thanks for your help, Scott."

The boy was gone in a flash.

"Just a minute!" Sawyer leapt off his stool. "Man, why didn't I think of this sooner? I've got the perfect solution for you."

Matt was paying attention now. "You do?"

"Hot damn, I can't believe I didn't think of this sooner." Sawyer paced the floor, threading his way between the tables. He slapped his hand against his thigh. "One of the most romantic things Abbey and I ever did was fly out to Abbey Lake."

"Abbey Lake."

"Yeah, I named it after her. She got a real kick out of that."

"I don't own any lakes to name after Karen." Matt was losing confidence again. Unlike him, the O'Hallorans owned a lot of land in these parts and could easily afford to name lakes after the women in their lives. Besides, land wasn't available to the every-day citizen the way it used to be, before statehood.

Sawyer gave an exasperated sigh. "I'm not saying

you should name a lake after Karen. I'm saying you should take her into the wilderness with you.''

"Fishing?"

"Why not?" Sawyer asked.

"Yeah," Ben echoed, "why not?"

Matt couldn't think of a reason not to do it. "You seriously think she'd like that?"

"Abbey thought it was great fun. I flew her and the kids out to the lake. Must have been a little more than a year ago now," Sawyer continued. "It was one of those really hot summer days we get now and then."

"Had quite a hot spell last year about this time," Ben commented. "That was when I served sweet-and-sour meatballs with pineapple for dinner one night. Sort of my salute-to-the-tropics night. John Henderson ate two platefuls." Ben grinned proudly. "I had those little umbrellas sticking out of the meatballs. They looked real festive."

"Go on," Matt encouraged Sawyer, afraid that Ben might have distracted him.

"I remember it was one of the first times I ever kissed Abbey. The kids were there having a great time in the water." His eyes grew warm with the memory. "That was when I realized how much I liked being with her."

"You must have if you were kissing her," Ben muttered. He reached for the coffee and topped up their mugs.

Still, Matt was skeptical. "I'm not so sure if Karen's the outdoor type."

"You think Abbey is?" Sawyer asked.

Sawyer had a point. The idea started to build in Matt's mind. The two of them out in the Alaskan tundra. Alone... It led to all kinds of interesting possibilities.

"Tell her if she's going to be answering the phone at the lodge she should have fishing and camping experience herself," Ben counseled. "That way she can answer the travel agents' questions."

Matt nibbled his bottom lip. "That sounds plausible."

"Then take her out there the same way you would any tourist."

Well, yes, except that they'd share a tent. And a couple would zip their sleeping bags together. Oh, yes, the thought of them crowded in a two-man tent held plenty of appeal. Karen curled up against him in a double sleeping bag would be heaven after the frustrating nights he'd spent tossing and turning in his huge bed.

"You might have hit on something here," he murmured.

"Give it a try," Ben said, looking pleased with the outcome of their conversation. "I'd say let her do the cooking, though."

"But I generally do all that myself," Matt explained. When people paid him a thousand dollars or more for the Alaska fishing experience, they didn't expect to have to fry up their own dinners.

"Women are really particular when it comes to that sort of thing," Ben explained. "They like to do their own cooking."

It had proved true so far, Matt thought. Karen had done all the cooking unless they had guests, in which case he took over.

"I think you might be right." Matt eased himself off the stool. "Thanks for everything."

"No problem," Ben and Sawyer said together as Matt left the café.

"DID YOU GET everything settled with Matt?" Scott asked Sawyer over dinner that evening.

"Settled?" Abbey looked from her husband to her son.

Scott stabbed his fork into the soft, pink flesh of fresh salmon. "Dad was advising Matt Caldwell about how to romance Karen."

"Sawyer was giving Matt advice? On romance?" Abbey wasn't sure what to think.

Sawyer grinned from ear to ear. "Yup. The poor guy came into Ben's all down in the mouth. No idea how to get back his ex-wife."

"And you told him?" This should be interesting.

"Yup." Sawyer made an exaggerated display of polishing his fingernails against the flannel sleeve of his shirt.

"You?" Abbey almost choked holding back a giggle.

"And Ben," Sawyer added defensively.

"They asked me a bunch of questions, too," Scott informed her.

"They asked you?" This was getting better by the minute.

Scott nodded.

"And what did you tell these three great romantics?" she asked her son. It took considerable restraint to keep the laughter out of her voice. Although she was deeply in love with Sawyer, the man knew as much about romance as she did about flying a plane. To his credit he tried, but she'd had to coax him every step of the way.

"I told Matt he should be affectionate," Scott said.

Sawyer frowned and with an air of superiority said, "Well, Scott, to my way of thinking, affection is something you give a dog. Women require a whole lot more."

"Is that right?" Abbey asked, and took a bite of her dinner in an effort to hide her smile. "What else?"

Scott's eyes narrowed as he concentrated. "Um, I told Matt to flatter Karen. Tell her how pretty she is and that kind of stuff."

"That's good."

"You think so?" Sawyer looked surprised. "We had a problem with that one."

"Oh?" This didn't come as a surprise to Abbey.

"Karen's got blue eyes and we couldn't think of something poetic to compare her eyes to."

"What about the sky?" Susan suggested, joining in the conversation.

"The sky," Sawyer repeated, pointing his fork at the eight-year-old. "I'll have to remember to tell Matt about that one."

Abbey rolled her eyes. "Just what did you three masters of romance finally suggest?"

Sawyer set aside his fork and planted his elbows on the table. He leaned forward as if he was about to share a wonderful secret.

"We're all ears," Abbey told her husband.

Sawyer spoke to the children. "Remember the time I took you and your mother to Abbey Lake?"

Both children nodded enthusiastically.

Sawyer beamed. "That's it."

"You mean you suggested Matt take Karen swimming?" Abbey remembered how cold the water had been, and the water fight that had ensued.

"Not swimming exactly," Sawyer said.

Abbey studied him expectantly.

"I thought the most romantic thing he could do was take Karen camping."

"Camping?" Abbey exploded.

"And fishing. Ben made a point of telling him he should let Karen do all the cooking, too. Women feel real proprietorial about those sorts of things," he added as though he was an expert on the subject.

"Oh, Sawyer," Abbey groaned, closing her eyes.

"Yup," he boasted. "That's what romance is all about. Taking a woman into the wilds, letting her share the wilderness experience."

Abbey buried her face in her hands.

"Great idea, don't you think?"

Abbey slowly shook her head. "Where, oh, where did I go wrong?"

CHAPTER SEVEN

"YOU KNOW WHAT I was just thinking?" Karen said over dinner. She studied Matt, who sat across the round oak table from her. Without guests, it made sense for them to dine in the kitchen, something they'd done all week.

Matt's look was absent, and he seemed absorbed in his own thoughts.

"Matt?"

"Sorry," he said, glancing up.

"I went over your books this afternoon." Karen half expected him to complain that his finances were none of her affair, and he'd be right. The lodge was his business, not hers.

"Did I make a mistake, mark the debits as credits?" he joked.

Matt would never make such an error, not after the months of training he'd received while working for one of Anchorage's largest accounting firms. "No, of course not."

The fact was, Matt was far more qualified than she to handle the books.

"I'm surprised at how well you're doing financially."

"It looks promising, doesn't it?" According to his reservation list, the dogsledding tours were booked solid. He'd collected a nonrefundable advance fee from each client. Karen was impressed with the way he'd handled the lodge's finances.

"You might think about hiring someone to help you this winter."

"Really?" Her suggestion appeared to surprise him. "You mean other than house-keeping?"

"Eventually you'll need some help in the kitchen and a couple more maids," Karen said. "And I was thinking you might want someone to pinch-hit for you with the winter tours." Since the baby was due in January, shortly before the first tour was scheduled, Karen was beginning to worry that Matt would be too busy to be with her. Although he'd arranged for professional mushers to train, supply and escort the participants, he'd be on the trail himself, hauling food, tents and other essentials. He'd be the one setting up camp each evening, cooking the meals, getting everything ready for the arrival of the dog teams.

"Why would I want to hire anyone just yet?"

Karen studied her stir-fry and pushed the green pea pods around her plate. How could the man not realize that the dates of his winter tours conflicted with her due date? She wanted Matt with her when the baby was born, but more than that, she wanted him to *want* to be with her. However, it wasn't something she would ask of him.

"No reason," she murmured, doing her best to hide her disappointment. "Looking over your ledgers, I thought you'd be able to afford to take on a couple of extra employees."

"I don't see why," he said without elaborating.

"Oh." Her appetite gone, Karen carried her plate to the sink. She stood with her back to him, collecting her composure.

Karen had done everything she could think of to push Matt out of her life. It shouldn't surprise her that he planned not to be available when she needed him. Maybe she should let him know how she felt, but the words stuck like a fish bone trapped in her throat.

"You sound disappointed," Matt said.

"No, no, the lodge is your business. It was a suggestion, that's all. Don't worry about it."

Later that evening, Karen was sitting on the porch knitting a blanket for the baby when Matt eased himself into the chair next to hers.

"I've been doing some thinking," he said.

"About what?" The knitting needles made soft clicking noises, and she jerked the string to unravel the soft pastel-green yarn.

"You've been taking a few phone reservations for the fishing tours lately."

"Yes." It surprised Karen how many people booked their vacations a year or more in advance. If the orders coming in for the following summer were any indication of what was to follow, Matt would be sold out before the end of the current year. She'd had no idea that people would be willing spend this kind of money to catch a few measly fish.

"I, uh, suspect there's been the occasional question you couldn't answer." He knew that to be true. More than once, she'd had to write down questions, ask Matt for the answers and then phone back.

"Yes," she said.

"It seems to me you'd be able to deal with that type of question better if you'd gone out on a fishing trip yourself."

"You want me to fly hundreds of miles from here

to fish and camp so I can answer travel agents' questions?'' That seemed a little extreme to her.

"Sure," Matt replied as though this made perfect sense to him. "You'll love it."

"We'll camp...in a *tent?*" Perhaps there was some other accommodation he hadn't told her about.

"It's the only way to go," Matt said, looking delighted with the idea.

"We'll cook over a camp stove?"

"You've never had better-tasting meals."

Karen didn't quite believe that.

"Come on, sweetheart, what do you say?"

She looked at him in shock. They'd been married four years and he apparently hadn't noticed she wasn't the camping type. She opened her mouth to tell him exactly what she thought, then stopped herself.

Matt was right. This was exactly the sort of thing she should do.

"If you agree we can leave in the morning," Matt coaxed, his eyes twinkling.

"Will we be gone one night or two?"

"Whatever you want."

"One night... You're sure you want to do this?" Karen didn't want to be difficult, but she did enjoy the more basic comforts.

"Of course I'm sure," Matt said, sounding a bit surprised. "We'll have a wonderful time, just you wait and see."

Karen would have been more than willing to wait. But she wanted to support Matt, and if that meant traipsing around the tundra, then she'd prove what a good sport she was by doing it.

MARIAH DOUGLAS waited for the paper to come out of the printer, then reread the letter she'd composed on Sawyer's behalf.

The phone rang and she reached for the receiver. "Midnight Sons. This is Mariah speaking. How may I help you?" The static on the line told her it was a long-distance call.

"Mariah?"

"Tracy!"

She was thrilled to hear from Tracy Santiago. They'd become good friends and corresponded regularly. Tracy was the Seattle attorney Mariah's family had hired when they'd learned she'd accepted the position with Midnight Sons.

At the time there'd been a lot of publicity, some positive and some negative, about the O'Hallorans "luring" women north.

Although Mariah had repeatedly reassured her parents that everything was fine, they'd insisted on having the O'Hallorans investigated. They'd hired Tracy to fly up and check everything out. The attorney had asked a lot of questions, which made some people uneasy, and she'd inadvertently stirred up bad feelings. Mariah didn't blame her; Tracy was only doing her job.

Unfortunately Mariah had already started out on the wrong foot with one of her bosses—Christian O'Halloran. When Tracy showed up, the youngest O'Halloran brother held Mariah personally responsible and labeled her a troublemaker. From that day forward, he'd actively looked for an excuse to fire her. Mariah was certain she would've been laid off long before now if it hadn't been for Charles and Sawyer.

From that rocky beginning, things had quickly deteriorated. Lately her relationship with Christian was worse than usual. The incident at the wedding—when he'd spilled punch on himself—hadn't helped. He hadn't actually said so, but she knew he blamed her.

"I'm calling in an official capacity," Tracy explained. "It's been a year now, and your commitment to Midnight Sons is over."

"Yes, I know."

"Will you be moving back to Seattle?"

Mariah's family had probably put Tracy up to this. She didn't even consider the suggestion. In the past twelve months, she'd come to love Alaska and Hard Luck. For the first time in her life, she was out from under her family's dominance. She made her own decisions—and, consequently, her own mistakes.

"I'm staying right here," Mariah said.

"You're happy, then?" Tracy asked, sounding unsurprised, perhaps even a bit wistful.

"Very happy."

"What about the other women?"

"So far, everything's worked out just great. Mitch and Bethany were married this summer."

The door swung open, and Duke Porter walked into the mobile office. Mariah's gaze followed the bush pilot. She didn't know what it was about Tracy and Duke, but those two definitely rubbed each other the wrong way. Mariah had watched the sparks flash whenever they were together—and yet they each seemed to gravitate toward the other. It was an interesting phenomenon.

Personally Mariah liked Duke. True, he was a bit of a chauvinist, but a lot of what he said was simply for show. Or provocation. He'd toss out the most ridiculous comments just to rile everyone, then sit back and look pleased with himself. Tracy's problem was that she'd taken Duke at his word.

"I don't know if you remember Matt," Mariah said conversationally. "He's the one who bought the old lodge from the O'Hallorans. It's in full operation now, and his ex-wife, Karen, is back with him. Oh, and Abbey's pregnant. Karen, too. So how's everything with you, Tracy?" She purposely used the other woman's name, expecting a reaction from Duke.

He didn't disappoint her. No sooner had the lawyer's name left her lips when Duke wheeled around. "Is that highfalutin lawyer bugging you again?" he demanded.

"Just a minute, Tracy," Mariah said and held her hand over the mouthpiece. "Did you say something, Duke?"

"Is that Tracy Santiago?" he asked.

"Yes." Mariah nearly laughed out loud at the way fire seemed to ignite in Duke's eyes. Tracy was probably the only woman to ever challenge the laughable things Duke said and did. He didn't much like it.

Mariah always got a chuckle out of Duke's heated response to the lawyer. In fact, everyone laughed, but nevertheless, Mariah sensed that Duke and Tracy could be good friends if they'd only put their differences aside.

"What's she want?" Duke demanded.

"To talk to me," Mariah informed him sweetly, turning her back to him. "I'm here," she told Tracy.

Duke strolled purposely over to Mariah's desk in a blatant effort to catch what he could of the conversation. He didn't bother to hide his eavesdropping.

"Is that Duke Porter I hear?" Tracy's usually controlled voice went chilly.

"If you two ever made the effort, you might be friends," Mariah said to them both.

"I'd rather be friends with a skunk," Duke said loudly enough to be heard in Fairbanks.

"You tell Mr. Chauvinist I'd rather clean fish than have anything to do with him," Tracy snapped.

"Does she have a reason for calling or is she just hoping to stir up more trouble?" Duke asked, making sure Tracy heard that, as well.

"Mariah, listen, this doesn't sound like a good time for us to talk. Why don't you give me a call if you need anything." Tracy hesitated. "You know, I've come to think of you and the other women as my friends."

"You *are* a friend," Mariah assured her.

"With a friend like that, who needs—"

"Duke, enough," Mariah said, glaring at him.

"All right, all right," he muttered as he moved away from her desk.

"You'll keep in touch?" Tracy asked.

"Of course," Mariah promised. "Thanks for calling, Trace. It was good to hear from you."

She was about to replace the receiver when Tracy giggled and said, "Mariah?"

"Yeah?"

"Is Duke still there?"

"Yup."

Tracy giggled again. "Do something for me, would you?"

"Sure."

"Walk over to him and kiss him and tell him it's from me. Then ask if I'm still his favorite feminist."

Mariah grinned. "You're sure you want me to do this?"

"Positive. I just wish I could be there to see the look on his face when you tell him that kiss is from me."

"You got it," Mariah said, and she hung up the phone.

Duke studied her quizzically. "What was it she wanted this time?"

Mariah rolled back her chair. Her eyes on his, she stood and slowly made her way toward him. He was obviously uncomfortable with the way she'd focused her attention on him.

"Mariah?" Duke glanced around, then started moving backward as she continued her approach. He cleared his throat and glanced both ways. "What's the matter with you? You look like something out of *The Exorcist*."

"Tracy asked me to give you something," she said, making her voice low and sultry.

When Duke was backed right up to the wall, Mariah braced her hands on both sides of his face. Duke's eyes widened, and he opened his mouth to speak. He didn't get a chance.

Angling her head, Mariah planted her mouth firmly over his.

Duke squirmed.

Mariah heard the door open, but paid it no heed.

"Mariah!" Christian yelped. "Duke! What the hell is going on here?"

"YOU DIDN'T TELL ME my feet were going to get wet," Karen complained as they trudged along the marshy banks of the lake. Sawyer had delivered them by float plane to the same prime fishing area Matt brought his clients. The plane had taxied as close to the shore as possible, but they'd had to walk the rest of the way in. Through the water. No one had bothered to tell her this, Karen thought with some bitterness.

Something bit her and Karen slapped her neck. The mosquitoes swarming about her face were evidently thrilled with her arrival. Already she had two huge swellings on her neck. She'd be lucky to get out of this place whole at the rate the bugs were dining.

"If your feet are wet you'd better put on a fresh pair of shoes," Matt said after he finished unloading their supplies.

"I only have the one pair. You told me to pack light, remember?" If Sawyer was late picking them up the following afternoon, Karen swore she'd kill him. Her enthusiasm for this undertaking had never been high. The little interest she did feel was vanishing quickly.

"We'll make camp by that cluster of trees," Matt told her, pointing into the far distance. "The river's directly behind there."

Karen drew a deep breath as she remembered Lanni's adventure with the brown bear when she'd taken Abbey's children out to gather wildflowers on the tundra. Scott had delighted in telling Karen how he was sure they were about to become "dead meat" that afternoon.

Matt had tried to reassure her about bears, but she wasn't taking any chances. She'd had Mitch Harris teach her how to shoot off the can of pepper spray herself. Karen gave a heartfelt sigh. Matt seemed to believe this trek in the wilds would be one grand adventure. He'd talked excitedly about the wildlife they might see, mentioning moose, caribou, Dall sheep and wolves. Then he'd blithely told her she didn't have a thing to worry about.

"Why do mosquitoes love me so much?" she grumbled, although she didn't really expect an answer.

"You'd think they were holding a dinner party and I was the main course."

"They're always more of a problem by the water," he reminded her.

Karen's feet made squishy sounds with every step she took. Matt might have advised her about adding an extra pair of shoes to her pack, she thought again—but she didn't want to be a complainer.

He was trying to make this a positive experience for her, and she felt guilty every time she found something else to gripe about. Unfortunately a camping-and-fishing trip wasn't even close to anything she considered fun. If Matt and his buddies enjoyed this kind of stuff, fine. Just leave her out of it.

"I brought along a bottle of wine," he said.

Good, Karen muttered to herself, she could use it for medicinal purposes; maybe dabbing it on her mosquito bites would relieve the itch. Had Matt forgotten she was pregnant and therefore wasn't drinking?

It seemed they'd been walking for miles, but in actuality, she realized, it couldn't have been more than a few hundred yards.

Matt slid the large backpack from his shoulder and set it on the ground. "We'll make camp here." Quickly and efficiently, he began to unpack.

He'd carried almost everything, and feeling equal parts guilt and exhaustion, Karen leaned against a large boulder and simply watched him.

"First I'll pitch the tent and then we'll do some fishing."

"What about dinner?" She was already hungry. It must have something to do with running around in the great outdoors, breathing fresh air. But then, you couldn't find air any purer than what she'd been breathing in good ol' Hard Luck. It seemed a crying shame to travel hundreds of miles north when the air at home was just as fresh and unpolluted. Besides, she could feel a cold coming on and would have preferred the comfort of her own surroundings. The truth was, she wouldn't mind crawling into bed right this minute. A *real* bed. *Her* bed.

"Dinner?" Matt said, his eyes twinkling with mischief. "That's why we're doing the fishing first."

Karen groaned. He honestly expected her to catch her own dinner. A crucial question occurred to her. Namely, what would she do if she struck out—did no fish mean no dinner? This was the first time she'd ever fished. Surely she should've taken lessons, gone to summer camp, something like that.

She felt decidedly annoyed that her very own ex-husband would assume she knew anything about this camping and fishing business when she'd never so much as baited a hook.

"It won't take me long to set up camp," he said, removing a few more things from the huge backpack.

Karen was astonished that he could carry everything they'd need for the night in that contraption. And she was impressed at how easily he assembled the small tent. Before she knew it, Matt stood in front of her, holding two fishing poles. "Ready?"

She wasn't. The new millennium could arrive, and she had the feeling she wouldn't be ready then, either. "I guess so," she said, forcing some enthusiasm into her voice.

It took effort to ease herself away from the rock.

Matt offered her his hand.

"I'm not good at this kind of thing," she muttered,

slapping at another mosquito. Then she sneezed. Twice.

Matt led her to the river, whose rushing water emptied into the lake, and in no time Karen had a fishing pole in her hand. However, she soon learned that whatever it was that attracted fish—and she refused to believe it was the offensive-smelling egg at the end of her hook—she lacked it.

Clearly Matt didn't suffer the same affliction. He cast his line into the water and almost immediately got his first bite. He'd brought in two fish, one after the other, and all Karen had caught was a cold.

She sneezed once more and rubbed her nose with her sleeve.

Matt stood in the middle of the river—or "stream," as he called it—wearing rubber hip boots. Water swirled around him like a witch's caldron. He held his fishing pole in one hand and fed the line with the other. He glanced over at her and smiled in perfect contentment.

"It doesn't get any better than this!" He shouted over the sound of the surging water.

"You mean it gets worse?" she shouted back. Matt laughed; he seemed to think she was joking, but she was serious. Dead serious.

Uneasy about walking into the middle of a river, despite the protection of the hip boots Matt had given her, Karen remained close to shore, feeding her line into the clear, tumbling water. She'd about given up hope of snagging one of the rainbow trout that seemed to migrate toward Matt's line when she felt something nibble at her bait. She actually *felt* the fish nibble. Her eyes lit up, and she gasped with excitement.

"Matt." She didn't dare shout for fear of alerting

the fish that it was about to become their main course. Matt didn't respond, so she raised her arm above her head and waved.

At that precise moment, the fish decided to take the bait and the fishing pole shot out of her hand.

"Matt!" she screamed, alerting him to what had happened.

"Grab that pole," he yelled, wading toward her, his eyes filled with panic. His expression told her she was replaceable, but the reel and rod were not.

Karen didn't have any choice but to go splashing into the fast-rushing stream after the rod. It would have been lost if the reel hadn't caught between two rocks. She just managed to rescue it, but lost her fish.

By the time she made her way back to shore, she was drenched.

Matt reached her side and jerked the pole away from her. "I thought I explained that this is expensive equipment! I can't afford to lose a rod and reel, so hold on to it, will you?"

She looked up at him and blinked back tears. When she spoke her voice sounded muffled—probably because she was struggling not to cry. Or sneeze. "I had a fish on the line. I...I wanted you to watch me bring it in."

He exhaled sharply, then placed his arm around her shoulders. "I'm sorry, honey. I shouldn't have yelled at you."

Karen sniffled, more than ready to abandon the whole venture, but Matt wouldn't hear of it. Against her will she was standing on the edge of the flowing water less than five minutes later. Sneezing. It seemed to take an eternity to attract another trout.

Soon, however, she experienced the same sense of

exhilaration as a fish nibbled at her bait. This time she was ready when the trout encountered the hook. She gripped the fishing pole with both hands, prepared to catch a trout or die trying.

"That's it, honey!" Matt hollered, his excited voice carried on the wind. "Give the line more slack," he ordered.

Karen had no idea what he was talking about, but she must have done something right, because she didn't lose the fish. The muscles in her arms ached with the strain, but she held on as the fish leapt and fought.

Matt was there to lift her prize out of the water, using the net. "He's a beauty," her ex-husband told her with a proud grin.

"He sure is." Karen gazed at the fish fondly as he flopped around in the net.

Matt deftly removed the hook from the trout's mouth and was about to place it in the basket when Karen stopped him.

"Put him back," she said.

"*Back?*" Matt's eyes held a look that said he must have misunderstood her.

"He's too beautiful to eat. And too brave and noble."

"Karen...you're not serious."

"I mean it, Matt!" she cried. "I don't want him killed." Not after the way he'd struggled to live. Not after she'd looked him in the eye.

Matt did as she asked, but he wasn't pleased.

From that point forward their afternoon went downhill. Karen thought wryly that from her vantage point there was nowhere else for it to go. By dinnertime she was tired, hungry and in no mood to commune with nature. She wanted dinner, a hot bath and her own bed, in that order. No luck on any score, however.

Her contribution to dinner was a disaster. Fortunately, Matt had caught a couple of trout, which he cleaned while Karen prepared the vegetables. She dumped a can of beans into a pot, then sliced some potatoes to fry in a pan. By accident, she charred them. Smoke got in her eyes, blinding her, and she coughed and hacked. When she could actually see the potatoes again, they resembled dried cow chips. And the beans had become a mass of soggy lumps. To her relief, Matt took over then, and handled the frying of the fish. The result was delicious—even though Karen's misery didn't allow her to truly enjoy it.

Even Matt's festive mood had dissipated by the time they crawled into the tent that night. Tired as she was, Karen had assumed she'd immediately fall asleep. That wasn't the case.

For one thing the atmosphere in the tent was... intimate. If she'd understood that they were going to be holed up inside this tiny space together, she would have insisted they bring an additional tent.

"Something smells," she said after a few minutes. Every time she closed her eyes, her nose was assaulted by a repugnant scent. It reminded her of skunk.

"It's your mosquito lotion," Matt suggested.

"No, it isn't."

"It is, Karen. I've been smelling it on you all day."

"Fine." She rolled away from him, presenting him with her back. Just like a man to stink up a place and then claim it was the woman's fault. Anyway, if it *was* the bug repellent, which she doubted, he had it on, too. Maybe not as much as she did, but still...

Ten minutes must have passed before Matt spoke again. "I didn't mean that as an insult," he said gently.

"I know. I'm just tired and cranky." What she wouldn't give for a hot bath and clean sheets...

"You comfortable?" he asked next.

"No." She itched and her back hurt. Matt had placed an air mattress beneath the sleeping bag, but it was a poor substitute for a real bed. The ground was still hard.

Five minutes later she announced, "I've got to go to the bathroom."

"You just went half an hour ago," he reminded her.

"I can't help it. These things happen when a woman's pregnant. You don't need to come—I'm perfectly capable of marking my own territory."

Matt chuckled, but followed her out of the tent nonetheless. When they crept back inside, the smell of the bug repellent wasn't as strong as it'd been earlier. Or maybe she'd just grown used to it.

Matt sprawled out atop the sleeping bag. He lay on his back, hands tucked behind his head.

Karen glanced at him, then released a slow, pent-up sigh and lay back down. She was careful to keep a respectable distance between them.

This wasn't so bad, she decided. It wasn't nearly as comfortable as the lodge, but she'd survive for one night. Barely. As long as they weren't attacked by any wildlife.

"Are you asleep?" Matt asked.

"No."

"Why don't you put your head on my shoulder?"

In other circumstances Karen might have worried that Matt was planning to seduce her. She doubted it now, though, since she wore half a bottle of bug repellent and hadn't bathed. Tentatively she rested her head on his shoulder and closed her eyes.

That felt better. A lot better.

"I'm a disappointment to you, aren't I?" she asked softly.

"No."

"I don't think I'm a good advertisement for the business. If any of the travel agents ask me about the fishing, I guess I can tell them about the one I set free."

Matt ran his hand along her hair. "You're doing okay."

"Well...I do have to confess this isn't my idea of a fun time."

"Really?" Matt seemed surprised.

"I'm sure plenty of women enjoy camping-and-fishing trips, but unfortunately I'm not one of them."

"But I thought—" He bit off the statement.

"What did you think?" she prodded.

He hesitated.

"Matt?"

"I thought...you'd consider this...romantic."

"Romantic?" The man was in need of therapy. Or maybe just a good dictionary.

"You said you wanted to be wooed."

"I do," she said, "but not like this."

Matt pulled away from her, raising himself up on one arm. Karen was unprepared for the sudden movement, and her head hit the hard ground.

"Ouch." Her eyes smarted. She rubbed the back of her head.

"Why isn't this romantic?" Matt demanded.

"You honestly have to ask?" She made a sweeping gesture with one hand. "My feet have developed jungle rot. I've been the main course and every other course

for the entire mosquito population. Then you set me
next to the Hoover Dam and when I nearly lose your
precious rod and reel, you make it clear that the damn
thing's worth more than I am!''

''I'll have you know that reel cost five hundred dollars.''

Karen gasped at the news, but it didn't slow her
down. ''*Then* you insist I cook dinner, probably to pun-
ish me because I had the audacity to set free a beautiful, brave trout who deserved to live.''

''Oh, please.''

''And you call this romantic?'' she sat up, crossing
her arms in a huff. ''I call it torture.''

The silence fell like a landslide between them.

''All right,'' Matt said after an awkward few
minutes. ''We got off to a bad start. I'll do better next
time.''

''Next time?'' There was more?

''You wanted wooing, didn't you?'' He had the
nerve to sound angry. ''And wooing means romance,
right?''

''Right.''

''Then that's what you're getting.''

''Wouldn't it be easier,'' she said between clenched
teeth, ''to torture me on a rack? At this rate I don't
know how much longer I'll survive.''

CHAPTER EIGHT

"JUST LOOK AT ME," Karen told Lanni, holding out her bare arms for inspection. A number of red, swollen mosquito bites marked her pale skin. "The bugs ate me alive."

Lanni walked over to the library table where Abbey kept the newest hardcover releases. She chose a murder mystery Duke Porter had returned earlier that afternoon. "Are you telling me you didn't have a good time?"

Karen shrugged, not sure how to answer her friend, who also happened to be Matt's sister. She realized she was placing Lanni in an uncomfortable position by asking her to side against her own brother.

"I had the experience of a lifetime—and I've never been more miserable." Karen sighed heavily and made a dismissive gesture. "I didn't mean to put you on the spot. It's just that this whole fishing business has left me flustered. And cranky." She sighed again. "Matt seemed to think he was doing me a favor."

Karen began to look through the library books, grateful for an excuse to get away from the lodge. Matt had been sullen and uncommunicative ever since they'd returned. Granted, she hadn't exactly been cheerful herself. She didn't understand how two people who clearly loved each other could find themselves at odds over something as ridiculous as a fishing trip. Matt had been trying to share his vision of the future. And she'd... well, she'd been looking for a way to survive a night in the wilderness.

"It may not have been the vacation of your dreams," Lanni commented, "but now you'll be able to answer any questions the travel agents ask, won't you?"

"I'm convinced that was just a ploy Matt used to get me to come with him," Karen muttered. "His sole purpose in all this was to romance me, if you can believe it."

Abbey returned just then, carrying a tray filled with tea things from the library kitchen. "I'm afraid Sawyer and Ben are to blame for that," she said, setting the tray down on the desk.

"What do those two have to do with this?" Karen wanted to know.

As she poured them each a cup of tea, Abbey said, "Apparently Matt decided to, uh, seek their advice on how to win you back."

"Ben and Sawyer?" Lanni cried. "Why, Ben's never been married!"

"I know," Abbey said, making an effort to conceal a smile and failing. "Frankly Sawyer isn't much better when it comes to being romantic. He tries, but I'm afraid he was a bachelor for far too many years. I planned to warn you, but one thing led to another, and before I realized it you and Matt had already left."

"He dragged me into the wilds in the name of romance." Karen shook her head. How could Matt possibly have believed she'd consider it romantic to traipse around for two days in wet shoes, with mosquitoes, the threat of bears and no hot water?

"I'm crazy in love with Charles," Lanni said, "and

I do happen to like camping. Nothing romantic about it, though. In fact, I can safely say Charles knows as much about romance as Matt. In other words, nothing.''

"What man really does?" Abbey asked as she handed around a plate of homemade cookies to accompany the tea.

Karen shook her head. "I guess I was asking the impossible when I suggested Matt woo me. Instead, he's woed me." She chuckled at her own witticism.

Both of the other women laughed, too.

"When we were first married," Abbey said, "I could see that this romance business was going to be a problem. I love Sawyer so much—he's a good man, a wonderful husband and father. I guess women are more sentimental than men. We occasionally want a symbol or an expression of love. I mean, I want him to realize there are certain dates that are important to me—dates I want him to remember. Not that I expect anything extravagant. The price of the gift isn't important.''

Karen and Lanni nodded in agreement.

"It's the thought that goes into it," Karen added for good measure. "And knowing that he cares enough to make the effort. No woman likes to be taken for granted.''

"Exactly," Abbey said.

"What dates did you give him?" Lanni asked. "That is, if you don't mind my prying.''

"Not at all." Abbey stirred a spoonful of sugar into her tea. "I explained to Sawyer that Valentine Day, my birthday, our anniversary and Christmas were important to me. I asked that he remember me on those days." Her gaze grew soft and warm. "He said there wasn't a chance on this green earth that he'd forget me any day of his life—which was sweet, but not the point.''

"How'd you clue him in on buying you a gift?" Karen asked.

"Actually Scott was the one who told him that when I said I wanted to be remembered I was really saying he should buy me something."

"What did Sawyer say to that?"

Abbey grinned. "He took out a pen and a piece of paper and wrote down all the dates, then tucked it in his wallet."

"So, has he remembered?" Lanni asked eagerly. "You know, this is good advice."

"Yeah, he has." Abbey grinned widely. "He's never had to buy a woman presents before—apart from his mother—so he generally seeks advice from the kids."

"Scott and Susan?" Karen couldn't suppress a laugh.

"I know. At least my husband had the sense to realize I wouldn't be interested in Barbie's Playhouse or a new computer game. For my birthday this year he bought me a cookbook about homemade bread."

"Not bad," Karen said, impressed. She recalled that for her birthday the last year she and Matt were married, he'd bought her a lens for his camera.

"It *was* a thoughtful gesture," Abbey agreed, "but he had an ulterior motive. He was mostly interested in having fresh-baked bread," Abbey explained. "Like his mother used to make."

"What did he give you on Valentine Day?" Lanni asked.

Abbey sipped from her tea. "He wasn't very imaginative. He bought me a box of chocolates and then promptly picked out his favorites.''

"Matt mailed me a card for Valentine Day,'' Karen murmured, remembering how keenly the simple card had affected her. She'd dug it out of the garbage and kept it, too.

''I know why he did,'' Lanni told her. ''At least I think I do. You sent a Christmas card for Matt last year, along with your gifts to the family, remember?''

Karen wasn't likely to forget. She'd agonized over that card. She hadn't wanted to ignore him, but at the same time, she didn't feel it would be a good idea to encourage him to think there was any possibility of a reconciliation. He'd never mentioned the card, or said anything about the note she'd sent with it. She wondered if he'd kept it, the way she had his valentine message.

The valentine card was meant to be a reminder that he still loved her and wanted her with him, she suspected. It had come when she was most vulnerable, when she'd been trying her hardest to put Matt and their marriage behind her. As if she could *ever* forget Matt, no matter how hard she tried.

''What's going to happen between you and my brother?'' Lanni asked, her expression serious. ''Will you really go back to California after the baby's born?''

Karen didn't know how to answer that. ''I don't know... I want us to make a new start together. Heaven knows I love him enough, but we still have some things to work out.''

''He's trying,'' Lanni reminded her.

Karen scratched at the mosquito bites on her arms. ''I'm afraid if he tries any harder it'll do me in.''

CHARLES WAS READING a scientific journal when he heard someone on the porch. Setting aside the magazine, he walked into the living room, half expecting Lanni's return from the library.

To his surprise his visitor was his youngest brother. "Well, hello, Christian. Come on in."

"Thanks." Christian stepped inside and glanced around. "Where's Lanni?"

"Over at the library."

Christian seemed relieved. "I hope I'm not disturbing you," he said, with an uneasiness that wasn't like him.

"Not at all. Can I get you anything?"

"Yeah," Christian said stiffly. "A new secretary."

Charles didn't bother to conceal his impatience. "What's the matter with Mariah?"

"We don't get along," he spat out. He sank onto the sofa. "I don't know what's wrong, but I don't like the woman. Never have."

"What does Sawyer think?"

Christian shrugged. "He doesn't seem to have a problem with her, and since we went to the expense of flying her up to Alaska, he isn't that keen on firing her."

"So you've come to me, hoping I'd talk Sawyer into agreeing with you."

Christian's eyes brightened. "Yes," he blurted, and then shook his head. "No. Hell, I don't know what I want. Yes, I do. I want Mariah out of that office. If she chooses to stay in Hard Luck, fine. As far as I'm concerned, she has as much right to stay here as anyone else."

"What about employment?"

A pained expression came over Christian's face. "Ben's been talking about hiring some help."

"But Mariah's not a waitress."

Christian rubbed a hand along the back of his neck. Charles could tell he'd given the matter thought. "Matt will need to take on an employee or two at some point. Let him deal with her. Just get her out of my sight."

Charles mulled this over, unsure how to respond. "It could be some time before Matt can afford to take on an employee. It wouldn't surprise me if Karen decides to stay after the baby's born. That'll mean extra expenses—and an extra person to help out at the lodge. Karen's already filling a lot of the gaps. Do you honestly think Mariah can afford to wait around till Matt's ready to hire her?"

"No." Christian frowned. "The hell if I know what to do with her. There's got to be somewhere she can go. I wish Sawyer and I could agree on this."

Charles sat on a chair across from his brother, gazing down at his feet. He was reluctant to involve himself in areas like hiring—and firing. Although he was a full partner with his two brothers in Midnight Sons, he was a silent one. Generally he left these types of decisions to Sawyer and Christian.

"Has Mariah made expensive mistakes?" he asked, buying time to consider the situation. Charles couldn't remember ever seeing Christian this flustered. That he'd sought him out for advice said quite a bit.

It took Christian several long moments to answer. "Mistakes," he finally repeated. "She made plenty of those in the beginning, but she seems to manage everything adequately enough now."

If the increase in profits was an indication, the woman had been a godsend, Charles mused. She'd skillfully organized the office and developed a system of rotation for the pilots that they considered fair. That was something Sawyer and Christian had never managed to accomplish. Mariah had even started an advertising program that had attracted new business. But Charles didn't think Christian would appreciate his singing Mariah's praises.

"Her year's up," Christian pointed out. With a deepening scowl, he said, "She's fulfilled her contractual obligation. The property and the cabin are legally hers."

"But you'd prefer it if she left."

"No," Christian muttered, then almost as if he wasn't aware he was speaking, added, "She spilled punch down the front of my suit at Mitch and Bethany's reception."

"The way I heard it you were as much to blame for that as she was."

Christian didn't respond, apparently caught up in his own thoughts. "I've reviewed a number of the applications I took last year, and there's another woman I'd like to invite up here."

"To take Mariah's job?"

"Yes," Christian admitted. "You probably don't remember, but I never intended to hire Mariah. I wanted Allison Reynolds."

"Who?"

"You never met Allison. She flew up and only stayed one night, but she was perfect, Charles. I took one look at her and...well..." He shook his head. "That no longer matters."

"Then how'd you happen to hire Mariah?"

Christian stood and walked around the living room, pausing in front of the fireplace. "As I said, Allison left after a…short stay. I was discouraged, so I reached for the first application on the top of the pile. In retrospect, I'm fairly sure I didn't read it.''

''But you phoned and asked Mariah if she wanted the job?''

''Yeah. I didn't even remember who she was. I can't be expected to recall every person in every interview, can I?''

''No, I suppose not.''

''Mariah's the one responsible for that lawyer snooping around, asking questions.'' Christian seemed to be looking for excuses to get rid of her.

''I know,'' Charles said. But in his opinion, Tracy Santiago had been a blessing in disguise. Without realizing what they were doing, his brothers had set themselves up for trouble with this scheme of theirs. Tracy Santiago had opened their eyes to the legal problems they'd invited with this venture. Luckily, as it turned out, any women who might have created serious difficulties for them had quickly moved on.

''You're sure firing her is what you want?'' Charles asked, sympathetic to both sides. He liked and respected Mariah, but he'd known for a long while that Christian didn't get along with her. He was also aware that it could be damned uncomfortable to work with someone who was a constant source of irritation, for whatever reason.

The intense look in his brother's eyes revealed just how uncomfortable he was. ''I don't know,'' he muttered. ''I just don't know.''

''Can you figure out what it is about Mariah that bothers you so much?'' Charles asked, hoping Christian could come up with a solution of his own.

''That's the crux of the matter,'' Christian confessed.

"When everything's said and done, Mariah's turned out to be a pretty decent secretary. The truth is, I simply don't want to be around her."

His brother was one contradiction after another.

"Never mind," Christian said with a deep sigh. "I have a feeling the problem will take care of itself, anyway."

Now Charles was confused. "What do you mean?"

"I think Duke's going to marry her."

"Duke?"

"Yeah, I found the two of them kissing the other day."

"Duke and Mariah?" Charles couldn't picture it.

"That's what I said," Christian snapped.

"You're sure?"

"I happened on them myself. This isn't hearsay, Charlie. I saw them kissing with my own two eyes."

Charles scratched the side of his head as he struggled to visualize them as a couple. Certainly stranger things had happened. Lanni had fallen in love with him, hadn't she? Heaven knew, she could have had any man she wanted. That she fell in love with him struck Charles even now as nothing short of incredible—but a blessing he wasn't about to question.

"Forget we had this conversation." Christian sounded eager to be on his way. "I suspect I just needed a sounding board and you were handy."

"Fine. I've wiped it from my memory."

"Good." Christian was at the door. "I don't begrudge them happiness, you know."

"Who?"

Christian cast a baffled glance at Charles on his way out the door. "Mariah and Duke. Who else?"

"Right," Charles called after him. He stood in the

open doorway and watched his youngest brother head off down the dirt road. Charles recognized that woebegone look. The first time he'd seen it, Sawyer had it plastered all over his face. Abbey was about to leave Hard Luck and Sawyer was beside himself, wondering how he could persuade her and the kids to stay.

Charles knew he'd worn that look himself the afternoon he discovered Lanni was Catherine Fletcher's granddaughter. It had felt as if his entire world had come crashing down.

Now that same look was in Christian's eyes. Charles chuckled, almost pitying his brother. Christian didn't have a clue what was about to hit him.

MATT STEPPED into the Hard Luck Café and let the screen door slam in his wake. He didn't walk up to the counter the way he usually did, but stared out the window at the airfield. John Henderson was picking up guests for the lodge, two retired college professors, who'd taken the afternoon flight into Fairbanks. John and company were due at Hard Luck within ten minutes.

"You want any coffee?" Ben called from behind the counter.

"No, but I'd like a refund for the last cup."

"A refund? What the hell for? I make the best coffee in town and you know it." Ben sounded insulted.

"The coffee was fine, but the advice stunk."

Ben chuckled, but Matt didn't find this at all amusing. He should have known better than to take advice on romance from a confirmed bachelor. And Sawyer hadn't been much better. Matt didn't know what the hell he'd been thinking; he'd been desperate, he decided. Desperate enough to seek the counsel of two men who were as ignorant in the ways of women as he was himself.

With guests at the lodge, Matt feared his relationship with Karen would become even more strained. He'd genuinely wanted her to enjoy their camping-and-fishing adventure. What he'd hoped, he admitted now, was that she'd be so impressed with him and his operation here she'd throw her arms around his neck, declare how much she loved him and promise never to leave him again.

Instead, they were barely on speaking terms.

Matt's intention had been to romance her, but he'd consider himself fortunate if she didn't pack up and return to California by the end of the week.

"I guess things didn't work out the way you wanted," Ben said.

At least the old coot had the good grace to sound contrite. "You could say that. Now on top of everything else, Karen's furious with me because she got a couple of bug bites and because her feet were wet for two days."

Ben chuckled, and if the situation hadn't been so critical, Matt was sure he would've seen the humor in it himself.

"Did she catch any fish?" Ben asked.

"One." Matt still had trouble believing Karen had set the trout free. Leave it to a woman to assign human characteristics to a fish. Brave and noble. For crying out loud, she was talking about a trout. A trout! Karen looked at this fish and saw a poor, maligned creature of God. Matt looked at the same fish and saw dinner.

If that two-day trek in the wilds was any indication of how their relationship was going, Matt might as well give up now.

"I take it you've got guests flying in."

"A couple of college professors," Matt explained, his thoughts still on Karen. He hadn't seen her since early that morning. He'd gotten everything ready for the evening meal himself, then spent the remainder of the day gathering the necessary supplies for the trip. He'd be away three days this time. He'd venture a guess that Karen would be pleased to have him gone. His biggest fear was that she'd leave before he returned.

He wished he could find a way to settle their differences once and for all, but every attempt he made seemed to backfire.

EARLY THAT EVENING, as the four of them sat down for dinner in the lodge dining room, Matt felt torn. Despite his natural sociability, he would've liked nothing better than to spend a quiet evening with his wife; he wanted a chance to right any wrong he'd unintentionally committed against her.

Unfortunately he found himself reluctantly sitting across the table from the two white-haired professors—likable though they were—and chatting with them. Both men, Donald and Derrick, were in their early sixties and full of vigor. They'd apparently been friends for years and often traveled together. One was married, the other divorced. They talked freely about their lives in a relaxed, companionable way.

Karen was her usual gracious self throughout the meal. She asked a question now and then in that thoughtful way of hers and listened intently to the answer. She was a perfect hostess, making their guests feel interesting, valued, important. It was her gift, one that had touched him from the first moment they'd met.

"I hope Matt had you sign the guest book," Karen said as she passed around the basket of fresh-baked rolls. They were still warm from the oven.

"I had them sign it first thing," Matt answered on their behalf, since both were busy eating.

"I understand this is your first season operating the lodge," Donald, the more animated of the two, said after a moment.

"That's right."

"We're still pretty new at this," Karen added.

"So far, it's been a delightful experience," Derrick said, smiling at Karen. "I must say, Mrs. Caldwell, dinner is delicious."

"Thank you, but I can't accept the credit. Matt's the chef at the lodge."

"The grilled salmon is excellent," Donald told him.

Matt shrugged off the compliment. "Thanks," he said gruffly.

"I'd be interested in knowing your background," Derrick said conversationally. "It seems to me you must be a jack-of-all-trades."

"And a master of none," Matt said, completing the old saying. "Actually that pretty well sizes up the situation. I've dabbled in a number of careers in the past few years."

"When I first met Matt he was a psychology major," Karen explained, avoiding meeting his eyes.

"Did you graduate?" Derrick directed the question to Matt.

"No." If he was uncomfortable with compliments, he was even more uncomfortable discussing the twists and turns his life had taken since college.

"He knows just enough about human nature to make him dangerous," Karen teased affectionately.

Matt couldn't take his eyes off his ex-wife. She looked radiant that evening. He wondered if she was ready to put their differences behind them. He knew *he* was. He hoped that if he got down on his knees and promised never to take her camping again, she'd be willing to forget and forgive. If she wanted romance he'd find some other method of providing it. He didn't know what, but he'd figure it out.

"You're an excellent cook, as well," Donald was saying.

"At one point in my illustrious past I decided I wanted to cook. That was soon after Karen and I were married." He saw no need to mention that they were currently divorced.

"Matt developed a number of excellent recipes and an extensive repertoire," Karen said.

It actually sounded as though Karen was boasting, but Matt was sure he was mistaken. He remembered how furious she'd been the day he'd announced he didn't want to be a chef, after all. When he'd finished his course at a culinary institute, he'd been hired as a sous-chef by a major hotel. The job had allowed for no creative freedom, and after ten months, Matt felt that his inventiveness had been stifled to the point that he could barely stand going into work.

Karen hadn't been pleased when he'd quit, but she'd supported his decision. That was when he'd decided to become a commercial fisherman and had hired on with a fishing vessel. The money was good—no, great—but the dangers were high. Fishing some of the roughest seas in the world was risky, and a number of vessels were lost every year.

"Not exactly," Matt said, and glanced toward Karen. This conversation had become disquieting. The last thing Matt wanted was to have his lack of direction discussed and dissected by his guests. It had always been such a contentious issue between him and Karen. He didn't want her to recite the litany of his failings. Not now when he was struggling to get back into her good graces.

"After leaving cooking school Matt decided to become a commercial fisherman," she announced.

"Where'd you fish?" Once more the question was directed to him.

"The Bering Straits," Matt answered with little enthusiasm. His gaze briefly met Karen's and he realized she was thinking the same thing he was. Those months apart while he'd been at sea had been some of the most difficult in their marriage.

Sure, the money had helped them meet their bills, but it hadn't been worth the strain on their marriage.

"How long did you fish commercially?" Donald asked.

"One season." He didn't elaborate, didn't say that when he'd first gone into the trade he'd dreamed of one day owning his own boat. But then, he'd also fantasized about running his own restaurant.

Although he was sure Karen would deny it, he'd given up fishing for her. She'd worried herself sick the entire time he was at sea, and Matt realized he couldn't do that to her. So he'd left at the end of the season and joined an accounting firm.

"After that Matt worked for an accountant—for a while," Karen said.

"Accounting," Derrick echoed. "My, but you have led a varied life."

"It's interesting to note how everything has pulled together for you now," Donald said thoughtfully. He helped himself to seconds of the salmon and while he was at it reached for another roll.

Matt looked at him curiously.

"You're happy with the lodge?" Donald asked.

"Perfectly happy." Matt said this as much for Karen's benefit as to answer the question.

"Yes, it's all pulled together for you now," Donald repeated. He had everyone's attention.

"How do you mean?" Karen pressed. She made it sound as though Matt couldn't be trusted not to sell the lodge at the drop of a hat. Not that he would've blamed her. He'd certainly given her enough grief with his erratic work history during their marriage.

"You were interested in psychology first, isn't that right?" Donald asked.

"Yes," Matt murmured, wondering how their conversation could have veered so far off course.

"Then cooking school?"

"Yes." Karen was the one to answer this time.

"For which he shows remarkable talent." Another dinner roll disappeared.

"Followed by a stint as a commercial fisherman," Donald went on.

"One season was all," Matt insisted. He'd tried to make that clear in his arguments with Karen. While the fishing had been adventurous and lucrative, it hadn't been a real career.

"Followed by accounting."

"Nine months' worth." Again it was Karen who supplied the details. "And now the lodge."

"This lodge means everything to me," Matt said. He yearned to explain that he'd invested his entire trust fund in the venture, rebuilt the place with his own two hands and was personally involved with every phase of its operation.

The professors exchanged looks.

"If anyone were to design a course on opening a lodge, I'm convinced they'd follow this exact same pattern," Donald said. "It's as if everything you've done in the past five or six years has steered you in this direction. I predict that Hard Luck Lodge is destined to be a success."

"You have a basic understanding of human nature," Derrick added. "Naturally Donald and I came up for the fishing, but if you continue to feed us meals like this, we'll certainly be coming back—even if we don't catch a thing."

Both men chuckled. "The fact that you've fished commercially is bound to be an asset."

"True," Matt admitted.

"Plus your accounting experience."

"It's a perfect fit." Donald nodded with evident satisfaction.

"Thank you," Matt said. Funny, he'd never realized all this before. The two men were absolutely right. It was as though he'd spent the past years in training for this very thing.

"If you gentlemen would kindly excuse me?" Unexpectedly Karen stood up.

"By all means." The professors rose politely to their feet and thanked her for her hospitality.

She threw them a quick smile and rushed into the kitchen.

Matt didn't know what was wrong, but knew he'd better find out. He decided he'd give her a couple of minutes, then excuse himself from the table, too.

Fortunately the professors made some comment

about heading up to bed, since they'd spent the better part of the day traveling. Matt waited until they were on their way up the stairs, then hurried into the kitchen.

"Karen, what's wrong—" He'd no sooner walked through the door when Karen hurled a wet sponge at him. It stuck to his shirt.

"What was that for?" he asked, stunned.

CHAPTER NINE

"Karen," Matt whispered, approaching her slowly.

She reached for the next-closest item at hand, which happened to be half a head of lettuce. "Stay away from me, Matthew Caldwell." Her cheeks were streaked with tears.

"Why are you so upset?"

She flung the lettuce at him, but Matt ducked in the nick of time. Not that she really wanted to hit him. She wasn't sure *what* she wanted to do.

"Karen?"

She couldn't bear it when he said her name like that. As if she was the most precious, the most beautiful woman on the face of the earth. As if he'd treasure her until eternity.

"I'm warning you—stay away from me." She backed up, edging toward the door, hoping to make a clean escape. If she got past him, she'd run up the stairs and flee to the haven of her room. Then, and only then, would she try to analyze the reason for her tears. She experienced a confusing mix of emotions—anger, guilt and a sudden, overpowering sadness that she could neither define nor explain.

"Tell me what's upsetting you," he pleaded.

"I can't." She shook her head helplessly; she didn't understand it herself. She didn't know *why* she felt so furious, or where to direct her anger.

But everything was somehow linked to their dinner conversation. The two professors had taken the apparent chaos that had ruled her marriage and Matt's life and seemed to find logic in it. Karen had been blinded by her complete lack of faith in her husband. A problem, she suspected, that was a result of her childhood.

"Why can't you explain?" he coaxed.

"Just leave me alone, Matt Caldwell," she wailed.

"No." His stubborn streak was showing. "You know I can't stand to see you cry."

"Then I'll stop." She sniffled hard in an effort to stem the tears. Matt wasn't the only one upset with her crying; it troubled her, too. Karen *hated* to cry. It made her nose red and runny, it made her eyes puffy and, worst of all, it made her weak. Vulnerable. Whenever she wept she wanted to be held. When they were married, it was Matt who held her. His comforting often led to lovemaking, which only complicated the issues between them.

Matt stretched out his arms to her. "Honey, let's talk about this."

She wavered, the lure of his embrace strong. It demanded every ounce of fortitude she possessed to shake her head. She was at the kitchen wall now, easing her way toward the door.

"Karen, I love you so damned much."

She pressed her hands over her ears. "Don't tell me that," she sobbed.

"Why not?" he demanded. "Don't you know by now that I'd move heaven and earth to have you back? I want you and our baby here, with me. I want us married."

"You only want me because of the baby."

"That's not true," he argued vehemently. "Do you

know any other man who'd have agreed to live the way we do? Damn it, Karen, I'm going crazy. Do you think it's been easy living with you day after day, loving you the way I do and not touching you? We hardly even kiss.''

''We can't kiss,'' she mumbled. Kissing was always the beginning for them; the lovemaking rarely stopped there.

''If you want to be angry with me, fine, but let me at least hold you.''

That was generally the way their fights went. She'd be unhappy over something that Matt found trivial and unimportant, and she'd explode. She'd usually throw things, and in an effort to calm her, Matt would comfort her. The comforting led to kissing and the kissing to much more. She didn't want it to happen that way now.

''No,'' she said. ''Not again. You seem to forget I'm not your wife any longer.''

''The hell you aren't,'' Matt growled. ''Sure, you've got some judge's decree in your hot little hands, but that doesn't change the way I think of you. You're my wife as much tonight as you were the day we married. I never understood this whole divorce business. You're the one who wanted it, but are you happy?''

She couldn't answer. Besides, he already knew. She'd divorced him, moved to California—and had never been more miserable in her life.

Removing herself from the temptation of being close to Matt simply hadn't worked. Here, she was, pregnant with his child, living with him. Difficult as this was to admit, she was happier than she'd been in two years. And it infuriated her.

The tears came in earnest then.

"Karen, for heaven's sake…"

She hadn't the energy to run from him, and she slumped against the wall. In giant strides, Matt crossed the kitchen and gathered her in his arms. "Honey, listen, nothing can be that terrible."

"Yes, it can," she sobbed, hiding her face in her hands.

The warm feel of his body pressing her against the wall seeped into her bones, chasing away the chill that centered in her heart. Karen could feel his breath at her temple, gently mussing her hair.

She didn't know who reached out first; it didn't matter. She was as hungry for him, as needy for her husband, as he was for her. His touch no longer merely comforted but excited. His lips were warm as they covered her mouth. His tongue traced her lips, then explored with eager thrusts. Soon their need for each other was consuming them.

"Matt, oh, Matt…" She breathed his name again and again as he buried his face in her neck. She slid her arms around him and pressed her body against his solid strength.

"I've been crazy for you for weeks," he muttered, whisking open the buttons of her blouse. Her breasts peaked, yearning for his touch. "But I'll be damned if I'll make love to you in the kitchen."

"Do you think this is such a good idea?" she asked as Matt swung her up in his arms. He opened the swinging door with a push of his shoulder and carried her past the registration desk and toward his private quarters.

"Our making love is a brilliant idea," he said, walking past the dining-room table.

"Matt, the dishes," she said, pointing.

"To hell with the dishes."

"You're angry." She was always the one who flew off the handle. Not Matt.

"Not angry," he corrected, "frustrated with this foolishness. I want my wife back."

She looped her arms around his neck and kissed him hungrily. His eyes met hers briefly before his strides took them into his darkened bedroom. His eyes filled with tenderness as he placed her gently on the mattress and knelt over her. "You asked for romance. I swear I'd do anything in the world to give it to you if I could only figure out what the hell it is," he said before he kissed her again.

"You seem to be doing a pretty good job at the moment," she whispered, her arms looped around his neck.

"I am?" He sounded both surprised and pleased.

"But I still think we should talk first."

"Not on your life," he said, removing her shoes and carelessly tossing them aside. He kicked off his own. "Not when there's a chance you might change your mind about us making love."

"I...I promised myself we wouldn't."

"You can unpromise yourself just as easily."

Karen held out her arms to him in open invitation. "I guess I'll have to."

WHEN KAREN AWOKE it was still dark. The space beside her on the bed was empty. "Matt," she whispered, sitting up and clutching the sheet to her chest. She saw his shadowy figure in the dim light and realized he was dressing.

"Is it morning already?" she asked, yawning luxuriously.

"Unfortunately, yes." He sat on the edge of the bed. "I've got to get the professors up and fed before Sawyer flies us out."

"You're leaving?" She'd completely forgotten about the professors and that Matt would be taking them fishing. "But we need to talk," she said urgently.

"It'll have to wait until later. I'm sorry, honey, but I don't have any choice."

"How long do we have to wait?"

"Three days," he told her. "Besides, what's there to discuss? Everything's already settled, isn't it? You're moving into this bedroom with me and we're getting married again as soon as I can arrange it."

"Aren't you taking a lot for granted?" she asked, piqued that he'd assume everything was settled simply because they'd made love. She wanted to right their relationship, remarry him, too. But contrary to Matt's assertion, there remained a great deal to discuss.

"You love me. I love you. There's nothing more to be said."

"Listen to me, Matthew Caldwell, we have to clear the air. We need to—"

"I don't have time, honey," he said. "Hold that thought and I'll be back in three days."

Discouraged, Karen fell back against the pillows and exhaled sharply.

Nothing was settled, although thanks to what the two professors had pointed out, Karen had a far better understanding of Matt, of their history and his ambitions for the lodge...and of her own reactions the night before.

The professors were right, but neither she nor Matt had seen the obvious. He'd found his calling, had unconsciously been working toward this for as long as she'd known him. The lodge wasn't another phase; it was his life's work. And it had taken two strangers to make both Matt and her aware of that.

Now Karen understood the reason for her tears the night before—they'd been prompted by both anger and sadness. And, she had to admit, guilt. She hadn't trusted Matt to find his own way, to find the work that suited him. She'd allowed her mother's experience to cloud her judgment. Her fears and insecurities had controlled her life, and she'd suffered because of it. Not only had she brought grief into her own life, but into Matt's, as well.

LANNI STOOD at the kitchen sink staring unseeingly at the world outside the window. Her thoughts were troubled as she reviewed her conversation with Karen the day before.

Charles stepped up behind her and slipped his arms around her waist. "You're thoughtful this morning," he said, kissing her neck. "Is something bothering you?"

"It's Matt and Karen," Lanni murmured. She set aside her cup and turned to wrap her arms around her husband, hugging him close. "Something's happened between them."

"Good or bad?"

"I don't know," Lanni confessed. She closed her eyes and savored the feel of Charles's arms. When Matt and Karen had separated she'd been careful not to take sides. Karen was one of her best friends, but Matt was a brother she idolized.

Following the divorce, she knew he was feeling lost and confused. In retrospect, Lanni wished she'd been more sympathetic. Karen's leaving him had undermined the very foundation of his life.

"I saw Karen, but where's Matt?" Charles asked, breaking into her thoughts.

"He's off doing his wilderness thing." Lanni leaned her head back far enough to look into her husband's eyes. "I couldn't bear to ever lose you," she said fervently, offering him a blurry smile.

Charles stroked her back lovingly. "What brought that on?"

"I was just thinking about my brother and Karen. When Karen left him and filed for divorce, it was as if someone had pulled the rug out from under him. He was miserable.

"Yet when I saw Karen soon after they'd separated, I realized she was just as heartbroken. I couldn't take sides or interfere—at least I didn't feel I could—and now I wonder if that was a mistake."

Charles kissed the top of her head. "What I hear you asking, oh, wife of mine, is whether you should involve yourself now."

"Yes." It astonished Lanni that Charles understood her so well. Until he'd spoken, she wasn't sure exactly where her thoughts were leading. "That is what I'm wondering. My brother's a private person, and I don't think he'd appreciate my meddling in his affairs, but at the same time..." She hesitated.

"What makes you think you should?"

"I was over to see Karen yesterday," Lanni said, then bit her lower lip. "I knew Matt was gone, and I thought I'd pop in and see how she was doing. At first everything was fine. We chatted and laughed the way we normally do, and then out of the blue Karen started to cry."

"Karen? About what?"

"That's the sixty-four thousand dollar question," Lanni said, more confused now than ever. "When I asked her what was wrong, she shook her head, hugged me and told me I was the best friend she'd ever had."

"Hmm."

"What's 'hmm' mean?"

"Nothing," Charles answered. "Do you think this bout of melancholy is related to her pregnancy? I've heard a woman's emotions sometimes go a little screwy with a pregnancy."

"How would I know? I've never been pregnant."

She felt Charles smile against her hair. "Not from lack of trying."

"Stop, Charles. We're talking about Matt and Karen here, not my insatiable appetite for my husband."

"Being that husband, I should mention how grateful I am for a loving wife."

"That's just it," Lanni said urgently. "Can you imagine how awful it would be if something were ever to drive us apart?"

The smile in her husband's eyes faded. "I couldn't bear it, Lanni. Loving you has changed my life for the better in so many ways. It's transformed everything. For the first time I have a healthy relationship with my mother. I have you to thank for that. Even the way I feel toward my brothers is different because of you."

Charles dropped his arms and pulled out a kitchen chair and sat down heavily. "I remember when I learned that Sawyer and Christian had brought women to Hard Luck. I was furious. Then I talked to Abbey and discovered my two brothers had expected her and those children to live in one of those old cabins. I was outraged. I decided to put an immediate end to this ridiculous idea of theirs.''

Lanni pulled out a chair for herself and sat opposite him. ''Don't forget about those twenty acres the women were promised.''

He snickered at that, but the amusement soon faded. ''I was the one who suggested Abbey leave Hard Luck. When Sawyer heard what I'd done, the most incredible look came over him. It was as if I'd stabbed him in the back, betrayed him. Then he told me something I've never forgotten.''

''What did he say?'' Lanni asked when he didn't continue right away.

''Sawyer told me I was tempting the fates with my arrogance. He'd never expected to fall in love, and if it happened to him, then I was just as vulnerable. Someday I was going to fall in love myself, and he hoped he'd be there to see it, because then and only then would I appreciate what he was feeling.'' Charles laughed softly and shook his head. ''Not long after that I met you, and I felt I'd been smacked upside the head with a two-by-four.''

''I felt the same way after meeting you,'' she said.

Charles reached for her hand and kissed her fingertips.

''Remember how Matt tried to bring us back together?'' Lanni asked.

Charles nodded.

''I can understand now why he did something so uncharacteristic.'' Her throat seemed to close and she blinked back tears at the memory. ''He was hoping to spare us the same kind of heartache he was suffering.''

''Now you want to help him?''

''Yes,'' Lanni said fervently. ''But I don't know

how, and I'm afraid that if I say or do something it might hurt more than it helps."

"I don't know what to tell you, sweetheart."

"I just wish I knew what to do."

"Perhaps if you talked it over with another woman," he suggested. "Someone you trust and respect."

Lanni's eyes brightened; she leapt out of the chair and planted a grateful kiss on his lips. "You mean someone like Abbey."

FAT RAINDROPS plopped down on the dirt road. Karen studied the pattern they made on the hard ground as she leaned against the support beam on the lodge porch.

She wrapped her arms around her waist and gazed up at the dark, angry sky. Matt and the professors weren't due back until the following day. In her loneliness it felt like an eternity.

Scott O'Halloran came racing down the road on his bicycle, with Ronny Gold behind him. Their young legs pumped the pedals furiously. Eagle Catcher easily kept pace with the two boys, staying closest to Scott's side.

Scott saw Karen and slammed on his brakes. "Hi, Mrs. Caldwell."

"Hello, Scott."

"Do you have a name for your baby yet?" he wanted to know.

"Not yet," she told him. "Do you have any suggestions?"

Scott pinched his lips as he mulled over the question. Then, with a look of excitement, he suggested, "Scott's a good name."

"So's Ronny," the other boy shouted.

"I'll keep both of those in mind," she assured them. "Don't you think you should get out of the rain?"

"Nah," Scott said, answering for them both. "I used to live in Seattle. I'm used to this sort of thing. Once you've lived in the Pacific Northwest, you learn to take rain in your stride."

"I'll remember that," she said, smiling a little at his grown-up manner.

"Look," Ronny said, tugging at the sleeve of Scott's jacket. "The girls are right behind us. We gotta split."

"'Bye," Scott said, arching forward over the handlebars in an effort to make a fast getaway.

Chrissie Harris and Susan O'Halloran raced after them. "Hello, Mrs. Caldwell!" Chrissie shouted.

"Hello, Chrissie. Hello, Susan."

Susan gave her a swift wave and paused only briefly, saying, "Scott let Ronny read my journal, and he's gonna pay."

"You're sure your brother would do something like that?" Karen asked, not quite concealing a smile.

"I'm sure," Susan said with righteous indignation.

"Ronny wrote her a note in the margin of the page. Boys," Chrissie Harris said with wide-eyed wisdom, "are not to be trusted." The two girls disappeared, chasing after the boys.

Now for the first time it came to Karen that this Hard Luck was a good town to raise her child. Although the town was small, the sense of family and community was strong.

She knew there were occasional problems. Friday nights when Ben served alcohol, some of the local trappers and pipeline workers drifted into town and every now and again a fight broke out. But Mitch was routinely there to take care of things.

Karen remained on the porch, musing about life in Hard Luck, when Abbey strolled past, carrying an umbrella.

"Howdy, neighbor," her friend called.

When Karen returned her greeting Sawyer's wife stopped and studied her carefully. "How're you feeling?"

"Fine." She was, if a little lonely. She missed Matt and wished he was home. Her heart was full of all the things she wanted to tell him.

Abbey moved onto the porch. "Do you have time to sit and chat for a while?"

"Sure." Karen was grateful for the company.

They sat side by side on the porch steps. "So how's life treating you these days?" her friend asked.

Karen rolled her shoulders in a shrug. "I can't complain." But she could. In truth, Karen felt wretched, although her condition wasn't physical. The malady was one of the heart.

Tears filled her eyes, and she knew Abbey saw her struggle to keep them at bay. She was thankful that her friend didn't comment or ply her with questions. Instead, Abbey gave her a moment to compose herself.

"I imagine the lodge must feel empty when Matt's away," Abbey said in a quiet, conversational tone.

"It does." Days like this made Karen wonder how she'd managed without Matt during their year and a half apart. In her first months of pregnancy, she'd felt alone and afraid, and the harder she'd tried to convince herself she didn't need Matt, the less it became true. She did need him. The fact that she'd been tempted to keep the baby a secret from him proved as much— she'd been fighting the very thing she wanted most. It seemed to be a pattern in her life.

"I've been feeling so blue lately," Karen admitted softly.

Abbey reached for her hand and squeezed it. "Sounds to me like you could use a little cheering up."

Karen managed a watery smile. "What do you have in mind?"

Abbey gave her a knowing smile in return. "What does every woman do when the going gets tough?"

"Shop," Karen answered automatically.

"Sawyer's flying into Fairbanks later today. Why don't you and I tag along and check out baby furniture? It's time the two of us indulged ourselves at a real, live shopping mall."

"That," Karen said, brightening immediately, "is an offer too good to refuse."

MATT HAD NEVER in his life been so eager to head home. Good thing he wasn't responsible for the weather, because it had rained for two days solid, and there was no letup in sight. Donald and Derrick, his two clients, had called a halt to their expedition. They were wet, cold and miserable.

Luckily the fishing had been great, and the two men felt they'd gotten more than their money's worth. What they wanted now was a hot bath, a good dinner and a warm bed.

Matt was in complete agreement. He radioed in to Midnight Sons and requested that Sawyer fly out and pick them up a day early. Unfortunately Sawyer was in Fairbanks, but Christian agreed to meet them. It might have been Matt's imagination, but Christian sounded eager to get out of the office.

Although the weather was dismal, that wasn't the only reason Matt felt eager to get home. He missed

Karen. He wanted to be with her, hold her, make plans for the future. The last thing he wanted to do was discuss the past. It seemed to him that a lot of their problems had come as a result of these discussions. He'd always dreaded it when she wanted to clear the air, because those conversations invariably led to more problems between them. He never understood why women found it necessary to dissect every aspect of a relationship.

As far as he was concerned, the matter of Karen and him being together was simple. He loved her. He wanted her and the baby with him. If she didn't want that, too, well...

But Matt knew Karen. A man couldn't live with a woman for more than four years and not become well acquainted with her ways. She loved him so damned much it hurt. He knew that in the very depths of his heart. *She loved him.* What bothered Matt was her reason for holding out.

All right, he understood that his tendency to drift from one kind of job to another had troubled her. But all of that was tied to her childhood and her father.

Matt wasn't anything like Eric Rocklin, and if Karen hadn't figured that out by now, he thought with a spurt of anger, then she never would.

Christian arrived in the float plane late in the afternoon. It took the two of them more than an hour to load up the gear. Matt sat next to him in the copilot seat and watched as the landscape unfurled below them and the town of Hard Luck finally appeared. A swelling sense of pride filled him as the lodge came into view.

But it wasn't only the lodge that beckoned him. His wife would be there, and for the first time in a long while he felt like a husband again.

It seemed to take forever to reach the lodge. He imagined Karen rushing out to greet him, and the anticipation set his heart racing. He could hardly wait to take her in his arms again. They had a lot of lost time to make up for.

"Karen!" he shouted as he pushed open the heavy wooden door and strode through. "I'm home."

The two bedraggled professors followed close on his heels.

"Karen!" he repeated, louder this time.

No response.

"She must have gone out," he explained to the two men. The image of her rushing to greet him crumbled at his feet.

Donald and Derrick mumbled something about a bath and immediately headed up the stairs.

Matt wandered through the house, looking for his ex-wife. It wasn't as if she was expecting him; nevertheless, he felt a deep sense of disappointment that she wasn't home.

When she hadn't returned an hour later, he called the library. To his surprise his sister answered.

"I don't suppose you've seen Karen?" he asked without preamble.

"Not today," she told him, and it seemed to him that she stopped herself from saying more.

"Do you know where she might be?" he probed.

Lanni hesitated. "I haven't got a clue. Let me check around and see what I can find out for you."

"I'd appreciate it." He hung up and, because he didn't have any choice, he started the dinner preparations.

Peeling potatoes, he thought about his short conversation with his sister. It suddenly occurred to him that something wasn't right. Wedging the receiver between his shoulder and ear, he punched out the number for the library.

"What's going on with Karen?" He wanted the truth, and he wanted it now.

"What do you mean?" she asked.

"You're keeping something from me."

"I—" Lanni stopped.

"Tell me," he ordered.

"Something's happened between you two, hasn't it?" his sister asked.

"Yes," he said, but to his way of thinking, the changes were all good. She was back in his bed, and as soon as he could make the arrangements, they'd get remarried.

"Whatever it was must have really upset Karen," Lanni said gently.

"What do you mean?" he demanded. He'd thought, he'd hoped, that Karen would be excited. That she'd be happy. He realized she wanted to "clear the air,"— have one of those discussions he disliked so much— but he'd assumed they'd scaled the major hurdles by admitting how much they loved each other and wanted to be together.

"When I stopped by to see Karen she started crying for no reason."

"Crying? Just where the hell is she?" he asked, losing his patience.

"If you'd give me a chance I'd tell you," Lanni snapped. "I talked to Scott, and he told me Karen flew into Fairbanks with Abbey and Sawyer. They're due back anytime now, so don't worry."

By ten that night it became clear that Karen had no intention of returning.

She'd left him again.

Well, it wasn't the first time, but it as sure as hell would be the last.

CHAPTER TEN

ABBEY WAS RIGHT. A shopping spree in Fairbanks had done wonders for Karen's spirits. Sawyer had dropped the two of them off at the closest mall and arranged a time to meet them later.

Karen and Abbey had delighted in drifting from one store to another, from one baby department to the next. Karen felt like a child let loose in Toyland at Christmas.

The experience of shopping for baby clothes had produced a flood of tenderness for her unborn child. Choosing sleepers and nighties somehow made everything more immediate, made the baby seem *real*. Before she could stop herself she bought a number of things, almost more than she could carry comfortably. She put a crib and changing table on layaway and selected several other items for a layette.

The most fun she had was trying on maternity clothes with Abbey. Karen hadn't laughed this much in ages. The smocks were huge on her. But although she barely showed, she could no longer button her pants. Abbey was an old pro at this pregnancy business, and she assured Karen that before long, those smocks would be a perfect fit.

Sawyer met them at the scheduled time, and because of the rainstorm, suggested dinner in Fairbanks before flying back to Hard Luck. When they finally landed that evening it was after ten. The afternoon away had been the perfect remedy for her case of the blues. Karen felt happy—and exhausted.

Sawyer and Abbey dropped her off at the lodge. Sawyer climbed out of the truck, helped her down and sorted through the packages before handing Karen her purchases.

"Looks like someone's inside," Abbey said, gesturing toward the front window where a light showed in the growing dusk.

"Do you think Matt might be back?" Sawyer asked.

"I doubt it," Karen answered. Knowing her ex-husband, he'd probably consider the rain and wind something of a bonus. She'd heard it said that rain made for good fishing, but then, what she knew about the sport was minimal. She could imagine Matt standing in the middle of a raging river that very minute, happily soaked and hoping to lure breakfast toward his hook.

"Thanks again," Karen called as her friends drove off. She shifted the sacks in her arms, pleased with the things she'd purchased and looking forward to showing Matt.

"One thing's for sure," she said aloud to the baby, "whether you're a boy or a girl, you're going to be one of the best-dressed kids around."

She suddenly realized that she and Matt had never talked about the baby's sex. She didn't know if he had any preference; he'd never said.

No sooner was she inside than her eyes connected with those of her ex-husband. He was sprawled in the overstuffed chair in front of the fireplace. His feet were propped on the raised hearth and his outstretched arms dangled over the sides of the chair. One hand was holding the neck of a whiskey bottle, which seemed in danger of slipping from his fingers.

"Karen?" He stared at her as though she were an apparition.

"You're back early!" she said excitedly. "This is a surprise."

"You can say that again."

She ignored the sarcasm in his voice. "I've had the most marvelous day." Hurrying across the room, she set down her packages in the empty chair. "Just wait until you see what I bought the baby!"

He continued to stare at her. Although the liquor bottle appeared to be nearly full, Karen wondered how much Matt had been drinking. It wasn't like him to overindulge. As she recalled, he was easily hung over and generally avoided the hard stuff. He was more inclined to drink wine, but rarely to excess.

"Why are you buying these things now?" he asked in a snarling tone.

"Because I had the opportunity to fly into Fairbanks with Sawyer and Abbey," she explained with strained patience. Surely he wasn't upset because she'd bought things for the baby. Ignoring his sour mood, she pulled a yellow cotton sleeper from the sack. "Isn't this adorable? You wouldn't believe the incredible things they have for babies these days. I found the cutest pair of baby sunglasses. Abbey and I got a real kick out of them. You can flip up the lenses and everything."

"Baby sunglasses," he muttered, but he didn't sound impressed.

It was clear that her ex-husband—soon to be husband again—was in a rare temper. Karen lowered herself onto the hearth, facing him. "What happened?" she asked with a laborious sigh.

After the long, happy afternoon she was tired and disappointed by his lack of welcome. The last thing she wanted now was a confrontation with Matt. "Didn't the professors have a good time? Are they demanding their money back?"

"Hell, no," Matt said irritably, obviously taking offense at the question. "They had the time of their lives and made a point of telling me so. They would have stuck it out if the rain hadn't started coming down in buckets."

"So that's why you came back a day early?"

His eyes narrowed as he glared at her. "I surprised you, didn't I?" He set the bottle aside and stood, looming above her. She noticed that his balance was a little off, and he braced his feet wide apart in an effort to maintain it. "You figured to be out of here by then, didn't you?" he went on. "You were planning to be gone before I learned what you'd done."

"Out of here? Gone?" Karen had thought they'd be able to sit down and discuss where their lives were headed, how their relationship would change. But she had no intention of leaving him. It was the furthest thing from her mind.

"Sure," he said with more than a hint of belligerence. "You intended to sneak out of Hard Luck without telling me."

"You assumed because I wasn't here when you returned that I'd *left* you?" This was by far the most ridiculous thing he'd ever said. She leapt to her feet and stuffed the yellow sleeper back into the bag.

"What else was I to think?"

"If you'd bothered to look in your office you'd have found a note."

"You wrote me a note when I wasn't expected home?" he challenged, his eyes bright with disbelief.

"You or anyone else who happened to stop by and wanted to know where I was." She held the packages tightly against her stomach as if to protect herself from Matt's hostility. This wasn't like him; she didn't understand it, didn't know how to respond.

"You left me before," he reminded her. "What else am I to think when I return home and find you gone?"

"That was different," she said in her defense.

His short laugh was devoid of amusement. "The last time, you filed for divorce so fast you left my head spinning. Remember? You couldn't wait to be rid of me then. Nothing's changed. Certainly not you."

Karen almost gasped with pain at his accusation. Her knees felt weak, but she stood her ground. "I warned you, Matt, but you wouldn't listen. You hardly ever listened to me in those days." He didn't seem to have improved much now.

"You warned me?" he spat out.

Karen glanced over her shoulder and up the stairs, fearing his outburst would wake their guests. Well, so be it, if that was what Matt wanted.

"When you decided to become an accountant I told you to be very sure. You'd already gone through three other professions in short order, and I wasn't about to have you risk our financial security again."

"To be very sure is a long way from filing divorce papers," he said sullenly.

"You didn't even discuss it with me. I come home from work one night and you gleefully announce that you've quit." Tears threatened, but she held them back with sheer force of will. "Without a word of warning, without so much as hinting you were unhappy, you quit. If you'd once talked to me, explained that the job wasn't right for you... But you left me completely out of the decision.''

"And so the next day you packed up your bags and were gone,'' he said. He snapped his fingers as if to say her leaving had been a snap decision.

"Can you blame me?'' she cried. "Can you honestly blame me? I was tired of having you jerk our lives around. I'd had it up to here,'' she said, raising her hand above her head, "with your inability to stick to a job. Any job.'' She paused and dragged in a deep breath before she continued, "I'd grown up with a father who refused to accept responsibility. Then I'd made the mistake of marrying a man just like him.''

"I am not your father.'' Matt made each word loud and distinct.

"You're exactly like him. You didn't even think about the bills. They were supposed to pay themselves, I guess. Your 'Don't worry, be happy' attitude drove me *crazy*.''

"I was miserable working for the accounting firm!'' he shouted.

"Just as you were miserable continuing with college, with the chef's job, with commercial fishing and with everything else you dabbled in over the past five years? Or was this a *different* kind of misery?''

He didn't answer.

"The time had come to grow up, Matt. You didn't want a family, you drifted from job to job, without revealing an ounce of responsibility or any ambition, any plan for our future. What else was I supposed to do?''

"Answer me this, Karen. Would a responsible adult turn tail at the first sign of trouble? Would a responsible adult walk out on her husband and end her marriage on a whim?''

"Do you really think that was easy for me, Matt?'' Her voice shook as she stiffened against his accusations.

"Easy or not, you did it, and I don't trust you not to look for some excuse to do it again.''

"Is that what the bottle's all about?'' she demanded, pointing to the whiskey in his hand.

"Yes. I returned early and you were gone. When I called around all I could find out was that you'd been feeling low. Then I discovered you'd gone into Fairbanks with Sawyer and Abbey.''

"For heaven's sake, I went shopping!''

"I didn't know that. For all I knew, you could be returning to that wonderful job in California that you love so damned much.''

She couldn't believe what she was hearing. It hurt that he was saying such things. "Why would I do that?''

He shrugged. "Why do you do anything? What happened two years ago makes as little sense to me now as it did then.''

"You're being ridiculous.''

"Am I?'' he challenged. "The last thing you said to me before I left the other day was that I shouldn't take you for granted. Trust me, Karen, I don't. I never will again. You're as likely to walk out on me now as you were before, and I can't—I *won't*—forget that.''

"Just because I didn't leap back into marriage when I learned I was pregnant? As far as I could see—''

Matt didn't allow her to finish. "If you're going to go, Karen, I advise you to do it now. I haven't got the stomach to drink away my sorrows. Nor do I enjoy living with uncertainty."

"You honestly believe I'd do anything so underhand?"

"Why shouldn't I? You did it before."

She swallowed at the constriction blocking her throat. "Fine, then, I will." She moved toward the stairs. "You didn't need an excuse to get me to leave, Matt. All you had to do was ask."

MARIAH WAS HUMMING to herself when Duke Porter opened the office door and walked in. She looked up, relieved to find it wasn't Christian. Her boss appeared to be doing his utmost to avoid her these days. Which was just as well.

"Hello, Duke." She greeted him with a cheerful smile.

Duke stayed close to the door, as if he was ready to make a quick exit. "If I come in here you aren't going to kiss me again, are you?"

Mariah laughed. "A lot of guys around here wouldn't complain if I did."

"Maybe not," Duke agreed good-naturedly, "but you said the kiss was from that attorney friend of yours. Tracy something or other."

"It was." Duke wasn't fooling her; he knew Tracy's name as well as he did his own. He should—he'd been complaining about her for months.

Duke rubbed the back of his hand across his lips as if to wipe away anything having to do with the lawyer. "Let me set one thing straight right now. The last woman I want kissing me is that…that she-devil."

"She's not so bad."

"She wouldn't be if she knew her place."

"Knew her place?" Mariah echoed in disbelief. "What do you mean by that?"

"Exactly what I said." He walked over to the coffeepot, removed his mug from the peg and poured himself a cup. "She thinks just because she's an attorney, she knows better than anyone else. What that woman needs is a man to put her in her place."

Mariah opened her mouth in outrage, then felt a laugh gurgling up. Duke went out of his way to be provocative, and frankly she'd like to see him or any other man try to put Tracy in "her place." She didn't know what it was with those two. They hadn't gotten along from the very first moment they'd encountered each other.

Suddenly dejected, Mariah realized it had been that way with her and Christian, too. The first day she arrived in Hard Luck her suitcases had fallen open and her unmentionables had scattered across the runway. That beginning must have been an omen. Things had quickly gone from bad to worse between them. The man flustered her so much she'd made one mistake after another.

"Speaking of Tracy," Mariah said, forcefully taking her mind off Christian, "I received a letter from her this week."

"Oh." Duke sat on the edge of her desk. "She's not making a trip up here, I hope."

"She's got two weeks' vacation due her, and she wanted to know if I'd meet her somewhere."

"Like where?"

"I was thinking of Anchorage. I've always wanted to go on one of those glacier tour boats." She opened a bottom drawer and removed a brochure. "There's plenty I'd like to see in Anchorage, especially Earthquake Park. It's supposed to be quite something.''

''Any chance you might invite her up here again?''

''Here?'' She eyed the pilot, wondering if he was hoping to stir up a little trouble. Mariah sometimes thought Duke was attracted to Tracy, but she dismissed the idea. Not Duke and Tracy. Not the two people who couldn't exchange one civil word.

''Maybe I will,'' she said, studying him.

Duke scowled. ''In that case let me know so I can avoid her. I don't want to be within a two-hundred-mile radius of her.''

He sipped his coffee, grimaced as if he found it not to his liking and walked out of the office.

No more than a minute later the office door opened again. Without looking up she chided, ''Come on, Duke. Make up your mind, would you? You—'' She stopped abruptly when she did look up and saw not Duke, but Christian.

His gaze focused on her. ''Was that Duke I noticed coming out of here? Or should I say loverboy?''

''Yes,'' she answered stiffly. ''It was Duke.'' Judging by his expression, Christian seemed to be suggesting that she and Duke had been involved in something unseemly. ''And for your information, Duke isn't my loverboy.''

''The two of you were in here alone?''

''Yes.'' She rolled her eyes and sat down at the computer, presenting him with a view of her back. It did no good to reason with Christian. He'd already decided she and Duke were romantically involved, and he seemed unwilling to change his mind.

''Do you think that's such a good idea?'' he asked.

''What? Being in here alone with Duke? Really,

Christian, he's a pilot. It isn't like he doesn't have business here.'' She was about to point out that she was the one who scheduled the flights, took orders and handled numerous other details, but she realized her arguments were useless.

''The last time I caught the two of you together you were practically undressing one another.''

''That's not true!'' Mariah's cheeks reddened with embarrassment. ''You make it sound like I need a...a baby-sitter.''

''You do,'' Christian sneered. ''It's a miracle you haven't destroyed the airfield by now. You certainly have a habit of wreaking havoc wherever you go.''

''That's the most unfair and unkind thing you've ever said to me, Christian O'Halloran.'' Pride demanded she hold her head high, but it was difficult.

Mariah had known for a long time that Christian regretted hiring her. She was also aware that he'd approached Sawyer soon after her arrival, wanting to replace her. If anything, his dislike for her had spurred her on; she'd tried harder to please him, to fit into the office and prove herself. She'd hoped that in the past year she'd done that.

She had worked hard. When it came to Sawyer she had a near-flawless record. But with Christian everything had gone wrong. Spilling punch on him was just the tip of the iceberg. If she lost an important file it was inevitably one Christian needed. If she misplaced a phone message it was one Christian had been anxiously waiting to receive. It never failed; she was continually in conflict with him, when he was the very one she most wanted to please.

For nearly a year Mariah had lived with the threat of losing her job. Just when it seemed they were making progress and finding some common ground, Christian had stumbled on her kissing Duke. Everything had gone downhill since.

He avoided her whenever possible. When it wasn't possible and they were in the office alone at the same time, he rarely spoke to her, and then only about business. It made for an awkward situation, and Mariah didn't know what to do to change the situation for the better.

KAREN'S SUITCASES were packed and ready to be taken to the airfield. The two professors had left earlier that morning, and the lodge was strangely quiet.

Karen had been downstairs only once all morning; Matt wasn't there. Now she waited in her room, although for what she wasn't sure.

The tightness in her chest hadn't gone away from the moment she announced she was leaving. The phone call to her parents in Anchorage had assured her she was welcome to live with them as long as she needed.

She walked over to her window and stared out at the panoramic view of the tundra. She would miss all this. More important, she'd miss the friends she'd made here. Lanni, of course. Abbey and the children. Bethany, and although she didn't know Mitch well, she thought the world of his little girl. Then there was Ben. And the O'Halloran brothers. Duke and John and Ted, and the other pilots.

But she was fooling herself, Karen knew, if she believed it was the townsfolk she'd miss most. For the second time in her life she was about to walk away from the man she loved.

It had been difficult enough the first time. She didn't know if she could find the strength do it again.

A noise echoed up the stairway from below. The screen door slammed, indicating Matt was back.

Leaving her suitcases at the top of the stairs, Karen slowly made her way down.

Matt stood at the foot of the stairs watching her.

Neither spoke.

His eyes seemed huge, twice their normal size. It took Karen a moment to realize that the tears brimming in her own eyes had distorted his image.

"Are you ready to leave?" he asked starkly.

"No," she answered. Her fingers tightened around the railing. All at once, in a rush of pain, Karen knew she'd never be ready. She couldn't make herself do it. She couldn't leave him. Not again.

Her gaze scanned the room. During dinner the night before in Fairbanks Sawyer and Abbey had told her how hard Matt had worked to rebuild the lodge. How he'd taken on an impossible task and made this half-burned, abandoned place a promising enterprise. How pleased they were to have her and Matt as part of the community. They'd spoken of Hard Luck's future, and Karen had felt a vital part of that future. Until she'd arrived home. Until she'd faced Matt.

The moment she'd moved into the lodge with him she'd seen it all for herself. He'd found his calling. Everything he'd done in the last few years had steered him in this direction. The professors had revealed that truth to her. A truth that should have been obvious. All she'd had to do was watch her husband here in his lodge. His capability, the care he took, the responsibilities he assumed—they all should have told her that things were different for him now.

In all the time she and Matt had been married, she'd never seen him this happy, with himself or his work.

"What do you need?" he demanded.

"Need?"

"To get ready to leave."

It seemed he couldn't be rid of her fast enough. She didn't know how to answer him and glanced behind her.

"I'll get your suitcases," he said, and he took the stairs two at a time, roaring past her.

"No." The word nearly strangled her.

He stopped midway up the stairs. "No?"

"I don't want to leave you, Matt," she choked out. "Not again. The baby needs you. *I* need you."

A strained silence followed.

"How long?" he asked, his voice taut with emotion. "How long are you willing to stay this time?"

"Forever."

A deep breath of air filled his chest. "I don't know if forever will be long enough. Are you certain Karen? Be very certain because I won't have the strength to let you go again if that's what you want."

"I *am* sure," she said, and the tears ran down her face.

All at once they were wrapped in each other's arms. Matt was kissing her and she was crying and kissing him back.

They both tried to speak a number of times, but it seemed more important to reassure each other with kisses.

"Never again," Matt whispered between kisses.

"No. I'm here for a lifetime."

"Partner. Lover. Companion," Matt said between nibbling kisses.

"I am moving," she whispered, and laughed at the way his eyes lit up like fire, "into your bedroom."

"*Our* bedroom. I remodeled that room with you in mind."

"What about a family?"

"That, too," he agreed, smiling.

Tears of happiness sparkled on her lashes. "I have so many ideas for the lodge."

"Wonderful." He pressed his mouth hungrily to hers.

"But I have an even better idea for right now."

He lifted his head and his gaze probed hers. "You do?"

"It doesn't have a thing to do with the lodge, either." Gripping his hand, she led him down the stairs and toward their private quarters.

"Might I ask what you have in mind?"

She laughed joyously. "You'll find out soon enough, oh, husband of mine."

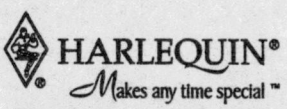

If you enjoyed what you just read,
then we've got an offer you can't resist!

Take 2
bestselling novels FREE!
Plus get a FREE surprise gift!

Clip this page and mail it to The Best of the Best™

IN U.S.A.
3010 Walden Ave.
P.O. Box 1867
Buffalo, N.Y. 14240-1867

IN CANADA
P.O. Box 609
Fort Erie, Ontario
L2A 5X3

YES! Please send me 2 free Best of the Best™ novels and my free surprise gift. Then send me 4 brand-new novels every month, which I will receive before they're available in stores. In the U.S.A., bill me at the bargain price of $4.24 plus 25¢ delivery per book and applicable sales tax, if any*. In Canada, bill me at the bargain price of $4.74 plus 25¢ delivery per book and applicable taxes**. That's the complete price and a savings of over 15% off the cover prices—what a great deal! I understand that accepting the 2 free books and gift places me under no obligation ever to buy any books. I can always return a shipment and cancel at any time. Even if I never buy another book from The Best of the Best™, the 2 free books and gift are mine to keep forever. So why not take us up on our invitation. You'll be glad you did!

185 MEN C229
385 MEN C23A

Name	(PLEASE PRINT)	
Address	Apt.#	
City	State/Prov.	Zip/Postal Code

* Terms and prices subject to change without notice. Sales tax applicable in N.Y.
** Canadian residents will be charged applicable provincial taxes and GST.
   All orders subject to approval. Offer limited to one per household.
   ® are registered trademarks of Harlequin Enterprises Limited.

BOB00   ©1998 Harlequin Enterprises Limited

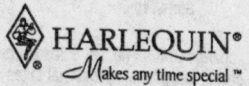

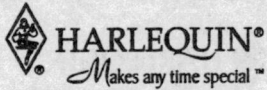

Three complete novels by bestselling author

DALLAS SCHULZE

Angel in your **EYES**

Half savior. Half sinner. *All hero!*

There's nothing like being safe in the arms
of the man you love.

Dallas Schulze turns up the heat
with these three stories of love and passion!

On sale June 2000 at your favorite retail outlet.

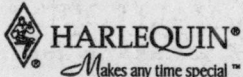

HARLEQUIN®
Makes any time special ™

Visit us at www.eHarlequin.com

PSBR3600

Return to the charm of the Regency era with

GEORGETTE HEYER,

creator of the modern Regency genre.

Enjoy six romantic collector's editions with forewords by some of today's bestselling romance authors,

Nora Roberts, Mary Jo Putney, Jo Beverley, Mary Balogh, Theresa Medeiros and Kasey Michaels.

Frederica
On sale February 2000

The Nonesuch
On sale March 2000

The Convenient Marriage
On sale April 2000

Cousin Kate
On sale May 2000

The Talisman Ring
On sale June 2000

The Corinthian
On sale July 2000

Available at your favorite retail outlet.

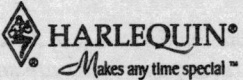

HARLEQUIN®
Makes any time special ™

Visit us at www.romance.net

PHGHGEN

THOM

THE VIENNA HOFBURG

THE HISTORY
THE BUILDINGS
THE SIGHTS

UEBERREUTER

Showpiece of the Treasury: The Imperial Crown (1602)

Contents

The Residence of the Habsburgs

The Hofburg was originally built as a fortress by Otakar II Přemysl, the king of Bohemia, who had begun construction by 1275. But it is inseparable from the House of Habsburg, a family of Alemannic counts who came from the Habichtsburg ("Hawk's Castle") in Aargau, in what is now Switzerland. Rudolf I, who had been elected German king in 1273, is said to have moved into the Hofburg in 1279. In 1918, after Austria had been defeated in World War I, the reign of the Habsburg Dynasty over Austria, which with Hungary had formed the Dual Monarchy, came to an end.

Over this period of just under 640 years, the Hofburg developed into a magnificent, if heterogeneous, residence, the center of a multinational empire and a monument to Austrian and Western history. In the Hofburg the Congress of Vienna was held, reorganizing Europe; here the precious symbols of the Holy Roman Empire of the German Nation were kept. This is where Maria Theresa and Sisi lived, Ludwig van Beethoven and Johann Strauss conducted, Antonio Salieri and Anton Bruckner composed. Since 1498, the Hofburg has been the home of the Vienna Boys' Choir and since 1562, that of the Lipizzaner horses as well.

Almost every ruler continued to expand the Hofburg. During the Renaissance period, at the end of the 16th century, it consisted of three separate buildings: the fortress (today

From the roof of the Neue Burg: St. Michael's Church and St. Stephen's Cathedral

the Schweizerhof ➤ Swiss Court); the residence of Maximilian II, which he adapted to stable his horses (the Stallburg); and the Amalienburg (named for the widow of Joseph I, Amalia of Brunswick). During the Baroque period, it grew into an ensemble of magnificent buildings (including the Court Library). The term "Hofburg" (literally: "court castle") was first used at the end of the 17th century. Each emperor in turn added new wings or remodeled existing apartments, because it was not customary to use the same rooms as one's immediate predecessor.

Thus every era left its traces behind – and every political system as well. The Hofburg, which today extends from the Albertina to Michaelertor (Michael's Gate) and on to the Offices of the Austrian President and from the Stallburg to Heldenplatz (Heroes' Square), the Kunsthistorisches and Naturhistorisches Museums (Museums of Art History and Natural History, respectively) and on to the Imperial Court Stables (now the MuseumsQuartier), has still not stopped growing, either above or below ground. Giant underground storage areas have been built and most recently, at the turn of the millennium, the MuseumsQuartier along with the new buildings of the Leopold Museum, the Kunsthalle Wien and the Museum of Modern Art.

With its 18 wings, 54 stairways, 19 courtyards and 2600 rooms, the Hofburg is the world's largest secular residential district. Together with the MuseumsQuartier it occupies an area of more than 500,000 m^2 (5,400,000 square feet), making it the world's largest complex of museums and monuments (with the possible exception of the Roman Forum). The museums and the Austrian National Library, which were founded for the most part on the collections of the Habsburgs, contain not only artworks from classical antiquity to the present but also magnificent weapons, precious manuscripts and extraordinary finds (papyrus documents, minerals and ethnological materials).

Practical Information

ADMISSION TICKETS: There is no general admission ticket for all the facilities in the Hofburg and MuseumsQuartier. There are individual tickets and several types of combination tickets (i.e. for the Kunsthistorisches Museum, the Schatzkammer (Treasury), the collections in the Neue Burg and the Austrian Theatre Museum, or for the Leopold Museum, the Museum of Modern Art, the Architekturzentrum and the Kunsthalle Wien). The ticket for the Imperial Apartments and the Sisi Museum is also valid for visiting the Imperial Silver Collection.

GUIDED TOURS: The organization "Walks in Vienna" offers several guided tours to the Hofburg with a focus on various aspects. Survey tour: every Sunday at 11:15 a.m., from April to October also every Wednesday at 10:30 a.m. (meeting place: Michaelerplatz near the excavations). Internet: www.wienguide.at, e-mail: office@wienfuehrung.at

CASH DISPENSERS: Raiffeisen, Michaelerplatz (corner of Kohlmarkt). MuseumsQuartier Main Entrance, Museumsplatz 1. Bank Austria Creditanstalt, Babenbergerstrasse 9.

KINDERINFO (CHILDREN'S INFORMATION): WienXtra-Kinderinfo is located in the MuseumsQuartier (in the wing between the Main Courtyard and Fürstenhof). It provides free information about leisure activities for children ages three to 13. Opening times: Tuesday to Thursday 2 p.m. to 7 p.m., Friday to Sunday 10 a.m. to 5 p.m. Phone: +43/1/4000-84 400. Internet: www.kinderinfowien.at.

MUSEUMSQUARTIER: phone: +43/1/523 58 81-1730, Infoline: 0820/600 600 (only in Austria), Internet: www.mqw.at. At the Main Entrance MQ Point (Info Tickets Shop), baby changing room, lost & found and free wheelchair service. Tours of the grounds: German, English, French, Italian and Spanish by prior arrangement at tour@mqw.at.

PUBLIC TRANSPORTATION: The quickest way to reach the Hofburg is by subway (U-Bahn) line U3 (station: Herrengasse). The MuseumsQuartier is next to the Volkstheater station of the U2 and U3. Bus line 2A connects the Hofburg with the Kunsthistorisches and Naturhistorisches Museums and the MQ (only until 8 p.m., on Saturday until 7 p.m.; bus does not operate on Sunday).

PARKING: Underground parking is provided right in front of the MuseumsQuartier (Museumsplatz). A reduction is available upon purchase of an MQ combination ticket. More underground parking is located at the Staatsoper, Rathausplatz (Dr. Karl-Lueger-Ring) and on Stiftgasse behind the MuseumsQuartier. Parking on Heldenplatz is usually only permitted with special permission (Wagenkarte).

POLICE: Goethegasse 1, phone: +43/1/313 10-21330. Stiftgasse 2a, phone: +43/1/313 10-22380.

POST OFFICES: A-1014 Vienna, Wallnerstrasse 5–7. A-1016 Vienna, Museumsstrasse 12.

TAXIS: On Reitschulgasse (next to Michaelerplatz), on Bellariastrasse and at the lower end of Mariahilfer Strasse.

Shops

CHEAP RECORDS & STORE in the Fischer von Erlach Wing on Electric Avenue (MQ). Opening times: Tuesday to Friday 12:30 p.m. to 7 p.m., Saturday and Sunday 1 p.m. to 6 p.m. Records and CDs, designer merchandise.

Next to the MQ's Main Entrance: Prachner Bookshop

KULTURBUCHHANDLUNG PRACHNER (cultural bookshop) in the Fischer von Erlach Wing next to the MQ-Point. Opening times: Monday to Saturday 10 a.m. to 7 p.m., Sundays and holidays 1 p.m. to 7 p.m. Books and magazines (architecture, art, landscape architecture, photography, Austrian themes).

LOMOSHOP next to the Kunsthalle Wien Shop (MQ) underneath the open-air staircase to the Museum of Modern Art. Opening times: daily 1 p.m. to 7 p.m. Various cameras, novelty items, gifts.

MÄDCHENPOP and LA FÁBRICA DE LA SUERTE in the Fischer von Erlach Wing on Electric Avenue (MQ). Opening times: Tuesday to Friday 1 p.m. to 7 p.m., Saturday and Sunday noon to 6 p.m. Fashion and the other things girls need.

MQ POINT (INFO & TICKET SHOP) in the Fischer von Erlach Wing at the Main Entrance (MQ). Opening times: daily 10 a.m. to 7 p.m. Information and brochures about the MQ, admission tickets, MQ products, gifts, toys, jewelry.

MUSEUM SHOPS in the Albertina, Architekturzentrum Wien (MQ), Imperial Apartments, Kunsthalle Wien (MQ), Kunsthistorisches Museum, Leopold Museum (MQ), Lipizzaner Museum, Museum of Modern Art (MQ), Naturhistorisches Museum, Treasury and Spanish Riding School. Opening times are usually the same as those of the respective institution.

SOUVENIR SHOPS in the pedestrian arcade between Heldenplatz and the inner courtyard (In der Burg). Opening times: generally Monday to Friday 9 a.m. to 6 p.m.; closing times on weekends are generally earlier.

TABAK TRAFIK (TOBACCONIST'S SHOPS) in the pedestrian arcade between Heldenplatz and the inner courtyard (In der Burg). Opening times: daily 8 a.m. to 6 p.m. Tobacco products, newspapers, magazines, souvenirs, postcards.

Cafés and Restaurants

AUGUSTINERKELLER and WEINMUSEUM next to the Albertina. Opening times: Sunday to Friday 11 a.m. to midnight, Saturday 11 a.m. to 3 p.m. Phone: +43/1/533 10 26. Traditional restaurant (Viennese cuisine) with new wine on tap.

CAFÉ ATELIER next to the escalator to the Albertina. Opening times: daily 8 a.m. to 2 a.m. Phone: +43/1/533 10 26. Café and bar. Outdoor seating.

CAFÉ LEOPOLD in the Leopold Museum (MQ). Opening times: daily 10 a.m. to 2 a.m. (Thursday to Saturday 10 a.m. to 4 a.m.). Phone: +43/1/523 67 32. Café, bar and restaurant with moderate prices (snacks, midday set meal). Two outdoor seating areas. DJ lines on weekends.

CAFÉ NAUTILUS in the Cupola Hall of the Naturhistorisches Museum (Maria-Theresien-Platz). Opening times: daily except Tuesday 10 a.m. to 6 p.m. Phone: +43/1/524 02 50. Café and restaurant.

CAFÉ RESTAURANT HALLE is located in the Kaiserloge (Emperor's Box) in the former Winter Riding Hall (MQ). Opening times: daily 10 a.m. to 2 a.m. (hot dishes until 11:30 p.m., Friday and Saturday until midnight). Phone: +43/1/523 70 01. Mediterranean cuisine, breakfast until 4 p.m. Two outdoor seating areas.

CAFÉ SPANISCHE HOFREITSCHULE on Michaelerplatz. Opening times: as a rule Tuesday to Sunday 9 a.m. to 5 p.m. Phone: +43/1/533 41 11. Operated by the Sacher Hotel. View of the Summer Riding School through the window.

DO & CO in the Albertina. Opening times: daily 10 a.m. to midnight. Phone: +43/1/532 96 69. Café, bar and restaurant (expensive). Outdoor seating on the Bastion.

EL MUSEO in the Museum of Modern Art (MQ). Opening times: daily 10 a.m. to 2 a.m. (hot dishes until 11:30 p.m.), Thursday to Saturday 10 a.m. to 4 a.m. Phone: +43/1/525 00 1440. Café and restaurant, Mediterranean and Latin American cuisine, clubbing, outdoor seating.

In the Cupola Hall of the Naturhistorisches Museum: Café Nautilus

GERSTNER in the Cupola Hall of the Kunsthistorisches Museum (Maria-Theresien-Platz). Opening times: daily except Monday

In the Burggarten: Palmenhaus Brasserie and Bar

10 a.m. to 6 p.m. (evening buffet on Thursday until 11 p.m.). Phone: +43/1/526 13 61. Café and restaurant.

GLACIS-BEISL at the Breite Gasse entrance (MQ). Opening times: daily 11 a.m. to 2 a.m. Traditional restaurant (Viennese cuisine), recently refurbished. Outdoor seating (unfortunately no longer as enchanting as it was before the MQ was built).

HOFBURG CAFÉ near the Imperial Apartments (In der Burg). Opening times: daily 9 a.m. to 8 p.m. Fine café-restaurant with outdoor seating.

HOFBURGSTÜBERL in the pedestrian arcade between Heldenplatz and the Inner Courtyard (In der Burg). Opening times: Monday to Friday 7 a.m. to 5 p.m., Saturday, Sunday and holidays 10 a.m. to 3 p.m. Stand-up snack bar.

KANTINE (cafeteria) in the Fischer von Erlach Wing (MQ). Opening times: Sunday to Wednesday 10 a.m. to midnight, Thursday to Saturday 10 a.m. to 2 a.m. Phone: +43/1/523 82 39. Snacks, including filled pita pockets, inexpensive daily plate (also vegetarian). Two outdoor seating areas.

MEIEREI in the Volksgarten. Opening times: April 1 to October 30, roughly 9 a.m. to 8 p.m. (depending on the weather). Phone: +43/1/533 21 05. Café, pastries and snacks. Formerly housed a water reservoir. Outdoor seating.

MQ-DAILY (UNDER'M HOLLERBUSCH) in the Fischer von Erlach Wing (MQ). Opening times: Monday to Friday 9 a.m. to 7 p.m., Saturday 9 a.m. to 6 p.m. Phone: +43/1/526 53 03. Food, beverages, take-out dishes and fixed midday meal of organic products.

PALMENHAUS in the Burggarten. Opening times: daily 10 a.m. to 2 a.m. (closed Mondays and Tuesdays from November to February). Phone: +43/1/533 10 33. Café, brasserie and bar in a Jugendstil greenhouse. Large outdoor seating area.

RESTAURANT UNA near the Architekturzentrum Wien (MQ). Opening times: Monday to Saturday 9 a.m. to midnight (hot dishes 9:30 a.m. to 10:30 p.m.), Saturday, Sunday and holidays 10 a.m. to 6 p.m. Phone: +43/1/523 65 66. Chic, with ceiling faced with Turkish tiles. Outdoor seating.

SOHO in the Neue Burg (entrance: Bibliothekshof). Opening times: Monday to Friday 9 a.m. to 4 p.m. (closed August). Phone: +43/676/309 51 61. Reasonably priced cafeteria of the Austrian National Library. Fine set meals at midday.

VOLKSGARTEN CLUBDISKOTHEK on Burgring. Opening times: as a rule starting at 11 p.m. Phone: +43/1/532 42 41. Bar and disco. Well preserved furnishings from the 1950s. Outdoor seating (café with dancing on summer weekends).

VOLKSGARTEN PAVILION. Opening times: April to September daily 10 a.m. to 2 a.m. Phone: +43/1/532 09 07. Espresso bar from the 1950s, in its original condition. Outdoor seating.

Faced with Turkish tiles: Una in the MuseumsQuartier

The History of the Hofburg

Prologue: The End of the Babenbergs

The Babenberg ruler Henry II Jasomirgott, who in 1156 had obtained for Austria the status of a duchy from Emperor Frederick I Barbarossa, built a palace in his new capital, Vienna. The building and walls surrounded a courtyard, today the square Am Hof. Under his son Leopold V and succeeding rulers, the ducal palace, which has vanished today, was expanded. It was financed in part with the English ransom paid for the release of Richard the Lion-Hearted, who was captured in Vienna in 1193 while returning from the Holy Land.

With the death of Frederick II on June 15, 1246, in the battle against the Hungarians at the Leitha River, the male line of the Babenberg family, which had ruled since 976, came to an end. In 1252, Frederick's sister Margaret, a widow since 1242, married Otakar II Přemysl of Bohemia, who assumed power in Vienna and expanded his sphere of influence from the Sudeten region to the Adriatic. But when he was excluded from voting in the 1273 election that chose Rudolf of Habsburg (1218–1291) to be the first German king (king of the Romans), he refused to recognize Rudolf. In 1276 the Imperial Diet launched a military campaign against Otakar, and Rudolf I marched on Vienna with an army of 20,000. The decisive Battle of Dürnkrut took place in 1278 on the Marchfeld plain, and Otakar was killed as he tried to flee.

The Fortress of Otakar II

By 1275 the king of Bohemia had begun construction of a fortress within the Vienna city wall (built between 1200 and 1207) on an elevation next to the Widmer Gate. It was a complex with four towers around a rectangular courtyard, which today is called the Schweizerhof (Swiss Court). Rudolf I is said to have moved into the fortress in 1279 because the ducal fortress of the Babenbergs had become uninhabitable following a large fire in 1276. His son Albert (1248–1308) built the Castle Chapel (first mentioned in 1296). To the southeast of the fortress, the Church of the Augustinian Friars was consecrated in 1349. There were two reasons why no other major architectural changes occurred during this period: firstly, the construction of St. Stephen's Cathedral required large sums of money, and secondly, Vienna had lost importance with the division of the Habsburg lands (1379). The fortress was then used only occasionally as a residence. The only major change occurred when Albert V (1379–1439) rebuilt the chapel (1423–1426). In 1452, Frederick III (1415–1493), who preferred Wiener Neustadt as his residence, was crowned emperor of the Holy Roman Empire by the Pope. The title remained in the Habsburg family (with a brief interruption between 1742 and 1745) until the Empire came to an end in 1806. In 1488, the "House of Austria" was reunited for 76 years. Maximilian I (1459–1519), the "Last Knight," was the founder of the Habsburg practice of conducting politics through matrimony. His motto was: *Bella gerant alii, tu felix Austria nube* ("Let others wage wars: you, fortunate Austria, marry"). In 1477, Maximilian married Mary of Burgundy, heiress to the rich duchy to which the Netherlands also belonged. His son Philip (1478–1506) married Joan, the heiress of Castile and Aragon, bringing Spain with its colonies in South America into the Habsburg realm. Ferdinand I (1503–1564), a grandson of Maximilian, married Anna, heiress to the kingdoms of Bohemia and Hungary. Thus within three generations the Habsburgs were in possession of a world empire on which "the sun never set." Ferdinand I made Vienna the capital of the archduchy. Following the Turkish siege of 1529, he built a ring of bastions and curtains along the ring wall in 1531. The bastion called

Mid-16th century: the Schweizertor (Swiss Gate) by Pietro Ferrabosco and on the right, the wing for the children of Ferdinand I

the Burg Bastion and later the "Spanier" (Spanish Bastion) was built in front of the Widmer Gate. Significant changes were also made within the fortress: the three existing wings were extended outwards and upwards, and the fortified wall on the northwest was replaced by a fourth wing with the Schweizertor (Swiss Gate, built in 1552, probably by Pietro Ferrabosco). Because there was still a shortage of space, a wing was added on the southwest, above the Widmer Gate and beyond, for Ferdinand's children (the "Kinderstöckl"). On the side towards the city, the Burgplatz (Castle Square), on which tournaments were held, was bordered by several buildings that housed the newly constituted administration, including the Court Treasury and the Court Chancellery. On the northwest, the Cillierhof, which had burned almost to the ground in 1525, was repaired and restored to its use as an armoury. Other additions were a room of natural arts and wonders in the palace, a hospital north of the Cillierhof, a corridor from the palace to the Church of the Augustinian Friars and a new Real (Royal) Tennis Court, because the old one had been destroyed in a devastating fire. This was a type of tennis that Ferdinand I had learned to play in Spain.

The Stallburg and the Amalienburg

In 1559, Ferdinand began building a residence for his son on the grounds of an abandoned church east of the palace. Construction of the free-standing building, however, proceeded slowly. Following the death of his father in 1564, Maximilian II (1527–1576) moved into the old residence, converting the new building to provide a stable for his Spanish horses. To this building, known as the Stallburg, a second storey was added in 1565. Hardly any changes were made to the fortress itself, which according to contemporary accounts must have been quite ugly. In 1554, Ferdinand I decided to divide the Habsburg lands among his three sons, which once again diminished the importance of Vienna. Maximilian II, who in addition to "Austria above and below the Enns River" had also received Bohemia and Hungary, spent much of his time in Prague. A year before his death in 1576, he decided to erect a new building to provide a court for his eldest son, replacing the Cillierhof. The armoury moved to Renngasse. But instead of holding court in Vienna, the son, Rudolf II (1552–1612), moved his residence to Prague. As governor, his brother Ernest occupied the third large freestanding building, which was constructed between 1575 and 1577. (The name the building has today, Amalienburg, was not used until the 18th century: the widow of Joseph I, Amalia of Brunswick, moved there in 1711 after her husband's death.)

To house the treasury and art collections, Rudolf II built a new wing (1583–1585) on the northeast of the palace. It was a three-storey building located behind the Real Tennis Court. Expansion of the Amalienburg continued until 1610–1611. Following the death of Rudolf II, his brother Matthias (1557–1619) moved his residence back to Vienna, but because of the Thirty Years' War few changes were made to the Hofburg. Under Ferdinand II (1578–1637) a ballroom was built (1629–1631) where the two Redoutensäle now stand. Most likely this was done at the request of Empress Eleonora Gonzaga.

This building, probably a wooden structure, was converted by Giovanni Burnacini between 1659 and 1660 into a theatre with the latest stage technology. He was commissioned to do so by Leopold I (1640–1705), who ruled for almost half a century (starting in 1657). On the occasion of Leopold's marriage to the infanta Margaret Theresa of Spain in 1666, a new three-tiered opera house with seating for 5000 was built on the "Cortina" (curtain) of the city wall in the area of what is today the Burggarten. The wedding is said to have been one of the most lavish celebrations ever staged in the Hofburg.

Mid-17th century: the Amalienburg with the Minorite Church behind it

The Leopoldine Wing

Leopold I was interested in far more than just Italian Baroque opera and theatre: in 1660 he decided to remodel

The Burghauptmannschaft

By virtue of its dimensions, the Hofburg with its 18 wings, 54 stairways and 19 courtyards is like a small town. It is administered by the Burghauptmannschaft, a department of the Economic Ministry. Among its duties are the negotiation and signing of rental agreements (there are around 50 apartments and several shops in the Hofburg), planning and supervising all construction activities, and maintaining the building complex. It also operates its own fire service, which is responsible for safety.

The first mention of a *Burggraf* (burgrave) appointed to command the Hofburg (Michael von Maidburg) dates from the year 1434. The name "*Burghauptmann*" to designate the office was used for the first time in 1443. In 1793, Francis II/I declined to nominate a burgrave, and those duties were then performed by a "*Burginspektor*" or castle inspector. In 1849, Emperor Francis Joseph I authorized a basic reform of court services. Subsequently the "*Hofburginspektion*" was renamed "*Burghauptmannschaft*." In 1850 Ludwig Montoyer was appointed director of the newly created department. He was the son of the court architect, Louis Montoyer. According to a detailed description of duties, which remained valid until the downfall of the monarchy in 1918, the Burghauptmannschaft had responsibility for taking care of the building complex itself but also for its furniture, security and cleaning. In 1870, Montoyer was succeeded by Ferdinand Kirschner, who deserves credit for the completion of the Michaelertrakt (Michael's Wing).

Since 2001, the Burghauptmannschaft has been responsible not only for the Hofburg, including the Albertina, Kunsthistorisches and Naturhistorisches Museums, but also for all state-owned historical buildings in Austria. These include the palaces in Marchfeld, the former Nazi concentration camp at Mauthausen, the Federal Chancellery, Belvedere Palace and several other palaces in Vienna, the Heldenberg (an Austrian Army memorial), the Hofburg in Innsbruck and Ambras Castle in Tirol. Around 180 employees administer all of these buildings and facilities.

the Hofburg and the courtyard that is now called "In der Burg." Modeled on the new residence in Munich, a long winged building was completed in 1667 between the Kindertrakt (Children's Wing) and the Amalienburg. Based on plans by Philiberto Lucchese, it replaced a section of the city wall. In February 1668, a large fire broke out that almost completely destroyed the new wing. The Jews were accused of arson, and in 1670 at the request of his wife, Margaret Theresa, Leopold I ordered the ghetto to be evacuated and closed in the "Corpus Christi expulsion." Since that time, the district has been called the "Leopoldstadt." By 1681, the Leopoldine Wing was rebuilt by Giovanni Pietro Tencala: it was a third longer than before and a mezzanine storey was added. In addition, the Widmer Tower was incorporated into the façade, so that the building was no longer free-standing. The design of the façade, which was identical to that of the previous building and harmonized with the old palace, was intended to create architectural uniformity.

The riding-school building on the Exercise Ground to the southeast of the palace was not renovated until the Leopoldine Wing had been completed, although plans had existed since 1663. A library floor was added, making it essentially the predecessor of the Court Library. The constant threat of attack from the east had ended with the defeat of the Turks in 1683. For the first time, it was possible to consider converting the Hofburg, which was still a fortress, into a more ostentatious building complex. Leopold I commissioned Johann Lucas von Hildebrandt, who had been Imperial Court Engineer since 1700, to create a model for the new complex. This project, however, was never realized. The Emperor had meanwhile become more interested in a new hunting lodge, which was built between 1695 and 1711 according to plans by Johann Bernhard Fischer von Erlach. The only changes made by Leopold's elder son, Joseph I (1678–1711), were to demolish the south tower, to replace the old sacristy of the Castle Chapel with a new addition, and to connect the Leopoldine Wing to the Amalienburg, which meanwhile had risen to a height of four storeys. Although Fischer von Erlach tutored the Emperor in architecture and was Inspektor der Kaiserlichen Gebäude (Supervisor of Imperial Buildings), architecture remained rather neglected as an art form at Joseph's court. That changed suddenly after his premature death. His brother Charles VI (1685–1740), who had been king of Spain since 1703,

Johann Bernhard Fischer von Erlach

was baptized on July 20, 1656, in St. Martin near Graz and died on April 5, 1723, in Vienna. After training as a sculptor with his father, he turned to architecture. In 1670 he went to Rome, where the work of Francesco Borromini and Gian Lorenzo Bernini deeply impressed him. In 1684 he moved to Naples, returning to Graz in 1686. Two years later he designed Frain Palace in southern Moravia. From 1689 he taught architecture to the Prince Imperial, Joseph I, in Vienna. His first design for Schönbrunn adopted the French style. From 1693, he was employed by the Prince-Archbishop of Salzburg, where his buildings include the Seminary with the Trinity Church (Dreifaltigkeitskirche; 1694–1702) and the University Church (Kollegienkirche; 1696–1707). In 1694 he was appointed Imperial Court Architect and Engineer in Vienna. In 1795 construction began on his second design for Schönbrunn Palace, completed in 1711. Raised to noble rank in 1696, the first artist to be thus honored, he added the name of his mother's first husband (Sebastian Erlacher) to his, calling himself "Fischer von Erlach." In the years that followed, he developed an increasingly independent style of intersecting building wings, whose spatial concept frequently emanated from an oval shape. In contrast to Johann Lukas von Hildebrandt, who was a generation younger, he placed little importance on sumptuous decoration. In 1705, following the accession of Joseph I to the throne, Fischer von Erlach was appointed Inspektor der Kaiserlichen Gebäude (Supervisor of Imperial Buildings). Thus he was in charge of the entire imperial building enterprise. In 1712 he was confirmed in office by Charles VI. In 1721 he published the first seminal monograph on architectural history. Entitled *Entwurf einer historischen Architektur* (*A Plan of Civil and Historical Architecture*), it contained the reconstructed designs of famous buildings. His most important buildings, besides the churches in Salzburg, are Clam-Gallas Palace in Prague (1707–1712), Batthyány-Schönborn Palace (1699–1711), the Böhmische Hofkanzlei (Bohemian Chancellery; 1708–1714) and Schwarzenberg Palace, which Hildebrandt had begun (completion 1720–1723) in Vienna. The strict unity of Trautson Palace (1710–1716) pointed the way to his culminating works in Vienna, the Karlskirche (Church of St. Charles Borromeo, begun in 1716) and the Hofbibliothek (Imperial Court Library, begun in 1722). Just as with the Imperial Stables, his son completed the latter two projects.

Joseph Emanuel Fischer von Erlach

was born on September 12, 1693, in Vienna, where he died on June 29, 1742. Following studies in Germany, Italy and probably in England and France as well, he returned to Vienna in 1722. A short time later he entered the service of Prince Schwarzenberg and took over supervision of the latter's palace from his father, who was gravely ill. In 1725 Charles VI appointed him to his father's office of Supervisor of Imperial Buildings, despite the opposition of Johann Lukas von Hildebrandt. His designs, such as the Reichskanzleitrakt (Imperial Chancellery Wing; 1726–30, which Hildebrandt had begun, and the Hofreitschule (Court Riding School, 1729–1735) in the Hofburg, were influenced by early French Classicism. He later abandoned architecture to pursue his technological talents as inventor, mine engineer and machine-builder.

Johann Lucas von Hildebrandt

was born on November 14, 1668, in Genoa and died on November 16, 1745, in Vienna. He studied with Carlo Fontana in Rome and was a fortifications engineer during the Italian campaigns of Prince Eugene of Savoy. Hildebrandt came to Vienna in 1696. In 1700 he became Court Engineer, in 1711 Director of the Court Department of Planning and Building, and in 1723 Court Architect. He was unable, however, to assert himself against the competition of the Fischers and worked primarily for the aristocracy: Among his buildings were Daun-Kinsky Palace (1713–1726) and Starhemberg-Schönburg Palace (1705–1706) as well as several palaces for

Prince Eugene, including the Lower (1714–1716) and grandiose Upper (1721–1723) Belvedere Palaces as well as completion of Prince Eugene's Winter Palace on Himmelpfortgasse (1702–1724), the core of which had been built by Johann Bernhard Fischer von Erlach (1695–1698). Other Vienna buildings designed by Hildebrandt are St. Peter's Church (1702), the Piarist Church of Maria Treu (1716) and the Geheime Hofkanzlei (Secret Chancellery, 1717–1719), today the Federal Chancellery. Compared to those of Johann Bernhard Fischer, Hildebrandt's buildings seem more pleasant and agreeable. The façades are often decorated with artistically entwined bands, uniting them in an artistic whole. Hildebrandt's architecture was widely popular in his day and had enormous lasting influence.

returned to Vienna in 1712 and immediately asked Hildebrandt to convert the gated structure between Kohlmarkt and the main courtyard into a monumental triumphal arch as a representative sign of imperial power. In 1714, Charles VI was forced to relinquish his claim to Spain (the Bourbons having won the War of the Spanish Succession). He maintained close ties to that country, however, and introduced Spanish court protocol in Vienna. Under his rule, the monarchy reached its greatest geographic expansion.

The Baroque Alterations

In 1713, Charles VI commissioned Fischer von Erlach, whom he had confirmed in office, to design the new Imperial Stables at the edge of the glacis, the defensive slope outside the city wall. Construction began in 1719. The model for the complex was Fischer von Erlach's reconstruction of Nero's Domus Aurea, the Golden House in Rome. The second project was construction of the new Court Library in 1722, built according to Fischer von Erlach's plans instead of a combined riding-school and library building.
With the death of Fischer in 1723, his most bitter rival, Johann Lucas von Hildebrandt, saw an opportunity to become involved in the remodeling of the Hofburg. In 1724 he presented the Emperor with a general plan that proposed striking alterations to the old fortress, including a large chapel in the courtyard. Hildebrandt's concept included a monumental façade facing the city, with sweeping corners, a rotunda and a cupola. But in 1725, Charles VI conferred the

office of Supervisor of Imperial Buildings upon Joseph
Emanuel Fischer, who had already assumed responsibility
from his father for the Imperial Stables and the Court
Library. In the same year the palatial façade of the Imperial
Stables was completed (the additional wings were never
realized, the imperial stud having become too small to
require them). The shell of the Court Library was finished
by 1726, and in 1730 Daniel Gran completed his frescoes.
It took until 1737 to completely furnish the building.
In 1723, the only contract remaining for Hildebrandt was
building the new Imperial Chancellery, the planning of
which he had begun the year before on a commission from
the Imperial Chancellor. But even this wing was never
completed according to his plans: in 1726 Charles VI took
responsibility for the construction away from the Imperial
Chancellor and entrusted it to his Court Chancellery in
order to allow Joseph Emanuel Fischer to design the
façade facing the Burgplatz, although, like the one facing
Schauflergasse, it had already been erected. It was intended
that Fischer should design the Court Treasury and thus the
façade facing the Michaelerkirche (St. Michael's Church).
The goal was twofold: a unification of the façades and a
demonstration of power: the Imperial Chancellery Wing
thus became a project of the Emperor and not of the
Empire. Starting in 1728, following a two-year break in
the planning, the Court Treasury and the façades of the
two buildings were realized. But Michael's Wing with its
dominant rotunda, for which Hildebrandt's triumphal arch
had to step aside so to speak, remained incomplete. By the
time construction was halted in 1735, only the southeastern section of the façade had been completed, with the
Winterreitschule (Winter Riding Hall) stretched out behind
it, having been built by Fischer between 1729 and 1733.
The rotunda, which remained half-finished for the next
one and a half centuries, resembled an ancient ruin.
In 1740 Maria Theresa (1717–1780), the eldest daughter
of Charles VI, ascended the throne. In the first years of
her reign she succeeded in defending her inheritance
against France and Prussia, but she was forced to relinquish the wealthy region of Silesia. The Empress adopted
the ideas of the Enlightenment, introduced compulsory
school attendance for all children and abolished torture.
She also continued the traditional Habsburg matrimonial
policy, marrying off most of her children to royal families
throughout Europe. In 1741, a year after her coronation,

she converted the Ballhaus (Real Tennis Court), which stood between the Winter Riding Hall and the torso of the Round Tower, into the Court Theatre. In the 1770s the Theatre Wing facing Kohlmarkt was given a blind façade, furthering strengthening the picturesque appearance of St. Michael's Square. The new Ballhaus was built next to the Imperial Hospital and remained there until 1903, giving Ballhausplatz its name. The name Bellaria survived as well: the Empress, who lived and reigned (often from her bed) on the second floor ("bel étage") of the Leopoldine Wing, had a special ramp built so that she would not have to climb any stairs, calling it the Bellaria.

The Redoutensäle and Joseph's Square

Once the Court Theatre and the Winterreitschule (Winter Riding Hall) had been built, there was no longer any need for Burnacini's theatre. Between 1744 and 1748 it was converted according to plans by Jean-Nicolas Jadot into a large and a small ballroom, the Redoutensäle. A decade later, Maria Theresa's preferred architect, Nikolaus Pacassi, received a commission to renovate them for the

The Hofburg at the time of Maria Theresa (by Josef Daniel Huber 1776, detail): Court Library, Winter Riding Hall, Court Theatre, Burg Platz (In der Burg)

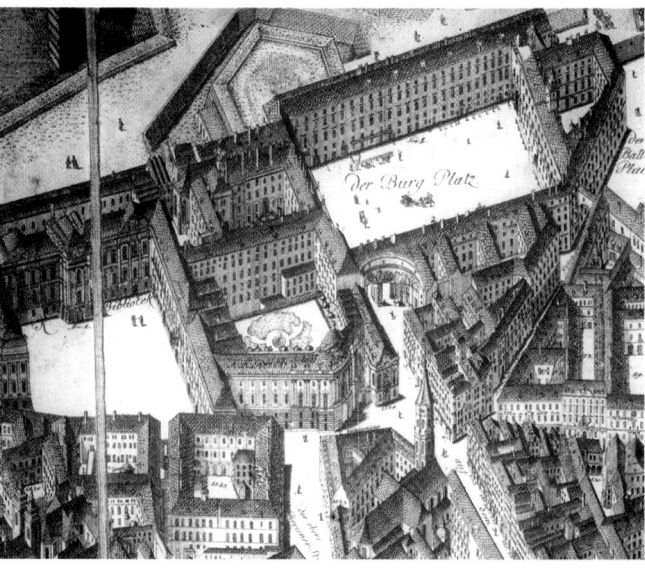

wedding of the heir to the throne, Joseph II. Pacassi was also given the job of renovating the Court Library, because the domed building had settled dangerously due to weak foundations. From 1769, Pacassi also focused on the completion of Joseph's Square, which was finally finished by Franz Anton Hillebrand in 1776. This strictly symmetrical square is considered one of the loveliest in Vienna. In order to provide additional space for the Court Library, the Augustinian Wing was added on the southeast, concealing the Church of the Augustinian Friars behind its façade. Under Empress Maria Theresa the Hofapotheke (Imperial Court Pharmacy) was installed in the Stallburg. The art collection that had been housed there by Emperor Charles VI was moved to the Obere Belvedere (Upper Belvedere Palace) in 1776. The remaining towers of the old fortress were torn down (the south tower had previously been demolished by Joseph I). Two stairways were built (the Botschafterstiege and the Säulenstiege, the Ambassador's and Pillar Staircases, respectively). Because a Swiss Guard kept watch at the gateway to the oldest part of the Hofburg from 1748 to 1767, the names Schweizerhof (Swiss Court) and Schweizertrakt (Swiss Wing) have been used ever since. Joseph II (1741–1790) opened the Augarten and the Prater to the public and shifted the focus of new construction from his residence to public facilities, such as the Allgemeines Krankenhaus (General Hospital). His apartments in the Leopoldine Wing were furnished with far less magnificence than those of his mother, which were parallel to them. Here he built the "Controllorgang" (Inspector's Corridor) and held his audiences, which were open to the public, on the mezzanine floor.

The Congress of Vienna and the Gardens

Leopold II (1747–1792), who reigned for only two years, was succeeded by his son Francis II (1768–1835). Francis gave Tarouca Palace, to the south of the Augustinian monastery, to Albert, Duke of Saxe-Teschen, and his wife, Marie Christine, Maria Theresa's favorite daughter. Starting in 1800, it was remodeled by Louis Montoyer and, with the addition of a new wing, became what is today the Albertina. Responding to the coronation of Napoleon as emperor in 1804, Francis II elevated Austria to the status of an empire and, as Francis I, he became the first Austrian emperor. In 1806, after being defeated by Napoleon, who dictated the

Mid-19th century (steel engraving by J. M. Kolb): the Hofburg with the Montoyer Wing

dissolution of the Holy Roman Empire, Francis abdicated his title. The Empire, which had more than a thousand years of history as a multinational Christian realm, ceased to exist. In 1807 an equestrian statue of Joseph II was unveiled on the former Tummelplatz (Exercise Ground), which was renamed Josefsplatz (Joseph's Square). Between 1805 and 1807 Montoyer built a ceremonial wing that was called disparagingly "the nose" because it was added piecemeal to the Widmer Gate on the side facing the suburbs. Napoleon occupied Vienna on May 13, 1809, and after concluding a peace treaty with the Austrians on October 14, he blew up the fortifications in front of the Hofburg.

In October 1813, Napoleon was defeated in the Battle of the Nations at Leipzig. The Congress of Vienna, which convened from 1814 to 1815 and established a new European order, was a magnificent event. According to a contemporary bon mot, it didn't meet, it danced. Among those residing in the Hofburg were Tsar Alexander, King Frederick William of Prussia and King Frederick VI of Denmark. Napoleon was banished and peace was restored. Between 1816 and 1819, the remains of the Burg Bastion and the Spanish Bastion as well as the old Burgtor (Castle Gate) were torn down, the glacis was leveled, and the Volksgarten was laid out. Between 1819 and 1823 Pietro Nobile built the Temple of Theseus and the Cortisches Kaffeehaus in the Volksgarten. During the same period, the new monumental gateway of the Äusseres Burgtor was built (begun by Luigi Cagnola in 1821 and completed in 1824 by Nobile). In the Neuer k. u. k. Hofgarten (New Imperial and Royal Court Garden, called the Burggarten since 1919), Louis von Remy built two greenhouses of iron and glass (1818–1820 and 1823–1826, respectively). They immediately became the "attractions" of the Biedermeier period.

Francis II/I died in 1835 and was succeeded by his eldest son, Ferdinand I (1793–1875), who had no descendants. He commissioned a grand monument to his father, which was built between 1842 and 1846 on the square In der Burg, which was renamed Franzensplatz (Francis Square), the name it kept until 1918. In March 1848, the Parisian February Revolution spread to Vienna. Although the dreaded chancellor Prince Clemens Lothar Metternich was forced to resign by Ferdinand, crowds of people rose up and stormed the Stallburg, where the National Guard was quartered. Austria's first legislature met in the Winterreitschule (Winter Riding Hall). At the end of October, the situation escalated when Prince Alfred Windisch-Graetz brought his troops into position to retake Vienna. During three days of fighting, which was concentrated around the outer square of the Hofburg (now Heldenplatz) and the Burgtor gateway, a fire broke out in the attic of the Court Library.

Ferdinand I abdicated on December 2, 1848, and his brother, Archduke Francis Charles, renounced the throne in favor of his 18-year-old son, who was to reign for almost 68 years. Francis Joseph (1830–1916), who continued the conservative policies of his predecessors, was confronted with the rising national aspirations of his multinational monarchy. In 1867

October 1848: the roof of the Court Library (Augustinian and State Hall Wings) is set on fire during the civil war

Shortly before its demolition in 1888: the Court Theatre (Rudolf von Alt)

a "compromise" was reached with Hungary, resulting in the founding of the *österreichisch-ungarische Doppelmonarchie*, the "imperial and royal Dual Monarchy," which gave the Hungarians a high degree of independence.

The appearance of the Hofburg changed decisively for a final time under Francis Joseph. First, between 1850 and 1854, the Imperial Stables were remodeled and expanded by Leopold Mayer according to the original plans of Fischer von Erlach. The Winter Riding Hall in the Classicist style was added, and later, at the end of the 19th century, an octagonal pony riding hall was built at the request of Empress Elisabeth, who had married Francis Joseph in 1854.

The Dream of the Imperial Forum

At the end of 1857, Francis Joseph ordered the demolition of the city wall, which had long since lost any military significance. This cleared the way for construction on the glacis. The Ringstrasse (Ring Road) was created – four kilometers (2.5 miles) long, 57 meters (187 feet) wide and flanked by chestnut trees – along with its monumental buildings and palaces. In 1862, the architect Ludwig Förster proposed building the Court Museums instead of purely utilitarian buildings in the area between the Hofburg and the Imperial Stables. In 1864, Francis Joseph gave his approval. These buildings were to become the Kunsthistorisches and the Naturhistorisches Museums (museums of art and natural history, respectively). On the outer square (now Heldenplatz) an equestrian statue of Archduke Charles was unveiled in 1860. He had vanquished Napoleon at the Battle of Aspern in May 1809 (and been defeated by him at the Battle of Wagram in July). Five years later it was joined by a monument to Prince Eugene of Savoy, who had defeated the Turks in the 17th century, and the area became Heldenplatz (officially, only in 1918). The architectural competition for the new museum buildings, however, had not produced an acceptable submission.

In 1869, Gottfried Semper was persuaded to develop a concept for a Kaisersforum (Imperial Forum), but at the request of the Emperor, he had to base his design on an existing project. This resulted in an involuntary and anything-but-frictionless collaboration with Carl von Hasenauer. The new plan, which was submitted in the same year (and altered in 1871), provided for a throne-room building in front of the Leopoldine Wing. It had two large, curved wings projecting at right angles from a central "nose" and was to be connected with the two museums by buildings similar to triumphal arches across the Ring. In 1871, excavation work on the museums began. In 1881, Francis Joseph approved construction of the "Kaisergartenflügel" ("Imperial Garden Wing": the Neue Burg), but construction proved to be laborious and costly because it required excavating 25 meters (82 feet) down. In 1889 the Naturhistorisches Museum opened, and two years later the Kunsthistorisches Museum followed. There were also changes on the side of the Hofburg facing the city centre. In 1888 the old Hoftheater (Court Theatre)

The Imperial Forum designed by Gottfried Semper and Carl von Hasenauer in 1869

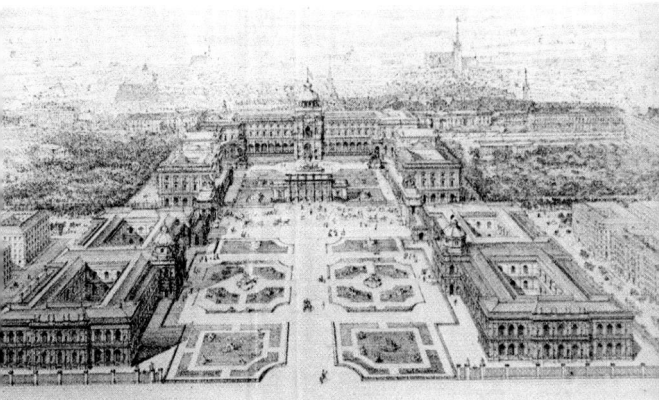

was torn down after the new Burgtheater by Semper and Hasenauer had been completed on the former Löwel Bastion. The concave Michaelertrakt (Michael's Wing) originally planned by Joseph Emanuel Fischer von Erlach could now be completed by Ferdinand Kirschner (following lengthy discussions about whether it should be topped with a dome). The cycle of statues by Lorenzo Mattielli on the façade of the Chancellery was extended with four additional "Labors of Hercules" beside the arched passageway, and by 1893 the Hofburg finally had a magnificent, showy façade. In 1898, the year that marked the 50th anniversary of Francis Joseph's reign, the Neue Burg was still under construction. In 1901 the old greenhouses were torn down and replaced with an Orangerie with Jugendstil elements according to plans by Friedrich Ohmann (completed in 1910). On the Ring, the Corps de Logis, which now houses the Museum of Ethnology, was finished in 1907, completing the Hofburg's new wing.

With the assassination of his wife, Elisabeth, in Geneva in 1898, the Emperor had lost interest in the protracted construction project. In 1906 the heir to the throne, Francis Ferdinand Archduke of Austria-Este, assumed responsibility and soon spoke out against construction of the throne-room building. In 1910 a much smaller Festival Hall Wing was built instead, connecting the Ceremonial Hall with the Neue Burg. In addition, plans for a second wing were abandoned, and a plan to substitute a colonnade was finally dropped as well. Thus the Imperial Forum envisioned by Semper and Hasenauer was to remain forever incomplete. In 1914, following the assassination of Francis Ferdinand in Sarajevo, World War I broke out. In November 1916, Francis Joseph died and was succeeded by his great nephew Charles (1887–1922). With the conclusion of World War I, the Austro-Hungarian monarchy came to an end, and the First Republic was proclaimed on November 11, 1918. Because Charles renounced governmental power but not the throne, he was forced with his family into exile.

The First Republic and the Nazi Period

In 1920 the Office of the Federal President was instituted as the highest office in the Republic of Austria. Some of the buildings in the Hofburg complex lost their usefulness, and many government employees had to be dismissed. Work to complete the interiors of the Festival Hall Wing and the

Neue Burg took until 1923 and 1926, respectively. In 1920, performances resumed at the Court Riding School. In 1921, the Wiener Messe GmbH (Vienna Exhibition and Fair Corporation) began using the Imperial Stables as exhibition space. Since 1922, the complex has been known as the Messepalast (Exhibition Palace). In 1928, the Museum of Ethnology, until that time housed in the Naturhistorisches Museum, opened in the Corps de Logis.

DER ADLER DES HELDENDENKMALS

In 1935, the Kunsthistorisches Museum's Collection of Arms and Armour moved into the Neue Burg.

In 1933 and 1934, at the time of the corporative state, the Äusseres Burgtor was redesigned by Rudolf Wondraček and became the Heldendenkmal (Heroes' Monument) to the Victims of World War I. In 1935, gateways with eagle sculptures by Wilhelm Frass were added on the left and right. On March 15, 1938, four days after the invasion of Austria by German troops, Adolf Hitler announced from the balcony of the Neue Burg the annexation of Austria by the German Reich. Some 250,000 people turned out to cheer the Führer on Heldenplatz. The National Socialists planned to redesign the square and convert it into a parade ground, aligned parallel to the Ring and facing the Neue Burg. They never got that far: towards the end of World War II, Heldenplatz, which had been excavated in the autumn of 1943 to create a pond for supplying water to firefighters, was being used for farming. Between 1940 and 1945 the Messepalast was used by the Nazi regime for staging propaganda events.

Four days after the German invasion: Hitler on Heroes' Square on March 15, 1938

Ortner+Ortner's 1990 design for the MuseumsQuartier (above) and the one on which construction finally began in 1998 (below)

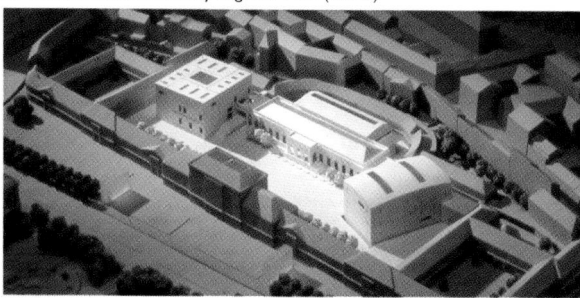

Reconstruction and the MuseumsQuartier

Allied bombing severely damaged not only the Stallburg, the Church of the Augustinian Friars and the Albertina but also the Offices of the Federal President in what is now the Federal Chancellery. In 1946, Karl Renner, who had been elected in December 1945 to be the first Federal President of the Second Republic, got approval from the Russians to move the President's Offices to the former living quarters of Maria Theresa and Joseph II in the Leopoldine Wing. From 1945 to 1955, the Neue Burg was the seat of the Inter-Allied Commission (symbolized to the Viennese by "four [nationalities riding together] in a Jeep"). In 1946, the Vienna Exhibition and Fair Corporation resumed its activities and subsequently built two large halls in the main courtyard of the Messepalast. The Hofburg was repaired and the Stallburg rebuilt. In 1955, following the signing of the Austrian State Treaty, the Lipizzaner horses returned to Vienna. In 1958, the Congress Centre was established in the Festival Hall Wing, and between 1962 and 1966 the Modern Library of the Austrian

National Library was installed in the Neue Burg.
In 1977, using the Imperial Stables to expand the capacity of the neighboring federal museums was considered for the first time. In 1983, it was decided to use the complex as a cultural forum, and in 1986 a two-stage architectural competition was announced. In 1989, Science Minister Erhard Busek (of the Austrian People's Party) referred to the site for the first time as the "MuseumsQuartier," setting the emphasis on contemporary art and culture. The jury recommended unanimously that the design by Laurids and Manfred Ortner be realized. It included two towers (a slender one with an elliptical ground-plan for the library and a cylindrical one for offices). But only a few weeks later, during the summer of 1990, a citizens' action group was formed, and in 1992 the populist newspaper *Kronen Zeitung* launched a campaign against the MuseumsQuartier project. As a result, it had to be downsized several times.

In the early hours of November 27, 1992, a fire broke out in the attic above the Redoutensäle, and the Large Hall was completely destroyed, although firefighters were able to prevent the flames from spreading to other wings. The attic was later converted to usable space. The Kleiner (Small) Redoutensaal was restored; the Grosser (Large) Redoutensaal was renovated and decorated with paintings by Josef Mikl. It reopened on October 26, 1997.

In December 1997 ground was broken for the Museums-Quartier, and in April 1998 construction began. In January 2001 the new buildings were handed over to their future tenants. The official opening of the grounds took place at the end of June. In September 2001 the Museum of Modern Art and the Leopold Museum opened. The renovation of the old buildings was completed in September 2002. Meanwhile in the autumn of 1999, renovation began on the Albertina, which had been closed since the mid-1990s. The museum was given a new study building, two exhibition halls and an underground storage area and reopened in March 2003. At the end of the year Hans Hollein's titanium roof projection was added to the building on the Augustinian Bastion.

Museum of Modern Art in June 2001:
a multimedia show to open the MQ

A Tour of the Grounds

In order to facilitate understanding of the complex architectural history of the Hofburg, the tour is organized chronologically. It begins in the oldest part of the complex, the Alte Burg (Old Castle). Today it is called the Schweizertrakt (Swiss Wing), because the Swiss Guard kept watch here for almost two decades, starting in 1748. Francis I Stephen of Lorraine, the husband of Empress Maria Theresa, had brought the Guard with him from Italy.

1st Loop:
The Middle Ages and the Renaissance

The core of the medieval Herzogsburg (Ducal Castle), which was probably founded by Otakar II Přemysl of Bohemia, was built between the 13th and 15th centuries. The stone fountain next to the gateway is decorated with a double-eagle relief in honor of a visit by Emperor Charles V in 1552. The Gothic ➤ **Hofburg Chapel** in the southern corner was consecrated in 1449. The ground-floor arcades and the Renaissance shape of the windows on the two main floors are the result of remodeling in the 1550s. The Säulenstiege (Pillar Staircase) in the northeast (like the Botschafterstiege – Ambassador's Staircase – on the opposite side) were built by Jean-Nicolas Jadot in the mid-18th century (it is worth having a look in the stairwell). This wing housed the apartments of Emperor Francis II/I (today it houses the Austrian Federal Office for the Care of Monuments). The Ecclesiastical and Secular ➤ **Schatzkammer (Treasury)** is located in the southeastern and northeastern wings.

A passageway on the southeast takes us across the Kapellenhof (Chapel Courtyard), where the chapel's choir, which was added later, is the only visible part of the façade, and on to Josefsplatz (Joseph's Square). This narrow courtyard was created in the second half of the 18th century when the moat was covered over. Joseph's Square was once the Exercise Ground. In the southeastern corner, hidden behind the Augustinian Wing of the Austrian

In the Swiss Court:
fountain with double eagle

National Library, is the ➤ **Augustinian Church,** built in the mid-14ᵗʰ century in Gothic style. We turn to the left (to the northeast) and come to the second large palace, the Stallburg, which was built in 1559 as a residence for Maximilian II. In 1565, the Emperor converted it into stables for his Spanish horses. The Stallburg, which is still the residence of the Lipizzaner horses today, is one of the few remaining Renaissance buildings in Vienna. The exterior façades have retained their original structure (apart from the enlarged windows on the ground floor). Because of the archway leading to the Winterreitschule (Winter Riding Hall), the entrance façade has lost the architectural effect it once had. The Hofapotheke (Imperial Court Pharmacy) was installed in the northern corner of the Stallburg in 1746. Today these rooms house the ➤ **Lipizzaner Museum.** The courtyard of the Stallburg is surrounded by a three-storey arcade with pilasters. The round fountain inscribed with the year 1675

Orientation maps of the Hofburg are posted throughout the grounds.
The point of departure for the tour depicted here is the Swiss Court.

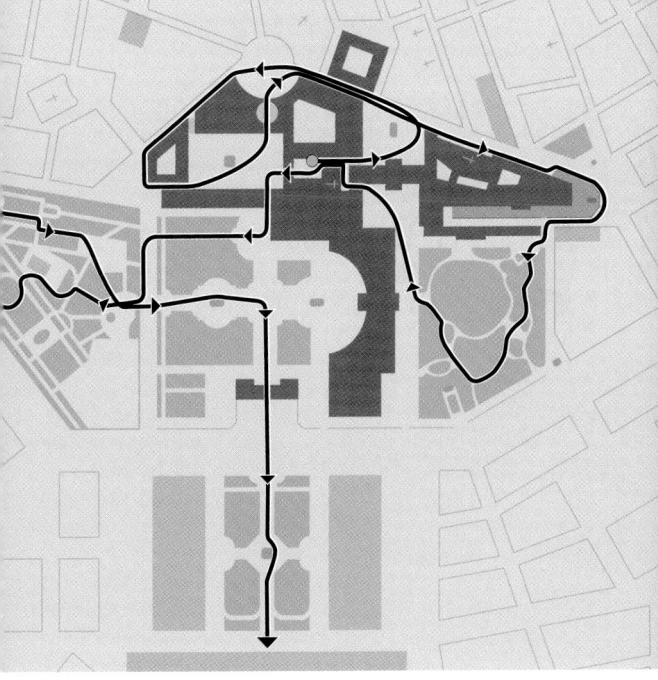

One of the few remaining Renaissance buildings in Vienna: the Stallburg with its arcaded courtyard

was originally in the Amalienburg (Amalia Residence). And that is where we go next: we head north on Reitschulgasse until we reach Michaelerplatz. In the middle of the square we can see excavated foundations from Roman times (2nd to 5th century) and of the first Ballhaus (Real Tennis Court, about 1530). This was the location of the original pleasure garden of the Hofburg, the Paradeisgartl. We turn to the northwest and walk down Schauflergasse.

On the left is the façade of the Imperial Chancellery Wing. It was built between 1723 and 1725 but is mentioned at this point because the Baroque façade with its bull's-eye panes bears the unmistakable signature of Johann Lucas von Hildebrandt. The last building on the right before we reach Bruno-Kreisky-Gasse is a Postmodern building (1982–1986) housing offices of the Foreign and Interior Ministries and the Federal Chancellery. In the mid-16th century, a hospital stood here and, after 1740, the new Imperial Ballhaus that gave the square its name. In media parlance, "Ballhausplatz" is used as a synonym for the Austrian government, much like "the White House" or "Downing Street." The **Federal Chancellery** (**➤ Environs**) was formerly the Geheime Hof- und Staatskanzlei (Secret Court and State Chancellery) and was built between 1717 and 1721 by Johann Lucas von Hildebrandt. The Court Hospital and the Ballhaus were torn down in 1903.

The Amalienburg is directly across from the Federal Chancellery. Construction began in 1575 and was completed by Pietro Ferrabosco in 1611. This Renaissance building, which Maximilian II built for his son Rudolf II, got its name in the first half of the 18th century when Empress Amalia, the widow of Joseph I, resided here. The irregular, four-winged complex has clean and simple façades with broad rustic work. The trapezoidal courtyard has a walled-up pergola and a simple Renaissance well.

The Leopoldine Wing adjoins the Amalienburg on the south, and we will discuss it presently. We walk through the flying buttress that connects the two buildings and back into the courtyard. This square, where tournaments were once held, is now called In der Burg. The façade of the Amalienburg is crowned by an octagonal tower with an early-Baroque helm roof. The lunar clock is said to have been designed by Tycho de Brahe, the court astronomer of Rudolf II. The apartments of Empress Elisabeth (➤ **Imperial Apartments**) are on the second floor (bel étage).

In 1552, two decades before construction of the Amalienburg began, the Schweizertor (Swiss Gate) of the Alte Burg was built by Pietro Ferrabosco at the opposite end of the square. This magnificent Renaissance portal still bears traces of the medieval fortress: for example, the winch for the chains of the drawbridge on either side of the gate. The inscription names Ferdinand I with his official titles (Roman and German King, King of Hungary and Bohemia, Spanish Infante, Archduke of Austria and Duke of Burgundy). The coat of arms is edged with the chain of the Order of the Golden Fleece and shows a one-headed eagle because Ferdinand was not yet emperor at the time.

The Swiss Gate: built in 1552 by Pietro Ferrabosco

Baroque show of imperial power: the façade of the Imperial Chancellery Wing

2nd Loop:
The Baroque Period and Classicism

For almost a century, the four great corner pillars of the Hofburg (Swiss Wing, Church of the Augustinian Friars, Stallburg and Amalienburg) stood separately without a wing to connect them. Only in 1660 did Leopold I decide to extend the Alte Burg to the southwest with a wing towards the Amalienburg. The Leopoldinische Trakt (Leopoldine Wing), under which the imperial wine cellar had been built, caught fire in 1668 only a few months after its completion. Restoration work by Giovanni Pietro Tencala was completed in 1681. The early-Baroque façade extends without accentuation across 29 sets of windows and was deliberately designed to conform to the façade of the Alte Burg. Since 1946 the Leopoldine Wing has been the office of the Austrian Federal President ➤ **Präsidentschaftskanzlei (Presidential Offices)**. The suite of rooms on the second floor (bel étage) facing the courtyard was the apartment of Empress Maria Theresa.

Much new construction occurred under Charles VI. First the Emperor commissioned Johann Bernhard Fischer von Erlach to build the Imperial Stables (1719–1725) and the Court Library (1722–1730), which we will be discussing later. Then Fischer's son, Joseph Emanuel, was entrusted with the Court Riding School (1729–1734) and the Michaelertrakt (Michael's Wing, (1728–1735) and was also commissioned to complete the Imperial Chancellery Wing, which Johann Lucas von Hildebrandt had begun on Schauflergasse in 1723. The façade on the courtyard side is magnificent and ostentatious. The central projection is topped with the coat of arms of Charles VI, with the imperial crown above it, surrounded by the personified virtues of the ruler. The pairs of sculptures on the side portals are by Lorenzo Mattielli: "Hercules and the Cretan Bull" and "Hercules and the Nemean Lion" on the northwest portal, "Hercules and Busiris" and "Hercules and Antaeus" on the southeast.

In addition to the police and the judicial administration of the Court, the Imperial Chancellery Wing housed the Imperial Court and State Archive from 1806 to 1902 as well as the most important of all Court offices, the Obersthofmeisteramt (Office of the Steward of the Household) with the ceremonial department. Following the dissolution of the Holy Roman Empire in 1806, part of the original chancellery rooms were converted into imperial apartments in which Emperor Francis Joseph later lived (➤ **Imperial Apartments**). On the ground floor is the former Court Porcelain and ➤ **Silver Collection**.

The monument to Emperor Francis II/I in the inner courtyard was created by Pompeo Marchesi between 1843 and 1846 on a commission from Ferdinand I in memory of his father. It was produced at the Manfredini bronze foundry in Milan and brought to Vienna in 33 days, drawn by eight pairs of oxen and nine pairs of horses. The four statues that surround the monument symbolize Faith (cross and star), Strength (lion's shield and club), Peace (sword and olive branch) and Justice (scales and sword). The Emperor is portrayed as Caesar Augustus in Roman robes. On the sides of the octagonal column are reliefs that depict the activities and qualities of the people (trade and commerce, mining and metallurgy, farming and stock-breeding, science, art and heroism). The inscription "Amorem meum populis meis" (To My People My Love) is taken from the last will and testament of Francis II/I.

We now walk through the Kaisertor (Emperor's Gate) at the eastern corner of the square to reach Michaelerplatz (St. Michael's Square). On the left we see the **Loos-Haus** built between 1909 and 1911; on the right, the Gothic

Michaelerkirche (St. Michael's Church) with its Classicist façade (➤ **Environs**). We really should have approached this area from **Kohlmarkt** (➤ **Environs**) in order to get the full effect of the façade of Michaelertrakt (Michael's Wing) with its mighty dome. The concave semicircular façade with its sweeping, convex corners closes the Hofburg off from the city center. Construction of this wing began in 1728 but was interrupted in 1735, and for the next 150 years it remained a picturesque torso, reminiscent of an ancient ruin. The original plan of Joseph Emanuel Fischer was completed in 1893 by Ferdinand Kirschner. The central area of the façade is like a triumphal arch with a central projection flanked by double columns. The sculptural decoration is completed by two

The Cellars of the Hofburg

In the old days it was allegedly possible to traverse the cellars of the Hofburg from the Albertina to the Secret Chancellery – today the Federal Chancellery – and from the Court Riding School across the Schweizertrakt (Swiss Wing) and the "Segmentgang" (Segment Corridor) of the Neue Burg to the Kunsthistorisches Museum. The giant subterranean depot of the Austrian National Library has blocked some of the passageways, but this underground labyrinth remains huge. Without a guide from the security service, one would undoubtedly lose one's way. Unfortunately, the cellar levels – meaning the first and second levels – are as a rule not open to the public. The wine cellar used to be in the Leopoldine Wing, near the connecting corridor to the Chancellery (which in February 2000 had to be used by officials because of demonstrations against Austria's new right-wing government). Following the downfall of the monarchy, thousands upon thousands of bottles of wine, spirits and Champagne that had been stored there were auctioned off for the benefit of war victims. Only a giant oak barrel and a magnificent tiled tank that holds an unbelievable 731.5 hectoliters remind us of the cellars' former purpose. Now hundreds of plaster models of statues, monuments and reliefs are stored here, including horses and angels, a massive head of Goethe and a Jesus on the Cross, a massive imperial crown and numerous double eagles. The white statues look, as the author Gerhard Roth wrote in his essay *Die zweite Stadt* ("The Second City"), "… like the props of a dream that are designed to haunt the minds of the dead emperors." And together with the eerie monumental fountains (on the left: "Austria, Ruler of the Sea" by Rudolf Weyer; on the right: Edmund von Hellmer's "Austria, Ruler of the Land"). The cycle of statues begun on the Imperial Chancellery Wing continues on either side of the gateway with four more "Labors of Hercules." The pediment is crowned with allegories of Wisdom, Justice and Power. Above the central gateway arcade is the coat of arms of Habsburg-Austria-Lorraine with trombone-playing figures on either side. Behind the façade of the left-hand wing lies the ➤ **Spanish Riding School**. The Winterreitschule (Winter Riding Hall), built by Joseph Emanuel Fischer between 1729 and 1734, fills the entire building along Reitschulgasse.

We now head down that street in a southerly direction.

In the cellars of the Leopoldine Wing: hundred of plaster models of statues, monuments and reliefs

vaulting, they provide an impressive setting for whodunits (for example, Austrian television's *Kommissar Rex*).

Heading towards the south, before we reach the semicircular choir of the Burgkapelle (Hofburg Chapel), we pass the old Zentralkesselhaus (Central Boiler Room), which in 1953 was converted into a coal-fired central heating plant for the complex but was taken out of service long ago, and the former ice cellar. Ice taken from the Danube was emptied through trap-doors in the barrel vaulting into two rooms that were a good eight meters (26 feet) high. There were semispherical metal humps in the floor, and food was stored directly beneath them.

Beyond the passageway we arrive again at Josefsplatz (Joseph's Square), one whole side of which is occupied by the originally free-standing Court Library (1722–1726), built on plans by Johann Bernhard Fischer. Its ➤ **Prunk-saal (State Hall)** consists of two naves and a large main hall, the central projection of which dominates the entire structure. The sculptural decorations are restricted to the attic zone. In the middle is Pallas Athena (Lorenzo Mattielli, around 1725), who is driving out Envy and Ignorance with her four-in-hand chariot. The atlases on either side are by Hans Gasser (around 1865). On the left they depict Atlas with the Celestial Sphere as well as Astronomy and Astrology, the Allegories of Astronomy; on the right we see Gaea with the Terrestrial Globe as well as Geometry and Geography, the Allegories of Metrology. In the mid-18th century Empress Maria Theresa commissioned Jean-Nicolas Jadot to convert the former Komödiensaal (Theatre) on the northeastern side of Joseph's Square into two ballrooms, the ➤ **Redoutensäle**. Nikolaus Pacassi began plans for the final architectural completion of the square in 1769, and by 1776 an apparently strictly symmetrical Ehrenhof (Court of Honor) had been built. The façades of the Augustinian and Redoutensaal Wings match the strict architectural design of the Court Library. The bronze equestrian monument to Emperor Joseph II, which was commissioned by Francis II/I, was made by Franz Anton Zauner (1795–1807). As can be seen from the clothing and footwear of the Emperor, it was inspired by the statue of Marcus Aurelius at the Capitol in Rome. Two palaces form the fourth side of Josefsplatz. The early-Classicist façade of Palavicini Palace (No. 5), which was built by Johann Ferdinand Hetzendorf (1783/1784), caused a scandal because of its revolutionary simplicity. Palffy Palace (No. 6), which underwent extensive alterations in 1956, was built in around 1575. The Classicist elements of the façade date from 1800.

We now walk down Augustinerstrasse past the Church and Monastery of the Augustinians to Lobkowitzplatz with the ➤ **Österreichisches Theatermuseum (Austrian Theatre Museum)** on the left and continue to the _ Albertina, which is also the home of the ➤ **Film Museum**. In around 1745, Emanuel Teles Count Sylva-Tarouca built a three-storey palace on the Bastion, which was 11 meters (36 feet) above street level. On a commission from Albert, Duke of Saxe-Teschen, Louis Montoyer began

Soaring into the square: Hans Hollein's flying roof for the Albertina

remodeling work in 1800, expanding the palace to the southwest with a wing that had a long, twenty-window façade. The projecting flying roof on the Bastion as well as the stairs were built between 2001 and 2003 in the course of the renovation and expansion of the Albertina on plans by Hans Hollein. He is also responsible for the Postmodern base zone with its bull's-eye windows on Augustinerstrasse. They make it clear that the two cellar basement levels of the palace were previously not exposed: a long ramp was torn down after World War II and replaced by a flight of steps.

On Albertinaplatz stands Alfred Hrdlicka's 1988 **Monument Against War and Fascism** (➤ Environs). The southeasternmost point of the Hofburg is the Danubiusbrunnen (Danube Fountain, 1864–1869), based on a design by Moritz von Löhr. Johann Meixner's figures in white Carrara marble are found in the nine – originally eleven – niches of the Augustinerbastei (Augustinian Bastion). They symbolize rivers, including the Danube, Mur, Salzach, March, Raab and Enns. On the Bastion stands a bronze equestrian statue of the Austrian field marshal Archduke Albert. It was made by Caspar von Zumbusch in 1899.

To the southeast we see the back of the **State Opera** (➤ Environs). We walk around the fountain in a clockwise direction and turn right on Hanuschgasse. From there a ramp leads up to the Albertina. We continue, however, through the Abrahamtor (Abraham's Gate) with the simple stone statue of the preacher Abraham a Santa

Built by Friedrich Ohmann in Jugendstil: the Palmenhaus

Clara, made in 1928 by Hans Schwarthe, and into the Burggarten. This garden was laid out between 1817 and 1819 after the Burg Bastion had been demolished by the French (1809) and the fortifications had been torn down. Until the downfall of the monarchy in 1918, it was reserved for the use of the imperial family. Francis I, who loved gardens and flowers, is said to have been personally involved in details of the planning. The garden had to be downsized on the northeast to make room for the monumental Neue Burg in 1881. In addition, the old glasshouses had to be torn down, and between 1902 and 1906 Friedrich Ohmann replaced them with the Jugendstil structure of the Palmenhaus (on the northwest, parallel to the Albertina). Today it houses a café-restaurant and the ➤ **Schmetterlinghaus (Butterfly House)**.

In the southern corner stands a bronze statue of Emperor Francis Joseph. The monument on the southwest to Wolfgang Amadeus Mozart, made in 1896 by Viktor Tilgner,

originally stood on Albertinaplatz, which was called Albrechtsplatz (Albert's Square) at the time, in front of the present Café Mozart. It was taken to safety after the bombing on March 12, 1945, and moved to the Burggarten in June 1953. The bas relief on the front depicts the invitation of the Stone Guest (Commenda-

In the Burggarten only since 1953: the Mozart Monument

tore) in the opera *Don Giovanni*. On the back is the six-year-old composer at the piano with his sister, Nannerl, and his father, Leopold, with his violin. On the west side of the garden, towards the Neue Burg, stands an equestrian statue of Francis I Stephen of Lorraine. Work on this monument in early-Classicist style by Balthasar Ferdinand Moll was begun during the Emperor's lifetime. It was first placed in the new Paradeisgartl on the Burg Bastion in 1797; in 1819 it was moved to the Kaisergarten.

A path leads to the north between the Neue Burg and the Palmenhaus to the Bibliothekshof (Library Courtyard), where we can see the rear façade of the former Court Library with the ➤ **Prunksaal (State Hall)**. In the northern corner of the so-called Verbindungstrakt (Connecting Wing), an inconspicuous passageway leads to the Kapellenhof (Chapel Courtyard) and from there we can re-enter the Schweizerhof (Swiss Court) and continue back to the inner courtyard (In der Burg). We now turn left and walk through the former Widmer Gate towards Heldenplatz (Heroes' Square). On the right, at the beginning of the pedestrian arcade, we see the exposed stonework of the medieval Widmerturm (Widmer Tower), which was torn down in 1753. The second part of the arcade is the Montoyer Wing, which used to be called the "Nase" (nose). The building, which used to project from the Leopoldine Wing into what is now Heldenplatz, was built by Louis Montoyer (1802–1806) and houses the Ceremonial Hall. Adjoining it is the Festival Hall Wing, built between 1910 and 1923 in the style of late historicism.

Heldenplatz and the Imperial Forum

We are now standing at the edge of Heldenplatz (Heroes' Square). On the far side is the Äusseres Burgtor. Its columned façade facing the Hofburg is an imitation of the Propylaeum in Athens. The building with its five arched gateways and two wings was built between 1821 and 1824 in the Classicist style. In 1934 it was redesigned as a ➤ **Heldendenkmal** (Heroes' Monument). After the destruction of the Burg Bastion, the huge area was intended to serve as a parade ground, but it was not completed until the early 20th century when the Neue Burg was built. Heldenplatz gets its name from the two monumental sculptures of heroes: on the northwest stands a monument to Archduke Charles, who defeated Napoleon

A reproduction of the one in Athens: The Temple of Theseus

at the Battle of Aspern in May 1809 and was defeated by him at Wagram in July. The outstanding equestrian statue made by Anton Dominik Fernkorn between 1853 and 1859 was unveiled in 1860. The monument to Prince Eugene of Savoy, the "Noble Knight" and commander to three emperors (Leopold I, Joseph I and Charles VI), was erected five years later on the southeast. The bronze equestrian statue (the Lipizzaner is executing the figure called a levade) on a pedestal of polished marble was begun by Fernkorn in 1860 and completed by Franz Pönninger. Instead of going straight ahead, we turn right towards the northwest. The façade of the Leopoldine Wing facing the suburbs is stepped and elaborately structured. The balcony was added in 1750 by Jean-Nicolas Jadot. Joseph II, a son of Maria Theresa, lived in the state rooms on this side. Since 1946 they have been part of the ➤ Präsidentschaftskanzlei (Presidential Offices). The projection on the narrow side was built in 1875 after the Bellaria ramp, which had been built to allow Empress Maria Theresa easy access to the second floor, was torn down.

We now walk across the Volksgarten (People's Park), to which we will return after the tour. In this area, where fortifications used to stand, Maria Theresa built the new Paradeisgartl atop the wall. After the destruction of the Burg Bastion, the park was laid out within the remaining city walls in 1819 and opened in 1823 as the exact counterpart of the private Kaisergarten (Imperial Garden). Instead of winding paths, the Court Architect Louis von Remy chose a strictly geometrical layout so as not to "open the way to indecency." This was part of efforts during the Biedermeier period – also called "Vormärz" (the period before the March 1848 revolution) – to allow the police to better monitor the Emperor's subjects. Between 1819 and 1823 Pietro Nobile built in the Volksgarten the ➤ Temple of Theseus – a smaller copy of the one in Athens – and the Cortisches Kaffeehaus with its semicircular colonnade. Expanded several times, it is now the ➤ **Volksgarten** Club Discothèque. Later a fountain with the "Triton and Nymph" bronze sculpture by Viktor Tilgner (1880) was added along with an octagonal water reservoir house (1890), which was converted in 1924 into the Meierei milk-bar.

Because the curtain wall that separated the park from the glacis had been torn down in 1860, it was now possible for the Hofburg complex to extend all the way to the new Ringstrasse. In this eastern area, which was laid out between 1863 and 1865, a central fountain by Anton Dominik Fernkorn was added in 1866. In 1889 a monument to Franz Grillparzer was unveiled (a larger-than-life seated figure by Carl Kundmann; the architectural design was by Carl von Hasenauer). The reliefs depict scenes from Grillparzer's dramas. Starting in 1884, the Volksgarten was extended towards Löwelstrasse. Since 1907 this area has been dominated by a monument to Empress Elisabeth with the remarkable Jugendstil architecture of Friedrich Ohmann (seated figure by Hans Bitterlich). Immediately behind it we see the **Burgtheater** (➤ **Environs**). In 1921 the bronze statue of a young athlete by Josef Müllner was placed in front of the Temple of Theseus. Next to the Volksgarten Restaurant, Oswald Haerdtl opened a "Milchbar" in 1951, a glass pavilion with a penthouse roof, still in its original condition.

After our tour through the park, we turn to the southeast and look across Heldenplatz to the historicist Neue Burg. This mighty structure with its curved façade is only one of two wings that were originally planned. In order to better understand the Imperial Forum project, which was based

With the Burgtheater in the background: the monument to Empress Elisabeth

The Imperial Forum was never finished: the Neue Burg with the Corps de Logis

on an 1860s concept, we go back to the street that runs from Michaelerplatz through Widmer Gate to the Äusseres Burgtor. It is the central axis of a gigantic symmetrical complex that is bounded on the southwest by the Imperial Stables, where the MuseumsQuartier opened in 2001. Implementation of the plans by Gottfried Semper and Carl von Hasenauer began in 1871. The first buildings outside the Ring were the Kunsthistorisches and the Naturhistorisches Museums. In 1881 work also got underway on the Kaisergartenflügel (Neue Burg), which 17 years later, on the 50th anniversary of the reign of Emperor Francis Joseph I, had still not been completed. In 1906 the heir to the throne, Francis Ferdinand, opposed the building of a domed "Throne Room Wing" because of the cost involved. It would have been placed in front of the Leopoldine Wing and the "nose." Instead, a smaller Festival Hall Wing was built between 1910 and 1923 to link the Montoyer Wing and Alte Burg with the Neue Burg. Since 1958, it has served (along with other rooms) as the ➤ **Hofburg Congress Centre**. In 1913, a year before the outbreak of World War I, plans to build the opposite wing in the Volksgarten were abandoned: the Imperial Forum was to remain only a torso.

The Neue Burg consists of a mighty central projection with two segmented wings, each with nine pairs of columns. Between the windows of the lower storey are 20 sculptures, symbolically representing the history and peoples of Austria. From the balcony, Adolf Hitler announced the annexation of Austria by the German Reich in March 1938. Access to the Modern Library of the ➤ **Österreichische Nationalbibliothek** as well as to three collections of the Kunsthistorisches Museum: the ➤ **Hofjagd- und Rüst-kammer (Collection of Arms and Armour)**, the ➤ **Ephesus Museum** and the ➤ **Sammlung alter Musikinstrumente (Collection of Ancient Musical Instruments)** is through the portico. Adjoining the Neue Burg towards the Ringstrasse is the Corps de Logis, which was completed in 1907. With its impressive, glassed-in courtyard, it was intended to provide lodging for guests. Today it houses the photo archive and portrait collection of the Austrian National Library. Since 1928 it has also been the home of the ➤ **Museum of Ethnology.**

We now pass through the Äusseres Burgtor and head in the direction of the former Imperial Stables. From the Ring we can see that the central axis of the strictly symmetrical Kaiserforum (Imperial Forum) leads not only to the main entrance of the MuseumsQuartier but past the former Imperial Stables and on to the district of Spittelberg beyond. In the courtyard of the Stiftskaserne military base stands a cylindrical anti-aircraft tower of steel-reinforced concrete. It was built during World War II as one of six such emplacements in Vienna. After the war the "shooting cathedral," as it was euphemistically called by Hitler's architect Friedrich Tamm, was supposed to become a "Totenburg" ("Fortress of the Dead"), a giant mausoleum for the fallen soldiers. Tamm planned to cover the outermost edge, with its extended bastions, with black marble that had already been selected. His vision for this practically indestructible "hall of glory" was taken in part from Castel del Monte in Apulia. We now cross the Ring to Maria Theresa Square. At the center is Anton Dominik von Fernkorn's monument to the Empress, which was unveiled in 1888. His pyramidal composition rises to a summit at her diadem. On the left is the ➤ **Kunsthistorisches Museum** (opened in 1891) and on the right the ➤ **Naturhistorisches Museum** (1889). They are mirror images of one another. Half columns provide structure to the central projection, and each has a large central dome and four satellite cupolas.

A mirror image of the Natural History Museum: the Museum of Art History

Heldenplatz as an Historic Focal Point

No other event is so closely associated with Heldenplatz (Heroes' Square) as the seemingly endless cheering of the population there after German troops invaded and occupied Austria. On March 15, 1938, Adolf Hitler announced the annexation of Austria by the Third Reich from the balcony of the Neue Burg. In his play *Heldenplatz*, which caused an unbelievable commotion in Austria before and after the 1988 première at the Burgtheater, Thomas Bernhard (1931–1989) lets this cheering rise to an almost unbearable level.

Abused by the National Socialists, Heldenplatz has always been used for important state events, regardless of the political system, and for large events of all kinds (Catholic conferences, open-air concerts, festivals, sporting events as well as by the army for parades and swearing-in ceremonies). It is regarded as the focal point and nucleus of recent Austrian history with all its contradictions and competing ideologies, a symbol of both power and defeat, of both psychological repression and political protest.

The square was created in an act of humiliation: Napoleon blew up the Burg Bastion and the Spanish Bastion in 1809. The rubble was cleared away and the area leveled after the Congress of Vienna. Called the Paradeplatz until 1821, it was intended for military parades. In the revolutionary year of 1848, the area became a battlefield on which more than 2000 lives were lost. The name Heldenplatz has been used only since 1865 when the second equestrian statue was unveiled: Archduke Charles and Prince Eugene of Savoy were among the monarchy's most successful commanders.

Heldenplatz, which is open on the north and separated from the Volksgarten only by a railing, is also part of a torso, because the Neue Burg was never completed. Thus even though the megalomaniac plans for the Imperial Forum project had already been abandoned in 1913, the square stands for the fall of the Habsburg empire and the dissolution of the multinational state of Austria-Hungary. In 1925, there was a mass demonstration on Heldenplatz in favor of Austria being annexed by the German Reich. In 1931 there was a "Völkische Kundgebung" ("national demonstration") by the National Socialists, and in 1934 a demonstration for Chancellor Engelbert Dollfuss, who had been assassinated by illegal Nazi Party members after he had dissolved Parliament and established an authoritarian regime ("Austro-Fascism"). In 1935 there was a parade by the Ostmärkische Sturmscharen (a Catholic paramilitary organization) at which Chancellor Kurt Schuschnigg spoke (on the steps in front of the Neue Burg's balcony), and in the autumn of 1938 there was a large demonstration of the NSDAP (Nazi Party). In February 1972, a huge crowd on Heldenplatz expressed its solidarity with the skier Karl Schranz, who had been excluded from participation in the Olympic Games for flimsy reasons. In September 1983, Pope John Paul II blessed Heldenplatz during a vesper service for Europe, and in June 1998, he said mass there. Nobel Peace laureate Elie Wiesel waved to the crowd from the "Hitler balcony" in June 1992 at a "Concert for Austria." In January 1993, 250,000 people holding burning candles ("The Sea of Lights") demonstrated against racism and a xenophobic petition sponsored by the rightwing, populist Freiheitliche Partei (Freedom Party). In February 2000 the crowd was demonstrating against the conservative People's Party's decision to enter into a coalition with the Freedomites. Meanwhile Heroes' Square has become the finish line of the Vienna Marathon and thus, perhaps, truly deserving of its name.

Thousands of burning candles to demonstrate against racism and xenophobia: the "Sea of Lights" on Heldenplatz in 1993

Dominating the skyline behind the MuseumsQuartier: the Nazi-era anti-aircraft tower at the Stiftskaserne military base in Spittelberg

The Imperial Stables and the MuseumsQuartier

The Imperial Stables, on which construction began in 1719, only appear to fit into the Imperial Forum, which is 150 years younger. They are not quite at a right angle to the axis between the two museums and the Neue Burg. Johann Bernhard Fischer von Erlach aligned his building with the old wing of the Hofburg Palace and not with Michaelerplatz (St. Michael's Square), as did the architects of the late 19th century. This cannot be seen from a distance, but for the architects of the MuseumsQuartier, Laurids and Manfred Ortner, this symmetric deviation was of great significance, as we shall see.

But first we approach the multi-axis façade. By giving the façade a rhythmical structure, Fischer von Erlach was somehow able to deal with its enormous size (a respectable 355 meters, 1129 feet). With their prominent central projection the Imperial Stables appear more like a palace than a utilitarian building. Fischer von Erlach's model, after all, was his reconstruction of Nero's palace in Rome, the Domus Aurea (Golden House). Nevertheless, there is a certain discrepancy between the width and the height of the two-storey building. During the war with Napoleon, the Imperial Stables were seriously damaged. In the course of renovation in 1815, two towers along the sides and the gable of the central building were demolished.

Between 1850 and 1854 other significant changes were made, especially to the interior of the complex. Leopold

Mayer enlarged the building, for the most part remaining true to Fischer von Erlach's design. But only the transverse wings were built in Neo-Baroque style. The central Winter Riding Hall clearly speaks the language of Classicism. Mayer changed the façade on the courtyard side of the old building, which used to be less ornamented. He inserted larger windows, added a balcony, and placed terraces between the staircases. In the course of the restoration in 2001, the building received a coat of salmon paint, similar to the color that the building is believed to have had during the Baroque period. If you cross into the courtyard, you will notice that some sections of the building are painted a lighter, yellow color, which is supposed to be that of 1854. The various nuances in the paint make it easy to recognize the period during which each part of the building was completed.

The Main Courtyard, which is the largest enclosed square in Vienna, is dominated by three free-standing buildings: in the center is the Winterreithalle (Winter Riding Hall), now the home of the two performance and event halls ➤ **Halls E + G**. Because this building was built at the same time as the Fischer von Erlach Wing, its central projection with the three-axis notched arcades and the horsehead shaped arch-stones is no longer oriented towards the axis of Michaelerplatz – Maria-Theresien-Platz. The ➤ **Leopold Museum** to the left of the Winter Riding Hall, however, is oriented parallel to the two Court Museums. Hence, it "docks" with the axis of the Imperial Forum. The outside surfaces, including the roof, are faced with white limestone. The interior structure of the building is evident on the façade as well: the walls of the rooms are indicated by slight grooves in the surface, creating an almost antique effect.

The ➤ **Museum of Modern Art**, a cube with a curved roof surface, is even more oriented towards the center of the square than the Leopold Museum. But this rotation was not an arbitrary decision either: the building reflects the structure of the Spittelberg. In contrast to the Leopold Museum, which is oriented towards imperial splendor, it points toward the bourgeois culture in which Modernism has its roots. The Museum with its curved roof, dark-gray basalt lava and narrow windows is in stark contrast to the Leopold Museum. It resembles a nearly impregnable fortress or a huge monolith that appears to have grown up from the ground. The size of the stone slabs, whose shading changes with the weather, increases towards the top, which lends the massive building a dynamic air. A small gap between the façade and the square provides an open view into the deep. The Museum had to be "pushed into the ground," according to the architectural theorist Friedrich Achleitner, so that the old silhouette would not be affected. Both museum buildings had to be repeatedly downsized in response to protests by preservationists. This also explains why they can hardly be seen from outside the complex: the height of the new buildings was not permitted to be greater than that of the central projection of the Fischer von Erlach Wing. It is especially sad that there is no outward sign – a tower or a column – to serve from afar as a symbol of contemporary architecture and of the MuseumsQuartier.

The third building by the brothers Ortner, the ➤ **Kunsthalle Wien**, is located behind the Winter Riding Hall and accessed through the latter. This municipal exhibition hall shares its foyer with the performance and event Halls E and G. The entrance area, a former gateway, was especially accentuated: it is lined with red clinker bricks, the surface material of the Kunsthalle. The two large museums can be approached via two open staircases on the left and right. Continuing across bridges, one can reach the finished attic of the Oval Wing, which is behind the Kunsthalle, and the entrance on Breite Gasse.

We continue our stroll on ground level, turn right, and walk through the Main Courtyard along the Fischer von Erlach Wing, in which we find the theme street Electric Avenue of ➤ **quartier21**. The second floor of the Baroque building was used by veterinarians, drivers, coachmen, blacksmiths, valets, stablemen, grooms, court servants, doorkeepers and stable masters. Through the gateway we reach the Staatsratshof (State Councilor's Courtyard) with the ➤ **Architekturzentrum Wien**. The event hall "Podium" was formerly the saddler's workshop; the information room of "basis wien" was formerly used for leather storage. We continue in a southeasterly direction and come to the Sattlerhof. Towards the end of the 19th century at the request of Empress Elisabeth, an octagonal riding hall was built, a half-timbered building with exposed brickwork. Today it houses the library of the Architekturzentrum. We turn left and pass a steep ramp, which leads to the Glacis-Beisl and continues in a semicircle to the second floor of the Neo-Baroque Imperial Stables.

Our path leads along the Museum of Modern Art to the rear entrance of the Kunsthalle. It was built as a free-standing building on the site of the open-air Summer Riding School. It stands close to the Winter Riding Hall, whose roof edge it overlaps with its brick roof. In contrast to the richly decorated edifice of the Winter Riding Hall, which was designed for purposes of traditional representation, the façade is reminiscent of a factory. On the other side of the "ravine" is the Oval Wing. The lateral wing, which adjoins it on the northeast, houses the ➤ **Tanzquartier Wien** on its upper floor.

We return to the Main Courtyard and see the southeastern wing of the Fischer von Erlach Wing with the theme street "transeuropa" of ➤ **quartier21**. The sculptural horse-heads on the portals of the building indicate its original use. Through one of the two gateways, we reach the Fürstenhof (Prince's Courtyard) with the ➤ **Zoom Kindermuseum** and the ➤ **Dschungel (Theatre for Young Audiences)**. Behind it is the Klosterhof (Cloister Courtyard). Today the former Klosterschule (Cloister School) is the studio of the TV station Puls TV. Another gateway leads to Mariahilfer Strasse. If you want a real overview of the complex, turn right and visit the cafeteria and roof terrace of the furniture store Leiner at Mariahilfer Strasse 18 (opening times: Mondays to Fridays 9:30 a.m. to 6:30 p.m., Saturdays 9 a.m. to 5 p.m.). The view, which takes in far more than just the MuseumsQuartier and the Hofburg, is impressive.

Evening rendezvous: the Main Courtyard of the MuseumsQuartier

Albertina

ADDRESS: Albertinaplatz 1
OPENING TIMES: daily 10 a.m. to 6 p.m., Wednesday until 9 p.m.
GUIDED TOURS: Saturday, Sunday and holidays at 3:30 p.m.
PHONE: +43/1/534 83 0
INTERNET: www.albertina.at, E-MAIL: info@albertina.at

Albrecht Dürer: "The Hare"
(watercolor, 1502)

The Albertina is the largest and most valuable collection of graphic arts in the world. At present it has around 65,000 drawings and almost a million graphic reproductions from the late Gothic to the contemporary modern period. The Albertina is generally associated with Albrecht Dürer's "Praying Hands" and "The Hare," but its collection of outstanding works ranges from Raphael, Michelangelo, Leonardo da Vinci, Rembrandt and Rubens to Eugène Delacroix, Edouard Manet and Paul Cézanne. In addition, the Albertina also has a large number of works by Egon Schiele, Gustav Klimt, Oskar Kokoschka, Pablo Picasso, Robert Rauschenberg and Anselm Kiefer.

The foundations were laid by the man who gave the Albertina its name: Albert Kasimir, Duke of Saxe-Teschen (1738–1822). Together with his wife, Marie Christine, the favorite daughter of Maria Theresa, he spent 50 years amassing his collection. In addition to the drawings and prints, there are two large special collections. The architectural collection consists of around 25,000 drawings, sketches and models, including a wealth of material from the estates of Francesco Borromini, Johann Bernhard Fischer von Erlach, Carl von Hasenauer, Adolf Loos and Clemens Holzmeister. The photographic collection, which was established in October 1999, contains the institution's own holdings as well as those of the Höhere Graphischen Bundes-Lehr- and Versuchsanstalt (Graphics School) in Vienna and the collection of the legendary publisher Langewiesche, famous for its photographic volumes *Die Blauen Bücher*, ("The Blue Books").

History: Around 1745, Emanuel Teles Graf Sylva-Tarouca, who was president of the Niederländische Kanzlei (Dutch Chancellery) and the Court Building Surveyor of Empress Maria Theresa, built a three-storey palace on the Augustinerbastei (Augustinian Bastion), which was 11 meters (36 feet) above street level. The trapezoidal outline of the foundations resulted from the previous building on the site, a mid-17th century storehouse for building materials.

Shortly before her death in 1780, Maria Theresa appointed the husband of Marie Christine – Albert, Duke of Saxe-Teschen – to be the new governor of the Austrian Netherlands. Albert initially gave up the use of his palace in Vienna and moved to Brussels, where he commissioned Charles de Wailly and Louis Montoyer to build Laeken Palace. In 1792, he and Marie Christine were forced by the Napoleonic Wars to flee Brussels. Emperor Francis II/I gave them Tarouca Palace and the adjoining part of the Augustinian monastery as a gift.

In 1800, two years after the death of his wife, the Duke commissioned Louis Montoyer to remodel it. First the Monastery Wing was modernized to provide a home for the Duke's growing collection of drawings and reproductions. In a second phase of construction, the palace was expanded, with a long wing with 20 sets of windows facing what is now the Burggarten.

At Albert's death in 1822, his heir was Archduke Charles, who had been adopted. He commissioned

The Albertina over the centuries: the palace of Count Sylva-Tarouca (c. 1800), the Danube Fountain (c. 1900) and the building after it was bombed in March 1945

Magnificent: the Gold Cabinet with its Sèvres table

Josef Kornhäusel to completely rearrange the palace and decorate the rooms in the style of Classicism. The entrance to the *piano nobile* (floor above the ground floor) was now via the Minerva Hall, the Colonnade and the Sphinx Staircase. Next to the Festival Hall, which was divided into two rooms, a ballroom was built. Today it is the home of a cycle by Joseph Klieber: *Apollo and the Nine Muses*. Although all the rooms were newly decorated with paneling, wall lamps and trellises as well as wall coverings and window drapes, some furnishings were used that Albert had brought with him from Laeken Palace when he returned to Vienna.

At the death of Charles in 1847, ownership was transferred to his eldest son, Archduke Albert. Between 1864 and 1868, after the demolition of the fortifications, Moritz von Löhr redesigned what remained of the Bastion, creating the Albrechtsrampe (Albert's Ramp) and the Danubiusbrunnen (Danube Fountain). Johann Meixner created the allegoric river figures in Carrara marble for the 11 arched niches, now only nine. In 1899, the equestrian statue of Albert by Carl von Zumbusch was installed on the Bastion. In 1906 Archduke Frederick decided to add to the palace. This was still in planning when World War I broke out in 1914, and the project was abandoned. With the downfall of the monarchy, ownership of the palace was transferred to the new Republic. In 1920 the collection was combined with the graphics collection of the former Imperial Court Library, and in 1921 it was given the name Staatliche Graphische Sammlung Albertina (Albertina State Graphics Collection). In March 1945, just before the end of World War II, the palace and the bastion were severely damaged by bombing. In the course of restoration between 1948 and 1950, massive changes were made. Although it had not been hit by bombing, the long ramp was torn down and replaced with a stairway. The main entrance was moved from the Bastion to Augustinerstrasse, and much of the decoration on the façade of the palace was removed.

In the mid-1990s, the museum had to be closed for long-overdue renovation, which took longer than expected. In 1999, a study building with a library and workshops as well as a subterranean depot were built on the Burggarten side. The change is almost unnoticeable from the exterior. Director Klaus Albrecht Schröder was also able to garner support for building two exhibition halls and restoring parts of the Baroque façade to their condition of 1822 and 1867, respectively. Thus the entrance was moved back to the front of the palace on the Bastion and the courtyard was roofed over. The Albertina reopened in March 2003. The titanium roof project, named "Soravia Wing" for its sponsor, was completed in the autumn of 2003. The "wing" was the work of Hans Hollein, who also designed the Postmodern base zone on Augustiner-strasse with its bull's eye windows and wave relief.

Tour: Crossing the Harriet Hartmann Court, which is the box office and center of activity (the restaurant on the left, the shop on the right), we reach the oval Minerva Hall, dominated by a statue of the goddess. On the left, an escalator leads to the subterranean Bastei Hall, which

The ballroom on the *piano nobile* with the cycle *Apollo and the Nine Muses*

is mainly used for displaying contemporary art and photography. Behind Minerva Hall, the Colonnade with its artificial-marble columns leads to the Sphinx Staircase. The Pfeiler Hall to the left as well as the Studio Gallery below on the mezzanine level are used for small individual shows. Above the stairway with its two sphinxes, we come to the *piano nobile*. On the right is the Propter Homines Hall in the Augustinian Monastery Wing. In this area were once the collection of Archduke Albert and a Classicistic library corridor.

We proceed straight ahead to the State Rooms (including the Muses' Hall, Tea Salon, Billiards Room, Audience Chamber, Study and Spanish Apartment). They look as they did between 1822 and 1825, but most of the furnishings are considerably older (e.g. in the mirrored Golden Cabinet and the ceramic panels in the Wedgwood Room), because they came from Laeken Palace. The Rococo Room, however, dates from around 1870: Matilda, the daughter of Archduke Albert, was a secret smoker and set herself on fire – much like Paulinchen in the German fairytale – and the furnishings with her. Thus the walls are covered not in silk but in satin. The Kaminzimmer (Fireplace Room) was furnished in 1897.

The small Sèvres table in the Golden Cabinet (a gift from King Louis XVI and Marie-Antoinette) and the center chandelier in the Muses' Hall are the only original items remaining. They were later purchased from the heirs of Archduke Frederick, who after the expropriation of 1919 had received permission to take furniture, carpets, vases, mantle clocks and other furnishings with him when he went into exile in Hungary. In 1936, his belongings were auctioned off and scattered around the world. For reasons of safety and conservation, the drawings on the walls of the State Rooms are generally facsimiles.

Architekturzentrum Wien

Address: MuseumsQuartier, Museumsplatz 1
OPENING TIMES: daily 10 a.m. to 7 p.m., Wednesday until 9 p.m.
LIBRARY: Monday, Wednesday and Friday 10 a.m. to 5:30 p.m., Saturday and Sunday 10 a.m. to 7 p.m. Phone: +43/1/522 31 15
INTERNET: www.azw.at, E-MAIL: office@azw.at

The Architekturzentrum Wien (Architecture Center Vienna) encloses three sides of the Staatsratshof (State

Once Empress Sisi's pony riding hall: the library of the Architecture Center

Councilor's Courtyard) in the northern part of the MuseumsQuartier. It has a total area of approximately 1,900 m² (20,000 square feet). It consists of three halls for exhibitions and presentations, the Podium lecture hall and an open-stack library in the Oktogon, the former pony riding hall built at the request of Empress Elisabeth. It has more than 4000 titles and some 80 architecture magazines from around the world. Cafeteria Una is extremely successful from an architectural point of view: the barrel vaulting was faced with Turkish tiles by the French architects Anne Lacaton and Jean Philippe Vassal.

History: In the spring of 1992, on a commission from the City of Vienna, the architectural theorist Dietmar Steiner began to create the concept for an architecture center. A year later, in June 1993, the interim Architekturzentrum was opened in the planned MuseumsQuartier. Two halls were available, an exhibition hall (today called "the old hall") and the meeting hall, called the Podium. In the following years, the Architekturzentrum developed an active exhibition and meeting program consisting of discussions, lectures and excursions. Since 1993, it has been organizing the Viennese Architecture Congress. The year 1995 marked the founding of the architecture library, the only such resource that is publicly accessible. Also in 1995, the Architektur Archiv Austria (AAA) database was started, which has been accessible via the Internet since 1997. In the course of the MQ construction, the Architekturzentrum was enlarged to its current size. It opened on October 10, 2001.

Augustinian Church and Heart Crypt

ADDRESS: Joseph's Square. Augustinian Monastery: Augustinerstrasse 3
MASS WITH CHOIR AND ORCHESTRA: Sunday at 11 a.m. (except July and August)
PHONE: +43/1/533 09 47-0
INTERNET: www.augustiner.at, www.kirchenmusik-augustin.at
E-MAIL: augustinerkloster.wien@augustiner.at, info@kirchenmusik-augustin.at

Among Vienna's medieval churches, St. Augustine's is second in size only to St. Stephen's Cathedral. It was the Court's parish church, where Abraham a Santa Clara preached his sermons in the 17th century. It was also the Habsburg matrimonial church and the scene of the wedding of Leopold I and Margaret Theresa of Spain in 1666, Maria Theresa and Francis Stephen of Lorraine in 1736, Napoleon (represented by Archduke Charles) and Marie-Louise in 1810, and Francis Joseph and Elisabeth in 1854.
On the wall of the right aisle is the tomb of Archduchess Marie Christine. Commissioned by her husband, Albert, Duke of Saxe-Teschen (founder of the ➤ **Albertina**), it was created by Antonio Canova between 1798 and 1805. The monument of Carrara marble depicts a funeral procession of six figures at the entrance of a tomb, a pyramid. Among

Restored to Gothic style at the end of the 18th century: the Augustinian Church

those depicted are Virtue (with the urn of ashes) and Mercy. An oval medallion above the illusionist scenery, bordered by a serpent as the symbol of eternity and held by the floating figure of Bliss, shows the departed.

Farther to the front is a curiosity, the Heart Crypt. In 1627, the Loreto Chapel was built in the middle of the nave, in imitation of the Santa Casa. It was commissioned by Eleonora Augusta, the second wife of Ferdinand II. King Ferdinand IV (1633–1654) specified that his heart was to be buried there, and almost all the Habsburgs have followed his example. In the course of restoring the church to Gothic style in 1784, the chapel was moved to a side room. The silver urns with the hearts were placed in a double row in the crypt behind it. Every Sunday after high mass – at around 12:20 p.m. – it is possible to view the 54 urns through the barred windows in the door. Emperor Francis Joseph was the first to break this tradition by having his mortal remains, including his heart, buried next to those of Empress Elisabeth in the **Kaisergruft** (Imperial Crypt) in the Kapuzinerkirche (Church of the Capuchin Friars) (➤ **Environs**). The Gothic St. George's Chapel, which adjoins the Loreto Chapel, is a remarkable structure with two naves. It contains the tomb of Leopold II but is not open to the public.

History: In 1327, Duke Frederick I provided land southeast of the castle so the Augustinian Hermits could build a monastery. Construction of the church with three naves began three years later (the architect was Dietrich Ladtner von Pirn), and the church was consecrated in 1349. Construction of St. George's Chapel, parallel to the nave, began in 1337 on a commission from Duke Otto. The cemetery in front of the church was abandoned in 1460 and replaced by an imperial garden, which Ferdinand I used as an exercise ground. In 1634, St. Augustine formally became the parish church of the Court, and soon the interior was remodeled in the early-Baroque style with 18 side chapels. The church tower was built in 1652, and between 1767 and 1769 the façade disappeared behind the left wing of the former Court Library ➤ **Prunksaal** (**State Hall**). On a commission from Emperor Joseph II in 1783, the church was restored to Gothic style by Johann Ferdinand Hetzendorf von Hohenberg and the number of monks was reduced. The last Augustinian prior died in 1837. During the fighting of the 1848 Revolution, the Court Library was set ablaze. The fire spread to the roof of the monastery and brought down the tower, which was rebuilt in 1852. The High Altar, made by Andreas Halbig between 1857 and 1870 and installed in 1874, was originally intended for the Votivkirche. After being damaged in bombing during World War II, the monastery and church were restored, and the work completed in 1950. Since 1951 the church has been back in the hands of the Augustinians. Interior restoration undertaken between 1996 and 1999 was intended to restore the church to the style of 1783.

Dschungel Wien
(Theatre for Young Audiences)

ADDRESS: MuseumsQuartier, Museumsplatz 1
PROGRAM: from early October until late May
PHONE: +43/1/522 07 20
INTERNET: www.thfk.at, E-MAIL: office@thfk.at

The 970 m² (10,400 square feet) Theatre for Young Audiences called Dschungel (Jungle), is located in the Klosterhof (Cloister Courtyard) of the MuseumsQuartier; the entrance is in the Fürstenhof (Prince's Courtyard). It has two multi-purpose halls (with seats for 100 and 180, respectively), a seminar area and a play corner. The Theatre offers guest performances as well as its own productions. In addition to conventional theatre for children and young people, it also offers marionette, puppet and dance theatre as well as music productions and plays of an experimental nature. It is also a center for providing information and continuing education in theatre for children and young people.

History: Since the early 1990s, those actively involved in staging children's theatre in Vienna had been calling for a children's playhouse of their own. Among other sites, a theatrical venue in the Spittelberg area was considered, but the project failed for lack of funds. The success of the Zoom Children's Museum led in 1997 to the idea of converting the empty premises of the former Residenz Cinema, adjoining the MuseumsQuartier on Mariahilfer Strasse, into a playhouse for children and young people. The concept and plans were presented in the summer of 2000, and in the autumn of 2002 the City of Vienna made a commitment to its realization. Construction began in the summer of 2003, and the Theatre opened on October 1, 2004.

Ephesus Museum

ADDRESS: Neue Burg, Heldenplatz (Middle Gate)
OPENING TIMES: daily except Tuesday 10 a.m. to 6 p.m.
PHONE: +43/1/525 24-476
INTERNET: www.khm.at, E-MAIL: info.as@khm.at

Ephesus, which was founded in Asia Minor by the Greeks in around 1000 BC, was one of the most important cities of classical antiquity. During its golden age (2nd century AD), some 300,000 people lived in the capital of the Roman province of Asia, where Heraclitus had once taught and where the Apostle Paul lived for two years. But it is worth visiting the Ephesus Museum not only because of the archaeological finds on display and the model of the reconstructed city (on a scale of 1:500). Not to be missed are the Neue Burg's monumental and magnificently decorated staircase, built between 1907 and 1913, in which most of the objects are exhibited, as well as the concave Marble Gallery. The admission ticket is also valid for the other collections of the ➤ **Kunsthistorisches Museum** in the Neue Burg and Corps de Logis.

Among the items on display are architectural models, reliefs, busts and small sculptures, including a bronze table candelabrum depicting the battle between Heracles and the Centaur. In addition to an

Life-size bronze statue of an athlete cleaning his strigil, or scraping iron (Roman copy)

octagonal tomb and a bronze statue of an athlete cleaning his strigil (scraping iron), the showpiece of the collection is the 40-meter (130-foot) long frieze of the Parthian Monument, built around 170 AD to celebrate the victory of the Roman troops over the Parthians. The reliefs glorify the life of Emperor Lucius Aurelius Verus, the adopted brother and son-in-law of Marcus Aurelius. A number of finds are on display from the Temple of Artemis, the goddess of nature and childbirth, which was numbered among the Seven Wonders of the World, and from the famous Library of Celsus, which was built above the tomb of the Roman senator Tiberius Iulius Celsus Ptolemaeanus, who died in 117 AD. Also in the collection are architectural fragments and sculptures connected with cult worship on the Greek island of Samothrace. They were excavated in 1873 and 1875 by Austrian archeologists.

History: In 1895 the Austrian Archeological Institute began excavation work that continues today at Ephesus (in modern Turkey). There near the village of Selçuk, British archeologist John Turtle Wood discovered the ruins of the Temple of Artemis in 1869. Until 1906, the Turkish authorities granted the Austrians permission to take numerous objects of high artistic quality to Vienna. The finds first entered the Collection of Greek and Roman Antiquities of the Kunsthistorisches Museum, but because of lack of space only a small number of them could be exhibited (sometimes in the ➤ **Temple of Theseus** in the Volksgarten). In 1978, following four years of planning and remodeling, the Ephesus Museum opened in the Neue Burg as a branch of the Collection of Greek and Roman Antiquities.

Esperanto Museum

ADDRESS: Hofburg, Michaelerkuppel
(Batthyány Staircase in Michael's Dome). From the summer of 2005: Mollard Palace, Herrengasse 9
OPENING TIMES: October to June: Monday to Wednesday 9 a.m. to 4 p.m., Thursday noon to 7 p.m., Friday 9 a.m. to 1 p.m. July to September: Monday to Friday 9 a.m. to 1 p.m.
PHONE: +43/1/535 51 45
(from the summer of 2005: +43/1/534 10 730)
INTERNET: www.onb.ac.at/sammlungen/plansprachen/
E-MAIL: plansprachen@onb.ac.at

The Esperanto Museum was founded in 1927 by Hugo Steiner and incorporated into the ➤ **Österreichische Nationalbibliothek (Austrian National Library)** in 1929. It has the world's largest collection of material on artificial languages, including 25,000 library volumes, 2500 periodical titles, 2000 museum objects, 2000 autographs and handwritten pieces, 20,000 photos and photo negatives, 1100 posters and 40,000 pamphlets . Esperanto is the most important of the world's 500 registered artificial languages, but the Museum documents the entire range, from Klingon (from the TV series *Star Trek*) to pan-Slavic languages developed during the period of the Austro-Hungarian Empire to the Lingua Ignota of Hildegard von Bingen.

The project Lingvo Internacia, which was presented in a thin brochure in 1887 by the Polish-Russian oculist Dr. L. L. Zamenhof writing under the pseudonym "Dr. Esperanto," has since developed into a complete language, used today by several million speakers. With the help of audiovisual media, historical documents and other objects, the Museum provides insights into the history and significance of the language. In 2005 the Esperanto Museum is moving to the recently renovated Mollard Palace, which is also the home of the ➤ **Globe Museum** and the Music Collection of the Austrian National Library.

The posters had already been printed, but the World Esperanto Congress of 1914 had to be cancelled because of the First World War

Film Museum

ADDRESS: Augustinerstrasse 1
OPENING TIMES OF THE LIBRARY:
Monday and Thursday noon to 6 p.m.
PHONE: +43/1/533 70 54
INTERNET: www.filmmuseum.at, E-MAIL: office@filmmuseum.at

The Film Museum was founded in 1964 by Peter Konlechner and film artist Peter Kubelka. Its principal focus is on the preservation, restoration, study and presentation of film as a medium. The German magazine *Der Spiegel* called the Film Museum "one of the most agile cinémathèques in Europe." Comprehensive retrospectives are devoted to avant-garde film, the comedians of the 1920s and 30s, Soviet Revolutionary films, classic American film genres and Japanese cinema.

Since 1965, these retrospectives have been shown in the Museum's own cinema. For the 25th anniversary in 1989, the "Invisible Cinema" based on a concept by Peter Kubelka was opened: a screening room in black-on-black design and intended as a "viewing and listening machine" permits viewers to focus their concentration with utmost intensity on the film being shown. Since November 2002, the Film Museum has been equipped with a completely renovated and extended projection and sound system.

The Museum has a collection of more than 20,000 films. In addition to classics of international cinema and avant-garde film, historical film documents and newsreels, propaganda films and commercials, it contains contemporary independent cinema as well as the works of German-speaking filmmakers in exile. The library of the Film Museum is the largest of its kind in

Austria, with more than 16,000 books and over 200 periodicals. Use of the library is free, but the books cannot be checked out. The Film Museum currently has more than 12,000 members.

A "viewing and listening machine": a screening room in black-on-black design makes for "Invisible Cinema"

Pocket globe with hinged case
(England 1750)
Diameter: 7 centimeters

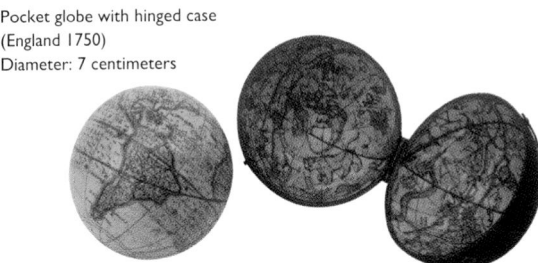

Globe Museum

ADDRESS: Josefsplatz 1, left side-gate.
From the summer of 2005: Mollard Palace, Herrengasse 9
OPENING TIMES: Monday to Wednesday and Friday 11 a.m.
to noon, Thursday 2 p.m. to 3 p.m.
PHONE: +43/1/534 10-297
(from the summer of 2005: +43/1/534 10-700)
INTERNET: www.onb.ac.at/sammlungen/globen/

The unique Globe Museum in the ➤ Österreichische
Nationalbibliothek (**Austrian National Library**) has a
collection of more than 400 globes and related instruments, such as armillary spheres, planetaria, lunaria and
telluria. With respect to the objects made before 1850,
the collection is the second most important in the world,
after the National Maritime Museum in Greenwich. The
oldest surviving globe in Austria (made by Rainer
Gemma Frisius about 1535) is on loan to the museum.
Around 200 exhibited objects reflect changing ideas
about cartography and cosmography as well as develop-
ments in the construction of globes down to the present
day. The museum records the history of our concept of
the shape of the earth and skies, bringing them to three-
dimensional life.

History: Globes were documented at the Imperial Court
Library from the beginning of the modern age (including an armillary sphere made by Martin Furtenbach
around 1535), but those items have been lost. The
Venetian globe-maker Vincenzo Coronelli gave Leopold
I a pair of his globes (each 110 centimeters, 43 inches in
diameter) that were lavishly colored and decorated with
a portrait of the Emperor. Together with a second,
almost identical pair of globes, they were exhibited
beneath the central dome of the State Hall in the Court
Library. A pair of globes by Gerard Mercator (1541 and

1551) were acquired from a private owner in 1875. But interest in models of the earth and planets remained limited, and in 1922 there were only 14 globes in the National Library.

The Globe Museum was founded as part of the Map Department of the National Library in 1953 and opened in 1956. An important part of the holdings had been collected by the Viennese globe researcher Robert Haardt, who had established a museum in his apartment after World War II. In its first three decades, the Globe Museum's original collection of 71 items more than doubled. In 1986 it moved to new space, but as new acquisitions and loans entered the collection, the quarters soon proved to be too small. In 2005 the Museum is moving to the recently renovated Mollard Palace, which is also the home of the ➤ **Esperanto Museum** and the Music Collection of the National Library.

Geocentric and heliocentric armillary sphere (Vienna 1764)

Halls E + G

ADDRESS: MuseumsQuartier, Museumsplatz 1
OPENING TIMES: vary depending on the event
BOX OFFICE AND ADVANCE SALES: Monday to Saturday from 10 a.m. to 7 p.m.
PHONE: +43/1/524 33 21
INTERNET: www.halleneg.at, E-MAIL: office@halleneg.at

The two performance halls, which opened in May 2001, are in and under the former Winter Riding Hall in the MuseumsQuartier. They share the entrance, box office and foyer with the ➤ **Kunsthalle Wien**, which was constructed directly behind the building. The underground Hall G is used by ➤ **Tanzquartier Wien** from September to April. In May and June both halls serve as venues for the Vienna Festival. During the remaining months, there are events of all kinds. The ingeniously illuminated foyer of Hall E is arguably the most successful architectural detail in the MuseumsQuartier.

History: The Vienna Festival is a large, comprehensive performing arts festival staged every year in early summer. Starting in 1985, various halls of the Messepalast were used as performance venues, including those called E and G. By October 1989, plans had been made to create a performance hall (in combination with the Kunsthalle), but it was not feasible to erect a dedicated building for this purpose. In the summer of 1995 it was decided to convert the Winter Riding Hall to a performance hall and to erect the Kunsthalle behind it. In 1997, a decision was made to create a second, underground hall to be used primarily for dance performances.

The Winter Riding Hall was divided into two separate spaces to improve the acoustics. Because of its length it would otherwise hardly have been suitable for spoken theatre. The separation is created by a steeply rising grandstand. Reminiscent of a ship's hull, it is set into the foyer with its central bar. The aluminum lining of the grandstand's lower surface is in contrast to the former Emperor's Box, now the home of Café-Restaurant Halle. Two free-standing staircases form a buffer between the two architectural styles: clean and contemporary on the one hand and ornamented Classicistic on the other.

Architecturally brilliant: the foyer of Hall E with the former Emperor's Box

Heldendenkmal (Heroes' Monument) and Crypt

ADDRESS: Heldenplatz
OPENING TIMES OF THE CRYPT: Tuesday to Friday
8 a.m. to 11:30 a.m. and 12:30 p.m. to 4 p.m.
MASS: every Sunday and holiday at 10 a.m.

In May 1809, a few days before the Battle of Aspern, which he was to lose, Napoleon bombarded the city of Vienna from the site of the Imperial Stables. Among the structures destroyed was the Burgtor gate. Between 1821 and 1824, in the course of converting the area to a parade ground, a new gate was built on plans by Luigi Cagnola, later modified by Pietro Nobile, to create a memorial to the Battle of the Nations at Leipzig (1813). The broad structure with five entrances separated by columns – the gateway in the middle was reserved for Court carriages – is considered the most important work of "Revolutionary Classicism" in Austria. In 1934 the Burgtor, which since 1916 had been a War Memorial (laurel wreaths with the names of fallen soldiers on the triglyph frieze), was redesigned by Rudolf Wondraček as a Heroes' Monument. Two basins for memorial flames were added on the side facing the Ring. Two monumental stairways were cut into the Burgtor on the side, leading to an open Ruhmeshalle (Hall of Glory) above the gate with its five entrances. It was dedicated to those who served in the Imperial Army from 1618 to 1918.
In the northwestern wing was the Crypt, an apsidal room flanked by columns, with the sculpture of a *Toter Krieger* (*Dead Warrior*, 1935) made by Wilhelm Frass of red marble. He also added the eagle sculptures to the gateways on either side of the Burgtor. In the Nazi daily *Völkischer Beobachter* ("People's Observer") of December 25-26, 1938, Frass, who was one of the most frequently employed

Austrian sculptors during the Nazi period, boasted that when the figure was erected, he had hidden a metal capsule with a declaration of faith in National Socialism. His wish came true on March 15, 1938,

Crypt with the sculpture of a
Dead Warrior

when Hitler laid a wreath at the feet of the statue. Despite repeated protests, the sculpture has not been removed and no one knows whether Frass's note actually exists. In the adjacent room are books with the names of Austria's fallen soldiers from both World Wars.

In 1965, the chapel for non-Catholics in the southwestern wing became a "shrine for the victims in the struggle for Austrian freedom" and since then it has also served as a mortuary. In 1991, a cast-iron cross designed by Gustav Peichl was installed on the south of the Burgtor in remembrance of the visits of Pope John Paul II to Vienna (1983 and 1998). Since 2002 there has been a metal monument north of the gate, dedicated to police officers and constables who have died in the line of duty.

Hofburg Congress Centre

ADDRESS: Heldenplatz
ADMISSION: only for public events
PHONE: +43/1/587 36 66
INTERNET: www.hofburg.com
E-MAIL: kongresszentrum@hofburg.com

The Hofburg Congress Centre is a complex of magnificent rooms that gradually grew together over the centuries. Directly connected to the ➤ **Redoutensäle** on Josefsplatz (Joseph's Square), it consists of 33 rooms that are used for staging events for between 60 and 3500 participants. The total area is 17,000 m² (183,000 square feet). The main entrance is in the Festival Hall Wing, which connects the Alte and the Neue Burg (Old and New Castle) with the Montoyer Wing (built between 1802 and 1806) and the Leopoldine Wing. The Festival Hall became necessary in the 20th century when the heir to the throne, Francis Ferdinand, opposed the building of an impressive throne hall as the heart of the Kaiserforum (Imperial Forum) planned by Gottfried Semper and Carl von Hasenauer. Construction of the Festival Hall Wing, which was designed by Ludwig Baumann in the style of late historicism, began in 1910. Work on the interior was halted during World War I and not completed until 1923, after the downfall of the monarchy. Since the renovation and modernization of the building in 1958, the rooms have been used primarily for holding national and international conferences. In 1969, a private company, the Vienna Congress Centre Hofburg Manage-

The Habsburg's final building project: the Festival Hall

ment Company Ltd., assumed managerial responsibility. In addition to the numerous congresses (Vienna has an outstanding reputation as a convention center), the Hofburg is also used for trade fairs (e.g. antiques), large banquets and a number of traditional Viennese balls (including those of the lawyers, doctors and hunters). The ball season opens each year with the Kaiserball (Imperial Ball) at New Year's.

Tour: On the second storey (*bel étage*) of the connecting wing are several halls, including the large Festival Hall, with three Neo-Baroque, monumental ceiling paintings executed by Alois Hans Schram between 1915 and 1918, octagonal paintings by Viktor Stauffer in the vaulting and lunettes by Eduard Veith. The decoration is an allegory of the House of Habsburg as the savior of the Christian West under the patronage of *Magna*

Mater Austriae and as the patron of art and science.
The Ceremonial Hall on the northwest is reached by crossing the Side Gallery. The hall was designed by Louis Montoyer and has 24 Corinthian columns of yellow faux marble and a coffered ceiling in the Classicist style. The 26 double crystal chandeliers formerly lit the room with 1300 wax candles. The hall was used as a throne room until 1918 as well as for concerts, wedding banquets and various balls. Here the Emperor conferred honors on noblemen, and the imperial couple conducted an annual foot-washing ceremony on Maundy Thursday. In this hall, Napoleon also courted Archduchess Marie-Louise, whom he married in 1810.

The Marble Hall on the northwest, which in imitation of the Ceremonial Hall was clad in faux marble in 1841, is in the Leopoldine Wing. It adjoins the Secret Privy Chamber with its original Rococo stucco ceiling. This is where Emperor Francis Joseph gave speeches to open the meetings of the Austro-Hungarian delegation. The other rooms of the Leopoldine Wing, which were the apartments of Empress Maria Theresa and Joseph II, have housed the President's Offices since 1946. The entrance to the ➤ **Präsidentschaftskanzlei (Presidential Offices)** is on Ballhausplatz.

On the southeast is the Trabantenstube (Chamber of the Guards, where the bodyguards kept watch) and the Rittersaal (Knights' Hall). These two rooms are in the oldest part of the complex, in the former "palas" of the late-medieval fortress, and together were once the Tanzhaus (Dance House). Starting in 1657, they were used by Leopold I for official functions, a purpose that continued after 1666 when the Leopoldine Wing was finished. Maria Theresa was christened in the Rittersaal in 1717. The baptismal font was set with precious stones and contained holy water to which five drops from the River Jordan had been added. In the course of general renovation in 1749, the room was redecorated in Rococo style.

The Rittersaal is adjoined by the Radetzky Apartments, where Field Marshal Johann Joseph Wenzel Count Radetzky, a personal friend of Emperor Francis Joseph I, lived after the revolutionary events of 1848. The Belgian tapestries are from the 16th and 17th centuries. Before the Neue Burg was built, the Botschafterstiege (Ambassador's Staircase) in the Schweizerhof (Swiss Court) provided access to the State Rooms. The staircase was built between 1749 and 1751 by Jean-Nicolas Jadot.

Hofburg Chapel

ADDRESS: Hofburg, Schweizerhof
OPEN TO VISITORS: from September to June, Monday to
Thursday 11 a.m. to 3 p.m., Friday 11 a.m. to 1 p.m.,
Sunday 8:15 a.m. to 10:45 a.m.
OPENING TIMES OF THE BOX OFFICE: Friday 11 a.m. to 1 p.m.
and 3 p.m. to 5 p.m., Sunday 8:15 a.m. to 9:15 a.m.
PHONE: +43/1/533 99 27
E-MAIL: hmk@aon.at, INTERNET: www.bmbwk.gv.at/hmk

The Hofburg Chapel, restored in 1977, is the home of the
Hofmusikkapelle (Court Orchestra and Choir) and thus also
of the Vienna Boys' Choir. Their musical performances can
be heard every Sunday at 9:15 a.m. from mid-September to
June (standing room is free), when the Hofmusikkapelle –
members of the Vienna Philharmonic, the men of the State
Opera Choir and the Vienna Boys' Choir – performs a mass.
On the tabernacle of the main altar is a wooden crucifix
with a legend: pursued by Protestants, the counter-
reformer Ferdinand II sought refuge beneath the black-
painted cross on June 19, 1619. It is said to have comforted him with the words "Ferdinand, I will not forsake
you." And in fact, Ferdinand was rescued from this difficult situation by the arrival of the Dampierre regiment.

History: Founded by Albert I, the Hofburg Chapel was first
mentioned in 1296. In 1424, the Gothic choir was added,
and interior improvements were made in the second quarter of the 15th century. The chapel was dedicated in 1449 to
the "Most Holy Trinity and All the Saints." On July 7,
1498, Maximilian I reorganized the Hofburg Chapel under
the direction of Bishop Slatkonia, a date that is considered
to mark the founding of the Hofmusikkapelle and the Hofsängerknaben (Court Orchestra and Boys' Choir). During
the Baroque period, music was accorded great importance:
Ferdinand III, Leopold I and Joseph I were composers
themselves, and under Charles VI, Johann Joseph Fux was
Hofkapellmeister (Court Composer and Music Director).
During the reign of Maria Theresa the orchestra's importance declined, its function being restricted to liturgical
services and entertaining the imperial household. In 1748
the Empress replaced the wooden altars with marble ones,
"Ferdinand's Cross" was mounted on the tabernacle, and
three new galleries as well as 12 oratories were added. The
richly decorated façade of the chapel was lost when the
Botschafterstiege (Ambassador's Staircase) was built

between 1749 and 1751. The renovations ordered by Francis II/I led to the restoration of the chapel to "Gothic" style as it was understood during the Romantic period: tracery was added to the galleries and oratories and a new pulpit in Gothic style was made. Almost nothing remains of the previous decoration, with the exception of 13 wooden statues (ca. 1480) that decorated the pillars. From 1788 to 1824 Antonio Salieri was Hofkapellmeister, but the Hofburg Chapel soon lost its significance once again: the Gesellschaft der Musikfreunde (Society of Friends of Music – the Musikverein) was founded in 1812 and became the focus of musical life. Even after the downfall of the monarchy, the Hofmusikkapelle continued to perform, responsibility for it having been transferred to the Education Ministry. The Institut der Hofsängerknaben (Boys' Choir Institute) was closed in 1920 but was reestablished in 1924 on a private basis. The name Wiener Sängerknaben (Vienna Boys' Choir) did not become established until 1928.

Hofjagd- und Rüstkammer (Collection of Arms and Armour)

ADDRESS: Neue Burg (Central Gate), Heldenplatz
OPENING TIMES: daily except Tuesday 10 a.m. to 6 p.m.
PHONE: +43/1/525 24-462
INTERNET: www.khm.at, E-MAIL: info.hjrk@khm.at

Unique: the "Eagle Armour" made by Jörg Seusenhofer (1547)

The Collection of Arms and Armour of the ➤ **Kunsthistorisches Museum** on the third floor of the Corps de Logis and in the Marble Gallery of the Neue Burg is the most important and best-documented collection of its kind in the Western world. There are objects representing almost every European monarch and prince from the 15th to the early 20th century, and the helmets and suits of armour on display were custom-made by the most renowned armourers. There are also decoratively etched swords, shields and daggers as well as beautifully ornamented rifles, pistols and shotguns from the 16th to the 19th century. Some of the suits of armour on display were intended for use in battle, but most of them – like the weapons – either resulted from the need for ostentation or were used for sport at court.

History: The armoury can be traced back to Emperor Frederick III (1425–1463). While the weapons were originally stored in the castle itself and in the abandoned Church of St. Paul, they were moved to the Stallburg at the end of the 16th century. The focus at that time was the collection of arms and armour of Emperor Maximilian II (1527–1576) and of his brothers, Ferdinand and Charles. Most of the objects – including the most beautiful ones – once belonged to them.

In 1606 Emperor Rudolf II acquired the collections at Ambras Castle near Innsbruck in Tirol. They had been accumulated by Ferdinand II (1529–1595) and included his extraordinary Heldenrüstkammer (the Atrium Hero-

icum – Armoury of Heroes). For the next two centuries they remained in Tirol. The armoury in the Stallburg continued to grow steadily as each new ruler added his splendid personal weapons and trophies (e. g. from the victorious battles against the Turks). In 1750, Empress Maria Theresa moved all of it to the armoury on Renngasse, putting it on display in a Baroque pantheon of Austrian and Habsburg history. On the orders of Joseph II, the armoury of Archduke Charles, which was stored in Graz, was added to the Vienna collection in 1765.

In 1859, the Renngasse armoury was torn down and the collection was moved to the newly constructed Arsenal, where it was combined with ostentatious weapons from Laxenburg Palace and the most beautiful items in the Hofjagd- und Sattelkammer (Collection of Arms, Armour and Saddles) to create the "k. u. k. Hof-Waffensammlung" (Imperial and Royal Court Arms Collection). Together with the Ambras collection, which had been moved to Vienna in 1806 and was on display at the Lower Belvedere Palace after 1814, these holdings were moved in 1888 to the Kunsthistorisches Museum, which opened three years later. After the downfall of the monarchy, the inventory continued to grow with additions from other court collections. Because there was no room for such a large collection, all of it was moved into the Neue Burg in 1935. The collection was removed and hidden during World War II and did not reopen until 1973.

Imperial magnificence and elegant materials: the Marble Gallery in the Neue Burg

Kaiserappartements (Imperial Apartments) and Sisi Museum

ADDRESS: Michael's Wing (entrance beneath the dome)
OPENING TIMES: daily 9 a.m. to 5 p.m. (in July and August
9 a.m. to 5:30 p.m.)
GUIDED TOURS (in German): daily at 10 a.m., 11:30 a.m. and 2 p.m.
PHONE: +43/1/533 75 70
E-MAIL: info@hofburg-wien.at, INTERNET: www.hofburg-wien.at

Visiting the apartments of Emperor Francis Joseph and
Empress Elisabeth (the ticket is also valid for admission to
the ➤ **Silver Collection**) is a highly recommended way to
begin exploring the Hofburg. The tour begins with information about the Habsburg dynasty and the architectural
history of the Hofburg. A model on a scale of 1:200,
which was made at the beginning of the 20th century, still
shows the Hofspital (Court Hospital) and the Ballhaus
(Real Tennis Courts, torn down in 1903) as well as the
downsized 1907 variant of the Kaiserforum (Imperial
Forum), with a sweeping colonnade instead of a second
wing. Like the earlier, more grandiose plans, this was
never realized either.

Tour: The entrance to the apartments is via the Kaiser-
stiege (Imperial Staircase) in the Imperial Chancellery
Wing, the same stairs that Francis Joseph used to gain

access to his apartments. In the first six rooms (Stephen's Apartment), the Sisi Museum was installed in 2004, not only maintaining the legend of the beautiful Empress but also offering a more critical view of her life. The focus of this theatrical production, which begins with her assassination in Geneva in 1898, is the private side of Elisabeth: rebelling against life at court, seeking refuge in the cult of her own beauty, dieting obsessively and writing effusive poetry.

Some 200 objects are on display. In addition to lots of memorabilia (medals, coins, commemorative pictures, small busts, etc.) and the well-known portraits, they also include the assassin's weapon – a triangular file with a wooden handle – and the death mask made by Franz von Matsch around 1900. The main focus is on the personal possessions of the Empress: we see her marriage contract, diamond stars and other jewelry, a dressing gown, fans, gloves and parasols, sets of writing utensils, a menu and scales, a black lace shawl, her death certificate and her last will and testament.

The tour takes us through 18 rooms, which either have their original furnishings or have been reconstructed from photographs. The imperial couple moved here after their wedding in 1854. The rooms were furnished according to the tastes of the time (furniture in the style of Neo-Rococo and walls clad in red silk damask). We reach the Audience Chamber via the Trabantenstube (Guard-room), where the body guards kept watch, and the Wartesaal (Waiting Room). Francis Joseph gave two general audiences a week, and every subject of the realm had the right to attend. Those attending an audience were required to appear in uniform, tail-coat or national costume. As a rule the Emperor received them at his standing desk. The Conference Room was used by the ministers for their meetings, which were

Emperor Francis Joseph always had eyes for Elisabeth: His Majesty's Study

Empress Elisabeth

Elisabeth Amalie Eugenie von Wittelsbach, called Sisi, was born in Munich on December 24, 1837. In the summer of 1853 she happened to accompany her mother and elder sister Helene to Ischl to celebrate the birthday of her cousin, Emperor Francis Joseph. Although Helene was intended to become the Emperor's bride, he fell head over heels in love with the shy Sisi and immediately became engaged. On April 24, 1854, they were married in the Church of the Augustinian Friars in Vienna. In 1855 their daughter Sophie was born (she died in 1857), in 1856 Gisela, and in 1858 Crown Prince Rudolf.

Elisabeth fulfilled her duties as Empress with reluctance. On official occasions she felt as though she were being paraded like a horse "in harness." In addition, her marriage with the pedantic and conservative Francis Joseph entered a crisis that reached its height in 1860. In 1866, Elisabeth spoke out in favor of greater autonomy for Hungary, and a year later the Dual Monarchy of Austria-Hungary was established. Francis Joseph and Elisabeth were crowned king and queen of Hungary. Elisabeth's favorite daughter, Marie Valerie, was born in 1868.

called "*Minister Conseils*." The Emperor, who usually arose at 3:30 a.m., spent most of his waking hours in his Study. Across from his writing-desk is his favorite portrait of the Empress. It was in this room on January 30, 1889, that he received the news of the suicide of his only son, Rudolf. The simple furnishings of the bedroom are evidence that Francis Joseph rejected luxury of every kind. He was perfectly happy with a simple dressing table and an iron bed.

When he wanted to visit the Empress, whose rooms were around the corner in the Amalia Wing, he had to ring a bell hidden behind a curtain in the Smoking Room (today a memorial room to Emperor Maximilian of Mexico) and ask to be admitted. This apartment with its large living room and bedroom was decorated in Neo-Rococo style,

Sisi suffered increasingly from the loss of her personal freedom and wrote poetry: "I have awakened in a dungeon/ With chains on my hands/And my longing ever stronger/ And Freedom! You, turned from me!" She reacted to the constraints of the Vienna Court by taking refuge in her own beauty, obsessive dieting and sporting manias (riding, fencing, swimming). She spent increasing time in travel. Although she was embarrassed by her dark teeth, Elisabeth allowed her portrait to be painted one last time in 1879 at the age of 42.

Elisabeth became even more withdrawn and eccentric after the suicide of her only son, Rudolf, in 1889, after he had shot and killed his mistress, Mary Vetsera, at Mayerling Hunting Lodge. Sisi's request to travel to America was denied. She gave away her jewelry and took to wearing only black. She even gave up writing poetry. On September 10, 1898, the Empress, who was traveling under the name Countess of Hohenembs, was assassinated in Geneva by the Italian anarchist Luigi Lucheni.

Her immortality began with her tragic death, and a legend grew up in keeping with the one fostered by the Empress's unconventional lifestyle. The memory today of the good, beautiful and selfless Empress has been strengthened by numerous films (including Ernest Marischka's *Sisi* series with Romy Schneider). But as we know from contemporary newspaper accounts, Elisabeth was neither particularly admired nor popular during her lifetime.

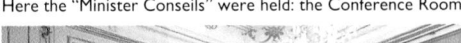

Here the "Minister Conseils" were held: the Conference Room

Wall-bars and rings: Elisabeth's dressing and exercise room

but some of the stucco decorations date from the 18th century. The wall-bars and rings that Elisabeth mounted in her dressing room and the doorway to the Large Salon create a rather strange impression. They were used for her daily program of exercises. In 1876, Elisabeth became the first member of the imperial family to have her own bathroom, with a bathtub of galvanized copper. Behind the bathroom are the two Bergl Rooms, which are covered in exotic landscape murals painted in 1766 by Johann Bergl. The original purpose of these rooms is not clear. In Elisabeth's day they were probably used by court servants as dressing rooms and lounges.

The Empress gained access to her apartments by climbing the Adlerstiege (Eagle's Staircase) in the adjoining Leopoldine Wing and by passing through the Türhüterzimmer (Doorkeeper's Room). The Large Antechamber that adjoins the Small Salon was a meeting place for the imperial family when they were going to a court ball. Led by the Master of Ceremonies, they crossed the State Rooms in the Leopoldine Wing (apartment of Maria Theresa, today the ➤ **Präsidentschaftskanzlei (Presidential Offices)** to the Ceremonial Hall.

Alexander's Apartments adjoined the Large Antechamber on the northwest. Here Tsar Alexander of Russia resided during the Congress of Vienna, and the last Austrian emperor, Charles I, lived here from 1916 to 1918. The Red Salon is decorated with Gobelin tapestries made in Paris; the medallions were modeled on paintings by François Boucher. The tapestries were a gift from Louis XVI to his brother-in-law Emperor Joseph II.

In Emperor Franz Joseph's day, the Dining Room was used mostly for family dinners, which followed strict court ceremonial, the Emperor sitting at mid-table. A dinner consisted of between nine and 13 courses and never lasted more than 45 minutes. The White Hall and an antechamber take us to the Alexanderstiege (Alexander's Staircase) on Schauflergasse, and we leave the Amalia Wing. The other rooms surrounding the courtyard were the private apartment of Emperor Charles. Today they are government offices.

Kunsthalle Wien

ADDRESS: MuseumsQuartier, Museumsplatz 1
OPENING TIMES: Friday to Tuesday 10 a.m. to 7 p.m.,
Thursday to 10 p.m.
PHONE: +43/1/521 89-33
INTERNET: www.kunsthallewien.at
E-MAIL: office@kunsthallewien.at

Kunsthalle Wien in the MuseumsQuartier is an urban exhibition space for international contemporary art. In the year 2002 the Italian art magazine *Arte* listed it on a footing with the Centre Pompidou in Paris and the Tate Modern in London as one of the six best institutions for exhibitions in Europe. The program focuses on photography, video, film, installations and new media. The Kunsthalle is a functional building, whose red brick emphasizes the workshop character of the art center. It is accessed through a converted gateway attached to the right side of the Winter Riding Hall. A shared entrance hall provides access to the Exhibition Hall and the Performance Halls (➤ **Halls E + G**). Hall 2, on the ground floor, serves primarily for presenta-

Vaulted ceiling: Hall 1 on the upper floor of Kunsthalle Wien

tions of contemporary expositions and retrospectives of young artists. Hall 1, on the upper floor, extends across the entire length (57 meters, 181 feet) of the building wing. Its hallmark is a vaulted ceiling that is more reminiscent of a cathedral than of an "art factory." Hall 1 is used primarily for large thematic exhibitions as well as for displaying important individual positions. The levels are connected by two prominent, free-standing staircases. The entrance hall provides access to the façade of the Kunsthalle. The band of illuminated display cases serves as a "project wall" in the public area.

History: The City of Vienna had been organizing exhibitions in the Messepalast since 1988 and planned to establish an arts center there. Because the MuseumsQuartier was not expected to open before 1994-95, an interim solution was found, a temporary arts center on Karlsplatz. When the yellow and blue painted container designed by Alfred Krischanitz opened in September 1992, many Viennese considered it to be an ugly box. Starting in December 1995, in order to create an immediate presence on the future cultural site, performances were continually staged in a hall of the Messepalast. The new Kunsthalle finally opened in February 2001 with a performance by Vanessa Beecroft. Regular programming began in May 2001. But the Karlsplatz location was not entirely abandoned. The "box" was replaced by a glass pavilion, also a very successful design by Krischanitz. Since January 2002 it has been serving as exhibition space for projects focused on specific topics.

Kunsthistorisches Museum

ADDRESS: Maria-Theresien-Platz
OPENING TIMES: daily except Monday 10 a.m. to 6 p.m.,
Picture Gallery and Egyptian and Near Eastern Collection,
Thursday 10 a.m. to 9 p.m.
GUIDED TOURS ON SPECIAL TOPICS: every Wednesday and Friday
10:15 a.m.; every Tuesday and Thursday 12:30 p.m. ("Mittags
im KHM"); every Thursday 6:30 p.m. ("Alte Meister")
PHONE: +43/1/525 24-0
INTERNET: www.khm.at, E-mail: info@khm.at

In Thomas Bernhard's novel *Alte Meister* ("Old Masters"),
the music philosopher Reger is heard to grumble at length
about the Kunsthistorisches Museum and the Habsburgs,
to whom the Museum owes its enormous collections,
because the Museum "doesn't even have a Goya, not even
an El Greco." The Museum gets along just fine without
an El Greco, who is not considered to have been among
the top echelon of painters, but not to have a Goya is
"downright fatal" for a museum like the Kunsthistorisches. Things are, of course, not as bad as Bernhard, a
master of exaggeration, would have one believe. The
KHM has a wonderful Vermeer ("Allegory of Painting"),
the world's largest collection of works by Pieter Bruegel
the Elder as well as countless other masterpieces, including works by Jan van Eyck, Hieronymus Bosch, Albrecht
Dürer, Titian, Tintoretto, Veronese, Parmigianino,
Giuseppe Arcimboldo,
Peter Paul Rubens and
Diego Rodríguez de Silva
y Velázquez.

Jan Vermeer:
"Allegory of Painting" (1665/1666)

In addition, the Kunsthistorisches Museum, which
was dedicated by Emperor
Francis Joseph to "the
monuments of art and
antiquity," consists of far
more than just its Picture
Gallery. It also has the Collection of Sculpture and
Decorative Arts, Collection
of Greek and Roman
Antiquities, Egyptian and
Near Eastern Collection
and a Coin Cabinet that

with 700,000 objects (coins, paper money, medals and decorations) is one of the most important in the world. Because of lack of space in the main building, the ➤ **Hofjagd- und Rüstkammer (Collection of Arms and Armour)** as well as the ➤ **Sammlung alter Musikinstrumente (Collection of Ancient Musical Instruments)** had to be moved. Together with the ➤ **Ephesus Museum (part of the Collection of Greek and Roman Antiquities)** and the ➤ **Museum**

Cupola Hall and Staircase: "Theseus and the Centaur" by Antonio Canova

of Ethnology they are across the street, in the Neue Burg and the Corps de Logis.

History: For centuries the imperial collections were scattered across various parts of the Hofburg and the Belvedere Palace, where the Picture Gallery was opened to the public in 1781. Plans to construct new buildings to house the collections date from the early 19th century. But the project did not become concrete until the city wall was demolished on the orders of Emperor Francis Joseph (1857) and the new Ringstrasse was laid out. In 1862 the architect Ludwig Förster proposed building two Court

Museums on the former glacis between the Hofburg and the Imperial Stables: the Kunsthistorisches and the ➤ **Naturhistorisches Museum**. In 1864 Francis Joseph gave his approval, and in 1866 four architects – Heinrich von Ferstel, Theophil von Hansen, Moritz Ritter von Löhr and Carl von Hasenauer – were invited to submit plans for two buildings that were to be mirror images of each other.

The jury, however, came to the conclusion that none of the four submitted designs was suitable. Thus they invited the German architect Gottfried Semper to come to Vienna to evaluate the plans. He criticized not only the plans themselves but also the competition's frame of reference and called for a comprehensive new concept that was to include the idea of a Kaiserforum (Imperial Forum). The Emperor commissioned him to develop a concept based on one of the existing plans. Semper chose Hasenauer's design, but made some fundamental changes that caused great tension between the two architects. In 1870 Francis Joseph approved the plan for the Kaiserforum, and ground was broken in the autumn of 1871. In 1880 the two buildings were finished, but the magnificent interior design, which Hasenauer undertook alone, was not yet complete. The Naturhistorisches Museum opened in 1889; the Kunsthistorisches Museum followed two years later.

All four façades of the Kunsthistorisches Museum are decorated with numerous figures. They depict allegories as well as historical personages and artists. The iconological program was designed by Semper and illustrates the conditions governing the creation of a work of art: material aspects dominate the ground floor, artistic ones the main floor, and both are surmounted on the attic floor and along the balustrade by the individual as the crowning glory, the statues depicting famous artists. The program is in chronological order, leading from classical antiquity (Babenbergerstrasse) to the Middle Ages (the side facing the MuseumsQuartier) to the Renaissance (Maria Theresa Square) to the Modern Age (Ring). The lantern in the cupola is crowned with a statue by Johann Benk of Pallas Athena as the protectress of the arts and sciences.

Tour: The view from the Entrance Hall through the circular opening in the Cupola Hall above it is breathtaking.

Before we climb the Main Staircase to the Picture Gallery, we turn right and enter the Egyptian and Near Eastern Collection on the mezzanine floor. The first two large Rooms (I and V) demonstrate the idea of an historical *Gesamtkunstwerk* ("total work of art") in an impressive manner. The painted ceilings are supported by three original papyrus columns of granite; the walls are decorated with scenic pictures and hieroglyphic inscriptions. Even the doorways are in Egyptian style.

The parts of the collection on display are organized into various subdivisions: the focus is on the Egyptian cult of the dead and religion as well as on the plastic arts, especially sculpture. The museum's rich holdings are based on a major acquisition in 1821 as well as the Miramar Collection of Archduke Ferdinand Max (who as Emperor Maximilian of Mexico was executed there in 1867). The important collection of monuments from the Old Kingdom is the result of Austrian excavations between 1912 and 1929 in the cemetery of Giza. Extremely interesting are the Tomb Chapel of Ka-ni-nisut and the False Door of Iha, which were found in the cemetery to the west of the Cheops Pyramid in Giza. In a small display case you'll find the mascot of the Kunsthistorisches Museum, a 20-centimeter (8-inch) long hippopotamus of blue faience (placed in a tomb around 2000 BC). Painted on the hippo's body are signs of its habitat (papyrus, lotus, a bird) to indicate that it is wallowing in a swampy landscape.

The Collection of Greek and Roman Antiquities is displayed in adjoining rooms to the south. The holdings range from Cypriot Bronze Age pottery from the 3rd millennium BC to Slavic finds from around 1000 AD. The architecture of Room XI is copied from the Roman imperial age. The imitative relief frieze with the legends of the gods is by August Eisenmenger. The collection, which will reopen in the autumn of 2004 after four years of renovation, is internationally renowned for its spectacular gems and cameos (Ptolemaic Cameo, Eagle Cameo, Gemma Augustea) as well as its finds from the time of the Great Migration (Tomb of the Princess of Untersiebenbrunn) and the

Middle Ages (Hoard of Gold from Nagyszentmiklós). Among the newly exhibited items are reliefs from the Heroon of Trysa, a tomb in ancient Lycia (today in southwestern Turkey), which is one of the most important objects in the collection of ancient sculpture. One gallery explains the development of the Roman portrait from the 1st century BC to painted mummy portraits. The smaller rooms have a thematic focus (Cyprus, Etruria, lower Italy as well as Austria Romana). The larger-than-life bronze statue of the *Youth from the Magdalensberg* has proved a disappointment in one respect: until the 1980s it was considered to be an original from the 1st century AD. But it is "only" a copy made after a farmer found the original while plowing in 1502. The genuine statue disappeared and was taken to Spain under mysterious circumstances.

The eastern wing, which originally housed the Münzkabinett (Coin Cabinet, now in three specially adapted and spacious rooms on the third floor) and the Collections of Arms and Armour and of Ancient Musical Instruments, is now home to the Collection of Sculpture and Decorative Arts, which includes some 800 tapestries. The high quality of the collection resulted from combining the Kunst- und Wunderkammer (arts and natural wonders rooms) of Archduke Ferdinand II at Ambras Castle near Innsbruck and of Emperor Rudolf II from Prague Castle as well as the collection

Gesamtkunstwerk: the rooms of the Egyptian and Near Eastern Collection

Impressive stairwell: lunettes by Hans Makart

of Archduke Leopold William and former holdings of the ➤ **Schatzkammer** (**Treasury**) in the Hofburg. The collection has an astonishing variety of objects: in addition to sculptures of every conceivable material, it has vessels of precious stones, ivory carvings and goldsmith work as well as games, cabinets, toilet and other caskets, clocks, automatons and other complicated instruments. It is still not clear what the "Püsterich" (Fire-Blower), a 25-centimeter (10-inch) bronze figure from the 12th century, was used for. The little man, who is reproduced on many KHM products, was filled with water and placed among the embers, where he puffed steam through small holes in his mouth and nose. The most famous item in the collection, the "Saliera" by Benvenuto Cellini (an ornate saltcellar of gold and enamel) was stolen in May 2003. The Collection of Sculpture and Decorative Arts, which has been closed for renovation since 2002, is to reopen in 2005. A staircase of white Carrara marble leads to the second floor. On the landing stands the sculpture "Theseus and the Centaur" by Antonio Canova. Created between 1805 and 1819, it was originally intended as a symbol of Napoleon; the symbolism was reinterpreted after his defeat. For this sculpture, made on a commission from Emperor Francis II/I, Pietro Nobile built the ➤ **Temple** of **Theseus** in the Volksgarten between 1819 and 1823. In 1890 the piece was moved to this central location in the Kunsthistorisches Museum to complete the interior furnishings.

The large ceiling fresco in the stairway is entitled "Apotheosis of the Renaissance" and was painted by the Hungarian artist Mihály von Munkácsy. The viewer steps into the painting like the man on the lower edge of the picture. The fanlights in the staircase present Renaissance masters, including Michelangelo, Veronese, Titian, Leonardo da Vinci and Raphael. Each of the four sides has three lunettes by Hans Makart. The spandrel pictures between the capitals of the huge columns are by Gustav Klimt, Ernest Klimt and Franz von Matsch. They depict the development of art (a sign near the Cupola Hall explains the individual pictures in detail). Gustav Klimt, who with his brother and Matsch also painted the ceiling frescoes above the Main Staircase of the **Burgtheater** (➤ **Environs**), was responsible here for "Egypt" and "Greek Classicism."

The Picture Gallery spreads across the entire second floor. Italian, Spanish and French pictures are found in the southwestern wing; the northeastern wing has

Dutch, Flemish and German paintings. The foundations for the Picture Gallery were laid by Archduke Leopold William during his governorship in the Netherlands from 1647 to 1656. He acquired some 1400 pictures, mostly Renaissance Venetian painting (Titian, Veronese, Tintoretto) as well as major works by Flemish masters of the 15th to the 17th century (van Eyck, Rubens, van Dyck). In 1651 David Teniers the Younger painted the Archduke with several visitors at his picture gallery in Brussels, and the 51 Italian paintings that are depicted are

Klimt painting: "Egypt"

Raphael: "Madonna in the Meadow" (1505 or 1506)

mostly in the Kunsthistorisches Museum today. The KHM's gallery portrait was one of a series that Leopold William commissioned to document his collection.

In addition, the Archduke tried to acquire paintings for the collection of his brother Emperor Ferdinand III at Prague Castle after it was looted by the Swedes. The collection had been founded decades earlier by Emperor Rudolf II (1552–1612), a great lover of art. In the early 18th century, Charles VI decided to bring together the Habsburg's painting collections in Vienna. Leopold William's collection was put on display in the Baroque manner in the Stallburg along with holdings from Prague Castle and several other palaces. In 1728 in the course of this rearrangement, Charles VI commissioned the Neapolitan painter Francesco Solimena to create a large painting that would be a monument to the Emperor and his artistic sensibilities: with a solemn gesture the Imperial Minister of Buildings, Gundacker Ludwig Joseph Count Althan, hands the Emperor a three-volume inventory of the Imperial Picture Gallery. This painting can be seen in Room VII, and if it seems a bit odd, that is because the court painter Johann Gottfried Auerbach added the faces of Charles VI and Althan to the otherwise finished painting.

In 1776, Empress Maria Theresa decided to open the Picture Gallery in the Upper Belvedere Palace to the public. By 1781, the paintings had been put on display in accordance with historical criteria. Under her son Joseph II, the collection grew rapidly as Flemish and Italian paintings were added, most of them large-format altar paintings taken from the monasteries and churches that had been dissolved. Many artworks were lost when Napoleon conquered Vienna in 1809, and during the next century almost nothing was added to the collection.

There are many paintings here that simply should not be missed: the Vermeer and Rembrandt's self-portraits, the "Madonna in the Meadow" by Raphael, the "Self-portrait in a Convex Mirror" by Parmigianino and "Christ Carrying the Cross" by Hieronymus Bosch. It is worth taking extra time to study the unbelievably detailed paintings by Pieter Bruegel the Elder, including "The Fight Between Carnival and Lent," "Children's Games" and "The Tower of Babel." Viewing the "Peasant Wedding" you may legitimately wonder why the red-jacketed man carrying the pies has three legs. Another strange detail is the superfluous river in "The Assumption of the Virgin Mary" by Peter Paul Rubens. According to the music philosopher Reger in Thomas Bernhard's novel *Old Masters*, if you study a painting long enough, you will eventually discover a serious mistake.

Or you can simply enjoy the fantastic details: for example, the wonderfully evil cat in "The Feast of the Bean King" by Jacob Jordaens or the mouth of the dragon at the feet of "Saint Margaret" by Raphael and his studio. And the allegorical depictions of the seasons and elements by Giuseppe Arcimboldo are always popular. He was court painter from 1562 to 1587 under the emperors Ferdinand I, Maximilian II and Rudolf II. The 13 views of Vienna and imperial palaces painted by Bernardo Bellotto (Canaletto) between 1758 and 1761 on a commission from Empress Maria Theresa give us a highly interesting impression of the city and palaces at the time.

Old masters: a room in the Picture Gallery on the upper floor

Leopold Museum

ADDRESS: MuseumsQuartier, Museumsplatz 1
OPENING TIMES: daily except Tuesday 10 a.m. to 7 p.m.,
Thursday 10 a.m. to 9 p.m.
GUIDED TOURS: group reservations available at
vermittlung@leopoldmuseum.org. Tours of the current special
exhibition are on Saturday, Sunday and holidays at 3 p.m. and
on Thursday at 7 p.m.
PHONE: +43/1/52570-0
INTERNET: www.leopoldmuseum.org
E-MAIL: office@leopoldmuseum.org

The collection of the Viennese ophthalmologist Rudolf
Leopold, which he assembled between the years 1947 and
1994 and which is now in the possession of the Republic

of Austria, amounts to approximately 5300 objects. The emphasis is on Austrian art of the 19th century (Georg Ferdinand Waldmüller, Anton Romako, Emil Jakob Schindler) and the first half of the 20th century. The Egon Schiele collection, with 47 paintings and almost 200 graphic works, is the largest in the world. Some of these exhibits, such as "Selbstseher" (Self-Seer; 1911), "Der Lyriker" (The Lyric Poet; 1911), "Kardinal und Nonne" (Cardinal and Nun; 1912), "Selbstbildnis mit Judenkirschen" (Self-Portrait with Winter-Cherries; 1912), "Eremiten" (Hermit; 1912) and "Entschwebung" (Floating Away; 1915) rank among Schiele's most important works. Little wonder that the museum chose as its logo the silhouette of a male nude, part of a work from the year 1910.

The collection also features masterpieces by Albin Egger Lienz, Oskar Kokoschka, Alfred Kubin, Gustav Klimt, Richard Gerstl, Herbert Boeckl and Anton Kolig. It is supplemented by arts and crafts objects as well as furniture by Otto Wagner, Adolf Loos, Josef Hoffmann, Koloman Moser und Dagobert Peche. Also on display are authentic objects from sub-Saharan Africa and Oceania as well as examples of Chinese and Japanese art that illustrate the influence of these styles on the ornamental art of Jugendstil (Austrian Art Nouveau). Only a few international examples of Expressionism are included (Edvard Munch, Ernest Ludwig Kirchner and Georges Rouault). About 1200 pieces are on permanent display: 600 of the 880 paintings, 100 of more than 3000 graphic works and 500 of the 1400 objects.

Tour: The museum with its almost square ground plan (40 by 45 meters; 127 by 143 feet) is accessible via a broad outside staircase in the Main Courtyard of the MuseumsQuartier. After passing through the entrance hall with the box office, the visitor enters a central, 21-meter-high (69 feet) atrium that is flooded with light. Its walls, like the exterior of the building, are lined with white Vraza limestone (Danube shell limestone from Bulgaria). The rectangular halls are arranged around the atrium and a second, lower-lying atrium like the blades of a windmill. Thus a direction of motion is set for the visitor in which three levels of the building can be visited continuously, without need to backtrack or enter a room twice.

The museum is nearly a cube, with two-thirds of its height (24 meters; 76 feet) rising from the inner courtyard of the MuseumsQuartier and the bottom third (13 meters, 41

Rudolf Leopold and the Foundation

Numerous important art collectors lived in Vienna until the seizure of power by Adolf Hitler in March 1938. The most important among them were Alphonse Rothschild, Prince Franz Josef II of Liechtenstein, the industrial magnate Ferdinand Bloch-Bauer, the librettist Fritz Grünbaum as well as the dentist Heinrich Rieger, who treated the destitute Egon Schiele in exchange for pictures. All of them were forced to emigrate or were murdered in the concentration camps. The tradition of upper-middle-class patronage was generally not continued after World War II and few private collectors emerged. Among the few who did, Rudolf Leopold stood out from the rest. By the mid-1980s, his collection – primarily of Austrian art from the Biedermeier period to Expressionism – illustrated the deficiencies of the Austrian state collections.

Rudolf Leopold was born in Vienna in 1925, studied medicine in the post-war years, received his medical degree in 1953, and finally specialized in ophthalmology. In 1947 he began to attend lectures on art history and to collect works of the 19th century. At an auction in 1950, he happened upon a forgotten catalogue of Egon Schiele's works, which had been published by the art dealer Otto Kallir-Nirenstein. Until 1938, Kallir-Nirenstein had exhibited at his Neue Gallerie pictures by the most important Austrian artists of the modern period. Rudolf Leopold was excited by the radical visual language of Schiele, whose art had been labeled "pornographic" in his own day. Leopold cared little about the lack of interest that the international art world showed for Schiele and the disparaging opinion that most art historians held of his work. He acquired practically every work of Schiele he could lay his hands on.

Leopold's passion for collecting, which was shared by his wife, Elisabeth, grew ever larger, sometimes bordering on fanaticism. In addition, he expanded the focus of his collection to Jugendstil, the period between the world wars, and after World War II. Leopold took out considerable bank loans, securing them with masterpieces. His spacious home in the Viennese suburb of Grinzing slowly turned into an art warehouse. Thousands of drawings were stored on cabinets and under

beds, and multiple layers of paintings leaned against the walls. Because his house was filled far beyond capacity and the mountain of debt had assumed dangerous levels, Leopold considered selling his collection to the Republic of Austria. On the occasion of the exhibition Egon Schiele and His Time, Chancellor Franz Vranitzky announced in March 1989 that negotiations for the

Rudolf and Elisabeth Leopold

acquisition of the collection would be initiated.

For a long time the negotiations failed to produce a satisfying result: Leopold's expectations far exceeded the amount that had been considered by the government. Furthermore, Leopold was not willing to have his collection added to the holdings of a museum of Austrian modern art: he wanted to see his life's work preserved as a whole. Hans Dichand, the publisher of the newspaper *Kronen Zeitung*, turned out to be a powerful ally. The widely read daily repeatedly called for the purchase of the collection.

In 1992 the *Kronen Zeitung*, together with the Freedom Party, launched a huge campaign against construction of the planned MuseumsQuartier. Even with all the downsizing, the project did not seem feasible. Erhard Busek, at that time minister of science, solved the conundrum by linking the two projects: in October 1993 the government decided to establish a Leopold Museum in the MuseumsQuartier, which to a certain extent owes its existence to Rudolf Leopold. Leopold had rejected the idea of housing his collection in the Baroque wing of the Imperial Stables. Instead, he insisted on a new building. Even the *Kronen Zeitung* had to accept this, and in the spring of 1994, planning resumed.

The negotiations between Busek and Leopold must have been rather nerve-racking for both sides. To establish an accurate value of the collection and the exact number of artworks, two experts were entrusted with drawing up an inventory and estimate. They arrived at a total of approximately 574 million euros for 5266 objects. This appraisal was not completely accurate, because it was based on the expected price of each artwork sold individually. The auction of the collection as a whole could scarcely have achieved that price.

In the early summer of 1994, an agreement was reached: Leopold agreed to transfer the entire collection to a foundation. In return he would receive 160 million euros in a series of annual, indexed partial payments until May 2007. Furthermore it was agreed that Leopold would hold for life the director's position of the museum bearing his name. He also had the right to name four of the eight board members of his foundation. With that, Parliament voted to purchase the collection, and in August 1994 the charter of the foundation was signed. Soon after the collection was moved from Leopold's home to the MuseumsQuartier, where a temporary high-security storage facility had been built, Leopold began assembling his "Collection II." It includes not only works by Schiele, Klimt and Kokoschka, but also acquisitions down to the present (Günter Brus, Otto Mühl and Hermann Nitsch).

Being director of the museum gave Leopold the opportunity to play an active role in the detailed planning of the building. He fought for every floor, for every square meter. In March 1997 the draft design was submitted and in May 1999 the cornerstone was laid. In September 2001, scarcely three months after the official opening of the MuseumsQuartier, the Leopold Museum opened as well.

feet) underground. It encompasses five storeys and another two intermediate levels on which the shop, café and information lounge are located. The entrance level and the two upper levels are dedicated to 20th-century art. Nineteenth-century art is exhibited on the two lower levels, which also house a 117-seat auditorium and the magazine (not open to the public). Management, administration and workshops found a home in the adjacent existing building. The entrance level serves as a symbolic threshold between the 19th and 20th centuries and exhibits works of Viennese Jugendstil by members of the Secession, foremost among them Gustav Klimt, and representatives of the Wiener

Egon Schiele: "Seated Nude with Green Headscarf" (1914).

Werkstätte such as Josef Hoffmann and Koloman Moser. Works by the loner Richard Gerstl complete the presentation. Next chronologically come the exhibits of the top floor. Works by Anton Faistauer, Anton Kolig, Hans Boehler, Herbert Boeckl, Lovis Corinth, Ernest Ludwig Kirchner, Oskar Kokoschka and Albert Paris Guetersloh are featured along with the world's largest collection of paintings by Egon Schiele. The panoramic window offers a wonderful view of the city center and the MuseumsQuartier.

A highlight is provided on the second storey by two halls displaying the paintings of Albin Egger-Lienz and pictures by Maria Lassnig and Oswald Oberhuber that serve as a connection between the post-war period and the present. Paintings by Josef Dobrowsky, Alfons Walde, Gustav Hessing and other artists can be seen as well. Rudolf Leopold wants to raise awareness for "artists who have been unduly forgotten or are unknown to today's public" by the presentation of their work within the context of Schiele, Klimt and Kokoschka.

On display on the first basement level are 19th-century paintings by artists that include Ferdinand Georg Waldmüller, Friedrich Gauermann, Michael Neder, August von Pettenkofen, Anton Romako, Emil Jacob Schindler, Tina Blau, Olga Wisinger-Florian and Carl Schuch. The second basement level accommodates light-sensitive graphic works, including some by Gustav Klimt, Egon Schiele and Alfred Kubin, and it is also used for special exhibitions.

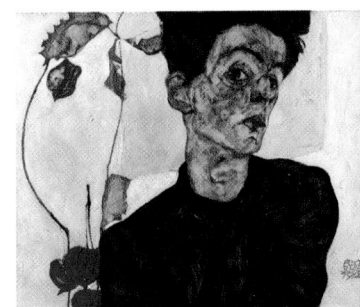

Egon Schiele: "Self-Portrait with Winter-Cherries" (1912).

Lipizzaner Museum

ADDRESS: Stallburg, Reitschulgasse 2
OPENING TIMES: daily 9 a.m. to 6 p.m.
GUIDED TOURS: Saturday at noon
PHONE: +43/1/525 24-583
INTERNET: www.lipizzaner.at
E-MAIL: lipizzaner@khm.at

Since 1997, the rooms of the former Hofapotheke (Imperial Court Pharmacy, 1746–1991) in the southwestern corner of the Stallburg have housed the Lipizzaner Museum. A permanent exhibition mounted by the ➤ **Kunsthistorisches Museum** as a joint project with the ➤ **Spanish Riding School** explains the history, breeding and training of the famous horses from the 16th century to the present. The tour takes us from the former sales room (now the Museum Shop and under preservation order) through the basement, where the medicinal wines were formerly stored. It begins with information about the famous Spanish Horses as well as the stud at Lipica (Lipizza) and covers such themes as riding skills, the Winterreitschule (Winter Riding Hall) and celebrations at court. Among the exhibits are drawings, photographs and sculptures as well as oil paintings by Johann Georg von Hamilton, who painted the favorite horses of Emperor Charles VI, and copperplate engravings by Johann Elias Ridinger. The Spanish Riding School has provided uniforms, harnesses, magnificent saddle cloths and studbooks. Large-screen monitors show the Lipizzaner horses, whose stables are right next door.

The former Imperial Court Pharmacy (below). Johann Georg von Hamilton: "Neput, the Horse of Emperor Charles VI" (above)

Museum of Modern Art Ludwig Foundation Vienna

ADDRESS: MuseumsQuartier, Museumsplatz 1
OPENING TIMES: Tuesday to Sunday 10 a.m. to 6 p.m.,
Thursday 10 a.m. to 9 p.m.
LIBRARY: Tuesday to Thursday 10 a.m. to 3:30 p.m.
GUIDED TOURS (overall view): Sunday at 2 p.m. (in German)
PHONE: +43/1/525 00
INTERNET: www.mumok.at
E-MAIL: info@mumok.at or kunstvermittlung@mumok.at

The Museum of Modern Art with its rectangular ground plan and its façade of rough, dark basalt rock is as much the opposite of the Leopold Museum in appearance as it is in its holdings. While the ➤ **Leopold Museum** concentrates on Austrian art since the Biedermeier period, the Museum of Modern Art specializes in international art of the 20th century to the present.
The collection is built around a core of Fluxus and Nouveau Réalisme (formerly the Hahn Collection) and Pop Art and Photorealism (the Ludwig Collection). Also of note are the holdings of Arte Povera, Minimal Art, Land Art and Deconstructivism. In addition, during the 1990s an extensive collection of Central and Eastern European art was assembled. Classic modernism (Expressionism, Cubism) is represented by only a few examples. No other museum, however, has as many masterpieces of Viennese Actionism, which is considered to be the most important contribution of Austria to avant-garde art. In total, the holdings of the Museum of Modern Art number about 7000 objects.

History: In February 1958, Heinrich Drimmel, the People's Party (ÖVP) minister of education at the time, announced his intention to establish a museum for contemporary art in Vienna. "For the time being" it was to be accommodated in the Austria Pavilion built for the World's Fair in Brussels, a structure for which a suitable use was sought. In 1959, the art historian Werner Hofmann was given responsibility for establishing the museum and assembling the collection. The Museum des 20. Jahrhunderts (Museum of the 20th Century) opened in September 1962 near the South Station with the exhibition Art from 1900 to Today. Two-thirds of the 328 works shown were on loan. A detailed and balanced collection could no longer

Enormous machine: the Museum's light and lift shaft

be acquired: despite skillful purchasing, many gaping holes in the collection (e.g. Expressionism, Cubism, Neue Sachlichkeit) could not be closed in the decades that followed.

In the spring of 1977, the Wiener Künstlerhaus presented the exhibition Art Around 1970, which was a selection from the collection of Irene and Peter Ludwig, a German chocolate manufacturer. Stylistically, the emphasis was on Pop Art and Photo Realism. Subsequently, negotiations began, with the goal of securing loans for a museum of modern art in Vienna. Agreement was reached with Peter Ludwig in February 1978. But he issued an ultimatum to the Republic of Austria: he would make approximately 120 works available, but only if a suitable home could be found within one year for the new collection, which also would include objects from the Museum of the 20th Century. First an extension of the World's Fair Pavilion was considered, but a location in the Messepalast was discussed as well. Then, however, the Liechtenstein royal family offered its Baroque palace in Vienna's 9th district, which had been the home of its art collection until 1945.

With the additional building, which was opened in April 1979, the institution was reorganized as the Museum of Modern Art, which consisted organizationally and conceptually of the two houses. The goal by that time was to combine the two collections in a suitable building in the former Imperial Stables.

While the preparations for the first exhibition were underway, negotiations had come to a standstill between the City of Cologne and Wolfgang Hahn, then the chief restorer of the Wallraff Richartz Museum, over the purchase of the latter's art collection. Hertha Firnberg (Socialist Party), who was science minister at the time, reacted quickly, purchasing in 1978 approximately 400 works with an emphasis on Fluxus and Nouveau Réalisme for the Museum of Modern Art. This enormous addition suddenly gave the collection an almost completely new face.

The Ludwigs immediately communicated their willingness to donate the artworks that were on loan. In January 1981, the Österreichische Ludwig Stiftung für Kunst und Wissenschaft (Austrian Ludwig Foundation for Art and Science) was created. On condition that the Republic of Austria would create a fund for expanding the collection and transfer to it 10 million schillings (726,000 euros) each year for 15 years, they agreed to donate 129 works. The Ludwigs made a second donation in 1991. The funding agreement was extended to 30 years (until 2021), and the name of the institution changed to Museum Moderner Kunst: Stiftung Ludwig Wien (Museum of Modern Art Ludwig Foundation Vienna). This arrangement has made important purchases possible every year (including works by Paul Klee, Francis Bacon, Gerhard Richter, Michelangelo Pistoletto, Mario Merz and Andy Warhol).

From the first phase of the architectural competition (1986), the Museum has been an essential part of the MuseumsQuartier. Nevertheless, its inclusion was challenged several times. In addition, several space reductions had to be endured. In January 1993, pressured by a citizens' action group instigated by the newspaper *Kronen Zeitung* and the Freedom Party, the building volume had to be reduced by 20 percent. A whole floor was lost in March 1995. Construction of the MuseumsQuartier started in April 1998. The new building opened in September 2001.

Existential: a sculpture by Alberto Giacometti

Tour: An outside staircase ten meters (31 feet) wide leads to the entrance level, four meters (13 feet) above the level of the MQ Main Courtyard and vertically aligned with the center of the building. Two main exhibition levels are above the entrance level, two below. A 35-meter (111-foot) high atrium, which is illuminated from above, cuts the museum across all levels into two differently proportioned space groups. On one side are five exhibition levels, each with approximately 700 m² (7500 square feet) of floor space five meters (16 feet) high. On the other side are the more intimate "cabinets" 3.5 meters (11 feet) high.

The arrangement of space is not immediately obvious to the visitor. In addition, it is not possible to tour the building in a logical sequence of rooms. Upon entering, it becomes immediately obvious, however, that this museum is an enormous machine from a time long past. This impression is created by the materials used (cast iron for the stairs and wall linings; glass and basalt lava), and the central shaft with the three elevator systems and the bridges that lead to the exhibition halls. The architectural concept of the huge shaft has been massively impaired since June 2002 by a white, tunnel-like bridge. This intervention by Heimo Zobernig created a direct connection between two exhibition halls, which have been used for changing exhibitions ever since.

The most sensible course of action is to approach the museum from the top floor: the imposing Cupola Hall with its panoramic window is flooded with daylight and has a gallery that primarily features exhibitions related to the permanent collection. The level beneath is dedicated to special exhibitions. The best way of accessing the other areas of the museum is by walking down the staircase and taking a look inside each doorway as it presents itself. Thus one also arrives on the entrance level, which appears brutally cut into the shaft. The descent continues to exhibition Level 3 and finally to the "Factory" deep underground, reserved for young viewpoints and contemporary currents.

Towards the rear of the entrance level is the access to the shop and to the restaurant with its bar and reading lounge. The library, which is open to the public, can be reached via the adjacent "Spange." The separate conference hall "Hofstallung" is located in the Oval Wing of the MuseumsQuartier. It can be reached by means of a more recently built bridge along the rear of the museum.

Museum of Ethnology

ADDRESS: Neue Burg (Corps de Logis), Heldenplatz
REOPENING: early 2007
PHONE: +43/1/534 30-0
INTERNET: www.ethno-museum.ac.at
E-MAIL: v*@ethno-museum.ac.at

The most famous object in the Museum für Völkerkunde (Museum of Ethnology) is also one of the oldest and most fragile. It is a headdress made out of 450 tail feathers of the quetzal bird. There is a persistent rumor that it once belonged to the penultimate Aztec ruler, Montezuma, but that is not supported by the facts. In the late 16th century it was listed as a "Moorish hat" in the collection of Archduke Ferdinand in Ambras Castle in Tirol. Among the other holdings of international importance are the 238 artifacts brought back by the British explorer James Cook (1728–1779) from his three research expeditions around the world, the bronze statues from the Benin kingdom of West Africa (today Nigeria), and Johann Natterer's Brazilian Collection assembled between 1817 and 1835 with more than 2000 ethnographic items from over 60 various Indian tribes, most of which no longer exist or have lost their cultural identity.

Glass-roofed courtyard: the Corps de Logis in the Neue Burg

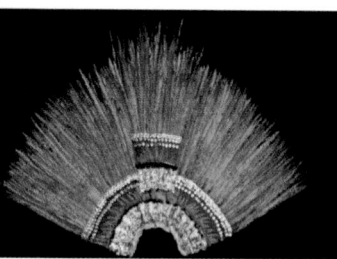

The best-known exhibit:
Aztec feather headdress from
the 16th century

History: In 1806 the Austrian naturalist Leopold von Fichtel was commissioned by Emperor Francis I to buy part of the collection of James Cook at auction in London. In the following decades, the holdings were enlarged by the addition of a number of other collections These included the Asian-Oceanic collection of Baron Karl von Hügel (1839) and the collection that had originated during the circumnavigation of the globe by the frigate *Novara* between 1857 and 1859. The main problem was the lack of a special museum: the artifacts were usually packed away in crates. In addition, compared with other departments of the Court Natural History Cabinet, the ethnographic collection did not have a specialized curator.

With the founding of the ➤ **Naturhistorisches Museum** in 1876, the stock of the anthropological-ethnographic collections found a permanent place at that institution. By 1918, the holdings had grown from fewer than 5000 to more than 94,000 objects. This expansion, however, led to a pressing shortage of space and thus to considerations about moving the ethnographic collections to the Corps de Logis. Since 1908, it had housed the collections assembled during the journey around the world by Francis Ferdinand, Archduke of Austria-Este (1892–93).

The transfer of the Ethnographic Department to the Emperor's guesthouse with its impressive glassed-over courtyard began in 1926; two years later the first show-rooms of the Ethnological Museum opened. The ➤ **Kunsthistorisches Museum** also began to spread successively into the Neue Burg: in 1935, the ➤ **Hofjagd- und Rüstkammer (Collection of Arms and Armour)** was set up. It was followed in 1947 by the ➤ **Sammlung alter Musikinstrumente (Collection of Ancient Musical Instruments)** and in 1978 by the ➤ **Ephesus Museum.** The Museum of Ethnology became part of the Kunsthistorisches Museum in 2002. Because the building is undergoing a complete overhaul that began in 1999, the Museum has been closed since the spring of 2004. Its collections currently contain around 240,000 objects, 72,000 photographs and 132,000 printed works.

Naturhistorisches Museum

ADDRESS: Burgring 7 (entrance: Maria-Theresien-Platz)
OPENING TIMES: daily except Tuesday 9 a.m. to 6:30 p.m.
(Wednesday 9 a.m. to 9 p.m.)
GUIDED HISTORICAL TOURS ALL THE WAY TO THE ROOF:
Wednesday 5 p.m. and 6:30 p.m., Sunday 2 p.m. and 4 p.m.
Insights into the museum's scientific research:
Saturday 2:30 p.m., Sunday 10:30 a.m.
EVENING EVENTS (guided tours, lectures): Wednesday 7 p.m.
Children's program: Saturday 2 p.m., Sunday 10 a.m. and 2 p.m.
PHONE: +43/1/521 77-0
INTERNET: www.nhm-wien.ac.at
E-MAIL: waswannwo@nhm-wien.ac.at

The Naturhistorisches Museum is a world unto itself:
only a fraction of its 20 million objects can be displayed,
and yet the great variety of beautifully presented displays
is still astonishing. In addition, there are times when you
feel as though you've entered another age: the furniture
and wooden display cases have remained unchanged since
the Museum opened in 1889. But there is a special quality
about this feeling of dustiness, of anachronism: the
Museum, which is one of the loveliest in Vienna, is also a
museum to the concept of museums.

The giant show-rooms cover a total area of 8700 m²
(94,000 square feet). Wandering through them, you constantly stumble across some special item or curiosity: a

A museum to the concept of museums: the Geology-Paleontology Department

giant topaz weighing 117 kilograms (257 pounds) or an ostrich egg that is almost the size of a medicine ball, a silver bandfish with pink gills and a record length of 5.5 meters (18 feet) or the 4.8-meter (16-foot) long lower jawbone of a fin whale. The most important object, however, is the 25,000-year-old figurine of the "Venus of Willendorf," which has its own small room. And despite the thousands upon thousands of stuffed animals, the Naturhistorisches Museum never seems dead: in the basement, for example, is a vivarium with many separate areas for fish, birds and lizards. And visitors can use the Museum's microscopes to their heart's content. A guided tour to the roof is especially recommended.

History: In 1750 Emperor Francis I Stephen of Lorraine (1708–1765), the husband of Maria Theresa, acquired from the Florentine scholar Johann Ritter von Baillou what at that time was the biggest and most famous collection of natural-history objects in the world. It consisted of around 30,000 items, including rare fossils, snails, mussels and corals as well as minerals and precious stones. In contrast to many other Wunderkammer (natural wonders rooms) this collection had already been classified according to scientific criteria.

Francis Stephen, who also founded the Menagerie at Schönbrunn Palace in 1752 and the Botanical Garden a year later, also equipped Austria's first overseas scientific expedition. In 1755 Nicolaus Joseph Jacquin brought back

from his journey to the Caribbean, the Antilles, Venezuela and Colombia many living plants and animals as well 67 crates of natural wonders. Following the premature death of the Emperor, the collection became the property of the state. It was rearranged and put on public display two days a week. In 1776 Empress Maria Theresa, who took a great interest in the earth sciences as the basis of mining and industry,

Venus of Willendorf: 25,000 years old

invited the mineralogist Ignaz von Born to come to Vienna to organize and expand the collections. He began buying minerals of every provenance, and the natural-history cabinet became a center of practice-oriented research.

Emperor Francis II/I (1768–1835) added a cabinet of animals to the natural-science collection. The basic holdings were provided by the Habsburg's hunting trophies, which dated from the time of Emperor Maximilian II (1564–1576). After several reorganizations, a cabinet of plants was founded in 1807. The stuffed animals at that time were displayed in artificial landscape dioramas and thus within an ecological context. Next to them, however, were stuffed examples of people from foreign races, including the "Princely Moor" Angelo Soliman.

On the occasion of the marriage of his daughter Leopoldine to Pedro I of Brazil, Emperor Francis sent an expedition to that country in 1817. Two Austrian frigates accompanied the Archduchess to Rio de Janeiro. Among the participants on this voyage was the taxidermist Johann Natterer, who ended up spending 18 years in the rain forests of South America instead of the two years that he had planned. During his research travels he collected huge quantities of exotic animals, plants, minerals and ethnologic items. Because there was not enough room in the Hofburg for these objects, consideration was given to building a "Brazilian Museum."

The most ambitious expedition in the history of Austrian research was the circumnavigation of the globe by the frigate *Novara* (1857–1859). It was proposed by Archduke Ferdinand Maximilian, the commander of the Navy, who provided use of the ship for two years to the Academy of Sciences and the Geographic Society. The expedition came back with an enormous quantity of items. The last important research journey was the expedition to the North Pole by the *Tegetthoff* between 1872 and 1874. It was led by Julius von Payer and Karl Weyprecht, who discovered Franz Joseph Land on August 30, 1873.

Meanwhile, construction of a new Naturhistorisches Museum had become a necessity. In the plan for the Kaiserforum (Imperial Forum) by Gottfried Semper and Carl von Hasenauer, it was the mirror image of the ➤ **Kunsthistorisches Museum** (q.v. for the architectural history). In 1871 excavation began and on August 10, 1889, the Museum opened.

The 170-meter (560-foot) long and 70-meter (230-foot)

wide building was crowned by a drum cupola bearing a colossal bronze statue of the Greek sun god, Helios. On the lower and middle levels (Intermediate Floor and Upper Floor), the figural decoration of the façade consists of allegorical and mythological depictions of the Development of the World and of the Cosmos. On the balustrade stand 34 chalky-limestone statues of scientists from classical antiquity to the 19th century as signs of progress. The figures and decorations in the Cupola Hall and in the Staircase as well as the ceiling fresco "The Cycle of Life" by Hans Canon are based on similar themes. In the showrooms more than 100 oil paintings illustrate the places the objects were found, depicting primeval landscapes and distant lands.

The Ethnographic Department, whose holdings had grown tremendously, were separated from the rest of the objects and moved in 1926 to the Corps de Logis in the Neue Burg. Two years the ➤ **Museum of Ethnology** opened its first show-rooms. In 1990, a subterranean depot with four levels was built beneath the Naturhistorisches Museum. The attic was finished between 1991 and 1995.

Tour: The internal structure of the Museum is characterized by the strictly systematic arrangement of the displays. On the Hochparterre (Intermediate Floor) they range from the realm of inanimate nature to traces of life from ancient geological eras to human beings. The Ober-

Zoological Collection: 600 mammals, 3200 birds, 700 fish, etc.

geschoss (Upper Floor) presents diverse forms of animal life as well as the world of microscopic organisms. Within the individual areas of the collection, the objects are arranged systematically: either according to natural relationships or their chronological sequence.

The Collection of Minerals (Rooms 1–5) is one of the most important in the world. Among its distinctive items are Colombian emeralds, diamonds and nuggets of gold and platinum. The Collection of Meteorites has more than 700 objects and is the oldest and biggest of its kind. In the Geology-Paleontology Department (Rooms 6–10) there is a complete skeleton of a 17-million-year-old elephant called a *Deinotherium*, a huge fossil palm leaf, a three-toed horse called a *Mesohippus*, the gigantic perissodactyl *Chalicotherium* and a diorama of a tropical coral reef 16 million years ago. Among the most spectacular objects in the dinosaur room are the skeletons of an *Allosaurus*, an *Iguanodon* and a *Diplodocus*. The 4.5-meter (15-foot) length of the fossilized *Archelon* makes it the biggest sea turtle ever found.

The corridors of the Hochparterre (Intermediate Floor) are dedicated to the Ice Age. The Prehistoric Department (Rooms 11–15) presents archaeological material from the Old Stone Age to the early Middle Ages, including, along with the "Venus of Willendorf," also the "Fanny of Galgenberg," a cult statuette from Stratzing. The Anthropology Department (Room 16) documents the development of humankind on the basis of skulls from the Middle Stone Age, New Stone Age, Bronze Age, Hallstatt culture, Celts, Romans, Germans, Slavs and Avars over a period of 35,000 years.

The "Mikrotheater" has been installed in Room 21 on the second floor. During demonstrations, microorganisms are magnified several thousand times and projected on a screen, and they can even be viewed three-dimensionally (every Saturday and Sunday at 1:30, 3 and 4:15 p.m.). The Invertebrate Collection (Rooms 22 and 23) with its tremendous variety of mussels and snails, corals, worms and arachnids leads to the insects (Room 24). This special collection alone has ten million objects, and even the relatively small part of the collection on display is impressive: more than 50,000 butterflies, grasshoppers, bees, gnats, flies and beetles in 224 giant display cases. Most of the upper floor (Rooms 25–39) is dedicated to vertebrate animals. The Zoological Collection displays 600 mammals, 3200 birds,

700 fish and 500 reptiles. Because many of them have meanwhile become extinct, some of the stuffed animals, which are as much as 200 years old (including the dodo, great auk and the Tasmanian wolf), are priceless rarities.

Österreichische Nationalbibliothek (Austrian National Library): The Modern Library

ADDRESS: Neue Burg (Middle Gate), Heldenplatz
OPENING TIMES MAIN READING ROOM: Monday to Friday
9 a.m. to 9 p.m. (July to September, 9 a.m. to 4 p.m., closed
September 1–7), Saturday 9 a.m. to 12:45 p.m.
PHONE: +43/1/534 10-252
INTERNET: www.onb.ac.at

The service facilities of the Austrian National Library are located in the Neue Burg: the local loan and borrowing desks, the Main Reading Room and other reading rooms, the periodical department, the catalogues and databases. The Picture Archive is next door in the Corps de Logis (entrance ➤ **Museum of Ethnology**). The collections of the ANL currently hold around 7.3 million objects, including 8000 incunabula and more than three million printed works. The library is divided into ten special collections. Of outstanding international importance are not only the manuscripts (including the Golden Bull of 1356 and the 2400-page Wenceslas Bible) and musical manuscripts (including the *Requiem* by Wolfgang Amadeus

In the Neue Burg: the service facilities of the National Library

Mozart and Ludwig van Beethoven's *Violin Concerto*), but also the incunabula and other old printed books (a Gutenberg Bible), historical maps, portraits and photographs, posters, bookplates and handbills as well as the literary estates of Austrian authors (Robert Musil, Ingeborg Bachmann, Erich Fried and many others).

History: The building for the Court Library that was completed in 1726 (with the ➤ **Prunksaal** or State Hall by Johann Bernhard Fischer von Erlach) soon became too small, on the one hand because of the demand that everything of importance be preserved and, on the other hand, the growth that occurred when Joseph II ordered the closing of the monastery libraries. The Court Library spread into adjoining buildings, including the Augustinian monastery. At the beginning of the 20th century, underground stacks for books were built as much as 14 meters (46 feet) deep beneath Joseph's Square. In 1920, following the downfall of the monarchy, the Court Library became the National Library and ownership was transferred to the Republic of Austria. Since 1945 it has been known officially as the Austrian National Library.

Between 1962 and 1966, several reading rooms as well as the borrowing desk were established in the Neue Burg, and two collections were moved there (Department of Papyri and the Department of Broadsheets, Posters and Exlibris). Since 1992, the air-conditioned subterranean depot beneath the Burggarten has been in use, with room on four levels for around four million volumes. In an essay, Gerhard Roth describes the subterranean stacks of the ANL as a "book mine." With the library growing at an annual rate of around 50,000 volumes, the present storage capacity will remain sufficient only until 2010. Plans are being made for another subterranean depot (beneath Heldenplatz).

Since January 2002, the ANL has been managed along the same model as the Federal Museums as an independent, non-profit and scholarly institution. Modernization and renovation of the service facilities in the Neue Burg are underway (installation of new wiring and cabling in the reading rooms, doubling the number of research terminals, remodeling the borrowing desks, creating a copy center and a reading lounge). Since 2003 the entire printed collection from 1501 to the present has been retrievable via the Internet. A long-term project is to digitize the books and periodicals.

Österreichisches Theatermuseum (Austrian Theatre Museum)

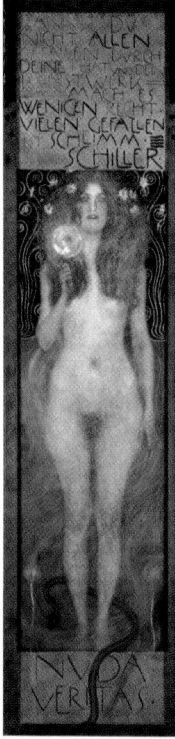

Gustav Klimt:
"Nuda Veritas" (1899)

ADDRESS: Lobkowitzplatz 2
OPENING TIMES: Tuesday to Sunday
10 a.m. to 6 p.m.
PHONE: +43/1/512 88 00-610
INTERNET: www.theatermuseum.at
E-MAIL: info@theatermuseum.at

A visit to the Theatre Museum is anything but boring: Herbert Kappelmüller designed the tour on the second floor of Lobkowitz Palace to be a theatrical and entertaining production. You stroll across the cobblestones and come across an old advertising pillar with posters; you suddenly find yourself in an orchestra pit where the musicians are tuning their instruments; or you enter a photo lab to find trays of developer with old pictures floating in them. Rockets explode to the tune of fireworks music, and through the velvet-lined doors of the boxes you can look down on the stage (or on the stage models). In the cemetery-like memorial room with personal effects from estates, the gravel crunches beneath your feet.

The Theatre Museum has more than 1.6 million objects, including more than 100,000 sketches and drawings, almost 1000 architectural and stage models, over 700,000 photos and around 2000 souvenirs of famous actors, authors and composers. The oldest playbill in the collection dates from the year 1713 and is an announcement of a harlequinade. Among the autographs are originals by Beethoven, Goethe, Richard Wagner, Richard Strauss and Gustav Mahler. Gustav Klimt's painting "Nuda Veritas" came to the museum from Hermann Bahr's estate. In addition, there are many costumes, some of them designed by Oskar Kokoschka, Fritz Wotruba and Pablo Picasso, as well as marionettes and shadow figures. One room is dedicated to the Jugendstil artist Richard

Teschner (1879–1948) and his revolutionary rod-puppet theatre called Figurenspiegel (Figure Mirror). Evening performances are occasionally staged. The Library contains around 80,000 books and periodicals (open from Tuesday to Friday 10 a.m. to 1 p.m. and 2 p.m. to 4:45 p.m., on Saturday 10 a.m. to 1 p.m.). The memorial rooms at Hanuschgasse 3 include tributes to Carl Michael Ziehrer, Emmerich Kálmán, Hugo Thimig, Hermann Bahr, Max Reinhardt, Caspar Neher and Fritz Wotruba (open by appointment).

History: The Theatre Museum was created in 1991 from the Theatre Collection of the ➤ **Österreichische National-bibliothek (Austrian National Library)**. While the Theatre Collection was not founded until 1922, it was based on several preliminary stages of collecting at the Court Library dating as far back as the Baroque period. As a result of an exhibition on comedy in the Library's State Hall, the extensive collection of Hugo Thimig, director of the Burgtheater, was purchased in 1923. In 1931 several rooms in the **Burgtheater (➤ Environs)** became available for the Federal Theatre Museum. The museum was closed, however, in 1938.

There has been a real Austrian Theatre Museum only since 1975. In 1982 a decision was made to combine the Theatre Collection of the National Library and the Theatre Museum. The obvious place to put it was Lobkowitz Palace, which had just been purchased by the Republic of Austria. The Theatre Collection was finally separated from the National Library, and the Theatre Museum acquired the status of a Federal Museum. It opened on October 26, 1991. A decade later the Theatre Museum lost its independence. At the beginning of 2001, it became

Theatralical presentation: varied historical costumes

Eroica Hall: ceiling painting by Jakob van Schuppen (around 1730)

part of the ➤ **Kunsthistorisches Museum**.

On a commission from Philipp Sigmund Count Dietrichstein, the architect Giovanni Pietro Tencala began planning Lobkowitz Palace in 1687. It was built between 1690 and 1694 with the participation of Johann Bernhard Fischer von Erlach, who designed the central projection, portal and attic. In 1745, the Baroque palace came into the possession of the Lobkowitz family. Prince Francis Joseph Maximilian Prince of Lobkowitz was an important patron of the music and theatre scene of that time. Himself a musician and later director of the Court Theatre, he built a concert hall in 1799. Ludwig van Beethoven often played at the palace and among the numerous works that he dedicated to the Prince was his *Third Symphony*, composed in 1804 and originally entitled *Bonaparte*. In Beethoven's honor the concert hall is called the Eroica Hall today. In 1807 Beethoven's *Fourth Symphony* was given its première at Lobkowitz Palace, and in December 1812, the Gesellschaft der Musikfreunde (Society of the Friends of Music – Musikverein) was founded there. From 1869 on, the palace was rented to various tenants, including the French and the Czech embassies. After World War II it was rented to the French Cultural Institute. Since 1979 it has been the property of the Republic of Austria. The renovation and conversion to create the Theatre Museum took from 1985 to 1991.

Papyrus Museum

ADDRESS: Neue Burg (Middle Gate), Heldenplatz
OPENING TIMES: Monday and Wednesday to Friday
10 a.m. to 5 p.m. (July to September 10 a.m. to 4 p.m.)
PHONE: +43/1/534 10-425
INTERNET: www.onb.ac.at/sammlungen/papyrus/
E-MAIL: papyrus@onb.ac.at

The Papyrus Collection of the ➤ **Österreichische National-bibliothek (Austrian National Library)** is the largest of its kind in the world. It holds around 138,000 papyri (from the 15th century BC to the 16th century AD), more than 50,000 archaeological documents and 17,000 photographs. The 400 most interesting objects are presented in a permanent exhibition on the basement floor of the Neue Burg (entrance via the Modern Library). The 30 display cases present ten different themes, including school, magic, the hereafter, literature, the military and the police. Among the objects on display are the oldest surviving "police ticket" (issued because an old coat was discarded in the street) and a recipe for toothpaste from the 4th century AD. It was made of a dram each of rock salt and iris, two drams of mint and 30 peppercorns. Various processes are also explained, including the technique of writing on papyrus with a reed pen and methods for preserving the fragments.

History: About 95 percent of the holdings in the Papyrus Collection date back to the private collection of Archduke Rainer, a nephew of Emperor Francis Joseph. In the Winter of 1878–79, Egyptian agricultural laborers searching for fertile soil had dug up a sand dune where they discovered the refuse dump of the ancient city of Crocodilopolis. The

Parchment fragment: "ticket" issued because someone discarded an old coat in the street

papyrus fragments they found made their way to the antique market of Cairo, where they were discovered by the Viennese antiquities dealer Theodor Graf. He informed Josef von Karabacek, Professor of Oriental Languages at Vienna University, and the latter was able to awaken the interest of Archduke Rainer. In 1883, the first bundle of around 10,000 papyri was acquired. In 1899, after making further purchases, the Archduke gave the collection, which in part had been subjected to prior study and presented in an exhibition, to the Emperor as a gift to the Court Library.

Präsidentschaftskanzlei (Offices of the Austrian President)

Ostentatious suite:
the apartments of Maria Theresa

ADDRESS: Ballhausplatz
ADMISSION: only on special open days with permission.
PHONE: +43/1/53 422
INTERNET: www.hofburg.at

In 1920, after the downfall of the monarchy, the Office of the Federal President was instituted. Until 1938, the head of state had his offices in what is now the Federal Chancellery on Ballhausplatz. Because these rooms had been heavily damaged during World War II, the Presidential Offices were moved in 1946 with Russian permission to the Leopoldine Wing of the Hofburg, immediately across from the former Geheime Hofkanzlei (Secret Chancellery). The previous December, the Socialist Karl Renner had been elected the first president of Austria's Second Republic. The two parallel suites of rooms were once the apartments of Maria Theresa and Joseph II, respectively. When the President is present, the Austrian flag is hoisted on the roof.

Tour: The rooms adapted by Maria Theresa in the Leopoldine Wing, which had been completed in 1681, have generally kept the names they had in her day. On the courtyard side the Adlerstiege (Eagle Stairway) provides access to the First and Second Bellaria Rooms (Bellariazimmer). They got their name from the Bellaria ramp that Maria

Theresa installed in order to reach her apartments without having to climb stairs. The projection we see today on the narrow side of the building, the "Bellaria Gate," was not built until the second half of the 19th century.

In the Rosenzimmer, named for the rose ornament above the doors, is the Kaiserliche Vorstellungsuhr (Imperial Performance Clock), a mechanical clock that Maria Theresa received as a gift in 1750. It is considered one of the finest and most beautiful timepieces of the Baroque period and weighs 128 kilograms (282 pounds). The "performance" in the name takes place on a stage beneath the dial. Set in motion by a complicated mechanism, it pays homage to the imperial couple, Francis and Maria Theresa. The first room that was used for official functions is the Pietra-dura-Zimmer, named for the 67 mosaic pictures on the walls. They were assembled in Florence between 1737 and 1767 from colored semi-precious stones carefully cut to shape. This collection is by far the biggest in the world. The cabinets and tables are also of Florentine pietra-dura (literally "hard stone") work. The most beautiful table, however, is missing: during the Nazi period, the Italian foreign minister, Count Galeazzo

The President's reception room: the Empress died here in 1780

Ciano, presented it as a gift to the Gauleiter ("district leader") of Vienna, Baldur von Schirach.

The Miniaturenkabinett (Cabinet of Miniatures), which adjoins the Spiegelsaal (Hall of Mirrors), was Maria Theresa's study and contained her delicate escritoire. The room got its name from a collection of miniatures acquired by Maria Theresa's grandson Francis I. Many are images of members or relatives of the Imperial household.

The Maria Theresa Room was the Empress's bedroom after the death of her husband, and here she died in 1780 at the age of 63. The walls were hung with dark-red, gold-embroidered velvet. In the middle of the long wall stood her impressive bed with a heavy velvet canopy hung above it. Today the room is used by the President for receptions, for swearing in the government and for state visits. A tall astronomical clock is the most impressive piece in the room. Made in 1671, it is supposed to keep accurate time until 2160. The dial showing the local time has hands that move counter-clockwise, with the three on the left and the nine on the right. There was good reason for this: instead of having to turn to see the clock when she was lying in bed – where she often conducted state business – the Empress could see the time in a mirror across the room. When the room was restored in 1957, a niche was found to contain an altar. It is believed to have been built for Pope Pius VI, who visited Joseph II in 1782 to encourage him to adopt more lenient policies toward the monasteries.

The other adjoining rooms facing the courtyard were not part of Maria Theresa's apartments. The first, called the Jagdzimmer (Hunting Room), is now the conference room of the President. The suite of rooms facing Heldenplatz served as living quarters for Joseph II and were not nearly as lavish as those of his mother. The first room, the closest to the Swiss Court (Schweizerhof), was the Emperor's bedroom. Because of the color of the upholstery, it was called the Blue Salon. The next room, the Green Salon, was Joseph II's study and is now used by the President for the same purpose. An office area adjoins it. At the western end of the Leopoldine Wing is the almost unknown Josefskapelle (Joseph's Chapel), which Maria Theresa remodeled in 1772. A "closet door" allowed the Empress to enter the oratory without having to leave her apartment.

Prunksaal (State Hall) of the Austrian National Library

ADDRESS: Joseph's Square 1
OPENING TIMES: daily 10 a.m. to 2 p.m. Thursday 10 a.m. to
7 p.m. Starting January 2005: daily except Monday 10 a.m. to
6 p.m., Thursday 10 a.m. to 9 p.m.
PHONE: +43/1/534 10-397
INTERNET: www.onb.ac.at/siteseeing/prunksaal/

Don't be put off by the soberly decorated rooms on the
ground floor, which used to be stables and are now used
for events staged by the ➤ Österreichische Nationalbibliothek (Austrian National Library). The State Hall on the
second floor of the former Court Library is a Baroque
Gesamtkunstwerk (total work of art) with Daniel Gran's
ceiling frescoes, white marble statues by the brothers Paul
and Peter Strudel and walnut bookcases, and it is also one
of the most impressive library rooms in the world.
Designed by Johann Bernhard Fischer von Erlach, it has
extremely clear and attractive proportions: the room,
which opens in the middle to an oval space topped by a
cupola, is exactly 240 Wiener Schuh (Viennese feet) long

(77.7 meters, 255 feet) and 45 wide (14.6 meters, 48 feet). The height of the barrel vault is 60 Viennese feet (19 meters, 64 feet), the top of the dome 90 (29 meters, 96 feet). Around 200,000 volumes, mainly works from 1501 to 1850, are kept in the State Hall. The frescoes in the entrance wing are based on themes of the World and War. Those in the rear wing adjoining the Hofburg (with the entrance for the Emperor) are allegorical depictions of the Sky and Peace. In the dome is the *Apotheosis of Charles VI*, the builder of the Court Library, and the history of its construction.

Clear proportions: the State Hall by Johann Bernhard Fischer von Erlach

History: The origins of the former Court Library date from the late 14ᵗʰ century. The book considered to be the "founding volume" is the "Gospel Book of Johannes von Troppau" ordered by Duke Albert III and completed in 1368. It is written in gold letters and decorated in the Bohemian style of book illumination. It is the oldest book authenticated as a Habsburg-Austrian codex. The library experienced a big upswing under the direction of the Dutch scholar Hugo Blotius, who was hired in 1575 by Maximilian II to be the first official Court Librarian. A lack of space in the Minorite Monastery, where the library was housed from 1558 to 1623, forced a transfer to a building on the outer Burgplatz (Castle Square), where it remained until 1727.

In 1660, Leopold I planned to add a library storey to the riding-school building on the Tummelplatz (Exercise Ground) to the southeast of the Hofburg. But the plans drawn up in 1663 were not implemented until 1681. In 1683 the almost finished building was severely damaged during the Turkish siege, and it was apparently never repaired. In 1722, Johann Bernhard Fischer von Erlach began building the new Court Library on the foundations of the old riding-school building. His son Joseph Emanuel Fischer completed the structure in 1726, and Daniel Gran worked until 1730 to finished the wall and ceiling frescoes. Some 15,000 volumes of the recently acquired library of Prince Eugene of Savoy were installed in the central oval of the State Hall.

The foundations, however, proved inadequate and the dome threatened to collapse. From 1765 to 1767, Nikolaus Pacassi undertook measures to secure the building. The Main Staircase was rebuilt on a different design between 1767 and 1769. At the same time, Franz Anton Maulbertsch restored the damaged frescoes. Subsequently the Augustinian Wing and the façades of the side wings were built by Pacassi, who adapted them to harmonize with the architecture of the Court Library.

In 1829, the Late-Baroque Library Hall – with a 1775 ceiling fresco by Johann Bergl – of the adjoining Augustinian monastery was rented as storage space for books and copperplate engravings. From 1903 to 1906, it was remodeled to create the Augustinian Reading Room. It is not possible to simply visit this hall, which since 1995 has been the reading room of the Department of

The Library of Prince Eugene of Savoy

In 1737, a year after the death of Prince Eugene of Savoy, Emperor Charles VI purchased the famous Bibliotheca Eugeniana from the niece and heiress of the celebrated military commander. He paid the princess an annual pension of 10,000 florins, which proved to be an enormous sum because Victoria of Savoy lived another 26 years. The value of the library, which was housed in Prince Eugene's town palace on Himmelpfortgasse (today the Finance Ministry), was estimated to be "only" 150,000 florins.

The library comprised 15,000 printed works, 500 volumes and boxes of copperplate engravings and 240 precious manuscripts, which Prince Eugene – according to the poet Jean-Baptiste Rousseau – did not collect for ostentatious purposes but rather because he was a true friend of science, fine books and art. In addition to the personal interests and connections of the prince, the library also reflects the universal spectrum of fields of knowledge to be found in a princely library.

The books, which were uniformly bound in morocco leather, have the coat of arms of their owner stamped in gold on the front and back. The various fields of knowledge are distinguished by the color of the binding (history and literature in red, theology and law in blue, natural sciences in yellow/ochre). Among the most precious objects in the Bibliotheca Eugeniana is the "Tabula Peutingeriana" (Peutinger Table, a copy of a Roman map and now in the manuscript collection), the *Atlas Bleau van der Hem* (in the map collection) and a *Bible moralisée* with 2000 medallion illustrations.

Incunabula, Old and Precious Books. (Opening times: October to June, Monday, Wednesday and Friday 9 a.m. to 3:45 p.m. Tuesday and Thursday 9 a.m. to 7 p.m.; July to September, Monday to Friday 9 a.m. to 3:45 p.m., closed September 1–7.)

"quartier21"

ADDRESS: MuseumsQuartier, Museumsplatz 1
OPENING times of the theme streets Electric Avenue and
"transeuropa": daily from 10 a.m.
INTERNET: http://quartier21.mqw.at
E-MAIL: quartier21@mqw.at

INSTITUTIONS

"quartier21" encompasses all the spaces in the
MuseumsQuartier that are not permanently assigned
to institutions (a total of 4900 m², 53,000 square
feet). It includes the publicly accessible theme streets
Electric Avenue and "transeuropa" (including the
meeting areas of the Oval Hall and Erste Bank Arena)
as well as cultural offices and conference rooms in the
Fischer von Erlach Wing and several institutions
spread across the grounds.

History: In 1993 a number of small autonomous culture
institutions and associations began to establish offices
in the former Messepalast. They were assigned performance space free of charge, which they were allowed to
use until the MuseumsQuartier was built. With their
various activities, they helped enliven the run-down
area. Eventually, this made it politically impossible to
abandon the project MuseumsQuartier or the concept
of a multifunctional art and cultural center. Some ini-

Designer merchandise, fashions, CDs: Electric Avenue in "quartier21"

tially provisory organizations, such as the ➤ **Architekturzentrum Wien** and the ➤ **Zoom Kindermuseum**, quickly established themselves on a permanent basis. Others remained temporary, were forced to disband due to insufficient funding and subsidies, or moved away. Now that renovation of the old buildings is complete, for the sake of flexibility the MuseumsQuartier Company usually grants leases with a term of only two years. "quartier21" opened in September 2002 with approximately 30 partner organizations.

Tour: The ground floor of the Fischer von Erlach Wing is laid out in such a way that visitors can wander the entire length of the building (if no events are being staged). "transeuropa" begins in the south with an open space, which is available for exhibitions of all kinds. Next to it is the "A9-forum transeuropa," in which the provinces that make up the Federal Republic of Austria present projects to introduce themselves. The core "transeuropa" space follows, with interlocked booths leased to various cultural organizations. Above the Oval Hall, the Main Entrance with MQ Point Info, the cultural bookshop Prachner and the Kantine (cafeteria), one can reach Electric Avenue. The partner organizations focus on electronic music (Cheap Records & Store), with video art, fashion and design. Electric Avenue ends at the northeast entrance of the MuseumsQuartier.

In addition to the Architekturzentrum, the Staatsratshof (State Councilor's Courtyard) also contains the "forum experimentelle architektur" and "basis wien." This information center, which is dedicated to current art, opened in July 1997 in the MuseumsQuartier, but moved in 2001 to Fünfhausgasse 5. The space in the MQ is still used as an "infopool" for exhibitions and events. Opening times: Tuesday to Sunday 2 p.m. to 7 p.m. (Internet: www.basis-wien.at). The two outside staircases in the Main Courtyard and the entrance on Breite Gasse lead to the attic of the Oval Wing, which is home to the mathematics laboratory "math.space." It offers regular workshops and lectures for pupils of all age groups. Opening times: Monday 10 a.m. to noon, Friday 3 p.m. to 5 p.m. (Internet: http://math.space.or.at).

Redoutensäle

ADDRESS: Joseph's Square
ADMISSION: only to public events
PHONE: +43/1/587 36 66
INTERNET: www.hofburg.com
E-MAIL: kongresszentrum@hofburg.com

Between 1744 and 1748, Jean-Nicolas Jadot built two
ballrooms, the Kleiner and Grosser Redoutensaal, to
replace the Dancing Hall originally constructed between
1629 and 1631. It had previously been converted into a
theatre in 1652 and was adapted again in 1660 for

The Redoutensaal Wing in flames: the cause of the blaze is still unknown

The 1992 Fire in the Hofburg

On November 27, 1992, shortly after one o'clock in the morning, a night watchman discovered a fire in the Grosser Redoutensaal. The first fire engine arrived within three minutes, but soon the attic was in flames. While 240 firemen fought the blaze, police blocked off the city center. At around 2:30 a.m. the ceiling of the Grosser Redoutensaal collapsed. A half hour later the attic of the entire building was alight. Thousands of books were removed from the State Hall of the National Library, and 69 Lipizzaner horses were taken to safety in the Volksgarten. Fortunately, the fire did not spread to the library or the stables.

By 8:15 a.m. on November 28, the fire had been extin-

operatic performances. In 1759, a decade after the Redoutensäle were complete, Empress Maria Theresa commissioned Nikolaus Pacassi to remodel the two halls for the wedding of Joseph II and Isabella of Parma, and he added Late-Baroque stucco decorations.

The halls were the venue for numerous "Redouten" (masked balls), banquets, operatic performances and concerts: Ludwig van Beethoven's *Eighth Symphony* received its première in the Grosser Redoutensaal, Niccolò Paganini performed there in 1828, and the composers Josef Strauss and Franz Liszt conducted their works there as well. The guished, but about three percent of the Hofburg complex had been damaged. The most serious destruction was in the Grosser Redoutensaal: the historical stucco ceiling was destroyed, and the Baroque structure of the attic was gone. In the Kleiner Redoutensaal the fire destroyed a third of the stucco ceiling. The cause of the fire remains unclear.

A team of experts consisting of around 100 architects and engineers was immediately convened under the leadership of architect Manfred Wehdorn. By December 22, 1992, a provisional roof and heating system had been installed to keep the waterlogged stucco from freezing. By the spring of 1993, a study of the building's architectural history had been completed. Following a heated discussion of whether to restore or completely rebuild the Redoutensäle, a compromise was reached: the Kleiner Redoutensaal was restored to its original state, while the Grosse Redoutensaal was rebuilt, using modern technology. All the levels were connected with stairways and elevators. The booths for interpreters and audio engineers were hidden behind one-way mirrors.

In order to restore the Grosser Redoutensaal to one of its original uses – as a venue for operatic performances – it was given an orchestra pit that can be covered when not in use. Josef Mikl won an international competition to provide art for the decoration. By finishing the attic, the amount of available space was increased from 7500 to almost 11,200 m² (80,000 to 120,000 square feet). The Redoutensäle were formally reopened on October 26, 1997, with a performance by the Vienna State Opera.

saying about the Congress of Vienna having "danced" rather than "met" recalls the numerous (and very lavish) events staged during the Congress (1814–1815).

In 1961 the Redoutensäle were the venue for a summit conference between American President John F. Kennedy and his Soviet counterpart, Nikita S. Khrushchev. In 1973, the halls were remodeled to create a conference center, and in 1979 US President Jimmy Carter and the head of state of the USSR, Leonid Brezhnev, signed the SALT II treaty there. Following a devastating fire in November 1992, the halls were either restored to their original state or renovated.

The Blue Ball is an eyecatcher in the attic, finished after the 1992 fire

The architect Manfred Wehdorn remodeled the attic to create a space of 3 500 m² (38,000 square feet). An eyecatcher is the top floor with its Blue Ball. A glassed area of the roof looking towards the courtyard of the Summer Riding School offers a fantastic view of the dome of Michael's Gate and surrounding roof areas.

The stucco ceiling of the Grosser Redoutensaal was replaced with a 404 m² (4300 square feet) abstract oil painting by Josef Mikl in memory of the Austrian journalist, critic, playwright and poet Karl Kraus: the painter used a typical "scrawl," which the viewer can hardly read, to write out the 34 verses of the poem "Jugend" ("Youth"). In Mikl's 22 paintings on the walls, he depicts scenes from works by his favorite authors: Elias Canetti, Johann Nestroy and Ferdinand Raimund.

After the facility reopened in 1998, the Vienna Congress Centre Hofburg Management Company Ltd. assumed managerial responsibility for the Redoutensäle. Nine conference areas offer meeting facilities for up to 1 300 participants. The Redoutensaal Wing is directly connected to the ➤ **Hofburg Congress Centre.**

Sammlung alter Musikinstrumente (Collection of Ancient Musical Instruments)

ADDRESS: Neue Burg (Middle Gate), Heldenplatz
OPENING TIMES: daily except Tuesday 10 a.m. to 6 p.m.
PHONE: +43/1/525 24-471
INTERNET: www.khm.at, E-MAIL: info.sam@khm.at

The Collection of Ancient Musical Instruments was founded with two significant 16th-century inventories: the Kunst- und Wunderkammer (arts and natural wonders room) of Archduke Ferdinand at Ambras Castle in Tirol and the art collection of the House of Este at Catajo Castle near Padua. The collection of Renaissance instruments, some of which are true rarities, makes this collection of the ➤ **Kunsthistorisches Museum** one of the most important in the world. In 1947, it was installed on the upper floor of the Neue Burg close to the ➤ **Hofjagd- und Rüstkammer (Collection of Arms and Armour)**. In contrast to earlier systems of displaying instruments (in which instruments were grouped according to the way they produced a tone), the permanent exhibition, which was reorganized in 1993 according to musical periods, takes us through the history of instrument-making and thus of music itself and the most important Austrian composers.

Tour: Our point of departure is the right side-gallery, which explains the origins of music in prehistoric times. To be seen here (and thanks to the audio guide, to be heard as well) are a bone pipe (16,000–10,000 BC), a clay pipe and a fibula (around 600–500 BC). The first three rooms are related to Emperor Maximilian I, who founded the Hofburg Chapel and thus also the institution of the Wiener Sängerknaben (Vienna Boys' Choir), and three other emperors who were composers themselves: Ferdinand III, Leopold I and Joseph I. One of the most precious items is a cittern

Tangent piano by Christoph Friedrich Schmahl (1798)

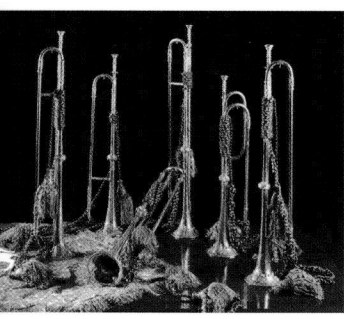

Trumpets by Franz and Michael Leichamschneider (1741 and 1746)

made in Brescia in 1574 by Girolamo de Virchi for Archduke Ferdinand.

A room is dedicated to each of the great composers of the Vienna classic period: Josef Haydn, Wolfgang Amadeus Mozart and Ludwig van Beethoven. Along with fortepianos and various other instruments (including the hurdy-gurdy, tangent piano, baryton, keyed trumpet, glass harmonica, basset horn and clarinet), there are also portraits and busts. The next rooms are dedicated to the Biedermeier period (Franz Schubert), Romantic period and Viennese dance music (Johann Strauss the Elder and the Younger, Joseph Lanner, Johann Schrammel). The 20th century is treated in a rather cursory manner: our journey through time ends with the twelve-tone technique of Arnold Schoenberg and a synthesizer as the supposedly "only new instrument of our time."

Schatzkammer (Treasury)

Address: Schweizerhof (Swiss Court)
Opening times: daily except Tuesday 10 a.m. to 6 p.m.
Phone: +43/1/525 24-486
Internet: www.khm.at
E-mail: info.kk@khm.at

There's a good reason why the entrance to the Treasury is protected by a massive safe-door in the Schweizerhof (Swiss Court). The objects that are stored there – jewels, medals, vestments, weapons, insignia and liturgical implements – are not only of extremely high material and symbolic value, they also reflect a millennium of European history.

The Secular Treasury holds the most important royal treasures that have been preserved from the Middle Ages: the insignia and jewels of the Holy Roman Empire, including the Imperial Crown. It was made in the second half of the 10th century, presumably for the coronation of Otto I in 962. The octagonal body is formed by eight gold plates set with precious stones and pearls, representing heavenly Jerusalem with its eight gates. The large brow and neck plates have 12 large precious stones each as symbols of the 12 Apostles and the Tribes of Israel. Among the imperial insignia are the golden Imperial Orb (around 1200), the Gothic Scepter, the Aspergilum (container used for sprinkling holy water on the altar), the Imperial Sword (blade from the 4th quarter of the 11th century), the Imperial Cross made around 1024–1025 and the Holy Lance. The leather cases in which the imperial jewels were kept can also be seen (Rooms 11 and 12). The set of coronation robes in the Secular Treasury provides a unique example of medieval textile artistry.

Because the imperial jewels did not belong to the Emperor even after his coronation (they were kept in Nuremberg from 1424 to 1796), the rulers had their own insignia made. Most of them got broken, but the Crown of Rudolf II by Jan Vermeyen of Antwerp (made between 1598 and 1602) survived the centuries. Between 1612 and 1615, Emperor Matthias, Rudolf's brother and successor, had a matching scepter and imperial orb made by Andreas Osenbruck. This set became the official insignia of the monarchy in 1804, when Emperor Francis II proclaimed the Hereditary Empire of Austria (thus becoming Francis I). The Crown, Scepter and Imperial Orb are in Room 2, together with Friedrich von Amerling's 1832 portrait of Francis wearing the Imperial Robes. The mantle with a train (1830) of red velvet has an ermine collar and is embroidered in gold. It can be seen in Room 3.

The Austrian Archducal Crown that was made in 1616 is kept at Klosterneuburg Abbey near Vienna, but the Scepter and the Imperial Orb are in the Treasury (both from the 14th century). They can be seen in Room 9 within the context of the Bohemian Elector's Robes. Another Archducal Crown was made for Joseph II in 1764, but only the carcass has been preserved (Room 1). Rooms 15 and 16 present the Liturgical Vestments and other precious items from the Order of the Golden Fleece as well as numerous memen-

The Crown of the Holy Roman Empire (2nd half of the 10th century)

tos of the Habsburgs and other dynasties.

The Ecclesiastical Treasury holds the liturgical implements of the ➤ **Hofburg Chapel** and religious memorabilia of the Habsburgs. The liturgical vestments, chalices, house altars, crucifixes, monstrances, lamps, reliquaries, Madonna statuettes and so on are in the old Rooms I–V with their tunnel vaulting and paneling. The large display cases are from the Baroque period. One of the most beautiful objects is the 123-cm (48-inch) copy of the Column to the Virgin Mary found on the square Am Hof in Vienna. It was made by Philipp Küsel around

Emperor Charles VI in the regalia of the Order of the Golden Fleece (c. 1730)

1670-80 of gilt silver decorated with painted enamel, precious stones and pearls.

History: As early as the beginning of the 14th century, at least part of the Habsburg's treasures must have been in the Hofburg, more precisely in the sacristy of the Hofburg Chapel. Under Ferdinand I a treasury was built in the northwestern wing with its Schweizertor (Swiss Gate). It was remodeled and completed between 1551 and 1554. Rudolf II,

The Orb of the Holy Roman Empire (around 1200)

whose residence was in Prague, built a wing between 1583 and 1585 that was first called Kunsthaus (Art House) and later Schatzkammer (Treasury) It adjoined the north tower of the fortress on the northeast. Even though the Treasury was moved several more times (e. g. because the threestorey gallery wing needed renovation), it stands in approximately the same place now as then. Access was via the Säulenstiege (Pillar Staircase) and through an iron door bearing the monogram of Charles VI (two intertwined Cs) and the date 1712. The lock is said to have been the most complicated one in Vienna.

Maria Theresa, a daughter of Charles VI, had her treasurer, Joseph Angelo de France, redisplay the holdings of the Secular Treasury between 1747 and 1750 (the rooms that were used for that purpose at the time are now part of the Ecclesiastical Treasury). Under Joseph II, Maria Theresa's son, the two collections were administratively separated after the Emperor transferred responsibility for the Ecclesiastical Treasury to the Hofburg parish priest in 1782. Because it was feared that the Treasure of the Order of the Golden Fleece could fall into the hands of Napoleon, it was moved from Brussels to Vienna in 1794. The Imperial Jewels were also moved from Aachen and Nuremberg in 1796 and placed in the Treasury in 1800 on the orders of Emperor Francis II. There they remained until the Holy Roman Empire was dissolved in 1806. When the imperial collections were reorganized under Francis Joseph in 1891, all the remaining art objects

Copy of the Column to the Virigin Mary by Philipp Küsel (c. 1670)

in the Treasury were transferred to the newly opened ➤ **Kunsthistorisches Museum**. The Treasury had already undergone a reorganization in 1886. The downfall of the monarchy was followed by further losses: Emperor Charles and his family took their private jewelry into exile with them. In addition, the Treaty of Saint-Germain specified that the robes and insignias of Napoleon as king of Italy had to be returned to that country. To Hungary went the robes and the diamond-encrusted cross of the Order of St. Stephen. Following the annexation of Austria in 1938, Adolf Hitler took the insignia and jewels of the Holy Roman Empire to Nuremberg, and the Treasury was closed.

In 1946, the insignia and jewels were returned to Vienna, and in 1952 the holdings of the Secular and Ecclesiastical Treasuries were reunited. Additional rooms in the eastern part of the Schweizerhof (Swiss Court) were adapted for the objects of the Secular Treasury. In 1954, the Treasury reopened. Between 1984 and 1987, there was further renovation (including putting the entrance under the stairway to the Hofburg Chapel).

Schmetterlinghaus/Palmenhaus (Butterfly House/Palm House)

ADDRESS: Burggarten
OPENING TIMES: November to March 10 a.m. to 3:45 p.m. April to October weekdays 10 a.m. to 4:45 p.m., Saturday, Sunday and holidays 10 a.m. to 6:15 p.m.
PHONE: +43/1/533 85 70
INTERNET: www.schmetterlinghaus.at
E-MAIL: schmetterling@netway.at

Between 1902 and 1906, the Palmenhaus (Palm House) in the former Imperial Garden was built by Court Architect Friedrich Ohmann parallel to the Augustinian Bastion, replacing two glasshouses. The terrace and the double stairway date from the year 1909, and the additions on the side from 1910. A one-storey connecting corridor to the Hofburg was torn down in 1918 because it disturbed Archduke Francis Ferdinand's view of the back of the Court Library.

The Neue Wintergarten, as the symmetrical Palmenhaus was first called, was considered an important example of Jugendstil glasshouse architecture. To the left and right of the high central section – a vaulted metal construction with a projecting stone façade (Ionic colonnade between rusticated pillars) – are two glassed wings with a sweeping stone balustrade. Masonry pavilions with rounded arches and stucco female figures are at the two ends.

In the 1980s, the Palmenhaus had to be closed for safety reasons. In 1998, following complete renovation, it reopened. There is a café-restaurant in the central section, a plant-storage facility operated by the Federal Garden Administration and the 280-m² (3000 square-foot) Schmetterlinghaus (Butterfly House). Hundreds of exotic butterflies live here in an almost natural tropical environment with a waterfall and small pools (temperature around 26°C or 79°F, humidity about 80 percent). The insects, all of which are bred here and are not endangered species, originally came from tropical butterfly farms in Thailand, Belize, Costa Rica and the Philippines. One of the most impressive species that can be admired here in its rain-forest setting is the Atlas moth, which has a wingspan of up to 30 centimeters (12 inches).

In the Palm House: tropical vegetation and hundreds of butterflies

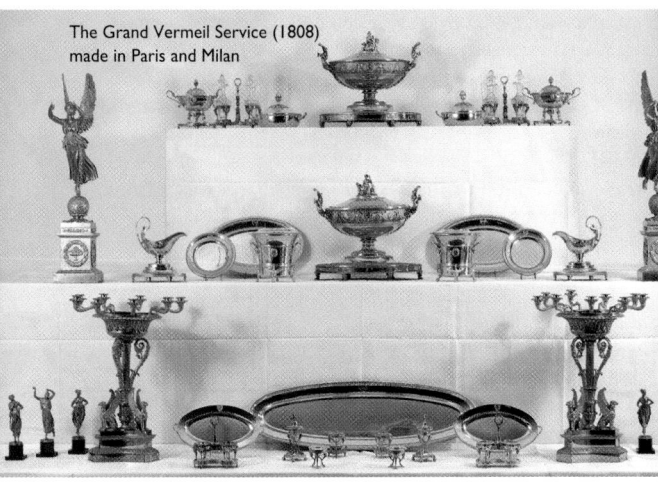

The Grand Vermeil Service (1808) made in Paris and Milan

Silver Collection

ADDRESS: Michael's Wing (entrance beneath the dome)
OPENING TIMES: daily 9 a.m. to 5 p.m. (July and August 9 a.m. to 5:30 p.m.)
GUIDED TOURS (in German): daily at 11:15 a.m. and 3:15 p.m.
PHONE: +43/1/533 75 70
E-MAIL: info@hofburg-wien.at, INTERNET: www.hofburg-wien.at

Since 1902 the Imperial Silver Collection has been housed on the ground floor of the Michaelertrakt (Michael's Wing). After the downfall of the monarchy in 1918, some of the holdings of the individual court offices (including the Court Kitchen, the Court Confectionery, the Court Cellars and the Court Linen Room) were sold, and the rest were transferred to the Silver Chamber. The imperial porcelain, linens and table decorations have been on public display since 1923. After complete renovation and the adaptation of adjacent rooms that had once housed the Royal and Imperial Gobelin Manufactory, the Silver Room was reopened in 1995 as the Imperial Silver Collection. The admission ticket is also valid for visiting the
➤ **Imperial Apartments and the Sisi Museum**.
Among the most magnificent pieces in the former Court Silver and Table Room is the Grand Vermeil Service, a completely gilded silver service. It was originally made for Napoleon in Paris and Milan in 1808. Emperor Francis II/I acquired the service during the Congress of Vienna

and replaced Napoleon's coat of arms with his own initials, FIA (Franciscus Imperator Austriae). It was brought to Vienna in 1816 on the occasion of Francis's marriage to Princess Caroline of Bavaria. The set was continually augmented so that the original service for 40 has been increased to 140 today. It is still displayed in the room that was created for it in 1902. The service has a total weight of 1200 kilograms.

In the spring 1814, when plans were being made to hold a huge peace conference in Vienna, the Hofburg did not have a service of precious metal, the flat silver having been melted down for coinage during the Napoleonic Wars. In order to preserve appearances, a completely gilt service was ordered from the Viennese porcelain manufactory. Not until the 1830s was another silver service acquired. The table silver of the Vienna Court was made by Stephan Mayerhofer. It was continually enlarged up to the outbreak of World War I (1914) and is still used today at state banquets.

Between 1821 and 1824, the Viennese porcelain manufactory created a Romantic-Neo-Gothic dessert service commissioned by Emperor Francis II/I. The Habsburg Service, almost all of which has been preserved, was decorated with portraits of the Habsburgs, fortresses and castles, including the dynasty's ancestral seat. In addition to numerous other porcelain services (made by Sèvres, Herend and Minton), cut crystal from Bohemia, table decorations and centerpieces up to 30 meters (100 feet) in length and Japanese Imari porcelain from the 17th and 18th centuries, the Imperial Silver Collection also has the individual set of cutlery in solid gold used personally by Empress Maria Theresa as well as Elisabeth's silver cutlery with a dolphin motif. It was originally made for Achilleion Palace on Corfu.

Terrine and ladle from a service made by Thun (1851); terrine and butter-dish from the service with green bands by Sèvres (1756/57)

Spanish Riding School

ADDRESS: Michaelerplatz 1
OPENING TIMES: Tuesday to Saturday 9 a.m. to 5:30 p.m.,
Sunday 9 a.m. to 1:30 p.m.
PERFORMANCES: in the spring and autumn,
usually on Sunday at 11 a.m.
PHONE: +43/1/533 90 31
INTERNET: www.srs.at

The Spanish Riding School is the only institute in the
world where the Renaissance tradition of training and riding has been maintained and practiced without interruption down to the present day. Training the white horses
takes four to six years. Once they have learned the "natural gaits" (walk, trot and canter) and have been through
their "campagne year" (second year of elementary but
thorough training), they learn more complicated movements, including the pirouette, the piaffe, the traversale
and the passage. Only a few animals have the necessary
talent for what is called the "*Schule über der Erde*" ("airs
above the ground"), meaning all the figures in which the
horse actually leaves terra firma. These include the levade,
the courbette and the capriole.

The maintenance of this tradition of *haute école* dressage
is in the hands of the riders. There are no textbooks or
written instructions; it is all handed down orally from
generation to generation. The traditional dress consists of

Training in the Baroque Winter Riding Hall: the quadrille

a black, two-cornered hat with diagonal gold trimming, a tailcoat of brown Trevira worsted, and pleated trousers of white buckskin as well as top boots of black leather and white suede gloves.

History: In 1562, Emperor Maximilian II brought the first Spanish horses to Austria because the breed, which was already famous in Roman times, had shown particular talent. Three years later, there is documentary evidence of a "Ross-Tumblplatz" (open practice run) in front of the Stallburg. The first riding hall was built around 1572. In 1580, Archduke Charles founded the imperial stud at Karst near Lipizza (today Lipica in Slovenia, near Trieste) for which he acquired Neapolitan as well as Spanish stallions.

In 1680, Emperor Leopold I decided to build a riding hall on the Exercise Ground (today Joseph's Square). But just before completion, the building was severely damaged during the Turkish siege of 1683 and was never restored. The Winterreitschule (Winter Riding Hall) as we know it today was built between 1729 and 1735 under Charles VI. It was based on plans by Joseph Emanuel Fischer von Erlach. From that time on, the Spanish Riding School got all of its horses from the stud at Lipica. The name Lipizzaner was not used, however, until the early 19th century: up to that time the horses were known as Spanish "Karster."

In 1743, Empress Maria Theresa used the new 55-meter (180-foot) long Winterreitschule (Winter Riding Hall), a venue otherwise used for ceremonial events (weddings, concerts and balls), for the first "carousel" and others followed, including one staged in 1814 during the Congress of Vienna. The last carousel was held in 1894.

After the fall of the monarchy, responsibility for the Court Riding School was assigned to the Agricultural Ministry. The Kingdom of Italy, to which Lipica now belonged, agreed after long and difficult negotiations to allow 87 stallions to remain in Austria. A new stud was built for the horses at Piber (in western Styria). Since June 1920, the performances have been open to the public.

During the Nazi period, responsibility for the Spanish Riding School was transferred to the German Agricultural Ministry in Berlin. The horses of the stud were moved in 1942 to Hostau in southern Bohemia (today Hostoun in the Czech Republic). In a secret operation, the horses

In the Stallburg since the 16th century: the Lipizzaner stables

were evacuated from the front line in 1945 and brought to safety (in 1963 Disney released a film about the dramatic rescue: *The Miracle of the White Stallions*). At the beginning of 1945, the Lipizzaner horses at the Court Riding School were also evacuated. They returned to the Stallburg in Vienna only after the signing of the Austria State Treaty in 1955. In 2001, the Spanish Riding School was privatized, and a year later a visitors' center was opened. There one can watch morning training (irregular schedule, Tuesday to Saturday from 10 a.m. to noon) and take a guided tour of the stables.

Tanzquartier Wien

ADDRESS: MuseumsQuartier, Museumsplatz 1
OPENING TIMES: visitor information/advance ticket sales daily except Sundays and holidays 10 a.m. to 7 p.m.
LIBRARY: Tuesday noon to 4 p.m., Wednesday to Friday 4 p.m. to 8 p.m.
PHONE: +43/1/581 35 91
INTERNET: www.tqw.at, E-MAIL: tanzquartier@tqw.at

In November 1992, several Viennese choreographers called for the adaptation of an old streetcar shed on Vienna's Vorgartenstrasse to be used as a dance theatre. After long discussions, the project was dropped, in part because of the high cost. This, however, did not alter the fact that a dance theatre was needed. In April 1997, the MuseumsQuartier Planning and Development Company suggested the creation of a dance theatre in the former

Imperial Stables. Eventually the cultural department of the City of Vienna was convinced of the suitability of the MuseumsQuartier location. The Tanzquartier opened in October 2001.

The Tanzquartier occupies the second floor of the old building wing between the Main Courtyard and the Fürstenhof. It includes three dance studios, which apart from providing space for professional training and workshops are also used for shows and lectures. There is also a theory and information center open to the public, with a library, video collection and magazine collection. Hall G is the venue for the Tanzquartier's major events (➤ **Halls E + G**). The season runs from September to April. Programs change weekly, and local as well as international dance and performance productions are presented.

Temple of Theseus

ADDRESS: Volksgarten
OPENING TIMES: no standard hours
PHONE: +43/1/525 24/407
INTERNET: www.khm.at, E-MAIL: info.pr@khm.at

With its simple, rectangular interior, the late-Classicistic Temple of Theseus by Pietro Nobile is a smaller copy of the eponymous Doric temple in Athens. It was built in the new Volksgarten between 1819 1823 to house the statue of "Theseus and the Centaur" by Antonio Canova, which Emperor Francis II/I had seen in the sculptor's studio in Rome and purchased. The sculpture, which was executed between 1805 and 1819, was actually intended to be a symbol of Napoleon. After his defeat, it was reinterpreted as a symbol of victory over the Revolution. Since 1890, the Theseus statue has been an eyecatcher in the Main Staircase of the ➤ **Kunsthistorisches Museum**. Until 1841 a lapidarium with Roman sculptures and inscriptions from the Antiquities Collection was displayed in the (now closed) catacombs of the Theseus Temple. Later the Temple served for several years as a venue for displaying a selection of the finds made in Ephesus starting in 1895. They are now in the ➤ **Ephesus Museum** in the Neue Burg. Today the Temple, which is administered by the Kunsthistorisches Museum, is used only occasionally for small exhibitions and events.

Volksgarten
(Club Discothèque and Pavilion)

Address: Burgring 1
Opening times: Club Discothèque: generally starting at 11 p.m.
Phone: +43/1/532 42 41
Internet: www.volksgarten.at, E-mail: info@volksgarten.at

Peter Corti was born around 1781 in Bergamo, Italy. In the summer he ran a coffee house in the Paradeisgartl atop the Löwel Bastion, and it became an extremely popular meeting place for Viennese society. Between 1820 and 1822, he added a semicircular foyer to the building. He also built a similar building only a few hundred meters away in the new Volksgarten. The second Cortisches Kaffeehaus (Corti's Café), a late-Classicistic building with a glassed-in Ionic colonnade and a terrace with space for dancing, was built according to plans by Pietro Nobile and opened on May 1, 1823. The musicians who played here during the Biedermeier period included Josef Lanner and Johann Strauss the Elder. In contrast to his first café, which was ➤torn down in 1872 to make room for the **Burgtheater** (➤ **Environs**), Corti's second café remained in the Volksgarten and was expanded in 1898.

Although severely damaged in the bombing of World War II, the building was reconstructed between 1947 and 1950 by Oswald Haerdtl, and a restaurant was added. In 1958 Haerdtl remodeled his establishment in the style of the day and added a conservatory with a retractable glass roof. For the most part, the remarkable interior has been preserved. Legendary for the appearances of artists such as Ella Fitzgerald and Joe Zawinul, the Volksgarten is now a discothèque. In summer the garden (with colored lamps on the tables) and the columned hall – now called "Banana" – are used for weekend dances. In 1951 Haerdtl added a "Milchbar" and the terrace and outdoor seating area were expanded in 1953. The glass Pavilion with its projecting penthouse roof is the only café by the architect that still exists in its original condition.

Zoom Kindermuseum

ADDRESS: MuseumsQuartier, Museumsplatz 1
OPENING TIMES: daily. Programs begin at various times; reservations are usually necessary.
PHONE: +43/1/524 79 08
INTERNET: www.kindermuseum.at
E-MAIL: info@kindermuseum.at

In 1992, art historian Claudia Haas suggested creating a children's museum in Vienna on the American model. Some 600 m² (6500 square feet) of space was made available in the Fischer von Erlach Wing of the MuseumsQuartier, and a temporary museum opened in November 1994. Due to the museum's success, major expansion became necessary, and the Zoom Children's Museum now occupies premises three times its 1993 size in the Fürstenhof. It opened in the autumn of 2001. Each year, Zoom stages two large exhibitions for children from seven to 12 years, in which a topic from the field of art, science or the culture of everyday life is presented in an interactive and playful manner. For kids under six, there is Zoom Ocean with installations and objects. And children from eight to 14 years also have access to the multimedia laboratory Zoomlab.

The Environs
Within Walking Distance

Sights

AM HOF: In Roman times this square was part of the military camp. Around 1155, Henry II Jasomirgott founded the Babenberg capital near what is today the Church of the Nine Choirs of Angels. Following construction of the Hofburg in the 13th century, the mint was housed in the former Babenberg palace. In 1365, Duke Albert III gave the area to the Carmelite order, which built a church and monastery. Today the square with its column dedicated to the Virgin Mary is remarkable for its Baroque architecture. To the right of the Urbanihaus (No. 12, façade in the style of Johann Lucas von Hildebrandt) is Collalto Palace (No. 13), where in 1762 the six-year-old Wolfgang Amadeus Mozart performed for the first time in Vienna. The church balconies are unusual for Austrian Baroque architecture. This was where Pope Pius VI gave his Easter blessing "Urbi et orbi" in 1782 and where the establishment of the Austrian Empire and the dissolution of the Holy Roman Empire were proclaimed in 1804 and 1806, respectively. Between 1912 and 1914, the former monastery building was replaced by the headquarters of the Österreichische Länderbank (now Bank Austria-Creditanstalt). On the opposite side of the square stand the Märklein'sches Haus (No. 7), built between 1727 and 1730 on a design by Hildebrandt – adaptation for the Fire Department in 1935), the Renaissance Schmales (Narrow) Haus (No. 8), the Unterkammeramtsgebäude (No. 9), heavily damaged during the Second World War, and in the north corner the Bürgerliches Zeughaus, which since 1884 has been the Central Fire Station. It was built in the mid-16th century and remodeled by Anton Ospel between 1731 and 1732. The sculptures on the façade are by Lorenzo Mattielli. The Fire Department Museum in the Märklein'sches Haus is open to visitors (Saturday and Sunday 11 a.m. to 1 p.m).

ATELIERHAUS DER AKADEMIE DER BILDENDEN KÜNSTE (ACADEMY OF FINE ARTS, ATELIERHAUS): Lehárgasse 6-8, telephone: +43/1/588 16-170. The former storage facility for sets and props of the Court Theater was built in 1873 by Gottfried Semper and Carl von Hasenauer. Now called the Semperdepot, it houses several of the Academy's classes. The impressive Prospekthof courtyard with its four-storey gallery of cast-iron columns and the Malersaal ("painter's hall") are open only for specific events or by appointment.

FEDERAL CHANCELLERY: Ballhausplatz 2, telephone: +43/1/53 115-4012. The Baroque building of the former Secret Court and State Chancellery was built by Johann Lucas von Hildebrandt between 1717 and 1721 and was a central venue for the Congress of Vienna in 1814 and 1815. Since 1919 it has been the office of the Austrian Foreign Minister and since 1922 also of the Federal Chancellor. In 1934 Chancellor Engelbert Dollfuss was assassinated by Nazis in the Marmoreck Salon on the second floor. During the Nazi period the building was the seat of the Gauleiter (district leader). The refurbishing of the Chancellery rooms, which had been destroyed in 1944, was undertaken between 1945 and 1950 by Oswald Haerdtl and Robert Obsieger. As a rule they are not open to the public.

BURGTHEATER: Dr.-Karl-Lueger-Ring 2, telephone: +43/1/51444-4140. The former Hoftheater (Court Theatre) was built between 1874 and 1888 by Gottfried Semper and Carl von Hasenauer in the style of the Italian High Renaissance with opulent decorations in the Baroque manner. The ceiling paintings in the stairwells of the two wings are by Gustav Klimt, Ernst Klimt and Franz von Matsch. The auditorium was severely damaged by bombing in 1945 and rebuilt between 1948 and 1955. Known to the Viennese simply as the "Burg," the theater is one of the most important in the German-speaking world. Tours: daily at 3 p.m. (in July and August also at 2 p.m.), on Sundays and holidays at 11 a.m. as well.

DENKMAL GEGEN KRIEG UND FASCHISMUS (MONUMENT AGAINST WAR AND FASCISM): The five-part group of sculp-

Burgtheater: one of the two wings with grand staircases

tures is on Albertinaplatz, where the Philipphof building stood until it was destroyed by incendiary bombs in 1945, killing hundreds of people in the cellars. The sculptures were created between 1983 and 1991 by Alfred Hrdlicka. Behind the "Tor der Gewalt" ("Gateway of Violence") is a bronze sculpture of a Jewish man bound in barbed wire and washing the street. The male figure emerging from a block of marble "Orpheus betritt den Hades" ("Orpheus Enters the Underworld") commemorates those who lost their lives in the resistance against the Nazi regime as well as the victims of wartime bombing. The group concludes with the "Stein der Republik" ("Stone of the Republic"), a granite stele with the declaration of government that re-established the Austrian Republic on April 27, 1945.

KAISERGRUFT (IMPERIAL CRYPT): Tegetthoffstrasse 2 (Neuer Markt), telephone: +43/1/512 68 53-0. Opening times: daily 9:30 a.m. to 4 p.m. The Kaisergruft in the Capuchin monastery is the most important tomb of a European ruling dynasty. It was founded in 1617 by Empress Anna, the wife of Emperor Matthias. Between 1633 and 1989, 145 members of the Habsburg family, including 12 emperors and 17 empresses, were buried there, generally without their entrails (their hearts are in the Herzgruft (Heart Crypt) of the Church of the Augustinians, their entrails in the Herzogsgruft (Ducal Crypt) of St. Stephen's Cathedral). The impressive double sarcophagus for the imperial couple Maria Theresa and Francis Stephen was designed, like many others, by Balthasar Ferdinand Moll. Directly in front of it stands the conspicuously frugal copper coffin of Joseph II.

KOHLMARKT: This expensive shopping street has been called Kohlmarkt ("Coal Market") since 1314 and was the place where wood and coal were sold. At the end of the 19th century – once Michaelertrakt (Michael's Wing) had been completed – a wave of construction activity got underway. A number of remarkable buildings were erected at the beginning of the 20th century in the style of the Viennese Secession (for example, No. 2 and No. 9). In 1964-65 Hans Hollein designed the former candle shop Retti (Nos. 8–10) and Schullin jewelers (No. 7). The Imperial and Royal Confectionary Demel was founded in 1786 on St. Michael's Square. Since 1887 it has been located in the former Blankenstein Palace (No. 14), and it remains Vienna's most elegant café and cake shop. The rooms are magnificently decorated in the style of late historicism.

Loos-Haus: Michaelerplatz 3, Opening hours of the bank: Monday to Friday 9 a.m. to 3 p.m., Thursday 9 a.m. to 5:30 p.m. The steel-framed structure was built by Adolf Loos between 1909 and 1911 for the men's tailor Goldman & Salatsch. The functional simplicity of the façade above the marble portal originally caused an uproar because of the glaring contrast with the Hofburg's Neo-Baroque Michaelertrakt, which had been completed in 1893, only a few years earlier. For a long time the office and apartment building was considered the major work by Loos and a monument of Neue Sachlichkeit (New Objectivity). In 1989, it was renovated and refurbished inside and out by Burkhardt Rukschcio for Austria's Raiffeisenbank. The magnificently appointed premises are well worth seeing.

Michaelerkirche (St. Michael's Church): The parish and monastery church (Salvatorian order) with a nave and two aisles on Michaelerplatz (St. Michael's Square) is an important early Gothic basilica with an early Classicist façade dating from 1792. It was built between 1220 and 1250 as the town's second parish church (in addition to St. Stephen's). Since the 14th century it has been one of Vienna's most important burial churches and has more than 100 gravestones and monuments. The main altar was designed by Johann Baptist d'Avrange in 1781–1782; the relief of the falling angel, which transitions into three-dimensional sculpture, is by Karl Georg Merville. In the passageway leading from Michaelerplatz to Habsburgergasse, there is a lovely late-15th century Mount of Olives relief.

MINORITENKIRCHE (CHURCH OF THE FRIARS MINOR):
The church on Minoritenplatz (Minorite Square) was
built in the mid-13th century, originally with two aisles.
Construction of the long chancel was completed in 1295.
It was demolished in 1903, and today its location is
marked by inset stones. In the mid-14th century, the
Gothic church with its projecting portal was remodeled,
giving it a nave and two aisles. The tower between the
two chancel apses was once crowned by a slender pyramidal top. In 1784. Joseph II gave the church to the Italian
congregation of Madonna della Neve. The interior, which
had been refurbished during the Baroque era, was later re-
Gothicized by Johann Ferdinand Hetzendorf von Hohenberg, who also designed the high altar. Since 1957, the
Friars Minor have been back in charge of what has
become the Italian church in Vienna. In the left aisle is an
altar of Carrara marble (1845–1847) with a mosaic copy
by Giacomo Raffaelli (1816) of the "Last Supper" by
Leonardo da Vinci.

PALAIS TRAUTSON (PALACE): Museumstrasse 7, telephone:
+43/1/521 52-0. This High-Baroque garden palace with
its mighty central projection and highly structured façade
was built for Johann Leopold Donat Prince Trautson
between 1710 and 1712 according to plans by Johann
Bernhard Fischer von Erlach. Today it houses the Ministry
of Justice and is not open to the public.

PARLIAMENT: Dr.-Karl-Renner-Ring 1–3, telephone:
+31/1/40 110-2715 and -2577. The Parliament was built
between 1871 and 1883 by the Danish architect Theophil
Hansen in the strict style of Neo-Renaissance historicism
as a representational building for the upper and lower
houses of the Austrian Parliament in the days of the
monarchy. A curved ramp leads around the fountain with
a statue of Pallas Athena (by Carl Kundmann, 1898–1902)
to the dominant central section of the building with its
mighty portico façade. Edmund von Hellmer created the
relief in the triangular pediment between 1879 and 1888.
It depicts the granting of the constitution to the peoples of
Austria's 17 crown lands by Emperor Francis Joseph I.
The building was partially destroyed during the Second
World War (reconstruction work lasted until 1956). It is
easy to lose one's way in the numerous corridors. Tours:
generally on weekdays when neither the upper nor the
lower house is in session.

PETERSKIRCHE (ST. PETER'S CHURCH): According to legend, the church was founded in 792 by Charlemagne. Remodeled several times, it was destroyed by fire in 1661. Rebuilding began in 1701 according to plans by Gabriele Montani, which included the dome. The plans were altered in 1703 by Johann Lucas von Hildebrandt. The church, which faces the Graben, was consecrated in 1733 and is considered one of the most important Baroque ecclesiastical buildings in Vienna. The frescoes in the dome are by Johann Michael Rottmayr, the sculptural decoration by Matthias Steinl.

STAATSOPER (VIENNA STATE OPERA): Opernring 2, telephone: +43/1751 444-2606 and -2421. Construction began in 1861 on plans by August Sicard von Sicardsburg and Eduard van der Null, who built the first monumental structure in historicism's "Renaissance arch style" on Vienna's Ring as a *Gesamtkunstwerk* ("total work of art"). Numerous artists, including Moritz von Schwind, were involved in the interior design. Neither of the two architects lived to hear the opening performance of *Don Giovanni* in May 1869: contemporary criticism of the building drove van der Null to suicide in 1868, and two months later his colleague died of a heart attack. The State Opera was severely damaged by bombing in 1945. It was rebuilt and partially redecorated between 1946 and 1955. Known to the Viennese as the "House on the Ring," the State Opera is one of the world's most important opera houses. Its orchestra is composed of members of the Vienna Philharmonic. Standing room is spectacularly cheap. The social highlight of carnival season in Vienna is the Opernball (Opera Ball). Tours: in summer several times a day on the hour (meeting place: Herbert von Karajan-Platz, first entrance under the arcade).

Museums and Exhibition Spaces

BA-CA KUNSTFORUM: Freyung 8, telephone: +43/1/53 733-0. Open daily 10 a.m. to 7 p.m., Friday 10 a.m. to 9 p.m. Designed by Gustav Peichl and opened in 1985, the Kunstforum specializes in Expressionist art.

GEMÄLDEGALERIE DER AKADEMIE DER BILDENDEN KÜNSTE (PICTURE GALLERY OF THE ACADEMY OF FINE ARTS): Schillerplatz 3, telephone: +43/1/588 16-228. Open Tuesday to Sunday 10 a.m. to 6 p.m. The building of the Academy, founded in 1692, was constructed between 1872 and 1877 on plans by Theophil Hansen. The Picture Gallery on the second floor has a collection of some 300 masterpieces from the 14th to the 20th century (Rubens, Titian, Cranach, etc.). The highlight is the "Last Judgment Triptych" by Hieronymus Bosch. Cafeteria (closed during school holidays).

JÜDISCHES MUSEUM DER STADT WIEN (JEWISH MUSEUM VIENNA): Dorotheergasse 11, telephone: +43/1/535 04 31. Open Sunday to Friday 10 a.m. to 6 p.m., Thursday 10 a.m. to 8 p.m. (closed for Rosh Hoshanah and Yom Kippur). The Museum, which opened in the former Eskeles Palace in 1993, sees part of its mission as bringing people together for changing exhibitions, symposia, readings and concerts. Most of the holdings are from synagogues, houses of prayer and private homes that were looted and destroyed by the Nazis.

KAISERLICHES HOFMOBILIENDEPOT (IMPERIAL FURNITURE COLLECTION): Andreasgasse 7, telephone: +43/1/524 33 57. Open Tuesday to Sunday 10 a.m. to 6 p.m. Since its founding by Empress Maria Theresa in 1747, the former "junk room of the monarchy" has become one of the world's most important collections of furniture. It features the personal belongings of famous Habsburgs and lots of other furniture from the Baroque era to the Jugendstil period. Special design exhibitions.

PROJECT SPACE OF THE KUNSTHALLE WIEN: Treitlstrasse 2 (Karlsplatz), telephone: +43/1/521 89-33. Open Tuesday to Saturday 4 p.m. to midnight, Sunday and Monday 1 p.m. to 7 p.m. The pavilion designed by Adolf Krischanitz is used for smaller, contemporary art projects.

SECESSION: Friedrichstrasse 12, telephone: +43/1/587 53 07. Open Tuesday to Sunday 10 a.m. to 6 p.m., Thursday 10 a.m. to 8 p.m. The Jugendstil building with its filigree cupola of laurel leaves was built between 1897 and 1898 by Joseph

Maria Olbrich. Above the entrance is the often-quoted inscription: "Der Zeit ihre Kunst – Der Kunst ihre Freiheit" ("To Every Age Its Art, To Every Art Its Freedom). It is the permanent home of Gustav Klimt's "Beethoven Frieze," an interpretation of the composer's *Ninth Symphony*.

Galleries

NEAR THE ALBERTINA:
Galerie bei der Albertina: Lobkowitzplatz 1. Open Monday to Friday 10 a.m. to 6 p.m., Saturday 10 a.m. to 1 p.m.
Galerie Wolfrum: Augustinerstrasse 10. Open Monday to Friday 10 a.m. to 6 p.m., Saturday 10 a.m. to 5 p.m.
Galerie am Opernring: Opernring 17. Open Monday to Friday 1 p.m. to 7 p.m., Saturday 10 a.m. to 5 p.m.
Galerie Karenina: Opernring 21. Open Tuesday to Friday 2 p.m. to 7 p.m., Saturday 11 a.m. to 2 p.m.
Galerie Ulysses: Opernring 21. Open Tuesday to Friday noon to 6 p.m., Saturday 10 a.m. to 1 p.m.

NEAR THE STALLBURG:
Charim Galerie: Dorotheergasse 12/1. Open Tuesday to Friday 11 a.m. to 6 p.m., Saturday 11 a.m. to 2 p.m.
Galerie Hilger: Dorotheergasse 5 and 12. Open Tuesday to Friday 10 a.m. to 6 p.m., Saturday 10 a.m. to 4 p.m.
Galerie Hofstätter: Bräunerstrasse 7. Open Tuesday to Friday 10 a.m. to 6 p.m., Saturday 10 a.m. to 1 p.m.
Suppan: Habsburgergasse 5. Open Monday to Friday 10 a.m. to 6 p.m., Saturday 10 a.m. to 12:30 p.m.

ON ESCHENBACHGASSE AND GUMPENDORFER STRASSE:
Raum aktueller Kunst Martin Janda, *Galerie Krobath Wimmer* and *Galerie Meyer Kainer:* Eschenbachgasse 3–9. Open Tuesday to Friday 1 p.m. to 6 p.m., Saturday 11 a.m. to 3 p.m. *IG*
Bildende Kunst: Gumpendorfer Strasse 10–12. Open Tuesday to Friday 10 a.m. to 6 p.m., Saturday 10 a.m. to 3 p.m.
Galerie Knoll: Gumpendorfer Strasse 18. Open Tuesday to Friday 2 p.m. to 6:30 p.m., Saturday 11 a.m. to 2 p.m.

NEAR THE MUSEUMSQUARTIER: *Galerie Mezzanin:* Karl-Schweighofer-Gasse 12. Open Tuesday to Friday noon to 6 p.m., Saturday 11 a.m. to 2 p.m. *Galerie Hubert Winter:* Breite Gasse 17. Open Tuesday to Friday 1 p.m. to 7 p.m., Saturday 11 a.m. to 2 p.m. *Layr: Wuestenhagen:* Bellariastrasse 6. Open Wednesday noon to 7 p.m., Thursday, Friday noon to 6 p.m., Saturday 11 a.m. to 3 p.m.

Index

Picture Credits

Most of the photographs were kindly made available by the institutions in the Hofburg.

Albertina: 54, 55 (3) – Albertina/Andreas Scheiblecker: 41 – Albertina/Shotview TimTom: 56, 57 – Austria Presse Agentur: 49, 128 – Bohatsch Visual Communication (map)/Fatih Aydogdu (adaptation): 33 – Bundesgärten: 42 (above), 44 – Burgtheater/Reinhard Werner: 147 – Filmmuseum: 66 – Ingrid Haslinger/ Marianne Haller: 138 – Heeresbild- und Filmstelle: 70, 118, 119 – Hofburg Kongresszentrum: 72, 127, 130 – Kunsthistorisches Museum: 2, 46, 47, 63, 75, 76/77, 85, 86, 88, 89, 90, 91, 92, 93, 100 (2), 131, 132, 133, 134, 135, 136 – Leopold Museum Privatstiftung: 99 (2) – Leopold Museum Privatstiftung/Peter Rigaud: 97 – MQ/Martin Gnedt: 31 – MQ/Lisi Gradnitzer: 53, 125 – MQ/Rupert Steiner: 7, 11, 50, 59, 69, 84, 94, 102, 103 – MQ/Gerald Zugmann: 21 – Museum für Völkerkunde: 105, 106 – Naturhistorisches Museum: 9, 107, 108, 110 – Österreichische Nationalbibliothek/Bildarchiv: 13, 15, 18, 19 (above), 22, 24, 25, 26, 27, 29 (2), 65, 67, 68, 117, 121, 122, 124 – Österreichisches Theatermuseum: 114, 115, 116 – Österreich Werbung: 4/5 – Ortner+Ortner/Josef Pausch: 30 (above) – Schloss Schönbrunn Kultur- und Betriebsges.m.b.H.: 78, 79, 80, 81, 82, 139 (2) –Wawel Castle, Kraków: 19 (below) – Spanische Hofreitschule: 140, 142 – Thomas Trenkler: 10, 32, 34, 35, 36, 39, 42 (below), 45, 60, 112, 137, 149, 151 – Volksgarten: 144 – Zoom Kindermuseum/Alexandra Einzinger: 145

Layout Map of the Hofburg: Joseph Koó
Chronological Map of Hofburg Construction: Fatih Aydogdu/ Thomas Trenkler

Many thanks to Christian Benedik, Edith Czap, Daniela Enzi, Barbara Goess, Ruth Gotthardt, Josefa Haselböck, Yvonne Katzenberger, Edyta Kostecka, Irina Kubadinow, Annita Mader, Hans Magenschab, Stefan Musil, Hans Petschar, Franz Pichorner, Monika Scheinost, Gudrun Spiegler, Gerhard Trenkler, Ingrid Viehberger und A+S.

ISBN 3-8000-7043-X
All rights reserved.
Translation: John Winbigler
Cover design: Franz Hanns
Photo: Österreich Werbung / Popp
Copyright © 2004 by Verlag Carl Ueberreuter, Wien
Printed in Austria
7 6 5 4 3 2 1

www.ueberreuter.at